ICARUS

Deon Meyer is the bestselling crime writer in South Africa. This translation occasionally uses colloquial phrases from his original Afrikaans. A glossary of terms can be found at the end of this book.

Also by Deon Meyer

Dead Before Dying
Dead at Daybreak
Heart of the Hunter
Devil's Peak
Blood Safari
Thirteen Hours
Trackers
7 Days
Cobra

ICARUS

Deon Meyer

*Translated from Afrikaans
by K. L. Seegers*

HODDER &
STOUGHTON

First published in Great Britain in 2015 by Hodder & Stoughton
An Hachette UK company

Originally published in Afrikaans in 2015 as *Ikarus* by Human & Rousseau

1

A CIP catalogue record for this title is available from the British Library

Hardback ISBN 978 1 473 61438 3
Trade Paperback ISBN 978 1 473 61439 0
Ebook ISBN 978 1 473 61437 6

Typeset in Plantin Light by Hewer Text UK Ltd, Edinburgh

Printed and bound by Clays Ltd, St Ives plc

Hodder & Stoughton policy is to use papers that are natural, renewable and recyclable
products and made from wood grown in sustainable forests. The logging and manufacturing
processes are expected to conform to the environmental regulations of the country of origin.

Hodder & Stoughton Ltd
Carmelite House
50 Victoria Embankment
London EC4Y 0DZ

www.hodder.co.uk

Les ennemis du vin sont ceux qui ne le connaissent pas.
(The enemies of wine are those who do not know it.)

Quote ascribed to both Prof. Dr Sellier, *Journal de Médecine* (Vlok Delport, *Boland, Wynland,* Nasionale Boekhandel, 1955), and Prof. Portman, probably Prof. Michel Portmann, a medical doctor from Bordeaux (www.alpes-flaveurs.com).

In clinical settings, some depressed people demonstrate a high prone-ness to survivor guilt, that is, guilt over surviving the death of a loved one, or guilt about being better off than others.

'Guilt, fear, submission, and empathy in depression' by Lynn E. O'Connor, Jack W. Berry, Joseph Weiss and Paul Gilbert, *Journal of Affective Disorders* 71 (2002) 19–27.

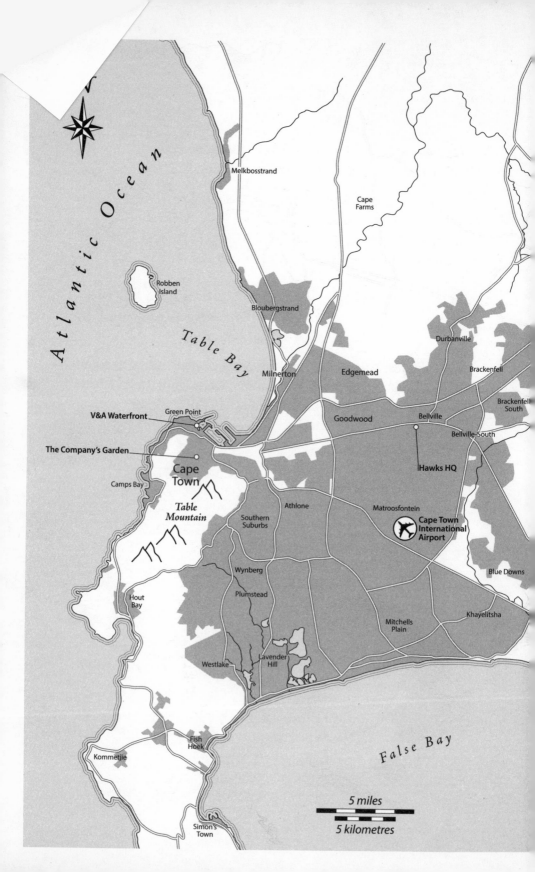

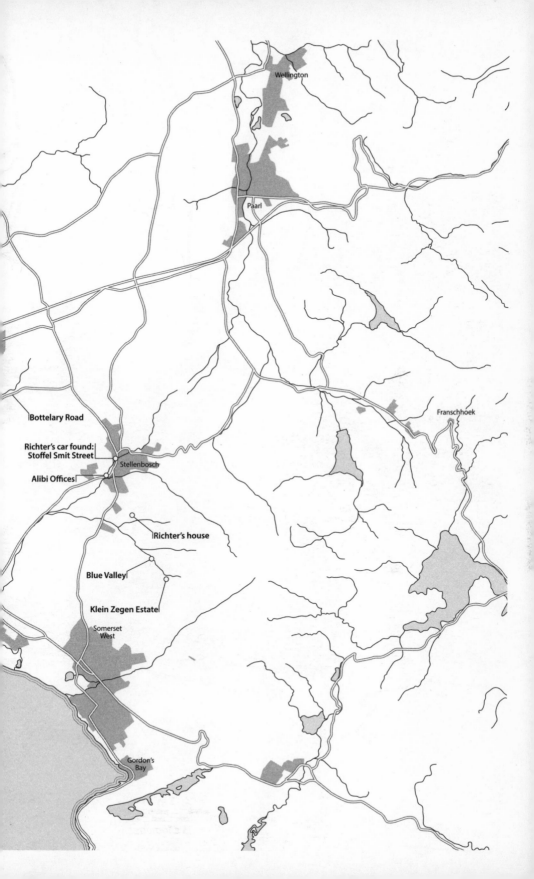

Wellington

Paarl

Franschhoek

Bottelary Road

Richter's car found:
Stoffel Smit Street

Stellenbosch

Alibi Offices

Richter's house

Blue Valley

Klein Zegen Estate

Somerset
West

Gordon's
Bay

I

Heaven and earth conspired to expose Ernst Richter's corpse, the universe seemingly intent on reaching out a helping hand for justice.

First came the storm of 17 December, blowing in at just past eight in the morning. It was a rare one, but not extraordinary, borne in on a cut-off low pressure cell: a blue-black, billowing monster that thundered in from the Atlantic Ocean just north of Robben Island.

The massed clouds shot spectacular white forked tongues down to sea and land, dragging a dense curtain of rain behind them. In under half an hour 71mm had deluged Blouberg Strand and Parklands, Killarney Gardens and Zeezicht.

There was flood damage and traffic chaos. The mainstream and social media would breathlessly repeat the big G-word: *Global Warming*.

But with regard to the body it revealed, the earth's contribution was more modest; simply the contours of the veld beyond Blouberg – where the southeaster had randomly moulded the dunes like a blind sculptor – channelling the flood. It eroded the sand away around Ernst Richter's feet: one bare and tragic, while from the other a black sock dangled, comically, at half-mast.

The last link in the causal chain was fate that made twenty-nine-year-old cameraman Craig Bannister stop nearby at 11.17, beside Otto du Plessis Drive: the coast road between Blouberg and Melkbosstrand. He got out of his vehicle and gauged the weather. The worst of the wind had died down; the clouds were breaking up. He wanted to test his new radio-controlled plane, the DJI Phantom 2 Vision Plus with its stabilised high-resolution video camera. The Phantom, a so-called 'quadcopter', was a technological miracle in miniature. It was equipped with GPS, and a Wi-Fi network that allowed Bannister to connect his iPhone to the camera. He could see the video on his phone screen mere milliseconds after the Phantom recorded it up there in the sky.

Just after 11.31 Bannister frowned at the strange image and manoeuvred the Phantom to fly lower and closer. He let it hover, just one metre above the anomaly, until he was certain.

Sand, black plastic and feet: it was quite clear.

He said nothing. He looked up from the iPhone to determine exactly where the Phantom was hovering, and began to walk swiftly in that direction. It felt as though the video image was a fiction, like a TV drama, in which he could not believe. He followed a winding route, between shrubs, up and down the dunes. Only when he crested the last rise did he see it first-hand. He walked closer, leaving a solitary line of footprints in the rain-smoothed sand.

The feet protruded from beneath the thick black plastic that the body had apparently been rolled up in. The rest was still buried under the sand.

'Shit,' said Craig Bannister, prophetically.

He reached for his phone, which was still clamped to the radio control. Then he realised the Phantom was still hovering a metre above ground, busy recording everything on video. He let the quadcopter land and switched everything off. Then he made the call.

At 13.14, in the Ocean Basket on Kloof Street, Detective Captain Benny Griessel's phone rang. He checked the screen, and saw that it was Major Mbali Kaleni calling: his new commander at the Directorate of Priority Crime Investigations – also known as the DPCI, or 'the Hawks' – Violent Crimes Group. A possible chance of escape. He answered promptly, with a faint feeling of hope.

'Benny, I'm sorry to interrupt your lunch . . .'

'It's not a problem,' he said.

'I need you in Edgemead. Farmersfield Road. Vaughn is on his way too.'

'I'll be there in twenty minutes.'

'Please apologise to your family.' Because she knew about the 'special occasion' that his girlfriend Alexa Barnard had arranged.

'I will.'

He rang off. Alexa, Carla and the Van Eck boy had overheard the conversation. They were looking at him. His son Fritz still had his nose buried in his cellphone.

'*Ai*, Pappa,' said Carla, his daughter, with a mixture of understanding and disappointment.

Alexa took his hand, and squeezed it in sympathy.

'I'm sorry,' said Benny, and stood up. He felt the ache in his side and arm. Not as bad as it had been earlier that morning. 'I have to go to Edgemead.'

'Big murder?' asked the Van Eck boy. He was Carla's new 'friend', a Jesus lookalike with shoulder-length hair and sparse beard.

Griessel ignored him. He took out his wallet, then his credit card. He handed the card to Alexa. He was relieved when she nodded and took it. 'Just give me a kiss,' she said. 'My master detective.'

In the veld east of Otto du Plessis Drive they carefully unearthed the remains of Ernst Richter, as the wind marked the drama by blustering for a few minutes and then died down again, and the sun suddenly emerged from behind the clouds, at once warm and blindingly bright, reflecting off the undulating dunes and the still turbulent Atlantic Ocean.

The video unit of the SAPS made their recordings, while Forensics busied themselves carefully scooping up the sand around the body, and putting it in marked plastic bags.

Detective Adjutant Jamie Keyter of Table View was the man in charge. He had had the area within ten metres of the find cordoned off with crime-scene tape. He had ordered two uniforms to control the traffic on Otto du Plessis Drive, and keep the inquisitive away. With the suspicious, vaguely accusing tone he reserved for occasions such as this, he had interrogated Craig Bannister thoroughly.

'Why did you come and test your little aeroplane here, hey?'

'There's no law against it.'

'I know that. But why didn't you go to the place up there by the Vlei, where they fly the little aeroplanes?'

'That's for the radio control hobbyists.'

'So?'

'Look, I just got this thing. I'm a professional DOP. This is a—'

'What is a DOP?'

'A Director of Photography. I work on TV and film productions. This is the latest technology in aerial camera platforms: a drone, with an HD camera. I need to practise with it, without dodging a hundred little aeroplanes.'

'Do you have a licence for it?'

'A licence? Nobody needs a licence for a little drone.'

'So you just stopped here?'

'That's right.'

'Big coincidence.' Jamie Keyter at his ironic best.

'What are you saying?'

'I'm not saying anything. I'm asking.'

'Look, I drove until I found a spot with a nice view,' said Bannister with extreme patience. 'The road, the sea, the mountain – just take a look. That's pretty spectacular. I needed to practise flying the thing, but I wanted to test the camera too, on something worthwhile. Like this scenery.'

Jamie Keyter lifted his Ferrari sunglasses off his nose, to give Bannister the I-can-see-right-through-you look.

The man just stood there, waiting uneasily.

'So you have everything on video?' asked Keyter at last.

'Yes.'

'Show me.'

Together they watched the video on the cellphone. Twice. 'Okay,' Keyter said, and ordered Bannister to go and wait at his car. The adjutant replaced his Ferrari sunglasses on his nose. In a black polo golf shirt that displayed his bulging biceps and black Edgars chino trousers with black leather belt, hands on hips, he stared at the two feet protruding from under the black plastic.

He was pleased with himself. The feet, despite the post-mortem discolouration, were clearly those of a white man. That meant media attention.

Jamie Keyter loved media attention.

Benny Griessel, forty-six years old, rehabilitating alcoholic, six hundred and two days on the wagon, sat and stared through the windscreen of his car, stuck in the traffic jamming up Buitengracht.

Usually he hated December.

Usually he would curse this holidaymakers' madhouse with a muttered '*Jissis*'. Especially the *fokken* Gautengers who raced down to Cape Town as fast as they could in their shiny new BMWs, their fat wallets ready to blow all their Christmas bonuses with that 'We're gonna shake the Cape awake' attitude; and the entire population of the Cape's northern suburbs who abandoned their regular inhibitions and streamed down to the beaches in droves. Along with the hordes of Europeans fleeing the winter cold.

Usually he would brood resentfully on the consequences of this invasion. There was no parking, the traffic stank, prices doubled and crime stats went up at least 12 per cent, because everyone drank like a fish, which unleashed all the wrong demons.

Usually. But not this year: the oppression was in him and over him and around him, like a disconsolate cloud. Again. Still.

The momentary relief of his escape from the Ocean Basket had evaporated. On the way to the car the melancholy in Mbali's voice had registered with him – the muted dismay, accentuated by her attempt to disguise it. In stark contrast to the positivity she had tried to radiate over the past two months as group commander.

I need you in Edgemead. Farmersfield Road. Vaughn is on his way too.

Something bad was brewing. And he didn't have the strength for disaster any more.

So today the December madness and the snail's pace traffic wasn't so much a thorn in his flesh, but a blessing.

The Forensic team had exposed the full length of Ernst Richter's corpse.

Adjutant Jamie Keyter called the video team closer so they could record it: the thick black plastic rolled around the body, just not long enough to cover the feet, and the blood red rope with which it had been so thoroughly bound – up near the head, around the waist and down at the ankles.

Keyter had seen the newspaper photographer trying to take photos from Otto du Plessis drive with his long lens. That was why he stood with legs apart, hands on hips: the image of a detective in control of his crime scene. He kept an eye on the video team, until he was satisfied that the recording covered all the suitable angles.

'Okay,' he said. 'You come out.' Then, to Forensics, with a wave of the hand, 'Cut him open.'

The two forensic analysts chose the right tools from their kit, lifted the crime tape and knelt beside the victim. One carefully cut the cord loose. The other picked up the cord and packed it in an evidence bag.

Jamie Keyter ducked under the tape himself now and walked up to the victim. 'Let's unroll him.'

It took nearly ten minutes, as they had to work carefully and the single sheet of plastic seemed endless. The forensics men folded up every two metres of the plastic to limit contamination.

The uniforms, the video unit, the two detective constables, ambulance men all stepped closer, curious.

Finally the body was revealed.

'He hasn't been here long,' said one forensic analyst, as there were relatively few signs of decay, just a general darkening of the skin, the blueish-purple network of livor mortis visible on the feet and the underside of the neck, and the sand grains that clung to the body from head to toe. A lean man of average height, with thick, dark brown hair, dressed in a black T-shirt – with the words *I refuse to engage in a battle of wits with an unarmed person* in big white letters – and blue jeans.

'Maybe a week or so,' said the other, and thought the face seemed vaguely familiar, but he couldn't place it at that moment. He suppressed the impulse to say something.

It was the closest anyone came to identifying Ernst Richter at the scene of the crime.

'He's been strangled with something,' said the other forensic analyst, and pointed at the deep discolouration that circled the throat.

'Obviously,' said Jamie Keyter.

2

Farmersfield Street had a quiet, middle-class sense of calm on this Wednesday afternoon, rows of white and cream three-bedroom developer's houses with tiled roofs and neat lawns. The morning's storm had left a trail of branches and leaves in the street.

Griessel didn't need to search for the address. He saw the neighbours standing across the road in small, dejected groups, and a huddle of police vehicles parked together. He stopped a few metres away, on the pavement. He remained sitting, hands on the steering wheel, his eyes downcast. Not keen to get out.

Something had happened to disturb the normality of suburban Edgemead; something that he knew would deepen the oppression he'd felt these past months. The minibus of PCSI, the elite Provincial Crime Scene Investigation unit, was also there. What were they doing here? And why had he and Vaughn of the Hawks been called in?

He took a deep breath, and slowly let go of the steering wheel. He got out reluctantly. Walked towards the house.

A white wall obscured his view, so that he first had to walk around to the driveway, where a constable was controlling access.

The house looked like most of the others in the street. More SAPS personnel in uniform stood at the door in a circle, heads down.

The constable stopped him with a forbidding palm. He showed his identity card.

The eyes widened suddenly: 'Oh, Captain Griessel. Captain Cupido asked that you just wait here. I will call him quickly . . .'

'What for?' asked Benny, and walked around the man.

'No, Captain, please.' Anxious. 'He gave me orders. I have to call him.'

'Get him then.' Annoyed – he wasn't in the mood for Vaughn's tricks.

In a loud voice the constable asked the uniforms at the door to call the 'Hawks Captain'. One of them hurried inside.

Griessel waited, impatient.

Cupido came hurrying out in his Hawk-in-Protest outfit – jeans, yellow T-shirt, blue jacket, and the shrill statement of his yellow-and-orange running shoes, that he had praised so enthusiastically to Benny yesterday: 'Nike Air Pegasus Plus, *pappie*, almost a thousand bucks regular price, but Tekkie Town had a sale. Cool comfort in Technicolor; it's like walking on air in a wet dream. Takes the "work" out of "foot-work" every time. But the real bonus is that these sneakers are going to piss off *Major* Mbali big time.'

For the past couple of weeks Vaughn had been protesting against the strict new edict on neatness laid down by *Major* Mbali (sarcastically accentuating the new rank every time). The previous Monday during a group meeting Kaleni had said solemnly, 'If you want to be professional, you have to look professional. We have a responsibility to the public.' And then she had asked them to wear suit and tie and 'formal shoes' – or at least a shirt with a collar and a jacket. That had been the last straw for Cupido who was already having trouble stomaching her appointment as group leader: 'You think it's a coincidence, just after the election? I don't think so. Because she's a Zulu, it's ethnic affirmative action; it's Zuma time, all the time, Benna. You *and* I have more experience, more years of service, more savvy. And she gets the promotion?'

Griessel knew the real problem was that Cupido was deeply concerned that the new commander would not put up with his nonsense. Mbali was conscientious and conservative. Vaughn was not. So he said she was the right person for the post, given the circumstances.

It had made no difference.

Despite his haste and the colourful outfit, Cupido's face was sombre as he approached.

'Benna, you don't need to go inside. Our work here is done.' Griessel could hear the tone in his colleague's voice, the false business-like note hiding his dismay.

'I didn't drive all this way to . . . What's going on, Vaughn? What happened here?'

'Trust me, Benna, please. It's an open-and-shut. Let's go.' Cupido put his hand protectively on Griessel's shoulder.

Benny felt his temper rising. What was wrong with Cupido? He shrugged him off his shoulder. 'Are you going to tell me what's going on, or must I see for myself?'

'Benna, for once in your life, trust me,' with a desperation that merely inflamed Benny's suspicions.

'*Jissis*,' said Griessel and began walking towards the front door.

'It's Vollie,' said Cupido.

Griessel froze. 'Vollie?'

'*Ja*. Our Vollie. Vollie Fish. And his family.'

Adjutant Tertius van Vollenhoven, who had worked with both of them before, back when the Provincial Detective Branch still existed. Vollie, who dished up his West Coast sayings sparely and dryly in his Namaqualand accent when the night was too long and morale too low. Vollie Fish, native of Lamberts Bay, who went home on weekends and brought back seafood for the whole team on Mondays, with precise instructions on the cooking, because 'to fuck up the preparation of a crayfish, that's sacrilege, my friend.'

The man had caught two serial killers on the Cape Flats in four years, through endless patience and dedication. And then he had left, for Bothasig Station. He said he had done his bit, he wanted a quieter life, wanted to save his marriage, wanted to see his children grow up. But everyone knew it was the trauma of the investigations, month after month of standing beside the mutilated body of another victim, knowing that only a stroke of luck would stop the monsters, whatever you did.

The old injustice awoke in Griessel, the rancour towards those responsible.

'Robbery?'

'No, Benna . . .'

'What happened, Vaughn?'

Cupido's voice was barely a whisper. He could not look Griessel in the eye. 'Vollie shot them, last night, and then shot himself.'

'Vollie?'

'Yes, Benna.'

He remembered, the two cute young girls, early teens, and Vollie's wife, plump, strong, supportive. Mercia, or Tersia . . . He wanted simply to reject it, he did not want to visualise it: Vollie with his service pistol at a child's bedside.

'Christ, Vaughn,' he said and felt the claustrophobia close in again, suffocating him.

'I know.'

Griessel wanted to keep on talking; he wanted to escape the pressure. 'But why? What happened?'

Cupido pointed at the uniforms at the door. 'Bothasig Station found a girl yesterday, in the veld, other side of Richwood. The second one – same MO as a murder a month ago. It's a serial. Bad stuff, Benna, very sick fucker. Vollie was there.'

Griessel put it all together, his hand on the back of his head. He tried to understand what happened – all the demons coming back to devour Vollie from inside.

'Come, Benna. Let's go.'

Griessel stood as if frozen. Cupido could see how his colleague's face had turned ashen.

'Benna, it's better if we—'

'Wait . . .' He looked sharply at Cupido. 'Why did Mbali send us here?'

'Bothasig OC asked her to let us check it out. He said he wanted to be sure they weren't missing something, because the media . . .'

'Oh.' And then: 'Why do you want to keep me away from there, Vaughn?'

Cupido looked him in the eye, and tapped an index finger on his temple. 'Because you're not yet right, Benna. I know it.'

Jamie Keyter and the two forensic analysts had gone through every pocket of the victim's jeans. There was nothing in them.

He had transferred the corpse to the big black body bag, zipped it up, and called for the stretcher. The body was carried to the ambulance. Forensics had packed up and carefully labelled the black plastic sheet and the red cord. One analyst fetched their metal detector and was busy walking in concentric circles around the crime scene, earphones on his head.

The other one stood with Jamie Keyter. Nobody else was within earshot. 'I swear he looks familiar,' said the analyst.

'Obviously. He works with you,' said Keyter, frowning behind his dark glasses.

'Not him, the victim.'

'As in, you know him?'

'No, not know. Just know of . . .'

'Like a celebrity?'

'I just know I've seen him before.'

'That's fuck-all help if you don't know where . . . Do you think he's a policeman?'

The analyst regretted opening his mouth. 'No, I . . . Maybe I'm wrong. Maybe he just looks like someone who—'

The analyst with the metal detector stopped. 'There's something here,' he said. He was about three metres from where the victim had been found.

The other one picked up a little spade, and climbed under the yellow crime tape. He used his hands to loosen the sand under the sensor of the detector, and scooped it away carefully. At first he could find nothing.

'Are you sure?' he asked his colleague.

'There's definitely something there.'

Forty centimetres under the surface he felt the metal. He worked with his fingers to get the sand out of the way. Then there it was.

'*Jis*, it's a cellphone.'

He stood up, fetched a brush from his tool kit then stooped again to brush the sand away, while Jamie Keyter called back the camera team.

'iPhone 5, looks like . . .' said the man from Forensics. He pressed a button on the phone but nothing happened. 'Dead as a *drol*.' At 15.07 on Wednesday, 17 December.

3

**Transcript of interview: Advocate Susan
Peires with Mr Francois du Toit**

*Wednesday, 24 December; 1604 Huguenot Chambers,
40 Queen Victoria Street, Cape Town*

Sound file 1

Adv. Susan Peires (SP): . . . Of course you may refuse. Then I'll just
make a note. But the recording is a much more reliable record, and
it's handled with exactly the same discretion. I will have it tran-
scribed, which can serve as reference notes as well. The rules of
privilege still apply.

Francois du Toit (FdT): Even if you don't take my case.

SP: That's correct.

FdT: Who transcribes it?

SP: My secretary, who is also subject to the privilege.

FdT: Very well, record me then.

SP: Thank you, Mr du Toit. Can you state your full name, date of
birth and your profession for the record.

FdT: I am Francois du Toit, born on 20 April 1987. I'm a wine farmer
from the Klein Zegen Estate in Stellenbosch . . . Out on the
Blaauklippen Road.

SP: You are now . . . twenty-seven?

FdT: That's right.

SP: Married?

FdT: Yes. To San . . . Susanne . . . We have a son of six weeks.
Guillaume.

SP: Thank you. I understand from your attorney that the police are
waiting for you right now? On the estate?

FdT: Yes . . .

SP: And you are requesting advice on how to handle the situation.

FdT: Yes.

SP: What is the police investigation about?

FdT: Gustav . . . my attorney . . . hasn't he told you?

SP: I gathered it was serious, but I asked Mr Kemp not to provide any details. I prefer to hear it from the client directly.

FdT: It . . . it's connected to the murder of Ernst Richter.

SP: The man who went missing? The Alibi Man?

FdT: That's right.

SP: And you are involved in that?

FdT: The police would surely not . . . I'm sorry. It . . . It's a long story . . . I have to tell you the whole . . . Please.

SP: I see . . . Mr du Toit, before we go any further, let me deliver the speech I give all my clients. I have been an advocate for twenty-eight years, and in that time I have represented more than two hundred people in criminal cases. Murder, manslaughter, rape, fraud – you name it. And my advice is always the same, and experience has shown over and over that it's good advice: You don't have to be honest with me, but eventually it makes my task that much easier. I don't—

FdT: I intend to be honest . . .

SP: Let me finish, please. I'm not here to judge you; I'm here to ensure that you get the best legal representation that I can offer. I believe steadfastly in a justice system where an accused is innocent, until the contrary is proven beyond reasonable doubt by the State. One of my greatest responsibilities is to set the standard of reasonable doubt as high as possible. And I have accepted cases where the accused has told me he is guilty, and I fought just as hard for him as for those who protested their innocence, because the system can only work if we are all equal before the law. Therefore, I don't object if you are guilty . . .

FdT: (Inaudible.)

SP: Please, Mr du Toit . . .

FdT: Call me Francois . . .

SP: No, I shall call you Mr du Toit. We are not friends; we are advocate and client. It is an official, professional relationship, for which you will pay me a lot of money. And I must maintain my distance and objectivity. I wanted to say, I don't object if you are innocent. It will make no difference to my dedication or the quality of my work. I do my absolute best, because that is what you pay for. I can't force you to be honest with me, but I would like to point out the implications to you. Undisclosed information has a way of coming out. Not always, but frequently. And when it comes out at an unsympathetic moment, it can do your defence incalculable harm. In terms of my role I can only take responsibility for what I know. I can only build your case and manage your defence on the basis of what you share with me. If it is your choice to present me with a fictitious version, I have no choice, I have to work with that. But in my opinion and based on my experience, that practically never has a positive influence. In short, Mr du Toit, the more frank you are with me, the better our chances are of keeping you out of jail. Do you understand that?

FdT: Yes.

SP: Would you like to think it over first?

FdT: No. I'm going to tell you everything. Everything.

SP: Very well. Where would you like to begin?

4

At 15.48 Benny Griessel walked into the Fireman's Arms, according to legend the second oldest watering hole in the Cape, after the Perseverance Tavern in Buitenkant Street.

The Fireman's had been serving alcoholics and other serious drinkers since 1864, which made the pub on this Wednesday 17 December about a hundred and fifty years old. Griessel didn't give a hoot about the history of drinking in the Cape. It was the available parking in Mechau Street that made him stop here.

With an air of resolve he strode between the dark wooden tables and benches to the long bar, sat down, and waited to be served. He inhaled the scents of the tavern. They released a thousand memories, all of them pleasant.

His elbows on the counter, he noticed the faint tremor in his hands. He folded them together so the approaching barman would not notice.

'Double Jack,' he said.

'Rocks?'

'No, thanks.'

The barman nodded and went off to pour it. Came back with the chunky glass and handed it over, with its two fingers of amber – mechanical, practised motions, utterly unaware of the significance of this moment.

Griessel did not hesitate. He didn't think of the six hundred and two days without alcohol that lay behind him. He picked up the glass and drank, deeply.

The flavour was a long lost friend; reunion was a joy.

But still it did nothing for him inside.

The comfort was not in that first swallow, he knew. That, and the anaesthesia and the calm and the order and the sense, the healing and the softening and the balance and that oneness with the universe only came later, near the end of the second divine glass.

★   ★   ★

The South African Police Service's forensic science laboratory had been situated in Silverboom Avenue, Plattekloof since 2011, more than 17,000 square metres of impressive steel and glass. The backbone of the building was a massive capital C, four storeys high, with five thick arms flowing out from it – one each for the departments of Ballistics, DNA Analysis, Scientific Analysis, Document Analysis and Chemical Analysis.

It was in the kitchen of the Department of Scientific Analysis, while he was pouring coffee into a mug, that it suddenly struck him. The forensic analyst remembered who the sand-specked face of the body in the dunes beyond Blouberg reminded him of.

Could it be?

He said nothing to his colleague, just hurried over to his work station, put the coffee down beside the keyboard, and Googled a name.

He clicked on a link, watched the photo loading. He knew it; he hadn't made a mistake. He searched in his notes of the day for Jamie Keyter's cellphone number and rang it.

'Jamie,' answered the detective, as though he didn't want to be bothered. He pronounced his name 'Yaa-mee', and not 'Jaymee', as the English would. The analyst found it mildly affected and irritating, like the man himself.

He identified himself and said: 'I think . . . I'm reasonably sure the victim is Ernst Richter.'

'Who is Ernst Richter?' asked Jamie Keyter.

'The guy from Alibi who went missing.'

Keyter was quiet for a moment. Then he answered with rising irritation, 'I haven't a clue who you're talking about, pal.'

'Then you had better call Stellenbosch Station.'

Griessel sat with both hands cradling his second *dop*.

He thought, this was his holiday, this. He needed nothing more. Mbali could quit her nonsense now.

On Monday she had examined his personnel file: 'You haven't had a holiday in three years, Benny'. Worried; the concern for him clear in her voice.

'I had more than three months of sick leave after . . .' and both of them knew he was referring to the shooting incident, where her predecessor had died, and Griessel had been wounded.

'That doesn't count. I want you to take a break between Christmas and New Year. You need to have a real holiday . . .'

A 'Real Holiday'? All he could afford was to sit at home, and that would drive him insane within a day.

'. . . And spend time with your loved ones.'

That was Kaleni's trump card.

His loved ones.

Before Mbali had phoned him this afternoon, he had sat for twenty minutes in the Ocean Basket with his *loved ones*. His daughter Carla had talked non-stop to Alexa about arty stuff he knew nothing about. His son Fritz sat with his cellphone, fingers dancing over the screen, giving a secret little laugh every now and then as a new SMS or WhatsApp or Facebook or Twitter or BBM or whatever it might be made the cellphone tinkle or chime. As if his father didn't exist. As if this wasn't a special occasion lunch that Alexa had taken great pains to arrange. Fritz, who was going to cost him a fortune to send to film school next year – not a figurative fortune, a literal fortune. AFDA charged R5,950 for registration alone. And R10,000 enrolment fees. And R55,995 tuition fees. For one year. He knew the figures; he could recite them in the middle of the fucking night, because he had had to present them to his bank manager. And the bank had deliberated for nearly a month before granting him the loan.

And Fritz had no appreciation for any of this, just stayed glued to his phone right through the special occasion lunch, and Griessel didn't know what to do.

Both of his children had a much better relationship with their mother. Sometimes he heard them talking on the phone with Anna, his ex. Conversations filled with laughter and shared experiences and intimate information. And he? What was he to do? His work was his life, and he couldn't talk about it. Because of his so-called altruism and his depression, according to the shrink.

And that Van Eck boy, Carla's new 'friend', who was studying Drama with her at Stellenbosch (at R29,145 a year, an amount that he had managed without a loan, but with some difficulty and extreme thrift, till now). Griessel could not stand Vincent van Eck. He had begun to wonder whether his daughter's previous love, the Etzebeth rugby player, hadn't been a better proposition. At least Etzebeth had known when to zip his lip.

Van Eck was full of chit-chat and opinions, and questions that Griessel did not want to answer. 'What was your most interesting case? What do you think of the Oscar verdict? Why is our crime rate so high?'

Not a respectful '*Oom*', it was 'you' and 'your', and his hair was too long and his eyes too sly and Alexa said he was a pretty boy and 'sweet' and Griessel didn't want to be ungracious, the kid was Carla's friend, after all, but he had a strong feeling that van Eck was a spoiled little prick.

Vincent van Eck. He could already hear Vaughn Cupido's reaction: What kind of *fokken* name is that? Who calls their kid Vincent, with a surname like that?

At 16.28 Adjutant Jamie Keyter sat opposite the heavily laden desk of the commander of SAPS Table View Station, and told him that the body they had so carefully dug out of the sand off Blouberg was most probably a man who went by the name of Ernst Richter.

'*The* Ernst Richter?' asked the colonel, sounding worried.

Keyter wondered why everyone but him had already heard of *the* Ernst Richter; maybe he should read the papers even when there wasn't a report on one of his cases. He confirmed that, and said that Richter had been reported missing just over three weeks earlier in Stellenbosch. The hair colour and features of the victim bore a strong likeness to the two head-and-shoulders photos that Stellenbosch Station had emailed ten minutes ago. And what's more, the corpse was dressed in the same clothes that Richter had been wearing just before his disappearance.

'Good work,' said the station commander, deep in thought.

'Thank you, Colonel. But Stellenbosch are talking jurisdiction now. I mean, it's our case, *finish and klaar*. Isn't it?'

'Do we have a positive identification?'

'I am going to phone his mother to see if she can come and identify him, Colonel. But he was discovered in our jurisdiction. So all that Stellenbosch need is a ninety-two, to close off their file . . .' Keyter's hopeful reference was to the SAPS form 92 that had to be filled in when a missing person was found.

The commander scratched the back of his neck while he thought it over. He knew Jamie Keyter's strengths and weaknesses. He knew the adjutant might not be the brightest bulb in Table View's detection chandelier, but he was dedicated, methodical and reliable, with a few successful investigations of uncomplicated murders notched up on his stick.

The big question was, if this was *the* Ernst Richter, could he entrust the case to him?

One problem was Keyter's ambition. After the heady positive publicity of a car theft syndicate exposé a year or three back, Jamie frequently over-estimated his own ability and potential. And in the Table View Station there was a lot of gossip about his love of the media spotlight (and his corresponding fondness for spending time in front of the mirror).

The other problem was work load. Table View was one of the fast-est-growing metropolitan areas in the Peninsula. And the growth was in the lower middle class: among others, thousands of immigrants from Nigeria, Malawi and Zimbabwe in the Parklands area, where nearly 60 per cent of the crimes were committed that his station had to handle. If it was definitely *the* Ernst Richter, he would have to deploy significant manpower, because the pressure from the Provincial Commissioner was going to be extreme once the media camped out on their doorstep.

It was manpower he did not have. And media attention that only Jamie Keyter wanted.

'Jamie, let me call Stellenbosch and see what I can do,' he lied.

At the end of the third glass Griessel's physical pains began to dissipate. The pain in his arm, the pain in his side, the dull ache of the bullet wounds, now six months old, from when they had shot Colonel Zola Nyathi dead – but not Benny.

The pain this morning, stoked by the stormy weather, had flared up into a fiercely throbbing memory of all of that.

And now here he sat, beginning to contemplate his fourth double.

He had known the drinking was close. Doc Barkhuizen, his sponsor at Alcoholics Anonymous for years, had also seen it coming. 'I know those glassy eyes, Benny. Confront the desire. When last were you at an AA meeting? Go and talk to the shrink again. Get your head right.'

He didn't want to go back to the shrink. In the first place, they had forced him to have therapy after the shooting. In the second place, he had completed the process, against his will. In the third place, psychologists didn't know a damn thing; they sat in their little, annoyingly decorated offices, carefully designed to make frightened, unstable people feel cosy and at home, with a box of tissues positioned nearby like a silent insult, and the teddy bear sitting on the windowsill.

A teddy bear: in the office of a shrink who treated policemen.

And they were oh-so-full of big words and book knowledge, but had any of them stood beside a mutilated body, time and again and again and again? Or lain and watched how the blood spurted and dribbled and dripped, as you knew for certain you were going to die, lying there with your colleague? And there was nothing you could do to save him.

She was an attractive woman, the shrink who had to counsel him. Mid-forties, just like Griessel. At first he thought it would be okay, despite the tissues and the teddy. But then she started with that *fokken* soothing voice, as though he was a madman who had to be kept calm. She asked her questions, about his whole life, his history as detective. And she listened attentively, her focus was so absolute, and she agreed with everything so compassionately and said she understood. After four weeks she told him he had post-traumatic stress, and survivor guilt. And it was his altruism and his depression that had made him drink.

He wasn't absolutely sure what 'altruism' meant.

'It's caring about others,' she said. 'To such an extent that you sacrifice something for them, without any expectation of advantage or reward.'

'That's why I drink?'

'It's a piece of the puzzle, Captain. The popular interpretation of depression, in a nutshell of course, is that people in whom it manifested could see no meaningful future. It was a depression of self-consequence and concern about status. But recent research shows there is another kind of depression – one where people feel terribly guilty and have a high level of empathy for the fate of others. Their altruism is so strong that they experience pathogenic perceptions, where they see themselves as a danger to the people close to them. I suspect that is what we must focus on.'

Griessel didn't like that one bit. People who suffered from depression walked around like zombies, heads down, thinking deep, dark thoughts, like wanting to slit their wrists. And that wasn't something he had ever considered doing. So he rejected her nonsense, but out of courtesy just shook his head slightly.

Then she said, in that soothing voice again, 'Everything you've told me points to it. Not only the incident where your colonel was shot. Every time you go to the scene of a murder, there's a feeling of complicity, that this was something you should have prevented. It is not exclusive to your profession. But the main factor is that you begin to feel responsible for all your loved ones; you develop an unnatural urge to protect them against the evils that you experience on a daily basis. On a certain level you realise that's impossible. We must explore whether that is causing your depression and drinking habits.'

Must explore. Fok. As if he were some kind of wilderness.

He sat in the pub and remembered these things. And he drank, in the hope that he would forget – because back in Edgemead that afternoon the demons that had possessed Vollie Fish had migrated into his head.

5

From her office in Suite 1604 of the Huguenot Chambers Advocate, Susan Peires had a perfect view over the green expanse of the historic Company's Garden. On this baking hot day before Christmas it was thronged with visitors. Sometimes, when she wanted to think a case over, she would open the blinds and look out. It helped her to order her thoughts. But now her full attention was on the young wine estate owner Francois du Toit.

She sat opposite him at the conference table. She listened to every word that he said, carefully noting his tone of voice, speech patterns and rhythms. He struggled to get going, but that was to be expected. She sometimes compared her work to that of a doctor in an emergency room. If they came in here, trauma was a given.

She gauged Du Toit's body language, his facial expressions, the eyes that glanced first at her, then stared at some fixed point on the wall.

All this, she knew, she must interpret with care.

As a young advocate, Peires had learned a valuable professional lesson. It was a pro bono case, in the last turbulent years of apartheid, a white municipal diesel mechanic who stood accused of the murder of his wife. The circumstantial evidence was strong – a day before the murder he had been told by an acquaintance that his wife had been unfaithful and there were neighbours close by in Goodwood's tightly packed houses who had heard the loud confrontation that followed. There were fingernail marks on his cheek, and he already had a suspended sentence for a seven-year-old assault case. And when she saw him for the first time in the interrogation room of the police station, Peires had known he was guilty. Because the man's face was rough, primitive. Under heavy brows his eyes shiftily evaded her gaze. He was tall and strong, with sledgehammer hands. And his manner was surly. He was verbally clumsy and vague. Peires, along with the investigating detectives, believed that his alibi – he swore that he was at his mother's house in Parow during the night of the murder – was a story concocted between mother and son.

She questioned the mother, a nervous chain smoker who would not make a good impression in court. Only when Peires told the woman that there was a good chance that her son would go to prison for life, did the mother break down in tears and confess, frightened. They hadn't been alone in her house: her lover, a coloured officer in the South African Defence Force Cape Corps, could confirm the alibi.

And he had – a dignified, well-spoken man with a quiet, resolute voice.

When the case against the mechanic was withdrawn and the attention of the police shifted to the victim's married lover, she asked her client if he had been so ashamed of the race of his mother's lover that he had been ready to go to jail.

'No,' he replied.

'Were you trying to protect your mother? Were you afraid people would talk?'

He shook his head.

'Then why didn't you tell me?'

'Because you have an angry face.'

That upset Susan Peires. That she, who saw herself as professional but compassionate, could be perceived to be an angry woman. That this apparently tough, burly man could be afraid of her because of the way she looked. That each of them had had their mutual perceptions of character warped by the influence of their facial form and expressions.

She thought it all over at length. She spent a long time in front of the mirror and systematically, unwillingly and slowly she had come to terms with her sharp features that were apparently, coupled with her profession, the reason she had not enjoyed any serious attention from the male of the species.

She tried to soften her appearance with make-up and clothes and a more relaxed approach in general.

She philosophised about people's tendency to categorise and label on the strength of appearance, she speculated over the influence of facial features on the formation of personality, but above all she resolved never to make the same mistake again.

As a result, she did not let herself be influenced by the fact that Francois du Toit was an attractive, tanned, well-spoken man. She listened and she observed.

Above all, she reserved all judgement about truth or falsehood.

6

Wednesday 17 December. Eight days to Christmas.

At 17.03 the Table View SAPS station commander phoned the office of the Directorate of Priority Crimes in Bellville, and asked to speak to the commanding officer.

'Brigadier Manie is on holiday, Colonel,' his secretary informed him.

The station commander sighed. It was that time of year. 'Who is head of Violent Crimes now?'

'Major Mbali Kaleni, Colonel.'

He had heard a lot about her. He suppressed yet another sigh. 'May I speak to her?'

'Please hold . . .'

Benny Griessel had spun his own little cocoon in the Fireman's Arms. He was unaware of people behind his back, the bar steadily filling up in the late afternoon. He didn't see the soccer matches on the huge flat screen TVs, he didn't hear the hubbub of fellow imbibers chatting and laughing in groups.

It was just him and the sixth double Jack, and the bravado and wisdom of the drunkard.

He bowed his head, trying to get his dancing thoughts in order.

He had stood there with Vaughn Cupido in front of that house in Edgemead and revelation pierced him slowly through the heart, with the stiletto of insight. The shrink was right.

Adjutant Tertius van Vollenhoven had committed the most terrible, unthinkable, heart-rending deed, because he wanted to protect his loved ones from the predatory evil that prowled the world with slavering jaws and bloodshot eyes. For no one could stop that hound, his hunger only grew.

The shrink was right. He, Benny Griessel, drank because it kept the dog from his and his loved ones' door. Drink was the bulwark, that prevented him from becoming what Vollie . . .

He wasn't drunk enough to venture into that place.

But he would get there, this very night.

Two collar-and-tie men in their thirties shifted in beside Griessel at the long bar. They looked at him, how he hunched over his glass. Their grins were scornful.

He didn't like that one bit.

His cellphone rang before he could say anything to them. It was Mbali Kaleni, he saw.

Fuck that. He was on a real holiday – just him and his good friend Jack.

He emptied his glass and beckoned to the barman.

Major Mbali Kaleni sat in her office and called Benny Griessel's cellphone number.

Cupido stood on the other side of her desk, breathing in the cauliflower aroma, and he thought, it's a disgrace. She was a group leader now, and her quarters smelled like this?

It was all because of her diet. She had lost eleven kilos already, but he couldn't see it; to him she looked as short and fat as ever.

Two weeks ago, he had known nothing about it. He came strolling down the passage, savouring a packet of Speckled Eggs, when Mbali walked past and said to him, in that irritating know-it-all way, 'Prof Tim says sugar is poison, you know.'

He let it go, because an argument with Mbali was like a Sumo wrestling match – you could never get a decent grip, and afterwards, it left you all sweaty and unsatisfied. But a day later, it was 'Prof Tim says low fat is a fraud,' when he was eating a tub of yoghurt at his desk for breakfast. He let that slide too. Until the following morning, when he and a packet of Simba salt-and-vinegar crisps walked out of the morning parade, and Mbali said, 'Prof Tim says it's the carbs that make you fat, you know,' and he couldn't take it any more and snapped: 'Prof Tim who?'

And so she told him. Everything. About this Prof Tim Noakes who once got the whole *fokken* world eating pasta, and then he did an about face and said, no, carbs are what's making everyone obese, and he wrote a book of recipes, and now he was Mbali's big hero, 'Because it takes a great man to admit that he was wrong', and she had already lost so much weight and she had so much more energy, and it wasn't all that hard, she didn't miss the carbs because now she ate cauliflower rice and cauliflower mash and flax seed bread.

Flax seed bread, for fuck's sake.

Mbali, with all the passion of the newly converted. As though he were fat too.

Every lunch time she bought two heads of cauliflower and left them exuding their odours in her office, and he missed the days when it smelled of KFC in here.

After an eternity Kaleni said, 'Benny isn't answering.'

Cupido stood there at the desk and he had to keep a grip on himself. Because he knew, Griessel always answered his phone. And if *Major* Mbali was less concerned about her new diet, and concentrated more on her people, he wouldn't have had to worry so much about Benny right now. This afternoon in Edgemead he had seen the shock and defeat on Griessel's face. And when his colleague left, he had wondered whether trouble was brewing.

Major Mbali should never have sent Benny there.

He suppressed his frustration, just looked at her.

'I've left him a message,' said Kaleni. 'Will you please get started? As soon as he calls back, I'll ask him to join you.'

'Yes, Major.' Since she had become his group commander, she was awfully nice to him. While in the old days she couldn't stand him. What's with that? But he just turned and left.

'Captain, I have a feeling they're dumping this one on us,' said Kaleni before he was out the door. 'When you're sure the deceased is definitely the Alibi Man, please involve Captain Cloete.'

John Cloete was the Hawks' media liaison.

'Okay,' said Cupido.

'I want you to take JOC.'

That caught him completely off guard; he'd never dreamed she would put him in charge, give him a joint operational command. 'Okay,' he repeated, and he wondered whether he had been made JOC leader just because Griessel hadn't answered his phone this time.

★   ★   ★

One suit-and-tie beside Griessel told the other one a story, loud enough for him to hear everything. He listened, because it was an escape from his own morbid thoughts.

'Noleen says, it's a friend of a friend. Nice girl, very pretty and . . .'

'If a chick says another girl is pretty, she usually isn't . . .'

'You know it. It's weird. Anyway, Noleen said the pretty girl broke up with her boyfriend six months back; she works at a small business, so she doesn't meet many guys, and she decided, she'll try internet dating . . .'

'Bad move . . .'

'You know it. Anyway, she had a few photies taken by a pro, checked out all the dating sites, and zoomed in on one. Made a profile with the nice new pics, wrote down her likes and dislikes, and the guys began chaffing her. Went through the whole thing, discarded the duds, and after a few weeks began chatting to this handsome dude on the site. The more they chatted, the more she realised he was actually quite cool. So she decided, okay, she would go out on a date with him. Very safe, drove there in her own car, met him at a restaurant. Dude arrived there, and he's helluva charming and intelligent. They chatted up a storm, had a great dinner, drank some wine, she falls a bit in love. Long story short, dude walks her to her car, she gives him the right signals and he kisses her. Nothing serious, just a semi-romantic kiss, the kind that says "I respect your boundaries on a first date". And she thinks, who said internet dating can't work. Two days later she starts getting small white sores on her lips . . .'

'Fuck, bru' . . .'

'You know it. Anyway, she goes to the doctor. Doctor says, you have to be honest with me, do you have contact with dead people. You know, corpses.'

'Fuck!'

'I'm telling you. Girl says, absolutely not, Doctor. He asks her, what contact have you had? She thought carefully, and she tells him about the handsome dude. He says, only way you get those sores, or can infect other people with them is when you have contact with corpses. As in kiss them . . .'

'Fuckit, bru'.'

'You know it, man. The doctor says to her, he will have to call the police. She says okay. Police come and they ask her, is she willing to go on a date with the dude again, so they can catch him. She says fine, and this time she lets the dude take her to his house, with the police following. When they walk in, it's SWAT team everywhere, and they search the place and they find three corpses, bru', with the tags still around the toes . . .'

'Can you fucking believe it?'

'Seems the dude works at the mortuary . . .'

'*Kak*,' said Benny Griessel. In his befuddled state it came out louder than he intended.

'What?' asked the storyteller.

'It's a *kak* story,' said Griessel. His tongue dragged on the 's'.

'How would you know?'

'I'm a policeman,' he said, struggling with the words.

'You're fucking drunk,' said the other suit-and-tie.

'Not drunk enough. But it's a shit story anyway.'

Then his cellphone began ringing. Benny took it out, looked at the screen. Vaughn Cupido. He put the phone back in his pocket.

'Why is it a shit story?' asked the guy who told it.

'Article 25 of the Criminal Prosh . . . Procedure . . .' He battled to form the words, said them slowly and methodically: 'Criminal. Procedure. Act. And we will never use a *Haas* . . . a civilish . . . civ.il.ian . . .'

'Pal, you're paralytic.'

'Where's your police badge?'

Griessel reached into his pocket, took out his wallet. It took a while. The two suits-and-ties watched him scornfully. He fumbled through the wallet, took out his SAPS identity card, smacked it down on the table.

They looked at it, then at him.

'No wonder our crime rate is the highest in the fucking world,' said the storyteller.

'Fuck you,' said Benny Griessel. 'That's not true.'

'Fuck you, *dronkgat*. If you weren't a policeman I would *moer* you.'

'You couldn't even put a dent in a *drol*,' said Griessel and rose to his feet unsteadily. He staggered, precariously, right up to the suit-and-tie.

The man hit him against the cheek with his fist. Griessel fell.

The storyteller said to his friend, 'You're my witness, he shoved me first.'

7

Transcript of interview: Advocate Susan Peires with Mr Francois du Toit

Wednesday, 24 December; 1604 Huguenot Chambers, 40 Queen Victoria Street, Cape Town

FdT: I . . . Maybe I should . . . Hell, I didn't see it coming. Two years ago I was still working overseas, I never dreamed . . . People do such stupid things and then you think, there's no other choice. Stress is a devil . . . and panic. It was more panic, I think, but when you're in it, and you don't know what to do, and a guy approaches you . . .

This story . . . How can I . . . ? It didn't start yesterday, not even last year. This story . . . I thought, now, the other day, when the papers were full of Richter's disappearance, then I thought, this story has been a long time coming. From my granddad's day already, my *oupa*. He was Jean du Toit, the Western Province scrum-half. I don't know if you . . . In 1949 and 1950 he . . . Never mind. There's so many . . . Klein Zegen – it's old Afrikaans for 'Small Blessing' – Klein Zegen has been in our family for seven generations. Before us it was the Vissers. The farm is over three hundred and thirty years old; it was established in 1682. Three hundred and thirty years: so much history and hard times and hard labour . . . Disease, pestilence . . . The vine blight of the 1890s; my great grandfather's father had to pull them all out – every vine, all ninety-six hectares . . . Last year I was thinking, the farm has a kind of curse on it, if you look at the history . . .

Sorry, just give me a chance. In the end it's all relevant . . .

SP: Take your time . . .

FdT: I'm really sorry. It's Christmas, I'm sure you would rather . . . you know, be with your family . . .

SP: I assure you, it's not a problem. Take your time; tell me everything that you think may be useful.

FdT: I just want you to understand . . . I suppose I'm looking for mitigating circumstances. Is that the right term?

SP: It is.

FdT: I want . . . I mean, the story played out in a certain context . . . I . . . It's all that I have. My story. And the court – I mean the legal process – it works on facts. This one did this, and that one did that, and that is the court's final judgement. I don't think the law listens to stories. But our stories are important. Our stories define us. We are the stories and the product of our stories.

Forgive me . . . I know I'm not making sense. I'm the reader in the family. Me and my grandma, Ouma Hettie. And my mother . . . I have a connection with stories, I think it has . . . if you read so much, from when you're small, then you want your life to be like a story-book, with a certain structure of struggle and history, from chaos to order – an ending that makes sense of it all. That's why I talk about the context of the story, because the context gives the final insight. Part of my context is . . . that thing about the sins of the fathers . . . and the firstborn son; it's kind of Biblical, the whole . . .

There are two things you have to understand. The first is the tradition of the firstborn son who inherits the farm. That's probably how most of the farms in this country operate. It's been passed down for seven generations of the Du Toit's, all the way back to 1776. It's just the way it is. My great-great-great-grandfather had six daughters before there was a son, he was in his forties before he could stop making children. It's a tradition with implications, but what can you do?

I was the second-born son . . .

My granddad, Oupa Jean had only one son – my father, Guillaume . . . Wait, maybe I should . . . Have you . . . Can I have that pen and a sheet of paper?

SP: Of course.

FdT: I want to draw a family tree . . . Not of all the ancestors. Just . . . six, but then you might be able to see . . . This is Oupa Jean and Ouma Hettie . . . Then my father Guillaume, and my mother Helena . . . and my brother Paul . . . and me . . . Here. Now you can see . . .

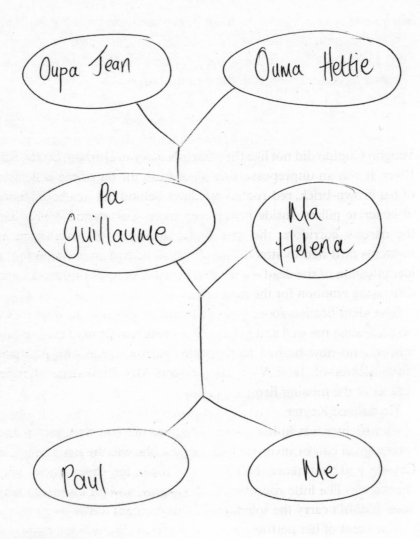

SP: Thank you . . .

FdT: My grandpa Jean, that's where it began. Oupa Jean was an only son. He inherited the farm. And he had it for a long time . . . He had to drink himself to death before my father could farm it, and then . . . This is the second thing you must understand, the influence of Oupa Jean. Genetically and psychologically and . . . let's say, financially. I . . . you can't look at this whole . . . you can't listen to my story without starting with my Oupa Jean. He casts a long shadow. As far as Ernst Richter.

So I'd better start with Oupa Jean.

8

Vaughn Cupido did not like the state mortuary in Durham Street, Salt River. It was an unprepossessing place from the outside: a collection of flat brown-brick, red-roofed buildings behind the weathered fence of concrete pillars. Inside it was even more spartan and depressing: the narrow corridors, the smells, the memories of macabre post-mortems he'd had to attend. But above all he had an aversion to the identification of the dead – a terrible moment of huge discomfort and distressing emotion for the next of kin.

The identification room was small and bare – only a rudimentary bench against the wall and a dusty blue curtain in front of the viewing mirror. And now he had to share this narrow space with Adjutant Jamie Keyter of Table View station, and Mrs Bernadette Richter, mother of the missing Ernst.

He disliked Keyter.

Mrs Richter was in her sixties. She dyed her hair dark brown and wore a small pair of silver-rimmed glasses. She was the same height as Cupido and very tense. Her face was made for cheerfulness, with cheekbones like little round *mosbolletjie* buns, and an unusually long nose. It didn't carry the solemnity of this moment well.

The scent of her perfume was overpowering in the small room.

'They will pull back the curtain and you will see the body,' said Jamie Keyter to her.

She nodded. Cupido could see her trembling.

'Are you ready?' asked Keyter.

Jissis, thought Cupido, what kind of bedside manner was this? 'Ma'am,' he said, 'Have you been informed that you don't have to do this?'

'No.'

He suppressed the urge to give Keyter a very dirty look. He said: 'If there is someone else . . . a family member, someone who works with him . . .'

'I am his mother.'

'I understand, ma'am, but we know how difficult it is. If you—'

'No. I am all he has. Let me do it.'

'You can take as much time as you like.'

She nodded.

'Is there someone who can support you . . . ?'

'Yes. My friends are here outside.'

'Thank you, ma'am.'

'I'm ready.'

Keyter knocked impatiently on the window. The curtain moved aside slowly.

Mrs Richter stood dead still. All three of them stared at the body. Cupido saw the body had not been prepared yet. Grains of sand were still stuck to the face.

It was deathly quiet in the room. From outside, somewhere in the corridor, the sound of a trolley being pushed along, one crooked wheel making an annoying squeak.

She stood motionless for so long that Cupido thought the identification wasn't going to be positive.

'It's Ernst.' Nearly inaudible. And then her legs gave way and he helped to steady her, one hand on her arm, one behind her back.

She only began to weep as they walked out into the parking lot, flanked by both her friends. At a white Honda Jazz they had to stop and wait uneasily while the women comforted her in a joint embrace. When she had calmed down, Cupido said he would like to talk to her.

'Just not today,' and she began to weep again, uncontrollably now. The friends looked at Vaughn reproachfully, as if he had brought all this upon her.

He asked for her contact numbers and address. She sobbed them out. He made notes on his cellphone.

It was after half past seven in the evening when the Honda drove out of the gates of the mortuary. The sun had not yet set.

'Are you sour because we are taking over the case, or are you always so unsympathetic with relatives of the victim?' Cupido asked Jamie Keyter.

'What did I do?' the reply came, full of innocent surprise.

'I'm genuinely not the most tactful cop in the Service, but *fokkit*, Jamie, it's a painful situation when a mother comes to identify her child, even if he is an adult. Any fool can work that one out. It takes a little finesse. You can *mos* see the woman was stressed, but it's just "Are you ready?" What kind of bedside manner is that?'

'That's why I asked her if she was okay.'

'There's ways and there's ways, Jamie, fuck knows . . . Did you bring the docket?'

'There isn't a docket yet, I haven't had time for anything, because nobody knows whose case it is and I first had to identify the victim . . .' Cursing under his breath.

'It's our case now. So I expect you to kick-start the docket. I want your Part A tonight, and I want a comprehensive SAPS 5 by tomorrow morning . . .'

'I just questioned the one guy, the one who found the body . . .'

'Then go and put that in your Part A, Jamie, or do you want us to do it all over from the beginning . . .'

Cupido's cellphone rang. He took it out, saw that it was Benny calling and the relief washed over him.

'Benna!'

'No, Vaughn, this is Arrie September from Cape Town Central.' An old colleague, now commander of the SAPS station that used to be known as Caledon Square. 'I'm phoning from Benny's phone, that's where I got your cellphone number.'

'Where's Benny?'

'I've got him here in the cells, they brought him in on a drunk and disorderly, and I don't want to phone his CO; you know what trouble that would create.'

'*Jissis*, Arrie, thanks a lot. Just keep him there, but don't book him, please. He's had a very bad day. I'm on my way, give me ten.'

'Apparently he assaulted a guy, Vaughn.'

'Assault? Benny?'

'I'll find out the details, but you had better come.' September rang off.

Cupido turned around to Keyter, and could see that the adjutant was listening intently.

★　★　★

On the way to Buitenkant Street Cupido phoned Major Mbali Kaleni. He heard the TV in the background when he answered. Probably at home already, with cauliflower boiling on the stove.

He told her he had a positive identification for Ernst Richter, he was waiting for the files from Table View and Stellenbosch, 'And I've just spoken to Benny, he's having cellphone issues. We're meeting in town in fifteen minutes.'

'Thank you, Captain. Have you called Cloete?'

'It's the next thing on my list.' Which was true, because though the name Ernst Richter rang a bell, he wasn't exactly sure who he was. He didn't want Kaleni to know that.

Why had she made him JOC leader?

He knew Kaleni. That Zulu was clever. Slow and anal, by-the-book, painfully irritating and conservative, but clever. She was a schemer. Scheming all the time. What was her scheme now, with him?

Make Vaughn JOC leader, let him prove how useless he was? Show him why she had got the senior job and not him?

Fuck that, my china. He would show her.

He called Captain Cloete's number as he drove.

'Vaughn?' answered the media liaison officer, in his calm, patient voice, even though he must know that a call at this time in the evening spelled trouble.

'John, you know about Ernst Richter who went missing a few weeks ago?'

'Yes,' with a certain resignation.

'He has just been ID-ed as the *ou* that Table View dug out of the sand this afternoon.'

Long silence.

'John, are you there?'

'I was just saying a quick prayer.'

'That bad?'

'I take it he didn't die of natural causes?'

'Definitely foul play, but we have to tread lightly, John. The docket is still in limbo. We only got the case a few hours ago, and I'm in transit.'

'Just a second . . . Okay, give me what you have.'

'Body of a man recovered from the dunes north of Blouberg this afternoon was positively identified as that of Ernst Richter, who went missing, and then you must put in the correct date. Directorate of Priority Crimes' Serious and Violent Crimes Group are investigating, more info as soon as blah, blah, blah. That's genuinely all that I have.'

The line went quiet while Cloete made notes. Then he asked: 'Who is JOC leader?'

'That would be me.'

'Vaughn, that's not enough.'

'What do you mean?'

'This thing is going to explode, Vaughn. It's the biggest story since Pistorius. And Dewani. The media are going to go crazy. I will have to feed them something.'

Cupido's heart sank. 'When Richter went missing, Uncle Frankie Fillander and I were on the Somerset West hijackings, so I missed all the hype. Can you get me the clippings?'

It took a second before Cloete realised: 'You don't know who Richter is.'

'Like I said, I haven't even seen the missing person report. I've been on this case for two hours. I know Richter was notorious for something on the Internet. Porn . . . ?'

'If only it was pornography. He's the guy from Alibi . . . Listen, the quickest and the easiest is if I send you a bunch of links. Before I issue the statement. Because once the cat is out of the bag, it's going to be chaos. For me and for you.'

Brigadier Arrie September unlocked the cell for Cupido and they went in. Benny Griessel lay on his back, mouth agape, eyes shut. He was snoring, long and loud.

'Ai, *fok*, Benna,' said Cupido.

'We'll have to get him out of here, Vaughn,' said September. 'Before I *tjaila*. I promised the missus I wouldn't be late home today.'

'Who all knows?' he asked as he sat down on the bare cement bench beside Griessel. He saw there was a blueish-purple bruise on his colleague's cheekbone.

'Just me and the two uniforms who brought him in. But they will keep quiet.'

'He had a really bad day. I don't know if you heard about Vollie Fish.'

'I did. It's tragic, my bru'. But Benny went and fought with two *hase*,' September said, using police slang, calling members of the public rabbits. 'And the Fireman's Arms people are very upset about the *moleste*. They talk about laying charges.'

'Benna should never have been sent out to Vollie Fish. His head hasn't been right since The Giraffe died.'

'Our lips are sealed, but if there's a formal complaint . . .'

'I'll go and talk to them.'

'Can I bring your car around to the courtyard?'

'Please.'

September went out.

Cupido put his hand on Griessel's arm, and shook lightly. 'Benna . . .'

Griessel's snore stopped abruptly. 'Fuck you,' he said. 'Fuck you all.'

9

**Transcript of interview: Advocate Susan
Peires with Mr Francois du Toit**

*Wednesday, 24 December; 1604 Huguenot Chambers,
40 Queen Victoria Street, Cape Town*

FdT: There is a framed cutting from *Huisgenoot* magazine of 1950
about my granddad, Oupa Jean. All down the years it hung in the
front room . . . San took it down recently. It's kind of, I don't know,
there's a tragic feel about it. The way the article and reality . . . the
title reads *Groot oesjaar wag vir jong Jean du Toit*, 'a good harvest
year awaits young Jean du Toit'. There's a photo of him. He's standing in the vineyard, in his WP rugby jersey, with a rugby ball in his
hands. When San saw it for the first time she asked, 'What happened
to those genes?' She said that if he had been alive today he would
have been a paparazzi's dream. He was blond, and very good looking, with deep blue eyes. He was a fantastic rugby player, but in the
photo you can see the other thing too. It's . . . a kind of self-confidence that borders on mischief, it's an attitude that says he will do
whatever he likes, the world belongs to him. San says there is a kind
of danger to this look, an irresistibility; there are women who go for
it, even though they know it just spells trouble.

    The photo was taken two years after my great grandpa's death.
Oupa Jean inherited the farm at twenty-two. In those days it wasn't
unusual, there were guys who took over the family farm at eighteen;
it's different today . . . The trouble was, Klein Zegen was a wine farm,
with all that entails. The mystique of wine, the history, the
culture . . . My Ouma Hettie said in those days, the early fifties, a
wine farmer was really somebody. There was a perception that they
were all filthy rich. And they weren't . . . but just imagine, twenty-two,

handsome, a sports star, and a wine farmer with an estate where the homestead was two hundred and twenty years old. It's like being a rock star today. And sooner or later it will go to your head . . .

Oupa Jean was not just the only son; he was the only child. Ever since he was a little boy he'd been aware that it all would come to him. And he was very spoiled, I think, the golden boy, the talented, handsome child who had a future without even having to try.

Now you must understand, back when Oupa Jean took over the farm, that was the golden age of the KWV — the Cooperative Wine-growers Union. Which was really the State controlling the whole wine industry. Up to 1956 the KWV would in any case buy up his whole harvest. In 1957 the KWV brought in the quota system, and with Oupa Jean's rugby contacts he made sure Klein Zegen got a big quota. His only goal was to fill that quota every year because Big Brother KWV would buy it all. Very few of the farmers those days worried about quality. There weren't many of them who made their own wine on the farm, it wasn't really financially rewarding . . . So you could farm part time, it was only at pruning and harvest time that you had to focus a bit. Which gave Oupa Jean time for rugby and women and drink. Not necessarily in that order.

And that's what he did, and everybody thought he would be chosen for the South African national team, and become a Springbok. But then two things happened. Oupa Jean got Ouma Hettie pregnant the next year, and he broke his leg, just before the Springbok tour to England and France . . .

In the car Cupido said, 'Benna, I need you on this one, please, partner.'

Griessel sat with his head down and swayed with the movement of the vehicle. He made a sound that sounded like a humourless laugh.

Cupido felt the tension in his gut. He had to get the Richter case going very fast, tomorrow morning Cloete would have to feed the media monster again, and he would have to report to Kaleni about what he and Benny had achieved. But first he had to go and talk to the Fireman's. The big problem was that, though the Hawks would tolerate a drunk member now and then, if you went around hitting a civilian in your drunken state, suspension was inevitable.

And Griessel would not be able to cope with that on top of everything.

He stopped in front of Alexa Barnard's big Victorian house in Brownlow Street, Tamboerskloof, walked around to the passenger side, and helped Benny get out. They struggled through the garden gate, to the front door. Cupido knocked urgently.

Alexa came to open up. She saw Benny hanging onto Vaughn Cupido and caught her breath.

'He's fine, he's just drunk,' said Cupido.

'A drunken altruist,' said Griessel, with difficulty, slurring the 's'.

'Oh, Lord,' said Alexa and began to cry.

'I think we had better go in, if you don't mind,' said Cupido.

Alexa nodded and stood aside. Cupido steered Griessel into the house. She closed the door behind them.

'A drunken altruist is better,' said Griessel. 'Much better.'

Cupido helped Benny to the couch, and let him sit down. Griessel lay back and closed his eyes.

'Can we talk somewhere?' Cupido asked her quietly.

She stared at Benny, tears running down her face.

'Vaughn, I heard a funny story,' said Griessel. '*Fokken* funny . . .'

'Okay, Benna.'

Griessel closed his eyes again.

'Come,' said Alexa, and led him to the kitchen.

'He's had a very bad day,' said Cupido, and told her about Vollie Fish and the family murder. 'They said Benny tapped a guy in the bar . . .'

'Hit someone? Benny?'

'I don't really know what happened, but the problem is if a complaint is laid, they will suspend Benny. And you and I know, that's not going to be good for him. I will try to fix things at the bar, but please, you must try to get him sober. And keep him sober. Major Mbali thinks he's out with me on a case. I can cover for him until tomorrow morning, but make sure he is at the office on time.'

Alexa stood, helpless and defeated, in the centre of the room. 'I don't know if I can . . .'

Cupido could see she was very confused. Then he remembered, she was also an alcoholic.

'Give him coffee . . .'

'Coffee doesn't help, Vaughn.'

'You'll have to try something. Call his AA sponsor. I really can't stay, we've got this huge case; I have to work. Don't let him answer his phone, no matter who calls. If there's big trouble, call me.'

She just stood there, utterly lost.

'Are you going to be okay?' he asked.

'I don't know.'

He drove to the Fireman's Arms and asked to speak to the manager. He told the man, 'He's a great detective and a good man. He hasn't had a drink in almost two years, but one of his colleagues shot himself today, so please, man, give the guy a break.'

'He assaulted one of my customers.'

'I get that, and on behalf of the police, I apologise. But please. You could ruin the man's career . . .'

'Okay. But I don't want him back.'

'I promise, thank you very much,' and he jogged out into the darkness, relieved, and he took the car, put on the siren and the blue lights and raced to Bellville, to go and read what John Cloete had sent him.

★　★　★

It took Alexa Barnard half an hour to gather the courage to call Doc Barkhuizen.

First she took off Benny's shoes, and helped him to lie comfortably on the couch. He gazed at her, a surreal moment when he looked at her without recognising her at all. And then he let his head fall back again and closed his eyes.

She said, 'Oh Jesus, Benny,' and she sat down in the easy chair beside the couch so that she could keep a watchful eye over him, and she thought, she was the weak one, she was the alcohol-risk, Benny was so strong. Why hadn't she seen this coming? He might have been quiet lately, but not that much quieter than usual, he had never been much of a talker. And after everything he had been through, and the work he did . . . there had been no sign.

She must phone Doc Barkhuizen, Benny's sponsor at Alcoholics Anonymous, the seventy-one-year-old, sinewy, eccentric medical doctor with long grey hair in a ponytail. Sometimes he wore an earring. He had thick glasses, wild eyebrows and a mischievous face. But she was careful of him, because he was so strict with Benny and he didn't like her, didn't like their relationship. He told Benny many times it was a recipe for disaster, two alcoholics together, and one of them a capricious, emotional, middle-aged singer. And Doc was right, because look at how helpless she was now; she must be strong, like Benny was when she relapsed.

All she could think of now was how much she wanted to have a drink too.

At last she stood up, looked carefully for Griessel's phone, took it out and looked up Doc's number. She saw it was the last one in his iPhone's 'Favourites'. She was first, then Carla, and Fritz and a few colleagues.

She was Benny's number one favourite. She had never known that, it made her want to cry again, but she fought against it, and made the call.

'Benny?' Doc Barkhuizen answered. 'This time of night it's never good news.'

'It's Alexa,' she said, with a catch in her voice, despite her best efforts.

'Oh, *magtig*,' he said.

'Doctor, Benny . . .' She wept.

'How many,' asked Barkhuizen, calmly.

'A lot.'

'There's not a lot I can do for him tonight, but it sounds as though you need help.'

'Yes.'

And then, to her infinite relief, he said, 'Where are you? I'll come right away.'

Vaughn Cupido clicked on the first link in Captain John Cloete's email. It was a news report on the Netwerk24 news website:

App helps you to get a bit on the side.

STELLENBOSCH – 'All Pleasure. No stress' is the motto and promise of a new smartphone app and website that will help South Africans to have a bit on the side – and get away with it.

Lovers who need a rock solid alibi for a dirty weekend, or who just need a verifiable excuse for a quick red-hot hour, can depend on Alibi. co.za in future to help them lie. But at a price, of course.

With membership at R62.50 per month, prospective cheaters will have access to a whole menu of dishonest options: a SMS calling you to a 'meeting', for example, can cost you R25, a telephone call from your 'office' is R125, while faux registration documents and a ficti- tious hotel account for the weekend's 'work conference' can cost up to R1,800.

'Clients can decide for themselves how comprehensive their alibi must be,' the founder and managing director of Alibi.co.za, Mr Ernst Richter, said during a press conference in Stellenbosch. 'Our task is to deliver it credibly and on time.'

'Slap me with a *snotsnoek*,' muttered Vaughn Cupido, and he thought, no wonder Cloete said this thing was going to explode. He read on.

In answer to a question whether this would encourage marital infidelity, Richter said websites like AshleyMadison.com and Maritalaffair.co.za already created the opportunity for South Africans to have extramarital affairs. 'Statistics show that hundreds of thousands have already regis- tered with these websites. Alibi.co.za just wants to keep them out of trouble and the divorce courts.'

It was precisely the local success of AshleyMadison.com that gave Richter the idea for his new company. Similar alibi services have existed for many years overseas, but South Africa had been behind the times until now. 'You need local knowledge to build a successful alibi for clients. On top of that the exchange rate makes it very expensive for South Africans to use the overseas alibi services. Our prices make it possible for Joe Bloggs to express his love life in a way that is stress free and affordable.'

'We invite people to supply as much information as possible when they register on the website or through the smartphone app, so that an alibi can have the maximum credibility. For instance, if you indicate that you work in banking, our sophisticated systems ensure that you never receive a fake call from the office outside of working hours.'

Richter said Alibi.co.za's security systems were highly sophisticated, and there was no chance that the users' information could end up in the wrong hands. 'Discretion is our driving force. Not even the employees have access to a client's full profile. We also offer the option of a pseudonym, so in most cases we don't even know who our clients really are.'

Over and above the extensive series of possible options from which clients can choose, users can also create their own alibi. 'We immediately send a quote for the execution of the alibi,' said Richter.

The company expects its user profile to be similar to that of the cheater websites – about 48% women, and 52% men. 'We accept that for socioeconomic reasons, our clients will mostly be over 35. The average age for women to begin thinking of an extramarital affair is 39. For men it is 42.'

Cupido typed in the web address in his Google Chrome search field.

The Hawks internet was faster than usual at this time of night and the page loaded quickly.

There was a large photograph of a good-looking couple in turquoise tropical waters. Their faces were turned towards each other, loving and satisfied. Behind them was a sandy beach with palm trees. Across the blue sky were the words:

Alibi.co.za
All pleasure. No stress.

The company logo was a white dove in flight, with a romantic heart icon in its beak. Below the photo, *Register now, and take the 'dangerous' out of dangerous liaisons, the 'ex' out of sex. Put the 'fair' back into affair. Satisfaction guaranteed or your money back!* – with fields where you could type in your name and email address.

11

Framed photos of Advocate Susan Peires hung on her office wall. Francois du Toit had seen them when he came in. One was of her graduation, a couple of decades ago. She was one of those women who age well, he thought. The years had softened her appearance, so that now, in middle age, she was attractive: strong and dignified.

As he told her his story, he had a vague sense that something about her gave him peace of mind. She *looked* like an instrument of justice. Perhaps it was her calmness, the inner strength that she radiated. Perhaps it was the fact that she didn't dye her hair, the salt-and-pepper mix of dark and grey gave her sophistication, wisdom. Or perhaps it was her face, the strength of its spare lines, the angle of her nose, the mouth neither too thin nor too full, in perfect neutral balance, so that it neither judged nor approved.

He talked more and more easily. He was swept along by the history, his enthusiasm growing as if somehow it really would serve as mitigation for his sins. He felt free enough to stand up from the chair – first behind it, with his hands on the leather backrest, and then, gradually, to begin moving around the large office.

He told her about the woman that his Oupa Jean had made pregnant.

His grandma, Ouma Hettie was a Malherbe from Calitzdorp. Her parents were humble people. 'Her father had a small shop; he struggled, he had to scrimp and save to send her to university. She had spoken of what a terrible thing the pregnancy was to her parents – a huge scandal. She was their passport to respectability; she was the symbol of their progress from backwardness and poverty. It must have been difficult in those days, 1951 . . . But she always said the one "klein zegen", the small blessing, was that she fell pregnant in September of her final year. She could still graduate, she had studied for a degree in Education. And of course the fact that it was a wine farmer who made her pregnant, a Western Province fly-half, that helped.

'Ouma was an incredible woman. I think it was her sense of humour that saved her – and the farm, and my father. Humour, and being down to earth . . .

'Oupa Jean . . . Ouma used to say that he was a magnet. Those eyes, that smile, that look that said the world was his oyster. She always said she was very proper, conservative, she'd barely kissed a man before Oupa Jean, but that evening when he asked her to dance, and he *could* dance, he made her look so good on the floor, and she smelled him and his face was against her hair and he said you are the most beautiful girl in the whole of Stellenbosch, then all of her careful upbringing flew out of the window.

'She was beautiful – very beautiful. Oupa Jean made a lot of mistakes, but his taste in women was not one of them . . .

'My father was conceived that very night, in the homestead. It was just about the last good thing that Oupa Jean did, except of course to marry Ouma, but he didn't really have a choice, back in those days.'

12

Cupido struggled to sit still. He wanted to get going, to be on the move, but the faded yellow file that Stellenbosch had delivered while he'd been out was a fair bit thicker than the average missing persons file.

So he stayed in his chair, pulled the file towards him and opened it. Inside he found a photo stapled to the first page, three statements in Section A and two forensic reports in Section B. Section C was so comprehensive he was impressed, but he knew that the media attention that Stellenbosch had received must have placed enormous pressure on the SC and his detectives to do a thorough job.

Right at the back was a signed SAPS 55(A) – the form that indemnified the police from fraudulent reports and gave them the right to circulate and publish the photo and description of the missing person.

He studied the photograph. It matched the face that he had seen at the mortuary. It showed Ernst Richter in jeans and a blue T-shirt with *H.T.M.L.* on it, and below that *(expert in) How To Meet Ladies*. He looked young: early thirties maybe. He was laughing, his hands gesturing to illustrate some point when the camera caught him; clean shaven; thick, dark hair almost touching his shoulders; lean body. He had his mother Bernadette's long nose, but his cheekbones were sharper and his mouth more prominent.

That was not how he imagined a guy who ran an alibi website would look, Cupido thought. Richter looked *decent*, normal; sort of the guy next door, if you lived in a middle-class white suburb, that is. But with whiteys, he had learned over the years, you couldn't go on looks. Very deceiving.

He deciphered the first statement, written by a charge office constable in nearly illegible handwriting. It was made on 27 November by a Cindy Senekal, described as a 'friend of the missing person'.

According to Cindy she had talked to Richter a number of times on the telephone on Wednesday 26 November. He was 'upbeat' and 'normal'. The last call was at 16.00. They had a date to have dinner at the Dorpstraat Deli in Stellenbosch at 19.00. When he was fifteen minutes late, she tried to call him, but only got his voicemail. Senekal tried again a number of times, and left two voice messages. She waited at the restaurant until 19.45, and then returned to her townhouse. Over the course of the evening she tried again to contact him by phone, without success. Senekal said Richter's cellphone had gone directly to voicemail around 20.30, and had stopped ringing. Her final call to him was at 00.24. 'I called again this morning at approximately 06.50. At that time, I was just getting his voicemail. So I drove to his house. The doors were locked. Nobody answered the door. Ernst was sometimes a little late for dates, but he's never disappeared like this,' the statement read.

His cellphone number and a description of his car, a grey Audi TT, were also written down.

Just after 08.00 Senekal drove to the offices of Alibi.co.za in Stellenbosch. Richter's car was not in its usual parking spot. She went into the offices, and asked after him. The staff did not know where Richter was. After talking to the operations manager of Alibi, Desiree Coetzee, she went back to her own place of work. Senekal and Coetzee communicated many times during the day of Thursday 27 November, and neither could make any contact with Richter. They agreed that Senekal would go to the police if there was still no news by 17.00, which she did.

The second statement was taken on 28 November by a detective of the Stellenbosch station at the Alibi offices, in an interview with the operations manager, Desiree Coetzee. It only added a few more details: Richter was last seen two days before, on 26 November around 17.15, when he left the Alibi offices. He was dressed in jeans, white trainers, and a black T-shirt with the words *I refuse to engage in a battle of wits with an unarmed person* in white letters on the front. He was, as always, in a good mood. There were no calendar entries on his computer for the rest of the day. His grey Audi TT was his only vehicle. His colleagues knew of no real enemies, but the company regularly received threats, from religious fanatics in particular. They had included death threats directed against Ernst Richter, but were, without exception, anonymous, and sent from temporary email accounts, or masked mail servers.

Cupido sighed. That was what he'd been afraid of. They'd have to follow up on each and every one of those threats.

The Coetzee statement went on to say that Richter had no notable record of absenteeism, although he was sometimes late for appointments, 'but never more than an hour'.

The third statement was from Bernadette Richter, the victim's mother, but Cupido hesitated before he read it. Something didn't fit. He pushed the docket away and leaned on the desk.

Something that Senekal or Coetzee had said in their statements?

No. The flaw wasn't there.

Cupido stood up. He hated sitting down, he just couldn't think like that. He walked out of his office and down the passage, without any particular destination.

Fokken Benna, why did he have to go on the booze again, where was his partner when he needed him?

He really wanted to talk to Griessel about this case. They were a team, the Yin and Yang of the Hawks, Batman and Robin. He often thought they worked so well together because he, Cupido, was the dancer: Twinkletoes, *pappie*, lightning mental footwork; he was the investigative artist, with everything that went along with it – creative, eccentric, a little touchy at times. And Benna was the philosopher, the thinker; man, that dude was methodical. And grounded, except for the *dop*, of course, but the drinking was only because Benna thought too much, and too deeply. In this job that was dangerous.

So their usual routine was that he, Cupido, tossed ideas around, a thousand miles a minute, and Benna was the screen, the filter, the gatekeeper. His sounding board.

And now his sounding board was dead drunk, and he would have to manage on his own for now.

So, something still didn't make sense.

It wasn't something in the statements.

Something this afternoon, at the mortuary.

He stood still for a second in the quiet twilit passage.

It was the dates.

He turned, jogged silently back to his office on his Nike Air Pegasus *takkies*. He clicked on the computer screen to open the Outlook diary, and counted the days from 26 November, when Richter had disappeared.

Twenty-one, until this morning, when Richter was found in the Blouberg dunes.

Trouble was, the body he'd seen in the mortuary this afternoon had definitely not been buried for twenty-two days. Not enough decomposition. He might have been dead a week or so, tops.

So where was Ernst Richter for the first fourteen days after he went missing?

The plot thickens.

He wanted to phone Cindy Senekal and talk to her, now.

He suppressed the urge, and pulled the docket closer again. He shifted his chair, put his feet up on the desk and leaned back comfortably. He balanced the folder on his belly, and read on.

The third statement was taken by the same detective, during an interview with the mother, Bernadette Richter. It provided nothing new, except that she expressed her deep concern, as her son had 'never run away before'.

Cupido paged over to the Investigation Diary in Section C.

It showed that on the morning of 28 November at 11.25 two detectives from Stellenbosch forced open the door of Richter's house in Mont Blanc, Paradyskloof, and searched it. There was no sign of a struggle and no clues to indicate what could have happened to the missing man.

Enquiries were made at the neighbours, but led nowhere.

On the same day, Richter's grey Audi TT was found, locked and parked at 16.42 in Stoffel Smit Street, Plankenbrug in Stellenbosch.

The offices of the light industries in the area were visited. Nobody knew Ernst Richter.

Audi Centre in Somerset West was called in to assist in unlocking the vehicle. After that the vehicle was processed. On the same day the detective also requested a forensic report on Richter's cellphone number, and issued an official missing persons bulletin, which included a statement to the media.

In the following week there were entries about fruitless attempts to trace the threats made against Richter and Alibi. The numbers on Richter's cellphone records were followed up on, but produced nothing significant.

Vaughn read the two reports in the docket's Section B. The first was a forensic report on the Audi TT Coupé. Only Richter's fingerprints, as retrieved from his office, and those of Cindy Senekal, were identified. Two other fingerprints were found, but the SAPS database produced no match. Which meant that the person or persons had no criminal records. Semen was found on the passenger seat. The report said it was probably not older than fourteen days. No blood spots were found. Richter's leather wallet was found in the glove compartment. It contained three Premier bank cards, his driver's licence, a reloadable Gautrain card, a Makro card, his medical aid fund card, 19 of his own business cards, R786.74 in cash, and seven receipts for general purchases. Also in the glove compartment were one marijuana cigarette and a small plastic bag with about ninety grams of marijuana, a packet of cigarette papers, two boxes of matches, a ballpoint pen and the car's official documentation.

The other report was about Richter's cellphone. On the evening of his disappearance it was in contact with both the Papegaaiberg and the Golf Course towers at Stellenbosch until 20.17, after which all contact was broken. The list of calls made and received showed that Richter had last talked to Cindy Senekal at 16.08.

On that day he also phoned two colleagues and his mother, or received calls from them.

Cupido swung his feet down from the desk, and put the folder back down.

He found Cindy Senekal's number and called.

'Hi, this is Cindy. You know what to do after the beep.'

He left a message, just his name and number, as he didn't know whether Richter's mother had let her know or not. He looked up the number of the Alibi.co.za operations manager, Desiree Coetzee.

It wasn't in the file.

He cursed softly, although he knew that happened sometimes. The detective probably had the number in his notebook or on his cellphone. He hadn't expected the docket to be passed on to the Hawks.

He turned to his computer, and clicked on the tab of Alibi.co.za that said *Contact Us*. He found a list of links to frequently asked questions, media enquiries and 'Client Service'. The latter provided three email addresses and a toll-free number.

There was no physical address.

He called the toll-free number. It rang for a long time.

'Alibi dot co dot za, Ashley speaking, I'd love to craft your alibi.' A woman's voice, very seductive.

He identified himself, using the Hawks' official name, the Directorate for Priority Crime Investigations. He didn't feel like having to explain himself to some young girlie. 'I'm working on an investigation concerning one of your staff members,' he told her. 'I need a physical address for your premises.'

'I am not at liberty to give you that information, sir.'

'I'm a Hawks detective.'

'I understand that, sir,' awfully polite. 'But we get a number of similar calls from people who say they are from the police. I am under instructions not to give out our address.'

'You can call me back. Just go the website of the Directorate, and call the number you see there, for the Cape Town office . . .'

'Sir, I'm sorry, but you'll have to call our office number tomorrow, after eight-thirty.'

'What is your office number?'

She read it out, an 880 landline in Stellenbosch. Cupido wrote it down.

'Now, is there anything else I can help you with?'

'I want to speak to your operations manager, Desiree Coetzee. Could you call her, and ask her to call me?'

'I don't have her number, sir.'

'Do you have a supervisor, or a manager or something?'

'I'll see what I can do, sir.' He could hear her lack of enthusiasm. 'Anything else?'

He said no thanks, and rang off.

13

Transcript of interview: Advocate Susan
Peires with Mr Francois du Toit

*Wednesday, 24 December; 1604 Huguenot Chambers,
40 Queen Victoria Street, Cape Town*

FdT: I think Grandpa Jean proved Shakespeare wrong. The fault was
in his stars *and* in himself . . .

SP: Shakespeare had a foot in each camp. Kent, in *King Lear* said:
'. . . the stars above us, govern our conditions'. And what about
'giddy Fortune's furious fickle wheel' . . .

FdT: Your Shakespeare is better than mine.

SP: A wine farmer who can quote Shakespeare is a pleasant surprise.

FdT: Grandma Hettie made me read Shakespeare. She and I were
the readers in our family . . . And my mother . . . I think I told you
that already. Sorry, it's the stress . . . Ouma Hettie was clever, she
would quote passages of Shakespeare, such interesting titbits, and
if I asked, then she would fetch the book, and say, *Read, Shakespeare
is better life orientation than life itself.* So I read Shakespeare. *Julius
Caesar* was my favourite, that's why I remember it best – and
because that quote always reminds me of Oupa Jean. Because he
didn't have complete control. If he hadn't broken his leg, or if it
had happened later . . . Everyone said he would have been a
Springbok, even people who weren't that keen on him. Three
months before the wedding . . . If you look carefully, you can see
one crutch sticking out in some of the wedding photos, and the
plaster of paris on his lower leg. And maybe it would still have
been okay, if he had recovered in time. But when they selected the
team at the end of the year tour to England in 1951, he wasn't
right yet. They picked Fonnie du Toit instead, and he was nearly

thirty. No relation, though. And Hansie Oelofse as the younger fly-half . . .

If he had been another sort of person . . . If he could have processed the setback, got over it. Maybe it was a combination of things, because there were a whole lot of changes all at once. Suddenly he was a married man and there was a bun in the oven, he doesn't get picked for the Boks, and he's trapped on the farm with a broken leg, a man who had always been on the go . . . Four months after the wedding, my father arrived and he was a colicky baby. Before all the troubles, Oupa Jean had apparently been a big party guy, it was all part of the rugby culture in those days. But then he started hitting the bottle hard, and Ouma said he wasn't a nice man to be around then.

He was never really the same player again. There were those who said his leg bothered him always, that it didn't mend properly. But Ouma Hettie said it was pride. And the fact that everything had come to him so easily, he had so much natural talent. He believed he was better than anyone else, he didn't want to put in all the hard work to earn his place from scratch again. And when he finally woke up in 1955 and began training seriously, it was too late. Because another chap, who was about half the size of Oupa, but with double the heart, made the WP and the Bok team instead. Tommy Gentles . . .

14

Vaughn Cupido followed another of the links that John Cloete had sent him – again to the website of Netwerk24.

It was a story that had appeared in the *Rapport* newspaper; the headline said: *Isabeau talks to Ernst Richter. Alibi Boss never wants to use his own product.*

He began reading:

On his black T-shirt are the words 'I went outside once. The graphics weren't that great'.

And now he is outside again, on the veranda of the Häzz coffee shop in Stellenbosch's Ryneveld Street ('because they have Wi-Fi', he says when we make the appointment). I ask whether the 'graphics' are better. He looks at me. 'Much better, now that you are here ...'

Ernst Richter laughs infectiously, holding up his hands defensively in front of him: 'That's too smooth, please don't write that I'm some kind of pick-up artist ...'

'Are you?'

'No! But I have a sense of humour. And you gave me the gap.'

'Do you always take the gap?'

'I wouldn't say always.'

But there's one gap he did take – the one he saw when South Africans in their hundreds began joining websites for adulterers. Richter has just made the headlines countrywide with Alibi.co.za, a website and smart phone app that sells infidelity, lies and alibis at a price.

'Sjoe, when you say it like that it sounds uncool even to me,' he says. But the broad smile does not waver for a second, maybe because fifteen thousand people have downloaded his app already?

'The support of the public is a big relief,' he says, swiftly and smoothly, as if coached by a media trainer. 'We didn't know what to expect. But it's just more proof: there's no such thing as bad publicity.'

And publicity he's had in abundance, from all sides: ministers, Christian and family organisations, even the Minister for Women in the Presidency; and a spokesperson for the Department of Justice who hinted that the company's products 'might not be legal'.

'We did our homework. There is not a single aspect of Alibi that is not absolutely legal. They can come and see.'

He doesn't look like the boss of a lie factory, this open-faced boy, the only child from Cape Town's northern suburbs who'd once nursed a dream of becoming an artist. How on earth has he got to this point?

'Aah, you know, life is strange ...'

Cupido's reading was interrupted by the sound of his cellphone – an unknown number. He checked the time display on the phone; it was nearly ten.

'Cupido.'

'This is Cindy Senekal.' Her voice was cautious and a little afraid.

He hated passing on news of a death. And the problem was that he didn't really know how close Senekal had been to Ernst Richter. The docket just said 'a friend of the missing person', but from the statement it seemed more like she was a girlfriend. This was where he needed Benna, with his greater diplomatic skills.

'Thank you for calling me back. I'm very sorry, but I don't have good news ...'

Total silence at the other end.

'Is there perhaps someone with you who can support you?'

No reaction, until he asked: 'Are you there?'

'Is Ernst dead?'

'I'm very sorry. His body was found this morning.'

There was a single sound, a cry of pain. Cupido didn't know what to say.

'I thought so,' she said at last.

A little weird, Cupido thought, sitting in Cindy Senekal's lounge a little bit later.

She was a blonde *poppie*: long, straight hair, slim body, big honey-brown eyes; mid-twenties, very pretty. A *mooi* girl, and she knew it.

Ten to eleven, in a white townhouse with a green roof in Kleingeluk,

Stellenbosch, she sat on the sofa across from Cupido. Her two female housemates perched like bookends on either side, each holding one of Cindy's hands. All three had been crying, all three were now under control.

Cindy, the sexy one, centre stage with the little fat one on the left, while on the right sat the wannabe. A lesser lookalike, not as pretty as Cindy, but trying hard – same blonde hair, style, the works. Cupido knew, you only had to look: pretty girls always come with that entourage, or a close facsimile thereof.

The *little weird* was the behaviour of the three whitey girls. Not the first time that he'd seen it though. You got it with the young ones who didn't know the deceased very well. They hadn't really yet experienced personal loss, they thought they knew how it must feel, and now they were faking it a bit. It was like they were mimicking some reaction they'd seen on a TV police drama. Not quite convincing, but that was because they weren't totally emotionally invested in the victim. He was just an acquaintance to them.

'We were starting to date in earnest,' said Senekal, unaware of the pun. 'We weren't seeing other people any more.'

'How long were you together?'

'We met in October on Tinder. But only around the beginning of November did we really . . . you know . . .'

Tubby and Wannabe nodded, a sober, pious pair.

He didn't know, actually. He'd only heard about Tinder, a dating app for smart phones. Apparently it was quite brutal, the way you could reject someone. Or block them.

'You only began dating in November?'

'*Ja*, you know . . . At first we only chatted on Tinder for a while. You have to be careful, there are so many weirdos out there . . .'

Tubby and Wannabe nodded in solemn agreement.

'Did you know who he was?'

'Obviously. You sign into Tinder with your Facebook profile.'

'And his Facebook profile says he's the boss of Alibi?'

'Obviously.'

'When did you begin dating just each other?'

'The twentieth of November,' swiftly, with certainty, as if it were a landmark date.

'A week before he disappeared?'

'Yes.'

They barely knew each other, he thought. But, hey, it's a brave new world.

'Okay, run me through your relationship . . . You chatted on Tinder until the end of October. And then you began seeing each other in early November.'

'*Ja*. Our first date was lunch at Liza's. You know, in Dorp Street. Their peanut butter cheesecake is divine. I'd told him it's my favourite, so he surprised me. Ernst loved surprises. He took me in a helicopter around Table Mountain, from the Waterfront. All he said was, bring your shades, Cin, and then we went flying . . .'

'He's a pilot?'

'No, no, he hired a helicopter.'

'How often did you see each other, after the first date?'

'The last two weeks before he . . . disappeared . . .' Her lovely face contorted and her two friends squeezed her hands and rubbed her arms. 'Sorry, I can't believe he's dead; he was so, like, alive. The last two weeks, almost every day. I'm a Wine Club Ambassador at Mooigelegen, so I work a lot at night, when we host wine club events, but Ernst was so . . . He *understood*, he always said, don't worry, Cin, I'm my own boss . . .' That was as far as she got before a flood of tears made her drop her head, body trembling.

Tubby and Wannabe comforted her, clucking and weeping a little in sympathy too.

Wannabe passed her a tissue. Cindy Senekal blew her nose.

'. . . He said, I'm my own boss, I plug into your schedule . . .'

'He talked about his work?'

She nodded. 'Obviously. His work, his start-up was his life. It was practically all he talked about.'

'He never said anything about trouble? Someone who was angry with him?'

'You didn't know him . . .'

Obviously, thought Cupido.

'Everyone was crazy about him. Everyone. He was never in a bad mood; he was just hyper, the whole time. He said, "Cindy, I'm on a permanent high, life's an adventure, just look where it's taken me."'

'But I heard there were people who made death threats against him.'

Eyes widened. 'Genuine?'

'He never said anything about that?'

'No! Who on earth would threaten him?'

'Alibi got emails. Anonymous ones.'

'I knew nothing of that. He . . . never said anything.'

'He never mentioned problems, a bit of tension at work? Or in his personal life?'

'No, I'm telling you, he was the most positive person in the whole world . . .'

'Okay. In your statement you say that on the evening he disappeared, you had a dinner date.'

'Yes.'

'His phone records say you were the last person he spoke to on his cell that day. Round about four. What did you talk about?'

'About that night's date.'

'Just the when and the where?'

'Yes.'

'You were supposed to meet him at the restaurant?'

'Yes.'

'He never picked you up at home?'

'Always.'

'Why not that night?'

'Oh. *Ja* . . . He asked me to meet him at the Deli.'

'Why? Did he say?'

She frowned. Both friends frowned too, empathy in stereo. 'No. That's weird, now that I think of it . . . On our first date I met him at Liza's. You know, I wanted to be sure he was legit . . . But from then on, he always picked me up. At work, or here. Until that evening.'

15

**Transcript of interview: Advocate Susan
Peires with Mr Francois du Toit**

*Wednesday, 24 December; 1604 Huguenot Chambers,
40 Queen Victoria Street, Cape Town*

FdT: My father got the family name, Guillaume. The sad thing was, that was just about all Pa did get from the Du Toit side. He took after Grandma Hettie's side of the family much more. He didn't inherit Grandpa Jean's sporting genes either. Well, that's probably not entirely . . .

When my son was born six weeks ago, I had a bit of a revelation. You look at your child and you look for yourself in him. Part of you wants him to be like you. God knows why; I've got so many faults, it must be an ego thing, or maybe we're just built like that. Like the evolution guys say, the more we see ourselves in our children, the more we want to nurture them, or something. But then you look at your child and you see bits of yourself and bits of your wife, but actually it's ridiculous, because children . . . People are like a complex blend of wine; there are parts of grandmas and grandpas, fathers and mothers, a whole mixture. But in truth they are completely new, unique – their own person.

Pa was . . . It's hard to describe him, precisely because of the hard time he had with Oupa Jean. Pa was soft, but not weak. Pa was sensitive. I don't know where it comes from, because Ouma Hettie was not really sensitive. She was strong. Maybe she couldn't afford to be sensitive. I don't know . . .

Now you must see how the stars lined up for Pa: Oupa Jean wasn't a farmer at heart. He didn't have a real love for the vineyard or winemaking. The allure of wine, its mystique, the secrets of viniculture, these meant nothing to him. But he wanted to be seen as a wine man, as the master of a historic wine estate, he wanted the aura of the big wine farmer when he went drinking with his mates at the Stellenbosch Club. He wanted his KWV quota . . .

If you had a quota, every year you could get so many cases of Roodeberg and other wines at KWV, and then everyone was your friend. He wanted that . . . Prestige too. And he clung to the aura of the almost Springbok, the *ou* who would have played for his country, if only he hadn't broken his leg.

He wanted that whole aura and status, that image when he flirted with women. That was his other thing, apart from boozing with his bosom buddies at the Club. The affairs he had. Compulsively, chronically, as though he couldn't make peace with the fact that his golden bachelor days had been snatched away by Ouma's pregnancy; he still wanted to be the player, the *ou* who could just take, and who would always get.

So Oupa Jean was absent, in the first six, seven years after my father's birth. And then Pa went to school, and around Grade Two or Three he played in his first rugby match and suddenly Oupa Jean saw how his son could restore the honour of the Du Toits, how his son would reach the heights that were stolen from him.

Ouma Hettie would tell how she felt equally sorry for her son, the coach and the referees, because Oupa Jean would stand at the side of the field, during practice and matches and shout at everyone. And all at once he began coaching Pa on the farm even. Passing the ball and kicking, but without a shred of patience. He wanted Pa to have the natural talent he'd had, and the more he realised it was just not there, the more he screamed and shouted. It went on like that for three rugby seasons. Ouma said she should have put a stop to it sooner, but by then she was pregnant with her third child, and she had to keep the farm and the household on the go, and at least there was some interaction between father and son, even though it wasn't positive.

But then she stepped in. When Pa was twelve and a half, she told Oupa Jean, it was enough. Accept that the child just doesn't have your talent. Support him. Let him enjoy the game in his own way.

Oupa Jean stormed out to the Club. And from then on he never really took an interest in his son again.

16

Cupido's first chance to talk to Cindy Senekal alone was when she walked with him to his car.

He had to ask her about the marijuana in Richter's Audi. And the sex in the car, because the forensic report said the semen on the seat was less than two weeks old. Touchy subject. Even in this day and age, you just didn't come out and ask, 'Listen, did you *njaps* Richter in the car,' cause there's loss and grief, even if half of it's a bit forced. If the *njaps* wasn't with her, she was going to freak out. But then, it was important for the investigation. So ask he must.

If only Benna were here . . .

'Miss,' he said, grateful for the half-darkness of the street, 'I have to clarify a bunch of forensic things. And some of them are a bit uncomfortable . . .'

She looked at him enquiringly. It didn't help.

'They found marijuana in his glove compartment . . .'

'*Dagga?*' Her query came back too fast and the stiffening of her body gave her away.

'I'm not here about recreational drugs. I don't care what he smoked, and who smoked with him, *daai moet jy mooi verstaan*. But I have to see if there isn't perhaps a drug deal somewhere here . . .'

'I don't know anything about *dagga*,' she said, and he knew she was lying.

Fair enough. If that was her attitude, it made the next question that much easier . . .

'Then I also have to ask, did you make love in his car in November?'

'Make love?' Half offended.

'That's right.'

'In his car?'

'*Ja*. The Audi.'

'Why do you want to know?' With an attitude that said now he was bordering on harassment. And for a moment he suspected it was because he was a coloured cop who was getting cheeky with a whitey. Maybe he was too sensitive, and Benna wasn't here to save him. Till now she hadn't been at all racist – give the girl the benefit of the doubt, he thought.

But he dropped the politeness: 'Do you think I would ask if it wasn't important to the investigation?'

Her eyes widened a bit, but she recovered quickly. She asked: 'Make love, as in kissing?'

'We're talking more intense than that.'

'No. We didn't.' Icy now.

It was midnight when he had to stop at the Dorp Street traffic lights. He used the time to send an SMS to Griessel's cell number.

You all still awake?

Four minutes later, as he drove out of Stellenbosch, the answer came back: *I am – Alexa.*

He pressed the hands-free of his HTC into his ear, and called.

'Hello, Vaughn. Benny's asleep,' said Alexa, but she sounded calm.

'Are you okay?'

'Yes. Doc Barkhuizen was here. Benny's AA sponsor. He helped me get Benny into bed. There's nothing more we can do tonight.'

'True. But I was thinking, it's very important for Benny to be at work the usual time tomorrow. Just in case the *hase* from the Fireman's make trouble.'

'I'll do my best . . .'

'I'm going to say Benny was out with me on the case tonight. Then no one can say he was so wasted that he couldn't work, if you get my drift.'

'Thanks, Vaughn.'

'*Daai's niks*, nothing to thank me for. But now I have to brief you, so you can prepare Benna in the morning.'

'I will.'

'Okay. Can you get a pen and paper?'

He drove down the Bottelary road, because Polkadraai was so choked up with roadworks, it had to be avoided at all costs.

He thought about Benna and Alexa.

Good people.

Because they had had a hard time. You only had to look, a whitey that hasn't had a hard time, was basically a *doos*. You had to suffer first, before you could connect, before you could see we are all just human, irrespective of race, colour, creed.

Alexa, the famous music star who was dragged down by the *dop*, faded from the scene, and then her husband was shot. She'd been through *kwaai* times. But now she was making an effort to get back on her feet again.

And Benna. He should have been group leader of Violent Crimes. He should have had that promotion long ago. Hell, he should have been a brigadier. But Benna's trouble was, he could not *see* himself there. Benna had a chip the size of Table Mountain on his shoulder, and Cupido could never quite work out why.

Just because he was a boozer? That didn't make sense; there were very senior members who drank like fishes too, but they didn't have that self-loathing that he could sometimes see in Benna. Where was it from? Everyone knew, he was a great detective, in his way. And Benna could work with people – with Mbali, with him, Vaughn, with witnesses, with suspects. It was like Benna was just plugged in, he had that sixth sense with people; he respected everyone, he knew what buttons to press.

But he hated himself . . .

Ours not to reason why, thought Cupido. Even if Benna made all the right moves, networked, believed, kissed ass a bit, he was white in a world of affirmative action. Basically fucked. Even the constitutional court said so recently, finding that affirmative action was all good and proper.

He thought about Alexa, still awake, there at Benny's bed. Not easy, you would also want a drink, now you had to sit and watch over your sozzled other half.

Strange couple, those two alkies.

But at least they were a couple. He wasn't even in a relationship, not of any kind.

Because he wouldn't use things like Tinder. The first problem was, there were twenty guys for every girl. The second problem was, if you wanted to stand out, you had to lie like your feet stink. The whole online dating thing was one massive fraud – you could weigh 200 kilo-grams and look like Dracula's grandma, but you just photoshopped your pic, or you stole a supermodel's, wrote all sorts of cute things in your profile, and off you go. So there was no credibility, and he, Vaughn Cupido, had personality. How do you show personality on a dating website?

The right thing to do was, just go out and meet someone. He had a lot to offer.

But where did the top detective of the Hawks find any time for going out, and meeting someone?

In his office he wrote his notes about the interview with Cindy Senekal. He wrote a lie, there in black and white, that Benny Griessel was with him.

And then he turned back to his computer screen and went on reading the *Rapport* article by Isabeau Bekker.

He didn't look like the boss of a lie factory, this open-faced boy, the only child from Cape Town's northern suburbs who'd once nursed a dream of becoming an artist. How on earth had he got to this point?

'Aah, you know, life is strange . . .'

How strange?

'No, the way you get these opportunities. My father died when I was fourteen. My mother was a housewife, then she had to step into his shoes. It wasn't easy. My father had a brokerage firm, short term insurance, it wasn't the sort of thing she could just take over. It had to be sold first, and then there wasn't much money, she had to find work, with a child in high school. We struggled at times, but she always just said, we have a roof over our heads and we have food on the table and that's more than a lot of people in this country have. We'll make a plan . . .'

I ask him what his mother says about the plan he made with Alibi, and the smile wavered for the first time.

'No, she asked me if that was really what I wanted to do.'

Is it?

'I'm an entrepreneur. Entrepreneurs see opportunities and grasp them. This is not my first business, and it won't be my last. Alibi is a stepping stone . . . My mother understands that,' and the smile is back.

In school he excelled at art, won competitions. He thought that paint-ing full time would be his career one day. His mother scrimped and saved so he could take extra classes with 'Oom Werner van Heerden', the famous artist of the Northern suburbs. 'But if you're alone at home in the after-noon, and you have a computer, then you discover gaming. And the internet. It becomes the place where you live, and you see the art in the games, and the aesthetics of websites, and you realise how the whole world comes to you on a screen – a PC screen, an iPad screen, a phone screen. And many of the designs are pure art, and many are pure . . . junk.'

In the Stellenbosch sunshine, at a table outside Häzz, Ernst Richter, the Great Sinner of Alibi.co.za, tells of his conversion to graphic design with an evangelical glow. 'It was like a thunderbolt, in the July holiday of my Grade Eleven year, I knew: this is what I want to do. I want to design games. I want to make the world wide web a more beautiful place. Graphic design is the future, everything will eventually be graphic design, just as our lives are becoming all the more digital, as we live more and more online.'

He went to study for a diploma in graphic design at the Cape Peninsula University of Technology. 'It was hard on me and my mother. There was only just enough money to pay for the classes. I took the train to the city; on weekends and holidays I was a waiter; my mother worked overtime so that we could afford the books and everything.

'In my second year, two of my friends and I started a small web design company. We used the Varsity computers for the first six months, but we could quote cheaper than anyone else, and our designs were cool, and I realised I could sell. I could sit down with a guy and say, usability and aesthetics are two sides of the same coin, the combination is a competitive advantage.

'We could stop being waiters. We made quite good money.

'And then we finished at Varsity and we went on with the business, and it was tough, because we weren't students any more, and we had to hire an office and buy our own hardware and software, and we had to increase our quotes. But we still believed. We had this big poster of Steve Jobs on the wall: "If you keep your eye on the profit, you're going to skimp on the product. But if you focus on making really great products, then the profits will follow."

'And then came the iPhone and the iPad, and because we were such total nerds, we quickly realised that app design was the next big wave. So we were

proactive. We started talking to the magazines. Half of the magazine apps you see on an iPad, we designed. We did okay . . . But about two years ago, I got restless. I felt that I needed a new challenge. So I sold my share, and went to see what hadn't been done yet. That's how Alibi was born.'

And the game design?

He laughed again. He said he designed the Alibi.co.za website. He said it was very attractive and functional. 'How many websites in the online dating industry can say the same?'

Game design would remain a dream, because there weren't big opportunities here on the southern tip of the Dark Continent.

But adultery apparently offered big opportunities?

Earnest Ernst again: 'Your time is limited, so don't waste it living someone else's life. Don't be trapped by dogma – which is just living with the results of other people's thinking. Don't let the noise of other's opinions drown out your own inner voice. And most important, have the courage to follow your heart and intuition.'

'Steve Jobs?' I ask.

'Yes,' he says.

'Do you feel a connection?'

'Absolutely.'

'Because of the money? Fifteen thousand clients at R62.50 a month is close on a million, just in basic income. And that's just the beginning. A lot of money for a young man.'

The smile evaporates. 'We're a long way from making a profit. There's a lot of hard work ahead. I will never be as rich as Steve Jobs. But I will always follow my heart.'

17

*Wednesday, 24 December; 1604 Huguenot Chambers,
40 Queen Victoria Street, Cape Town*

FdT: Pa is still a mystery to me.

Pa never really talked about all of this. Ouma Hettie would, but you never knew what *wasn't* said. You only knew what she saw and experienced, and that only from a certain perspective. That's another thing I learned and experienced in the past year or so: you can never see through someone else's eyes. And even if you try, it's a distorted view. So, Ouma Hettie looked through the eyes of a woman who was ... angry, probably. I don't know if that is the whole truth.

My mother would say something here and there, but Ma also comes from a wine estate; it's a closed community, you don't talk outside of it, you maintain a united front. Oom Dietrich ... He's our neighbour, on the estate next door, Blue Valley. Dietrich Venske. He and Pa worked together for a long time back then, I talk to him a lot about my father. He says, you could see the damage, earlier. And Pa used to tell him things ...

In any case, my father grew up on the farm in the sixties. And I have this image in my mind: my father had to watch Ouma struggle with Oupa Jean. Pa must have heard the big fights about the affairs, he must have experienced his father's rejection. He had to watch Ouma trying to raise his two younger sisters, how she had to manage the workers to get everything done on the farm.

And because Pa was sensitive, because he had a heart, he felt he wanted to help Ouma. When he was about fifteen, when he heard them fighting again one night, he couldn't take it any more. He went and told Oupa Jean, stop it, all of it: the sleeping around and the drinking, bullying Ouma, neglecting the farm.

And Oupa called him a *snotkop*, and what would a kid like him know? And to get out before he got a hiding. Then Pa said, 'Hit me.' And Oupa slapped him. Pa just stood there, and said, 'Is that the best you can do? Bully women and children?' Then Oupa hit him with his fist. And Ouma screamed and wept, because Pa's nose was bleeding. But Pa said, 'Hit me, I will get up again every time.'

Then Oupa Jean stormed out, and was gone for a week, no one ever knew where he went. Ouma Hettie used to say sometimes it was the best week of her marriage. But then Oupa came back, and he moved into the spare room, and that's how they lived, for the rest of his life. A sort of ceasefire between everyone, never officially declared, it just happened that way. Oupa came and went as he pleased, talked less and less to his wife and children, spent less and less time on the farm. And Ouma and Pa gradually took over more and more of the farming.

But Oupa Jean still had the final say, and the power of the chequebook.

The farm work was my father's refuge, I think. At first he worked with the farm labourers – you must understand, on a wine estate the labourers come down the generations on the same farm. They know everything, about pruning and spraying and harvest, the when and the how. So he learned from them, slowly and surely, methodically.

And in the process he grew to love the vineyards, the grapes. The workers had a very earthy relationship with the farm. I think they have a greater feel for the slow turning of the seasons, for the wind and the rain and the heat and the cold and the soil's influence – of terroir. We white South Africans want everything *now*, according to the day or month; we stare ourselves blind looking at the little squares on the calendar on the office wall. When the KWV says harvest, then you harvest. We don't have a thousand years of making wine behind us, like the French. Especially in those days we didn't have the patience or the will to make exceptional wines. We didn't have that understanding of the long term, of nature, of cycles and processes.

My father learned all this from the labourers. He saw that the grapes were never the same from year to year, and he wondered about that. When he was in Matric, he drove the truck with the grapes to KWV himself, because he wanted to know exactly what they did with them, what happened to our farm's produce. He saw how they were all thrown together, how our grapes lost their identity in the mass, and it bothered him.

I think he began to realise how great the potential was, because Klein Zegen was an incredible farm, and the strangest thing, down through the generations, was that not one of the Du Toits had really exploited that. They had just made a living. A good living, some of them . . .

The farm lay far back in the Blaauwklippen Valley, high up against the mountain. In the summer it was cooler than it was on the plain, the vineyard was well protected from the southeaster, so the grapes could take their time ripening, and the sugar content was lower. The soil was stony and hard, somewhere between Italy's Chianti region and the *croupes* of Bordeaux. It was unique, wine growing soil, if you planted the right cultivars.

Pa didn't have that insight. Not back then, in any case. But it was as if he had a premonition. As if somewhere deep inside he knew that piece of earth could do more. And love is a funny thing. Passion. It makes you wonder, it releases your creativity, so that you see other possibilities and outcomes. It makes you stop, focus and think. It helps you make choices about your future.

Pa's decision was that he wanted to study agriculture. Viticulture. Now, looking back, I wonder how much that contributed to breaking his heart.

18

As though he felt the intense gaze on him, Benny Griessel opened his eyes, an instant transition from sleep to waking, and there was Alexa beside him on the bed, her face so tightly drawn, so deeply concerned.

'Benny,' she said, the single word burdened with so much emotion that her voice cracked.

Along with the headache that hammered through his head with every heartbeat, came the consciousness of last night. He relived the taste of the Jack, and the effect of it – the anaesthesia, the euphoria. Even now, in his dry, sour mouth, it made the saliva spurt. He remembered with a sudden flood of relief and joy that he had a reason to drink, a good, defendable excuse. He could explain. Rationalise. He could give everyone insight into this thing.

He could drink.

'Alexa,' he said, his voice hoarse.

'Why, Benny?'

He wanted to tell her everything. The words gathered behind his tongue, they tangled in the dullness of his head. 'To protect you,' was all he could manage to utter.

He could see, from the fear on her face, that she didn't understand. Slowly he sat up in the bed. He took her hand. He said, 'You don't need to be afraid.'

'I am afraid, Benny. I'm not strong enough. Last night I realised that. I always believed, the day you needed me, I would be there for you. Like you were there for me, when I started drinking again. But I can't Benny. I—' The tear swelled suddenly from her eye, rolled slowly down her cheek.

Griessel reached out his hand and caught the drop with his index finger. 'I'm strong now,' he said.

'Thank God,' she said and embraced him.

'I want you to understand,' he said. 'I am strong enough now to drink.'

★   ★   ★

At 07.23 he walked into Cupido's office. 'I know you saved my *gat*, last night,' he said.

'*Jissis*, Benna . . .'

'Thanks, Vaughn.'

'It's Major Mbali's fault,' said Cupido. 'She should never have sent you to Vollie Fish yesterday. Are you okay? Did Alexa brief you?'

He shook his head. 'She . . . It was a difficult morning.'

'So you know nothing about Ernst Richter?'

'No.'

'You must have seen the posters on the lamp posts this morning?'

'No.'

Cupido checked his watch, and stood up. 'We must go and report, Benna, we'll have to wing it. Just say you were with me when we went to interview Richter's girlfriend. Her name is Cindy Senekal . . .'

'Why must I say that?'

'You know you tried to *moer* an *ou* in the Fireman's Arms last night.'

'I did not.'

'That's not what he says. *Jissis*, Benna, how drunk were you?'

'Drunk enough . . .'

Just then Captain Frankie Fillander walked into the office, and said: 'I hear you got JOC on the Ernst Richter case?'

'That's right, Uncle Frankie,' said Cupido, using the Cape Flats term of respect for older people. 'Now all the old *ballies* will see how things are really supposed to work.'

'Heaven help us,' said Fillander, a veteran with a long scar from a knife wound from his ear to his crown. 'Hey, Benny.' And then as he spotted the bruise on Griessel's cheek: 'Who tackled you?'

'It was my fault,' said Cupido hurriedly. 'Last night I dropped my phone and Benna and I both bent down at the same time to pick it up . . .'

They sat in Mbali's big office, the one that used to belong to the late Colonel Zola Nyathi. Around the table were John Cloete, the media liaison officer, Cupido, Griessel, Fillander, Mooiwillem Liebenberg and the small, neat Lieutenant 'Vusi' Ndabeni.

Griessel battled to concentrate.

Lord, his body and head were not used to the liquor any more, but that would change, he knew. He would get drinking fit again.

Kaleni said they were all assigned to the Richter JOC, 'because the Brigadier regards this as the highest priority in the Directorate. He has had calls from our national DPCI, and provincial commissioners this morning. The pressure is on. The PCSI and IMC have been notified, they are clearing the decks. Captain,' she said to Cupido, 'if there is anything you need, please tell me.'

Griessel wondered who the hell Ernst Richter was to warrant all this attention.

'I'll get to that in my report,' said Cupido.

Mbali asked John Cloete to sketch out the state of affairs. He said the Richter murder was headline news, in every newspaper and on every South African website, without exception. The radio stations were humming on every front, from news bulletins to phone-in programmes. 'And on Twitter, this thing is shaping up to be as big as Oscar. So please, be diligent in your endeavours, and in passing along information to me.'

Cupido began his report. He gave the basic background to Richter and Alibi.co.za. He said robbery as a motive could be ruled out, because the victim's wallet was still in his car, and his cellphone had been found beside him in the sand.

While Vaughn lied that he and Benny went to Stellenbosch together last night, Benny's thoughts began to wander. Had he really tried to hit some guy last night? In his forty-six years on this earth he had never become aggressive while drinking. In the old days it made him *los en lekker*, the happy-go-lucky comedian of Murder and Robbery.

But as for last night, he couldn't recall everything so well.

He focused on Cupido again, who was saying: 'Benny and I agree that the girlfriend is lying about the *dagga*. We're not sure about the sex in the car. But we need toxicology on the body, and we need it quickly.'

'I will do my best,' said Kaleni. But they knew, toxicology testing was one of the Hawks' greatest headaches. Unlike molecular diagnosis, which was done through the SAPS forensic laboratory, toxicology analysis fell under the Department of Health, and there were only three labs countrywide with that capacity. A report sometimes took six to twelve months to be returned to the detective.

'And we urgently need a post-mortem. Richter went missing twenty-two days ago, but I saw the body last night, and I'm pretty sure he's only been dead for about a week.'

'*Jissis*,' said Captain Frankie Fillander, then immediately, 'Sorry, Major,' because Kaleni would not tolerate strong language.

'That's the kind of thing we have to keep out of the media, please,' said Cloete. 'Don't discuss it with anybody outside this group. They'll go ballistic.'

'Yes. That is an order,' said Kaleni.

'Any torture marks on the body?' asked Vusi Ndabeni.

'Nothing obvious, but I only saw the front side of the upper body. It's clear he was strangled with something.'

'I'll talk to Salt River,' said Mbali. Then, with quiet confidence, 'You'll get your post-mortem report by tonight.'

'Okay, thanks,' said Cupido. 'There's a hell of a lot of work to be done, so let's get started. I've printed out all the articles on Richter that John sent me. If you could all read them, please.'

Major Kaleni nodded her head in approval. Cupido had to focus hard on not getting angry; had she thought he was a fool?

'Willem,' he said to Captain Liebenberg, 'if you could do all the interviews with the mother, Bernadette Richter. Uncle Frankie, I'd like you and Vusi to get all the forensic stuff to the PCSI, and all the cellphone records to Philip. We need a web . . .' Captain Philip van Wyk and his team from IMC, the Hawks' Information Management Centre, used computer programming to create a spider web showing connections between all cellphone calls or SMSes, from a central number.

'Right,' said Frankie Fillander.

'There was a phone found near Richter's body. The Table View docket says the phone is stone dead. It's currently with Forensics in Plattekloof. If you could get it to Lithpel, and see if he can get it going again. If it is Richter's phone, we also need Lithpel to look at his Tinder account.'

'What is Tinder?' asked Mbali Kaleni.

'It's a dating app for phones.'

'A dating app?'

'Yes, Major. To meet people. To get a boyfriend. Or a girlfriend.'

'*Hayi*,' said Mbali in disgust.

'Richter met the girlfriend, Cindy Senekal, through Tinder. But there might be other women as well . . .' He addressed himself to Fillander and Ndabeni again: 'Also, get Lithpel to look at Facebook, Twitter, Instagram, the usual suspects. Richter was in the tech industry, so he's probably into all that stuff. Benny and I are going to the Alibi offices now . . .'

In the car, on the way to the Alibi.co.za offices in Stellenbosch, Griessel said: 'Don't blame Mbali, Vaughn. She actually did me a favour.'

Cupido was driving. With a raised eyebrow he cast a sceptical glance at his colleague.

'Vollie . . . if Vollie had been drinking he wouldn't . . .'

Cupido snorted in total disbelief.

Griessel raised his hand, a gesture that said he didn't expect anyone to understand.

To his astonishment Cupido did not react. They drove in silence, until Vaughn said: 'If you want to read the dope on Richter,' and he pointed at the back seat.

Griessel wondered what had got into Vaughn. But he merely nodded, picked up the file, opened it and began to read.

The address that Cupido got from Cindy Senekal was in Distillery Street, past the Stellenbosch graveyard in Bosman's Crossing. They identified the building – an old factory that had been tastefully reno-vated – when they spotted the media herd crowding the entrance. Three security guards stood with their backs to the front door, arms crossed, to keep out the reporters, photographers, and one TV camera-man. There were no other visible signs that this was the Alibi office.

'The circus is here already,' said Cupido. 'Send in the clowns.'

The detectives parked in front of the Pane e Vino restaurant diago-nally opposite, took out their identification cards and walked towards the media. The questions were fired at them immediately. *Are you from the Hawks? Do you have a suspect? Was it someone at Alibi?* And the inevitable *Does everyone have an alibi?* followed by laughter and the clicking of camera shutters.

They walked heads down, ignoring it all, and showed their cards to Security. Only once they reached the front door could they see the bronze plaque: *Alibi.co.za. Head Office.*

Inside it was all big open spaces, a blend of the old and new facades, expanses of gleaming glass and splashes of bright colour from exuberant abstract art on huge snow-white canvasses.

And it was eerily quiet, only the muffled hubbub from outside to be heard. They could see small groups of employees – mostly young – talking in muted and defeated huddles. Some were in tears.

The reception desk was a long textured table of Oregon pine. The woman behind it looked as though she ought to be in school. Her face was drawn. Cupido flashed his identity card, and asked to speak to Desiree Coetzee. She whispered into the telephone, asked them to wait just a moment, and pointed at two elegant leather couches. Cupido thanked her. They sat down, aware that more and more of the staff were staring at them.

'Funny dress code,' said Vaughn, because it was just T-shirts, jeans, even some in shorts, everywhere you looked. 'Major Mbali's worst nightmare.'

'You should feel right at home,' said Griessel.

'She hasn't said a word yet about my clothes. And then she made me JOC leader. I swear she's got a scheme. I don't know what it is yet, but I'm telling you now, it's not going to work.'

The coloured woman who came down a flight of wooden stairs was beautiful. She was wearing knee length shorts, a white T-shirt and sandals, her legs long and slim. Pitch black hair hung down to her shoulders. But it was her eyes that captivated Cupido – shades and flecks of gold and copper, like those of a lioness.

'I'm Desiree Coetzee,' she said and held out her hand to Griessel first.

Why did it always work like that, Cupido wondered? Always assume the whitey cop is in charge. He had to make an effort to hide his surprise over Desiree Coetzee. He had expected a white woman – some sort of middle-aged managerial spinster type. Coetzee was not a very common surname for coloureds. And now, this bronzed beauty . . .

He waited his turn and shook her hand, noticing the flawless texture of her skin. 'I'm sorry for your loss. I am the Hawks Joint Operations Command leader on this case,' he explained. 'I tried to phone you last night; I didn't want you to read about this thing in the newspapers.'

'I got your message this morning, but there hasn't been enough time . . .'

'I understand, Miss Coetzee. Can we talk somewhere?'

Desiree looked at the media scrum outside and sighed. 'Come to my office.'

Cupido had to force himself not to look at her legs as they followed her up the stairs. How had such a classy chick ended up in a company like this? Thank God he had decided to babysit Benna this morning, and not brought 'Mooiwillem' Liebenberg along. Those were Vaughn Cupido's thoughts, just before nine o'clock on Thursday, 18 December.

19

Advocate Susan Peires had seen this behaviour before. It was usually the white-collar criminals who displayed it: those with education and property and status. Family men, who stood to lose everything after the crime, committed in a single moment – or an inexplicable stretch – of weakness or greed, jealousy or rage.

It was these men who, in detention, or here in her office, repeated the phrase 'you must understand' over and over, who told the long, drawn-out stories, taking wide detours, madly searching for understanding and insight into their indiscretion, already practising the rationalisation, justification and excuses for the moment when a spouse, child or family member would confront them with the big question: How could you?

It was not a good sign. This never-ending history was almost without exception the refuge of the guilty. But at least it meant that he was probably telling her the truth.

So she just listened attentively, keeping an eye on her body language, her face full of understanding.

20

Benny Griessel could feel the phone vibrating in his pocket.

He knew it was Doc Barkhuizen, who had been calling from early that morning, every half-hour or so. That was why he had set the phone to silent: he wasn't ready to talk to Doc. Maybe later this afternoon, when he had a drink or two inside him.

They were in Desiree's office. All the furniture was semi-restored Oregon pine to give an earthy texture to the otherwise modern surroundings. She invited them to sit and asked if they would like something to drink. They asked for coffee. Coetzee ordered it with a quiet voice over the phone.

'I know it's a very difficult time, Miss Coetzee,' said Cupido. 'But we have a lot of work to do.'

'How long will it go on like this?' she asked, waving a hand in the direction of the front door.

'With the media?' asked Cupido.

She nodded. 'Our PR agency issued a statement. I don't know what else we can do.'

'We will ask our liaison officer to call you. He knows all the tricks.'

'Thank you.'

Cupido made a note in his book. 'Miss Coetzee, I know the Stellenbosch detectives were here. We read the interview notes. But we're starting from the beginning again, because the missing person is now a murder case, and we are looking at this a little differently. We'll have to take Richter's PC, we'll have to bring our tech *outjies* in, we'll have to talk to all the employees. How many people are here?'

'We don't have Ernst's laptop. The police took it.'

'The Stellenbosch detectives?'

'Yes.'

He made another note. 'Okay. How many people work here?'

She had to think for a second. 'Sixty-seven in total. That includes the support people, the nightshift too.'

'Okay, let's take it from the top. Can you tell us how everything works?'

Forty-one-year-old Captain 'Mooiwillem' Liebenberg was known to his colleagues as the George Clooney of the Hawks — hence his nickname, meaning 'Pretty Willem'. The similarities with the famous actor were not so much in appearance – although Liebenberg also had a premature sprinkling of grey at his temples and in his immaculately trimmed stubble. It was more the charm and the knee-buckling reaction of women, the quiet self-confidence that it cultivated in him, and the fact that every six months he had a new, attractive girlfriend on his arm.

He knew he had been sent to Bernadette Richter, mother of the victim, for a reason. The belief was that he could elicit more information, more easily, when he questioned a woman. What Vaughn called his 'bedside manner': old world courtesy, a benevolent, bass voice, a sympathetic smile and, of course, the famous charm.

When he knocked on the door, her house in Schoongezicht, Durbanville was full of women in their sixties. They ushered him in, offered him tea and tart, they clucked over him and made him wait in the sitting room for Mrs Richter, and then they left him alone with her, although he could still hear their hushed, respectful voices from the kitchen while he conducted the interview.

Her son's death was taking its toll on Bernadette Richter. She had dark circles under her bloodshot eyes, her entire being seemed shrunken. A number of times she repeated that there had still been hope after his disappearance, but now there was none. Then she wept bitterly.

Willem Liebenberg stood up, and sat down beside her on the couch. He held her hand, gave her his snow-white handkerchief, his voice gentle and full of genuine empathy.

He drew the information out of her gradually. It was a story of regret. She blamed herself for not speaking out when she felt uneasy about Ernst's company. It didn't align with her principles. Those were not the morals and values she had taught him. Work, yes. Hard work. But not on something like that. She should have protested. She should have stopped him. Now it was too late. But he was so ... so terribly enthusiastic. And now the scum had killed him.

What scum?

She waved the hand that desperately clutched the handkerchief, in the general direction of Stellenbosch, and she shook her head and said, *that* lot – that job – that whole business, and the people who use the services.

Was there anyone specific that she suspected?

No.

Did she believe it was the people who worked there?

No, no, he didn't understand. She had absolutely no idea who it was, but she knew it had something to do with the business, because if you involved yourself in that sort of thing . . . And she let the sentence hang there, full of vague insinuations. And then she reproached herself again. Why hadn't she said something? Why didn't he have a father in the vital years? Why would the Lord bring all of this on her, take away her husband, and now her son, and the newspapers had already phoned a hundred times this morning, and what could she say, what could she say?

Mooiwillem Liebenberg let her calm down, and then he started at the beginning again.

She talked about the good times, when Ernst was doing 'the web design thing'. She said the words as if it were a noble career. She said that was who Ernst really was: the child who loved to draw beautiful things, ever since he was little. Who could sit for hours drawing or copying paintings from a book. She pointed at the bookshelf against the wall, she bought those art books for him, they used to sit on this couch and page through them together, and Ernst was like a sponge. And so terrifically talented; he made perfect replicas, totally perfect copies.

So in love with beautiful things – aesthetics – ever since he was little.

And clever. That was the problem: he was more intelligent than she or her late husband, more intelligent than his peers. And along with brains comes that need for stimulus. When he was still at school, she could provide stimulation with the books, extra classes. But he grew bored with the web design business. He had achieved everything that he could, they were making a lot of money, but then Ernst got bored, and sold his share, and spent a year travelling and then he came back with the Alibi story, and she should have spoken out, back then, but it was too late now. Much too late.

He asked her about her son's private life.

She admitted she didn't know much. Ernst had never brought a 'girlfriend' home in recent years. Every second or third Sunday he came to lunch; bobotie and pumpkin fritters, or apricot chicken. Those were his favourites, who would she cook them for now?

There had been a steady girlfriend, three years back, when he was still in the web design business. Nicola Gey van Pittius. Lovely child, a physiotherapist; they were mad about each other. Nicola started getting very serious. But Ernst was not ready to settle down yet. It was because he never had a carefree youth; at university he worked, then came the business and he worked even harder. When he sold his share, when he went travelling, he broke up with Nicola. She was here, in this sitting room. She came to ask Bernadette Richter, what should she do now? Give him time, give him space, Bernadette had said.

They never got together again.

She knew he took girls out, over the past year. But he'd never brought one of them to Sunday lunch.

Benny Griessel had to force himself to concentrate.

It was the slow poison of the hangover, the anticipation of the next glass of Jack, the upsetting early morning conversation with Alexa, and the coming confrontation with Doc Barkhuizen that threatened to occupy his mind.

But if he wanted to drink, he would have to show everyone that he could still function as a policeman. More than that, he would show them that he was at his very best; alcohol was his salvation, his shield against the perils of his job. So he resisted the invaders and listened as attentively as he could manage. And gradually he realised that he hadn't been imagining things in the car. Cupido was different – had been ever since this morning.

Was Vaughn angry because he'd been drinking? That would be strange; everyone knew he was an alcoholic. Or was Cupido cross because he hadn't been more grateful and apologetic about last night? That was possible; his colleague could sometimes be oversensitive. The problem was that he couldn't remember doing anything wrong. Granted, it was a hazy memory, but he wasn't the one who'd lashed out first.

And drinking is not against the law. He was not on duty. His private life had nothing to do with the Hawks.

Or was it the responsibility of being JOC leader that was making Vaughn so serious?

And when Cupido addressed the operations manager for the sixth time as Miss Coetzee, another truth began to dawn on Griessel: Vaughn was also different with her. He handled her with a certain . . . tact that Benny was not familiar with. Usually when they interviewed coloured people, Cupido would quickly try to win their trust and create a bond with forms of address like *sister* or *my bru'*. He would speak in Cape Flats Afrikaans; he would be much more informal and casual.

But not now.

Cupido was intimidated by Coetzee's beauty, he thought. That would be a first.

Mooiwillem Liebenberg understood the art of subtlety.

He wanted to ask Bernadette Richter if she knew her son smoked *dagga*, but he knew one didn't do that directly. Not with a mother from Durbanville who had just lost her only son.

So he asked her if Ernst used any medication.

Medication? She seemed confused about the reason for the question.

He told her he wanted to determine if the villains – he knew that was the right word to use, with her – might have sedated or drugged Ernst, that they had to test his blood for this. Medication could affect blood tests.

She understood. No, she said, Ernst had been very healthy.

Could she think of anything else that could affect the blood tests?

No. Nothing.

As Willem Liebenberg had expected.

Desiree Coetzee explained to Griessel and Cupido that Alibi.co.za consisted of five departments: Administration managed the overall finances of the company and the registration and payments of clients. IT managed the computer and network systems. Graphic Design was responsible for the appearance of the website, banner adverts, and the creation of alibi items like plane tickets and hotel bills. Client Services was the department with the most employees. They answered the telephone and emails, twenty-four hours a day. Marketing did the publicity, and liaised with the contracted public relations agency.

Each department had a head, and together they served on the executive management, and reported to Coetzee.

'So, if they report to you, what did Ernst Richter do?' asked Cupido.

'He was the managing director.'

'But what did he manage?'

'Everything. But as he always said, his job was to see the big picture. He didn't want to get involved in the day-to-day matters, because you sit in meetings all day and then you lose your vision.'

'So you were actually the main manager?'

'Yes.'

'What did his day look like?'

'It was never the same.'

'But more or less.'

'It's difficult, he . . . On Tuesdays he would attend the executive management meeting, because we look at the figures every Tuesday. How many new registrations, how many cancellations, how many special requests, how much graphic work, what the books look like . . .'

'What is a special request?'

'If a client requests a custom SMS, a telephone call or an email as an alibi.'

'And graphic work?'

'Those are the special alibi items that the clients pay extra for. Airline tickets, conference invites by email, hotel invoices, anything that Graphic Design has to create.'

'And they have to cough up a lot of money for those things?'

'It's not that expensive. It depends on the requirement. Most of the stuff is around a thousand.'

'But that's all counterfeit, Miss Coetzee. Fake documents. Is that within the law?'

She shrugged. 'That's what our lawyers say. It's the same if you . . . Let's say you're a romantic and you Photoshop a certificate for your girlfriend that says she has won the Nobel Prize for . . . for beauty. If the graphics are just for private use, it's completely legal.'

'I don't have a girlfriend,' said Vaughn Cupido.

21

Francois du Toit told Advocate Susan Peires about the day in 1969 when his father Guillaume announced that he was going to study Viticulture.

It caused a minor explosion.

Oupa Jean was forty-three years old. Only in name and in the eyes of the world was he still a wine farmer, with all the status that came with owning Klein Zegen. At home, he was an outcast, his only role on the farm now being to sign the cheques. In town, his minor celebrity past was largely forgotten. Middle age and years of living it up had taken the shine off his attractiveness, but he could still walk around in Stellenbosch as the The Big Land Baron, the man with a KWV quota.

Guillaume's studies were a threat to him. Jean knew in his heart that the farm had the potential for greater things. He sometimes heard his son talk about a special estate wine, and about other cultivars, about their own vats and ageing. He had his doubts, but if his son came back to farm and made a great success of it, it would unmask him, reveal him as just an empty shell.

So at first he refused to finance Guillaume's viticulture degree. He told his wife Hettie and his son that he would not hand over the farm, not until he keeled over. Guillaume would only inherit, literally, over his dead body. So he should go and get himself a job in the meantime, because Jean was not planning to die any time soon. And in any case, you didn't need a university education to know how to farm.

Ouma Hettie only issued the great ultimatum twice in her life. The first time was that day. She told her husband, either he paid the university fees or she took her children and left.

Jean shouted and swore and threatened, but she stood her ground, calm and unshakeable.

Hettie sent Guillaume to register the following year, and brought the account to Jean. She sat in the office and waited until he had written out the cheque. He did it with great reluctance and misgiving, but he did it. He knew only too well that if his wife left, everything would fall apart. But he paid the bare minimum, forcing Hettie to scrimp and save, to wangle a bit here and there in order to give Guillaume some pocket money.

Jean made his son pay in other ways too. He communicated even less with him, and refused to attend his graduation. (Eleven years later, when Guillaume married Helena Cronjé, Francois du Toit's mother, Jean tried to boycott that too. That was the second time that Ouma Hettie issued the big ultimatum.)

Oupa Jean's final revenge was that he lived up to his promise: He clung to the farm, for another twenty years.

22

Desiree Coetzee said Ernst Richter came and went as he pleased.

'He wanted to know the precise state of everything. He kept his eyes on the figures, but he often said he didn't want to be caught up in the office grind. He said that was how he lost perspective. So he mostly kept his calendar open. Sometimes he would come in in the morning, and then he would sit down in client services and answer the telephone himself when the alibi requests came in. Then he would tell the client, "this is the managing director," and he would process the whole alibi himself. Or he would just sit and listen to how they talked to the clients, and he would give advice. Or he would come in late, around ten or so, and he would have some new idea, and he would go and talk to the relevant department. But his big thing was the graphic design team; he devoted most of his time to them. He was big on the acquisitions people. Often he would come in and tell them he had a new trick . . .'

'Who are the acquisitions people?' Cupido asked.

'There are four at Graphic Design who have to search out genuine documents all the time. Let's say a client's alibi is that he stayed over in the Hilton Hotel in Sandton. He has to have a receipt that looks like the real thing. In that case, what the acquisition people do is to phone the Sandton Hilton, and ask to talk to room so-and-so, until they get someone on the line. Then they tell the one who answers, they will pay him a hundred rand if he will take a photo of his receipt and email the picture to them. They were also constantly busy on the Internet, acquiring logos and the right fonts and stuff. Ernst took great pride in the work, and the quality of the alibis. He would often spend many hours with the designers, making a master document that was exactly right. He was very good at it. They all said, he's the Photoshop king.'

'Who is his secretary?'

'He doesn't have one any more. There was a secretary, for about three months in the beginning. But when we had to downsize the first time, he let her go. He said he answered his own email and phone in any case.'

'So who would know best what was going on in his life?'

She thought about it. 'That would probably be me.'

Cupido nodded. She was comfortable now. It was time for the big questions.

'Thanks, Miss Coetzee, we understand better now. But now we have to ask a few hard questions.'

'It's fine. Ask.'

'Are there people in this company who were angry with Ernst Richter?'

'You mean, as in . . . wanted him dead?'

'We have to examine all the possibilities, Miss.'

'No. Never.'

'You sound very sure.'

'I am.'

'Why?'

'Because they liked him. And he was Alibi. Without him . . . I don't know what is going to happen to us.'

'He was the sole proprietor?'

'No, he had a 51 per cent share, but he was the driving force. And the brain.'

'Who owns the other 49 per cent?'

'I can't say. There's a non-disclosure agreement.'

'Miss Coetzee, with all due respect. This is a murder investigation. You will have to answer.'

'I will have to talk to our lawyers first.'

'Can you phone them now?'

She hesitated only for a moment. Then she reached for the phone.

Benny Griessel wondered why she was so calm and in control, under the circumstances.

Sergeant Reginald 'Lithpel' Davids was the resident genius of the Hawks Information Management Centre, or IMC. He was skinny and slight of build, with the face of a schoolboy, and a massive Afro hairstyle.

'Cappie, you're crowding my space,' he said as he scrabbled around in a box of cables.

Captain Frankie Fillander, who was leaning anxiously over Davids' worktop, took a small step back.

'Where are the days, Lithpel . . .'

'Cappie?'

'Back when we couldn't understand you. I'm telling you, one of these days they're going to write you up for insubordination.' Davids had had a serious speech impediment until about three months ago. But thanks to reconstructive jaw surgery at Tygerberg hospital, he now spoke normally, without the old lisp. His nickname, however, had survived.

'They won't, Cappie. You need me too much.'

'And *windgatgeit*,' said Frank Fillander. 'And I'll lock you up myself for being so cocky.'

Davids just laughed. He was going to try to resurrect the iPhone 5 that Forensics had dug out of the sand beside Ernst Richter's body.

'Your iPhone 5s is not nearly as watertight as your iPhone 6 or your Samsung S4 or 5, but sand is a great dehumidifier, Cappie. Did you know, if you drop your phone in the water, that you should put it in rice?'

'In rice?'

'That's right. Cover it in rice. The rice absorbs the water. Now, sand does the same job. And this phone doesn't look wet to me.' Davids selected a charger cable, and pushed one end into the USB port of his laptop, and the other end into the back of the phone.

'I see. Any luck?'

'Patience, Cappie, patience . . .'

Fillander couldn't help himself. He leaned forward again to see the screen of the phone.

It lit up suddenly, and the Apple icon appeared.

'It's working,' said Frank Fillander.

'Too soon to tell. It has to boot first . . .'

They stood waiting and watching in silence. The icon disappeared, and was replaced by a sign-in screen.

'Hallelujah,' said Fillander.

'Thank you, Lithpel,' said Davids, pointedly.

'Thank you,' said Fillander. 'But all you did was plug in a cable.'

'It's not just plugging in the cable. You have to know which cable . . .'

He pointed at the screen lock and said, 'We still have a problem. It's still locked.'

'Can you unlock it?'

'It's an iPhone 5s, and the owner used his fingerprint for the lock.'

'His fingerprint?'

'Apple's touch ID. Very cool.'

'So we need his finger?'

'Cappie, you're a genius.'

'We have ten of his fingers in Salt River . . .'

'You're not making me go into that mortuary, Cappie. That totally freaks me out.'

'*Windgat, maar bang-gat*, hey? You're so full of it, but it's all just hot air. Give me the phone, and tell me what I have to do.'

Desiree Coetzee put the phone down. 'The other two shareholders are Marlin Investments, and Cape Capital, 24.5 each,' she said.

'Who are they?' asked Cupido.

'Venture capital firms. They put up about half of the start-up capital for Alibi.'

'And the other half?'

'Ernst put it up.'

'How much was it?'

'The total start-up capital? I'm not sure, but it was around three million.'

Cupido's phone beeped in his pocket. 'Sorry,' he said and took it out. He read the SMS. It was from Vusi Ndabeni. He wanted to know where Ernst Richter's computer was.

'Miss Coetzee, what computer did Richter use?'

'His laptop. A MacBook Pro.'

'And the Stellenbosch SAPS took it?'

'Yes.'

'When?'

'When Ernst was reported missing: three weeks ago. They phoned later to ask if we knew what the password for the laptop is. We couldn't help them.'

'Okay . . .' Cupido typed an SMS in response to Ndabeni.

While he was busy, Benny Griessel asked a question for the first time: 'Miss, you said all the staff liked Ernst Richter.'

'Yes. He was really nice to them.'

'And you?'

'Sure.' But the answer was just a touch too light on enthusiasm, thought Griessel.

He kept his voice sympathetic: 'It must be hard to keep it all together this morning.'

'It is. The people are devastated. But the show must go on.'

'You're handling the shock very well.'

'I have no choice. I am the only one who can . . .' And then she stopped, and displeasure wrinkled the lovely smooth skin of her forehead. 'What are you trying to say?'

Cupido lowered his phone and looked with fresh interest at Griessel, who merely shrugged. He knew he had said enough.

Coetzee crossed her arms, clearly affronted. 'If you're insinuating that I'm not . . .' She shook her head, then leaned forward over the desk, her eyes angry, and focused on Griessel: 'He was missing for three weeks. Just gone, like that. His car was found in Plankenbrug. Here, near the township. This is Stellenbosch. Do you know what the crime statistics are? Muggings at the university, the Balaclava Gang on the farms, the varsity prof murdered in the Strand. What would *you* have thought? How long before you put two and two together? I did my grieving a week after he disappeared, in the privacy of my home. That's when I knew, something had happened. But I did not have the luxury of showing my sorrow in public because I had to go back to work, and manage sixty-seven people in very difficult circumstances. So please forgive me for not breaking down this morning, sir, and not living up to your high emotional standards.'

23

**Transcript of interview: Advocate Susan
Peires with Mr Francois du Toit**

*Wednesday, 24 December; 1604 Huguenot Chambers,
40 Queen Victoria Street, Cape Town*

FdT: Ouma Hettie did some careful creative accounting with the farm books, while Pa was swotting, and the year that he did national military service. The day of his passing-out parade, Ouma Hettie gave him a gift – a plane ticket to Europe, along with some spending money . . .

I wish I had known Pa when he was young. Or just knew more about him . . .

In all the farm photo albums there is practically nothing from my father's student years. He never talked about it; it was as if the student Guillaume du Toit had never existed, except for the graduation certificate that he eventually framed and hung in the cellar. When he was forty-four years old – two decades after he had graduated.

I wonder if Pa was a happy student. I wonder if he ever laughed or talked nonsense, if he partied, if he took girls out on dates, if he had fun. How much fun can a person have when your father hates and rejects you, if you know your mother had to make a terrible threat so that you could be at university? What sort of student life do you have when your passion is wine making, and you learn how to do it, but you might never get the chance, because your father is going to stubbornly cling to the farm until the day he dies?

As a child I was still too dumb to really know my father. He was just what he was. My father. And in those days Pa worked at the KWV, office hours. He travelled a lot, so he was to a certain extent absent. It was hard to form a proper idea of his character back then. But after my teens, when he eventually got the farm, when as an adult I began to see him as a person for the first time . . . He was a quiet man. Responsible, fair, calm. Maybe too calm. But unknowably quiet. Not completely sombre, he had a certain dry sense of humour, but I don't believe I ever heard my father laugh really spontaneously.

I often used to wonder, was he always like that? Was that his nature? Or was that how life had made him? I still believe it was life. When he smiled, there was a sort of . . . nostalgia, longing, almost as if at that moment he thought that things could have been different. *He* could have been different.

But life was cruel to Pa.

First there was Oupa Jean. And then there was his firstborn son. Paul.

24

Vaughn Cupido took a few minutes to realise that he and Benny Griessel had switched roles. For the first time since they had worked together, as far as he could remember.

Traditionally he had been the bad cop versus Benny's good cop, and he had enjoyed it, because he was good at it. He knew how to get under the skin of the suspects, how to tip them off balance. How to make them cross, so that in their anger and agitation they would say the wrong thing, or go seeking protection from a sympathetic Griessel, who would then winkle the information out of them more easily.

But he could play the good cop. Especially with Desiree Coetzee. 'Captain Griessel, that's a bit harsh; Miss Coetzee has a lot to deal with this morning,' he said and saw her glance gratefully at him.

'But you didn't like him as much as the others did,' said Griessel.

She looked to Cupido for help.

He said: 'It must be different when you work with someone in management.'

'Yes,' she said, and sank back slowly into her chair. 'We had our differences. I wished he would be more hands-on. And I said so. There were times . . .'

They didn't react, waited for her to elaborate. She shrugged again. 'The department heads will tell you, Ernst and I sometimes disagreed strongly in the exec meetings. And it's true. The trouble is, he wanted me to run the company, but then he made decisions that . . . He didn't consult . . .'

She looked out of the window. She breathed in slowly and deeply, and then let the breath out suddenly, explosively, as if somehow that brought her relief and release. 'He was like a child, sometimes. I mean no disrespect to the dead, honestly, but he . . . I think that it was more of a game to him. The whole thing – the company, the alibis, the fake documents – he was having a lot of fun. He wasn't a businessman. No, he wasn't a *manager*. When he sat with the staff, he made jokes, he wanted them to be his friends, to like him. You can't do that if you are the managing director. When we had to do the lay-offs, six months ago, he didn't want to. He was so afraid they would . . . not like him. That's the problem, if you rub shoulders with the staff. Appearances were important to him. Everything had to look right . . .'

And then she fell silent.

'But everything wasn't right?' Griessel asked.

'No, everything wasn't right.'

'Where was the problem?' asked Cupido.

'Ernst was cooking the books.'

Lithpel Davids had given Captain Frank Fillander very detailed instructions: keep Richter's iPhone plugged into the car charger on the way there, they didn't want the battery to give up the ghost just at the crucial finger moment. Make sure the thumb on the right hand of the corpse was properly clean. 'Phone me then, Cappie, and I'll talk you through it.'

Now Fillander was standing in the State Mortuary in Salt River, where the remains of Ernst Richter lay on a table of gleaming stainless steel, ready for the forensic pathologist's investigation. The body was covered with a green sheet, only the right arm was exposed. The thumb had been cleaned with alcohol. The smell of decomposition was powerful.

Fillander had rubber gloves on both hands. He took out his own phone, called Lithpel's number, and pinched the instrument between his chin and shoulder.

'Cappie,' Lithpel greeted him.

'Okay, I'm ready,' said Fillander.

'Take a deep breath, Cappie.'

'Don't mess with me, Lithpel.'

Davids said he must activate the screen by pressing the button on the top right of Richter's iPhone.

'Done,' said Fillander.

Davids told him to press the cushion of the right thumb lightly against the circular button below the screen of the phone.

Fillander bent down to see better, picked up Richter's phone and followed Davids's instructions.

Nothing happened.

'Shit,' said Fillander.

'What now?' asked Davids.

'Didn't work.'

'Just stay cool,' said Davids.

'Why didn't it work?'

'Cappie, you pressed the thumb too lightly. Or on the wrong spot. But now you must work nicely, because it's three strikes and out.'

'What do you mean?'

'Your iPhone works like this, if you give it the wrong fingerprint three times, then it asks for an access code, which we don't have. You can switch it off, and on again, but then you only get one chance at the fingerprint before it asks for the access code again.'

'*Fok,*' said Fillander.

'Just relax. Try it one more time. Make sure you have the meaty part of the finger, and press it a bit harder.'

'Okay. Hang on . . .' Fillander bent down further and the sickly-sweet odour threatened to overwhelm him. He had to swallow to suppress the urge to vomit.

He activated the screen again. He held Richter's phone in his right hand, brought the phone closer. He aimed and then pressed, his head turned so that he could see what was happening on the screen.

'*Fok,*' he said again.

'What?' asked Davids.

'This thing is shaking its head.'

Lithpel laughed. 'Yes, Cappie, the iPhone does that.'

'What do we do now?'

'There's one more possibility.'

'Yes?'

'Was Richter left or right handed?'

'How would I know?'

'Cappie, I thought you were the Great Coloured Detective of the Hawks?'

'That's Vaughn Cupido.'

'Fair enough. But we will have to find out. Maybe he used his left thumb.'

★   ★   ★

Desiree Coetzee told the two detectives that Alibi.co.za was not exactly a giant financial success.

A surprised Cupido quoted from the *Rapport* article, which said the company earned nearly a million rand a month, back then already, when they'd interviewed Richter.

Coetzee said the monthly subscription had nearly doubled since then. The trouble was that the business model was based on even stronger growth, and predictions of quicker economic recovery. And because income had increased more slowly than anticipated, expenses were the big fly in the ointment.

Alibi's salary account alone was R1.6 million per month. Then there were the costs of marketing and advertising, rent for the building, electricity, the ADSL lines, the toll-free number; and they weren't making as much out of the more expensive alibi options as they had initially anticipated. More than 80 per cent of their clients relied on SMSes or telephone calls as the basis for their alibis.

'In July 2013 we launched the website and the app. We knew it would take time to break even, so our agreement with the bank was an overdraft of half a million, until December 2013. Then it had to come down to three hundred thousand by July 2014, and two hundred thousand now, this month.

'Nine months ago, our overdraft was still over six hundred and eleven thousand. The bank said it could not continue like that, and the two venture capital firms were very unhappy. Everyone wanted a strategic recovery plan. We were forced to downsize; we let 20 per cent of the staff go. But by June Ernst could see that it was not enough. Seems like there's less fooling around in South Africa in the winter, because our income remained flat.'

'And then he cooked the books?' Cupido asked.

'Yes.'

'How?' asked Benny Griessel.

'He put some of his own money in, and said we must put it through as sales.'

'Of alibis?'

'Yes. Fictitious clients.'

'How much?'

'Just enough to get us into the black. Between thirty and fifty thousand a month, since June, until he . . .'

'And you were unhappy about that?' asked Griessel.

'Of course I was unhappy about it.' Coetzee still would not look at him, only at Cupido. 'It's not a sensible strategy at all. You can't keep on inflating the books, even if you use your own money. What we should have done was to let more staff go. But Ernst could not do it. He was such a people pleaser.'

'But why?' asked Cupido.

'Why what?'

'Why didn't he just put his money in as . . . What do you call it . . . ?'

'Investment capital?'

'Yes. Why lie about it?'

'Because the venture capital firms are relentless – if something is not working, they are quick to say fire more people. Those firms invest very big money: twenty, thirty million at a go. This company was small fry to them. In the meetings I got the idea Alibi was almost like a game to them. Their dirty little secret; dabbling in the slightly seedy online dating business. But they made it very clear: nobody was allowed to say they were involved. And get the finances right, or we close you down.'

'Who knew, about the book cooking?' asked Cupido.

'Just me and Ernst, and the chief financial officer, Vernon Visser. They both knew exactly how I felt about it, but Ernst kept on saying, it's only temporary, just to see us through, things will look up soon.'

'And did they?'

'Yes, but not enough.'

'Not enough for what?'

'Not enough for the bank. In October the overdraft was still half a million. Which was less than in May, but nowhere near the three hundred thousand in the agreement. Then they gave us until the end of the month.'

'This month?'

'Yes. The thirty-first of December. And I have no idea how we are going to make it.'

25

Advocate Susan Peires asked Francois du Toit to stop talking for a moment. 'I just want to stop the recorder. It's better if our sound files are not too big.'

He stood leaning against the bookshelf, and raised his hands in a gesture of apology. 'I'm sorry. I'm going on a bit . . .'

He reminded Peires of the doctor who had been courting her six or seven years ago, a divorced general practitioner looking for companionship, a partner to travel with and talk to. His attentions as a middle-aged man were pragmatic rather than romantic. 'I really love your mind,' he had said more than once. They went out to dinner two or three times a week, and the doctor would tell stories constantly – long anecdotes, but interesting.

She enjoyed it, for a few months, until he began to get serious. Then she had to let him know diplomatically that she wasn't interested. She gave professional reasons, but the truth was that she hungered for love, and passion: intellectual, emotional and sexual attraction. Not just camaraderie. And she had never been the kind of woman to live a compromise – she wasn't that desperate.

'Don't apologise. I need to hear everything,' she said to Du Toit, as she fiddled with the buttons of the recorder.

She looked up to nod at him to continue. And she saw him, in his grey trousers and white shirt and charcoal tweed jacket, suntanned, with intelligent eyes and large hands, his sensual mouth, from which his story emerged with such burning passion. He wanted so badly for her to understand, and to believe him.

If she were thirty years younger, and he were single. And not somehow involved in a murder case. He would have stirred her, on all the vital levels.

He continued with his story, and she had to suppress a smile at herself. Fifty-four years old, and nothing had really changed inside.

26

Captain Frank Fillander wiped the rubber gloves on the green mortuary sheet, and stroked the knife wound scar behind his ear with the tips of his fingers, as he sometimes did when he was nervous. He had let go of Ernst Richter's thumb and called his colleague Mooiwillem Liebenberg.

Liebenberg was on the way to the offices of Alibi.co.za to help Cupido and Griessel, and first had to call Mrs Bernadette Richter to hear whether her deceased son had been right- or left-handed.

He got the answer and let Fillander know, who received the news with huge relief.

He phoned Lithpel Davids: 'He was left-handed.'

'Well, that explains a lot, Cappie. You know what to do. But be careful.'

Fillander asked one of the pathologists to clean Richter's left thumb. And then he went through the ritual once more. He walked around to the left side of Ernst Richter's corpse. He activated the iPhone's screen with a faintly trembling hand, and picked up Richter's left thumb. He knew that the stiffness that rigor mortis caused in the body disappeared about eighteen hours after death. So it was easy to pick up the arm, and to turn the thumb so that it fitted snugly against the sensor.

He leaned in close for a better view, and brought the phone and the thumb pad together.

The screen changed, the familiar icons appeared.

'Hallelujah,' said Captain Frank Fillander.

'I'm assuming that signifies success, Cappie?'

'Damn straight.'

'Keep the phone activated, Cappie. Or cut off that thumb, and bring it along.'

'*Jirre,* Lithpel . . .'

*   *   *

Vaughn Cupido did not yet know that he was in love.

That insight would come later.

But the chemistry of the process was already in motion. His brain and adrenal glands had already begun excreting dopamine. His heart beat a fraction faster, he began to lightly perspire, his awareness of her was heightened. His subconscious was already measuring Desiree Coetzee – her shape, her beauty, her stance, all the involuntary measurements that evolution had laid down in his synapses. And at the same time, measuring himself against her genetic state. Would a woman like her be interested in a man like him?

There were positive signs. Just a bit earlier, when Benny Griessel had riled her, the Cape Afrikaans had come through in her accent and word choices. Which meant that she might not be too sophisticated for a Hawks detective from Mitchell's Plain. And she was focusing almost exclusively on him now, even though she had initially assumed that Benny was the boss of their partnership.

There was still the vague gnawing question in the back of his mind: why was this sensational person involved in the somewhat tacky Alibi. co.za? And how could he get an answer to that?

'I want to take you into my trust, Miss Coetzee,' he said.

'Desiree,' she said. 'Please.'

Cupido nodded, hiding his delight. 'Desiree, I am going to tell you things that no one knows, and I want to ask you to keep it confidential.'

'Of course,' she said.

'We are still waiting for the post-mortem, but the indications are that Richter lived a week or more after his disappearance.'

Her eyes widened.

'So there is the possibility of abduction too. It's possible that someone held him somewhere for over a week. Now I want you to think hard. Who would want to do that?'

She took a while to digest it all. 'I have no idea,' she shrugged, the confusion clear in her voice.

'You don't have to answer now. Think about it first.'

She nodded.

'I see in the Stellenbosch report that you received a lot of hate mail. Especially Richter,' Cupido said.

'Every day,' she said. 'And not just mail. Through the call centre too. People phoning.'

'And what do they say?'

'They are mostly religious fanatics. "God will smite you." We are all going to hell. And Ernst was the face of the company, so they called him by name. But the religious stuff wasn't that scary. The bad stuff, the death threats, were mostly from men who thought their wives were cheating on them, with our alibis. Those were the ones who said they were going to kill Ernst. In the most graphic and violent ways.'

'Were there some of those who said they would strangle him?'

'Is that how Ernst died?'

Cupido nodded.

She shook her head, as if to dispel the image. 'I don't see all the messages. But they are untraceable anyway. I told that to the other detectives.'

'Are you sure?'

'You can ask our IT people. They look at the stuff. It's all in the database.'

'I would appreciate it if you would take us to the IT people.'

She stood up, and they did too. She walked to the door, then halted. 'I don't know about the abduction thing. That's new to me. But when I began to suspect that Ernst was . . . That something had happened, I began to wonder. I didn't think it was a jealous husband or a religious fanatic. I think it was *dagga*.'

'We know he was a smoker,' said Cupido. 'What did you figure?'

'I knew he smoked, because he offered me some. Twice. But I don't do drugs. Then I thought, his car was found in the Plankenbrug. If a white *ou* wants to get *dagga* in the *dorp* . . . It's a logical place that. I think he met his dealer there.'

Of all the detectives in the Violent Crimes group of the Directorate for Priority Crimes, Lieutenant Vusumuzi 'Vusi' Ndabeni was the one who was the least bothered by their commanding officer Major Mbali Kaleni's insistence on neat attire.

This was because Vusi's 5ft 6in frame was permanently kitted out in a dark suit with wide lapels, a snow-white shirt and sober tie, with a matching handkerchief peeping out of the jacket pocket. (The fact that he was inspired by the style of a young Nelson Mandela, he revealed to no one.) He also spent considerable time grooming his Van Dyke-style beard and moustache, which he trimmed back neatly with an electric shaver every morning.

Not even his Hawks colleagues teased him about his appearance. Ndabeni was very popular, thanks to his even temper, and the fact that everyone knew he lived in a tiny Reconstruction and Development home, one of the RDP houses, in Gugulethu, so that he could send the lion's share of his paycheque to his mother, who lived in a township outside Knysna.

This moratorium on mockery did not apply to the SAPS Forensic Laboratory in Plattekloof. Especially not to two members of the PCSI, the Provincial Crime Scene Investigation unit: Arnold, the short fat one, and Jimmy, the tall thin one. Together they were known as Thick and Thin, as in the worn-out old joke that they themselves often told: the PCSI stands by you through Thick and Thin.

'We have some really bad news,' said Jimmy, and pointed at the roll of black plastic on the table.

'What?' asked Vusi.

'You're not going to like it, Vusi,' said fat Arnold.

'You see this material?' said Jimmy.

'Yes.'

'It's plastic.'

'I can see that.'

'Just by looking at it?' asked Arnold, in mock amazement.

Ndabeni knew their ways. He just smiled pleasantly.

'Ready for the bad news?'

'Yes.'

'We're really sorry, but there isn't enough for a suit.'

'A suit?'

'Yes, you know. For you. I mean, it's your favourite suit colour.'

'Okay, guys, that's a good one.'

'We can maybe get a tie out of it . . .'

'Or a hanky.'

'Or both.'

'Thanks, guys.'

'But not a suit . . . Not enough for the lapels.'

'Okay,' said Vusi.

'We do have a little bit of good news too . . .' said Jimmy, the skinny one.

'Because we are scientific giants,' said Arnold.

'And genius detectives.'

'The Eagles, to your Hawks.'

'That's nice, guys,' said Vusi.

'See that red string?'

'Yes.'

'It's called baling twine. The farmers use it to tie up the bales of hay, to stop them falling apart.'

'Hence the name, baling twine.'

'Elementary, my dear Watson.'

'It's a plastic compound, it's probably locally manufactured, it also comes in bright orange, and black. It's mainly sold by agricultural co-ops.'

'We will be doing spectrophotometry on the string, and the plastic, but already, we've made your job a lot easier.'

'How's that?'

'All you need to do is find a hay farmer, who was cheating on his wife.'

'Or maybe, find the wife.'

'Who needed an alibi.'

'That fell apart.'

'And your case is solved.'

'Please, don't thank us.'

'It's part of the service.'

'Just the way we roll.'

'In the hay.'

'But only with our own wives.'

'You guys are very funny,' said Vusumuzi Ndabeni.

'And clever,' said Jimmy.

'I am going to Salt River now, to pick up Richter's clothing. If you could test that for us too, please.'

27

In January 1975, Pa Guillaume went off backpacking in France, said Francois du Toit.

He organised jobs and accommodation for himself via his university professors' contacts, and for two years he worked in and around Bordeaux. In the winter, he worked as a waiter in the city, in summer on the wine estates. In harvest season, he picked grapes at Lafite.

'Lafite! Château Lafite Rothschild. The Holy Grail, the most famous estate in the world,' said Du Toit. 'Those weren't their best vintage years, they only had a great wine again in '82, but that didn't matter to Pa.'

The young Guillaume breathed it all in – the culture, the tradition, the pride, the incredibly focused striving of the French to make an extraordinary wine, year after year, one that truly reflected the terroir of the region and the estate.

'It had a massive influence on him, I am sure of that. And I think that was the happiest time of his life.

'He never said so specifically. But that was one of the parallels between us. I also went to Bordeaux, in 2009 and 2010. I so wished I could sit with Pa and talk about those times, if he had experienced it as I did. Because it was a revelation to me, such an incredibly big . . . enriching, enlightening experience. Wine. We had a passion for wine, both of us, and you can't be a wine fanatic in the Gironde for two years and not enjoy it. It's the Mecca . . . I know it was for him too. That's why I think he was happy, back then in Bordeaux.

'I had so many questions for him. I couldn't wait to get back and share it all with him . . . But I never had the chance . . .' Du Toit's voice faltered, and Advocate Peires looked at him with concern in her eyes.

'That was just before . . .' he said, but failed to complete that sentence too.

'Are you okay?' she asked.

'Yes. Sorry. It was two years ago that Pa . . . and it still gets me . . .'

'Perhaps it's time to order tea or coffee. What do you prefer?'

'Coffee . . . No, tea, please.'

**Transcript of interview: Advocate Susan
Peires with Mr Francois du Toit**

*Wednesday, 24 December; 1604 Huguenot Chambers,
40 Queen Victoria Street, Cape Town*

Sound file 3

FdT: In 1976 a big thing happened in the international wine industry.
Later it was called the *Judgement of Paris*. It was a wine tasting
arranged by the British wine dealer Steven Spurrier. He got nine of
the most influential French wine judges to take part in a blind tasting – of the best French Chardonnays against those of California,
and the best Bordeaux red wines against his choice of the best
Cabernet Sauvignon from California.

The incredible thing was that the American wines won in both
categories.

There was only one journalist at the wine tasting. But he was a
very influential writer – George Taber of *Time* magazine. And when
he published his article, it brought about a revolution in the wine
world.

The important thing was that it happened during Pa's last year
in France. He experienced it, and it made him believe even more
strongly: if California could do it, if they could make world class
wines, then it could be done in the Cape as well. Our climate and
our soil are better, we have a longer wine tradition; all we needed
was the will and the vision.

Pa wrote Ouma Hettie a letter, a couple of months before he
came back. About all the possibilities he saw, in France. About what
could be done at Klein Zegen, the dreams that he dreamed. Ouma
Hettie said that he asked in the letter if Oupa Jean had softened. If
there was any chance that he would let Pa be on the farm. He was
prepared to turn his hand to any kind of work – a labourer, or a
foreman. Or a winemaker, anything . . .

She wrote back and said he must come home and talk to Oupa Jean. She tried to lay the groundwork, she hinted at reconciliation and forgiveness.

So he came home, early in 1977. According to Ouma Hettie the discussion was behind closed doors, she would never know what was said there. Father and son talked for two hours. And when Pa walked out, he was in tears.

28

Benny Griessel was in need of a *regmakertjie*. Just a thimble of hair of the dog to set him right again. It wasn't that he couldn't concentrate. It was just that it got harder and harder to focus as the morning wore on.

He stood at the computer screen of the IT team leader of Alibi. co.za, along with Cupido, and Willem Liebenberg. Together they were reading the hundreds of threats, insults, reprimands, curses, and calls to repentance, peppered with Bible verses that the company had received over the past eighteen months. Griessel read, he listened, and time and again his thoughts drifted to the Pane e Vino restaurant across the street. It would be open already. When they'd arrived, he had seen through the window that there were wine bottles in a rack against the wall. That meant the place was licensed.

He didn't drink wine. Waste of time.

It made him think of the late, overweight Sergeant Tony 'Nougat' O'Grady. Shot on duty, nearly a decade ago. They had worked together at the then Murder and Robbery squad. O'Grady owed his nickname to the fact that he was constantly chewing on a stick of nougat.

A drinker of wine and a steak-and-chips man, O'Grady often said, there's a reason you should drink wine with your meal. Because brandy made you drunk before you were full, and beer made you full before you were drunk. But wine and food made you drunk and full together.

Griessel had never had a taste for wine; he preferred to be drunk first, full later. But he didn't want to be drunk now. He just wanted to shut his body up, calm it down. Its protests against the alcohol withdrawal were getting stronger and stronger.

The restaurant should serve the hard stuff too.

He wasn't going to drink tonight like he had last night, that only caused trouble. Just a Jack or two, or three, after work, every night – that was all that he needed. To function, to concentrate, and to keep the monster from his door, so that he wasn't reminded of Nougat O'Grady, because those thoughts reminded him of other deceased colleagues. Like Vollie Fish.

And the reason Vollie Fish was dead.

He had to get a *regmakertjie* into his body. Then those thoughts would leave him too.

Problem was, he had nothing for his breath. This morning there hadn't been time to buy Fisherman's Friend. It was the only thing that worked to mask alcohol on the breath. That old story that you should drink vodka or gin if you didn't want people to smell your breath was complete nonsense. He knew that from bitter experience. All alcohol stank. You had to camouflage it.

But where would he get a packet of Fisherman's Friend now?

'None of these mails are traceable?' asked Cupido.

'Just about all the religious ones are,' said the IT manager. 'But the death threats are all from anonymous mail servers. All of them. We check them when they come in.'

'And the telephone calls?'

'We can't see who is calling us. That's part of our privacy guarantee.'

'That doesn't help us at all,' said Mooiwillem Liebenberg.

'Are there any of the death threats that say they are going to strangle Richter?' asked Cupido.

The reaction was predictable: 'Is that how he . . . ?'

'That is *sub judice* information. Are there?'

'Not that I can recall. It's mostly people who want to shoot him or beat him to death.'

'Can you check?'

'Okay.'

Griessel listened to all of it, and he thought, they are wasting their time. He and Vaughn and Mooiwillem knew, working through all the death threats was really just to cover their butts. Because it was highly unlikely, the absolute exception, that the perpetrator would be someone who made anonymous threats in advance. Threateners were all cowards. They never had the courage to really commit murder.

He looked up and saw Desiree Coetzee standing on the stairs, arms crossed. She stared in concern at the cluster of detectives and IT people conferring together.

They could use their time better talking to her, Griessel thought. Because she knew more than she had shared with them up to now, he was certain of it.

But give her rope. Let her sweat a bit. It could do no harm.

Just before 14.00 on that Thursday, 18 December, Captain John Cloete, media liaison officer of the Hawks, sat in front of his computer. He had TweetDeck open on the screen, where he was following @ SAPoliceService – and all the important journalists and news media – and, since this morning, #ErnstRichter, #WhoKilledErnst, and #NoAlibi.

From eight o'clock that morning the news of Richter's death had been attracting a lot of attention on Twitter. But then the usual protests about crime levels and the government's inability to control it began; the speculations over who could have been responsible for his murder; and the carefully crafted jokes, most of them playing with the concept of 'alibi'. By twelve o'clock two camps had drawn up their lines – those against Richter and everything he had stood for, and those who defended him.

Up till this point there had been little from the media. A couple of journalists who were on the scene at the Alibi.co.za offices in Stellenbosch had tweeted that the Hawks had turned up – one with a photo of Vaughn Cupido and Benny Griessel entering the front door, their heads down.

Nothing to upset Cloete.

Then his cellphone rang.

He recognised the number and his heart sank.

It was the representative of the tabloid *Die Son*, the country's largest daily, with over a million readers. A man with way too many good contacts in all the right places in the SAPS. A writer whose call nearly always meant trouble.

'Hello, Maahir,' said Cloete, and lit up a reassuring cigarette. Smoking was not allowed in the office, but he was the one member of the DPCI for whom an exception was made as long as his door was closed and his window open, because they all knew how impossible his job was.

'*Hoezit*, John. How's things?'

'Can't complain, Maahir, can't complain.'

'This Richter thing, John . . .'

Of course. He had known it was going to be about the Richter thing.

'Yes?'

'He's been missing for over three weeks, but now I heard a little birdy say that he has only been dead a week. You know me, I listen when the birdy sings a reliable tune, John. And the trouble is, this is a very reliable birdy.'

Cloete sighed inwardly, drew on the cigarette for strength, and said: 'Maahir, the post-mortem is only taking place today. Unless your birdy is a pathologist, which I doubt.'

'Is that a denial, John?'

'The Directorate of Priority Crimes Investigation cannot comment on the time of death in the Richter case before the post-mortem investigation has been completed.'

'So you're not denying it?'

'I'm not going to play that game with you, Maahir. I can't confirm or deny Ernst Richter's estimated time of death before the pathological investigation is completed.'

'And that is later today?'

'The post-mortem is provisionally scheduled for later today. As you know, the report can take a day or so longer.'

'This is my scoop, John. I want to be the first one to know.'

'Okay.'

John Cloete walked to Major Mbali Kaleni's office. The door was open. He could hear her talking. She was on the phone, busy arguing with someone from the Department of Health. He knocked on the doorframe, and walked in.

Her desk was painfully neat. The in-trays were stacked high, but precisely. The out-tray pile was lower. The room smelled of cauliflower.

Cloete waited until she put the phone down with a sigh.

'I don't want to add to your troubles, Major, but we have a leak,' he said. 'And it might be someone on the team.'

'What kind of leak?'

He gave her the details.

She shook her head. 'It's not someone on the team. It might be the morgue, or Forensics.'

'Just thought I'd tell you.'

Benny Griessel spotted a computer programmer sitting and chewing gum. He asked the young man if he could spare him two sticks. The programmer nodded, took out some gum and handed it over. Then he asked: 'Do you know yet who did it?'

'No, but we know it's one of you. Here at IT.'

'Genuine?'

'Thanks for the chewing gum,' Griessel said and walked away, thinking; that was how he used to be, in the old days. *Lig en lekker.* Happy-go-lucky. A bit of a joker and teaser, because he drank in a controlled way. That was the thing with him and alcohol. It brought out the best in him. Yesterday at the Ocean Basket, if he had had just one single Jack inside him, he could have handled Carla's new 'friend' Vincent van Eck with ease and wit.

He went over to Vaughn Cupido and said he was going to get them takeaways at the restaurant.

'Thanks, Benna, I'm *lekker* hungry now.'

And then he was out the entrance and pushing through the media scrum. He ignored their questions, jogged across the road, and went into the Pane e Vino. He asked for the menu, and looked out through the window to see if the press could see him from there. Then he shifted position, out of sight. And ordered a double Jack, while he inspected the menu.

He ordered the food, and swallowed the drink in one clean gulp.

While he waited, he took out his cellphone and looked at the screen.

Nine missed calls.

Four SMSes.

Seven of the calls were from Doc Barkhuizen. Three from Alexa.

He read the text messages.

I love you, Benny. It doesn't matter what you do, I love you.

From Alexa.

Please, Benny, just talk to Doc, before you have another drink.

Alexa again.

Will you please call me when you have a chance. PLEASE, Benny.
Still Alexa.

And the single one from Doc Barkhuizen. *Sooner or later you will have to talk to me.*

He felt how the alcohol was starting to make him well again. He considered ordering another quick double. There were two risks. The first was, the more you drank, the greater the chance was that someone would smell it. The second was that one of those tabloid journalists could walk in here and ask what the policeman had just ordered. They published wild stories with headlines like *Cops at Alibi all day, just eating hamburgers.* What he really didn't need was *Cops drinking on the job in Alibi case.*

He took the chewing gum out of his pocket, unwrapped it and shoved it in his mouth.

As he walked back to the Alibi offices with the two brown paper bags of food in his hands, two photographers emerged from the media herd, and snapped him.

29

Guillaume du Toit went looking for a job in the wine industry in the seventies, and it was as if the gods were mocking him.

Because they gave him only one opportunity – a position as quota inspector at the Koöperatiewe Wynbouersvereniging: the narrow-minded, strict, conservative, prescriptive, rule-bound, Broederbond-controlled wine farmer's co-operative, the KWV, which at that time was merely an extension of the apartheid government.

And then they let Guillaume du Toit stand by and watch as a new movement – a revolution that represented everything that he believed in with such passion – fundamentally and permanently changed the South African wine landscape, while he was trapped in a job that he hated, as part of the repressive establishment.

'It must have been hell for Pa,' Francois du Toit said to Advocate Susan Peires.

He told her he had gained this insight from Oom Dietrich Venske, winemaker on the neighbouring estate Blue Valley, who worked with Guillaume at the KWV, back in the old days. In the past two years Venske had become friend and wine mentor to Francois – and on weekends around the *braai* fire, the source of information on his father's time of frustration.

Venske said there were two great frustrations in the Cape wine industry of the seventies.

The first was the KWV quota system. It had been instituted with good intentions: to stem the tide of overproduction in the country. But as with all governmental interference, there were frequently great disadvantages. The trouble was that a farm's quota was determined by its historical production, from the year dot. In other words, it took neither the terroir nor the quality into consideration. Nor did it give credit to a farmer who developed new vineyards. The KWV simply prescribed how much you were allowed to produce, of which cultivars.

Some farms had large quotas, others were so small that the farmers had to depend on sheep or lucerne or dairy cows to survive. And there was no solution. Your quota was your quota, for ever and ever.

A quota could not be sold to another farmer either. It was irrevocably tied to the farm.

Of course, the big problem with the quota system, was that it encouraged quantity, rather than quality. Overproduction of bad wine was rife.

The second big frustration was that the State and the KWV controlled the importation of new cultivars. A winemaker could not import a new kind of grape and start experimenting with it; it had to go through the official channels. And even when they followed those channels and miracle of miracles were given approval, the grapevine cuttings were quarantined for a long time. It often took a decade before you could get a new, imported cultivar into the ground.

In contrast, the winemakers in California had such fantastic success precisely because they could quickly and easily plant and cultivate Cabernet, Pinot Noir and Chardonnay. But the KWV in their omnipotence decided that Pinot Noir was too thin-skinned for South African conditions, and the process of importing Chardonnay was so onerous and drawn-out that it scuppered any progress.

And then the wine rebels arrived. They rebelled against the senseless regulations restricting the importation of noble cultivars, against the quantity principle, the restrictions on selling wine on the farm and, of course, the inferiority of South African wines.

It all started in 1971, when Frans Malan from Simonsig created the first Wine Route, to lure tourists to the wine estates themselves and start building their own brands. In 1972 the government passed the Wine of Origin law. Malan and a group of farmers with vision saw the potential to exploit the new legislation fully: to make exclusive wines, for people who were true wine connoisseurs. Original unique terroir wine.

Even if it was a niche market, they believed if you could build the brand of your estate, if you used the new laws to truly stand out, you could grow that market. The pioneers who began to do their own thing were among others Malan, Neil Joubert of Spier, Spatz Sperling of Delheim – an immigrant from Germany – and the two Jewish Back brothers from Backsberg and Fairview. Against the wishes and pressure of the KWV.

And then the smuggling started.

'More and more farmers began sneaking in noble cultivars,' Francois du Toit explained enthusiastically: 'a lot of Chardonnay, and Pinot Noir. Vine cuttings were flown to Swaziland from Europe, and then transported by road in *bakkies* and trucks, to the Boland. Other guys got theirs by post. They'd lost patience with officialdom, and their passion was as great as my father's. And we are talking about big, well-known farmers – Danie de Wet of De Wetshof, Nico Myburgh of Meerlust, Jan 'Boland' Coetzee . . .

All of these measures brought progress, and success. Big success.

'The biggest, best known, most daring of all the wine rebels was Tim Hamilton-Russell. He was an advertising man, the chairman of this massive advertising agency. And he was a wine fanatic. His drive to make wine was so great, he first started experimenting on a small plot of land just outside Johannesburg. But he dreamed much bigger dreams. He wanted to make wine as good as that from France and California, and he went looking for land where the climate was cooler . . .

'That's important . . . Our great challenge in South Africa is the heat. The hotter the temperature when the grapes ripen, the higher the sugar content. It has a big influence on the taste and the eventual alcohol content of the wine. That's why our red wines, for example, are so much more robust than those in France, America and Australia.

'And some of the noble cultivars like Chardonnay and Pinot Noir don't like the high temperatures, the vines struggle. The problem is, the world prefers the more subtle wines of Bordeaux and Burgundy. The best of those wines are in fact made from Chardonnay and Pinot Noir. If you want to export, if you want to compete over there, if you want to reach more than just the local market . . .

'In any case, Tim Hamilton-Russell bought land in the Hemel-en-Aarde valley near Hermanus, one of the coolest wine growing regions in the country. And then he smuggled Chardonnay in, and planted that and Pinot Noir, and the KWV said he was not allowed to produce wine because he did not have a quota.

'Then Hamilton-Russell bought a farm with a quota, and he outwitted the quota inspectors, and he made outstanding wine. And in the end KWV had to start changing their rules.

'All these things happened in the 1970s. And Pa knew about it all. In his heart, his whole being, he was a wine rebel and vine smuggler; he shared and admired the dreams and aspirations of all these men. But he was forced to work as a quota inspector at the KWV. That was the only work he could get.

'Now you will understand just how rotten his stars were.'

30

In the main room of the Hawks Information Management Centre Sergeant Reginald 'Lithpel' Davids was hard at work on Ernst Richter's iPhone.

While he worked, he said to Frank Fillander: 'Hell, Cappie, this Richter was quite the player.'

'What do you mean?'

'Chaffing girls on Tinder. *Wyd en syd*, left, right and centre.'

'Let me see.'

'Hang on, Cappie, let me capture the info first. We're working with a phone that locks if you don't keep it busy.'

'Okay.'

Lithpel laughed quietly and shook his head.

'What?' asked Fillander.

'No, I'm thinking of a story that my old *pêllie* tells . . . Digital dating is trouble, Cappie, I'm telling you.'

'Dating of any kind, if you ask me.'

'True. This mate of mine, he says, there's a dude he knows in Mitchell's Plain. About a year ago, this dude joined an SMS flirting service, and he began chatting up the cherries in a big way. But it's all anonymous, you give personal info as you choose, you understand, Cappie?'

'I'm old, but I'm not stupid,' said Fillander.

'Just checkin'. So, this dude is flirting and chatting something *vrees-lik*, and he checks out which cherries are witty and smart, because he's quite picky, you know, so he tries to weed out the dogs and the duds. He wouldn't mind a *njaps*, but actually his motives are noble, he's actually looking for a meaningful relationship . . .'

'On an SMS flirting service?'

'To each his own, Cappie. Anyway, after about two weeks, he real-ised this one cherry, she just gets him, if you catch my drift. Laughs at his little jokes, her own jokes are *lekker* sharp, there's a vibe, Cappie, a bit of chemistry . . .'

'Right,' said Fillander.

'So he begins focusing more and more on this cherry, and they have long chats, and finally he eases into the erotic zones, but carefully, slowly, slowly, catchee monkey, remember, he has a long-term plan, Cappie. That quest for a meaningful relationship. So he tests the sexy talk waters, and where he goes, she goes along, all the way, and it gets all hot and steamy, and he says to her, do you want to see my member, and she says, *ja, gooi* me a photo. And he goes for it, and she says, ai, a pretty member, do you want to see mine. And he says, of course. But it's still anonymous, Cappie, all the way, and it's one naughty pic after the other, but only the anonymous body parts, like it's a game to them. They both want to avoid the face photo, dead worried that it will be this *moerse* letdown. So the chat gets red hot, and they are so lus for each other's members for real that they can't stand it any more, and finally, after weeks of teasing she says, come and visit, and he says, a *fyndraai*, a special visit, and she says *jis*. And he says *gooi* me the address, and she sends it and he sees, but this is his sister's address.'

'*Jirre*,' said Frank Fillander.

'That's right, Cappie. *Hy skrik sy gat af*, huge fright, he schemed someone was having him on. And he says to her, okay, time to own up, what is your name and surname. And it's his own sister's name and surname.'

'*Fokkit*, Lithpel, that's sick.'

'I'm telling you, Cappie. That dude de-registered from the flirting service right then and there, and he deleted every photo on his phone, and it took him six weeks before he could talk about the thing, then he went and fessed up to his mate and, his mate told me, the dude hasn't yet seen his sister at all, he just can't face her. Who, by the way, was at least a single girl.'

'Now why are you telling me this story, Lithpel? How am I going to get those images out of my head?'

'Moral lesson, Cappie. Stay the fuck away from digital dating.'

'And you scheme I need that? I have been happily married for thirty-one years, and you want to give me a moral lesson on digital dating.'

'Cappie can pass it on to the children and grandchildren.'

'*Jirre.* You. What's taking so long on that phone anyway?'

'Screen shots of everything: Tinder conversations, emails, text messages, Facebook messages, Twitter DMs and mentions, Instagram pics, the works. Then I mail the screen shots to my mail account, then I send them to all of you. It's going to take time.'

'How much time?'

'Give me another hour or two.'

'Has Stellenbosch sent Richter's PC?'

'MacBook, Cappie.'

'What's the difference?'

Lithpel Davids shuddered, as if someone had walked over his grave. 'I'm working with Stone Age barbarians,' he said.

'That is insubordination,' said Frank Fillander. 'I'm a captain, you're just a lowly sergeant.'

'An indispensable genius of a lowly sergeant, and that's the truth. No, Cappie, nothing from Stellenbosch yet.'

'Let me go phone them. Then I'll find out how Philip and the team are getting on with the spider web.'

'Cool bananas, Cappie. Cool bananas.'

The young computer programmer, the one Benny Griessel had got the chewing gum from, was called Vaughn Stroebel. He sat nervously watching the three detectives doing their rounds from desk to desk. Like predators, he thought, three old lions on the African savannah moving through a herd of nervous springbok. The two white policemen looked like real detectives, in their jackets and ties. The coloured *ou* looked like he was trying hard to be young and cool, with his T-shirt and trainers. Probably a mid-life crisis, or maybe it was some kind of detective strategy, trying to look dumb, so that you underestimated him.

Each detective spoke to one of the IT guys, one by one. The coloured guy was only a desk away from him.

What was he to do?

They were from the Hawks.

Fuck.

The Hawks were the elite unit; that he knew. If there was a news report that said the Hawks had struck it was usually all over for the crooks. *Finish and klaar,* end of story. You didn't mess with the Hawks.

And the *ou* with the slightly bloodshot Slavic eyes, the messy hair and the bruise on the cheek had asked him for chewing gum. Did he really want the gum, or was it some clever cop trick. He had seen that a lot on TV: the detective asking to borrow something, but really it was to get your fingerprints, or your DNA, without you knowing.

Why would they want his fingerprints? Did they suspect something?

We know it's one of you. Here at IT. And the detective said it with the attitude of 'We're in no hurry, we'll get to you'.

He wiped his sweaty palms on his jeans.

Here came the coloured guy with the neon trainers.

'*Jis, pêllie,* what's your name?' asked the detective.

'Vaughn Stroebel?' He heard the question in his statement and he thought, *What the fuck, get a grip.*

'Vaughn Stroebel?' said the coloured guy, suspicious.

'I swear,' said Vaughn Stroebel. And he glanced at the door.

'Why are you looking so *katvoet?*'

'It wasn't me,' said Vaughn Stroebel. Somewhere in the back of his mind there was astonishment at how badly he was handling all this. He had thought he would be okay. But then the *ou* had asked for chewing gum, and . . .

'If your name is Vaughn, then you must be one of the good guys,' said the coloured detective with a faint smile.

What did that mean? Was he sarcastic? Or did he know everything? And now he was toying with him?

'Okay?'

'It wasn't you that did it?'

He knew. Vaughn Stroebel could see that clearly now in the detective's eyes.

Stroebel's courage deserted him. 'I only provided the dope,' he heard himself say, and disappointment washed over him. He was such a weenie. But, Lord, there was also relief, to be able to unburden himself of this heavy load. 'I swear. That's all that I did.' He spoke quietly, because he didn't want the other IT guys to hear what a coward he was. 'Ernst came and asked me if I had any dope. I don't know why he asked me. I wondered if perhaps he asked everybody, but how do you find that out? I gave him the dope. And he paid me. I didn't want to take money for it, but he said, please. Then he said, it was difficult for him to get weed, because of his high profile. And could I supply him. I could up the price a bit, make a profit. I didn't want to, I swear, I didn't like it one bit; I don't want to be a dealer, but he's the MD, he's my boss ... Sorry, he *was* my boss. But that's all. I only supplied him with the dope. Only to him. Nobody else. I'm not a dealer. I haven't got any dope with me now. I had two *zols*, in my rucksack, this morning. But I flushed them down the toilet. After you arrived.'

And then he shut up, and the coloured detective stared at him. He could see the disbelief on his face.

This *ou* also thought he was a total weenie.

'Vaughn Stroebel,' the detective said. 'Can you believe it?'

'Can you believe it?' asked Captain Frank Fillander.

'We will find it,' said the constable from Stellenbosch station over the phone.

'Wait, let me get this straight. The laptop was booked in as evidence with you?'

'That's right, Captain. On Friday 28 November, at 16.48. All good and proper.'

'All good and proper?'

'That's right, Captain.'

'And it was there, in your locker?'

'That's right, Captain.'

'How do you know that?'

'Because the register says so.'

'And now it's gone.'

'We'll find it, Captain. It must be here somewhere.'

'Does the register tell you that too?'

'No, Captain.'

'You know as well as I do that that laptop has been stolen.'

'No, Captain, it must be here somewhere.'

'Listen to me carefully. If I don't hear from your SC in the next ten minutes, if he does not tell me that you have found the laptop, there will be hell to pay. Do you understand?'

'Yes, Captain.'

'All good and proper *se gat*.'

'Yes, Captain.'

31

In January 1977 Dietrich Venske and Guillaume du Toit both began working at the KWV in Paarl – Venske in the accounts department and Guillaume as quota inspector. They were both single, young and shared a dream 'of making wine one day'. Till that one day came, they had to work together for the KWV. Guillaume had to inspect the quotas for wine and grapes on farms, and Dietrich had to pay the wine farmers for them.

Thirty years later the young Francois du Toit asked Venske to tell him what his father had been like in those days. Venske recalled the slowly developing friendship at KWV and his perceptions of Guillaume, the man he sketched through his reminiscences as 'a loner', quiet, reserved, incredibly private.

He carried out his duties as quota inspector with a dogged resignation and measured stoicism. He endured the dislike that the role elicited from many farmers, and simply stared into the distance whenever anyone asked him if he was *the* Guillaume du Toit, son of Jean du Toit of Klein Zegen.

It was as if he didn't want to be recognised, Venske recalled. Not yet. It was as if this job was a self-imposed exile, a message, a statement to his father Jean: 'I will do the work that you have the least respect for, and through that show the world how little I respect *you*.'

Or perhaps: 'I will endure anything while I wait for my inheritance. And I will do it for as long as I have to.'

'Something like that,' said Dietrich Venske. 'Maybe it was his way to unmask Jean as the bitter, jealous old man that he was. Perhaps it was because Guillaume did not want to make wine any other way than according to his own, clear vision. If he really wanted, he could have worked in the KWV's production unit. He had the degree, and they would have taken him, if he had been prepared to wait a while. But when I suggested it, he didn't even answer me. To him, compromise was impossible.'

And yet, said Venske, Guillaume was not unhappy. He was part of the wine world, he could steal with his eyes and his ears, he learned and secretly perfected his own plans, ready for the coming of that 'one day' when he could make his own wine. And the KWV was a pleasant place to work – fraternal, fair, tolerant, and not without status in wider society.

At first Guillaume rented a room in Paarl. Later he bought a small house in Nantes Street. But he was always the inspector who was willing to travel, to do the Robertson district inspections, to get away, to be on the move.

Until 1979. When he met Helena Cronjé.

32

'I probably need a lawyer now,' said the frightened programmer Vaughn Stroebel. And then as an afterthought: 'I don't even know where to find one.'

'I am deeply disappointed,' the detective said to him.

'I never needed a lawyer before,' the programmer said defensively.

'No, that's not why I'm disappointed. I'm disappointed that your name is Vaughn, and you're one of the bad guys.'

'Oh?' Total bafflement.

'My name is Vaughn too. And now you've shamed the name.'

'Oh. I . . . You . . . That's why you . . . Shit . . .'

'Where did you get the *dagga*?'

'I don't want to . . . It doesn't matter.'

'Do you know what the gangstas do to *outji*es like you in the *tjoekie*, Vaughn Stroebel?'

'No . . . ?'

'Unspeakable things.'

'But I'm cooperating with you now.'

'Then come clean, brother. Who supplied you?'

'It doesn't matter. He doesn't know anything about my arrangement with Ernst. Nothing. He just thought I was a big smoker.'

'Are you?'

'No!'

'How much do you smoke, Vaughn Stroebel?'

'I've got this trouble with my back. The dope helps my back.'

'Medicinal purposes,' said Vaughn the detective, as though he understood completely.

'That's right.'

'How sore is your back?' A pause, and then the detective laughed at him.

The realisation dawned on Stroebel, the cop was playing with him.

And he was such a complete weenie, he realised. He tried to pull himself together. 'I smoke very little.'

'How little?'

'Every third or fourth day.'

'I think you're lying,' said the policeman. 'I think Ernst Richter sat down with you guys, and he saw, *ja*, this *outjie* is a *roker*. Because of your red eyes and the sniffle and the snacks you sit and munch, all day long. I think you smoke heavily, Vaughn Shame-on-the-Name Stroebel. And I think, to feed your habit, you deal far and wide . . .'

The detective took a set of handcuffs out of his jacket pocket. 'Let me *gooi* a pair of cuffs on you, let's see if a few nights in the cells can make an honest Vaughn out of you . . .'

'I swear,' said the programmer, louder than he intended. All his colleagues looked at him. 'I swear,' he repeated, more quietly this time. 'On my word of honour, it was only Ernst. He smelled me. I went outside to smoke and when I came back in, he was sitting there and he smelled me, and then he asked me.'

'You smoke every day.'

'Yes.'

'A *zol* or two.'

'Yes.'

'And it's not for your back.'

'No.'

'Where were you on the evening of Wednesday 26 November?'

'I . . . I don't know. In my flat . . . Probably in my flat.'

'Busy with what?'

'DOTA 2.'

'Doe what?'

'DOTA 2.'

'What is Doe-tah two?'

'It's a game.'

'A computer game?'

'It's a MOBA: a multiplayer online battle arena. Defense of the Ancients: DOTA. A Warcraft three mod sequel.'

'Bullshit baffles brains.'

'No, I swear. I play every night . . . If I'm not working . . .'

'Or smoking . . .'

'Yes. No ... I ...'

'Or do you smoke when you play DOTA too?'

'I ...'

'Can you prove it, that you were on DOTA that night?'

'Yes! I have the logs.'

'What happened, Vaughn Stroebel? Did Ernst not want to pay for his *dagga*? So you strangled him?'

'No! I swear ...'

'Or were you so high that you didn't know what you were doing?'

He fought against the helplessness, the fear and tears. 'Please,' he said, shaking his head vehemently.

'Please what? Did you do it?'

He felt the tears come, he knew he wouldn't be able to hold them back.

Then he heard another voice, right behind the detective whose name was also Vaughn.

'I want to talk to you.' It was Stroebel's colleague, the sinewy Rick Grobler. He was the oldest of the programmers, and the quietest and most secretive – the guy who never mixed or squabbled with them.

'We'll get to you just now,' said the detective.

'I want to know if I'm going to need a lawyer,' said Rick Grobler.

'Why?'

'Because I threatened Ernst, in an email.'

'What about?'

'Money.'

'What money?'

'Money that he borrowed.'

'What amount are we talking about?'

'I don't think we should talk here ...'

Vaughn Stroebel saw the detective's attention shift to Rick Grobler. He swallowed back the tears and had an incredibly strong urge to get up and throw his arms around Grobler.

Lieutenant Vusumuzi Ndabeni stood beside the body of Ernst Richter, which now lay naked on the stainless steel autopsy table.

In his right hand he held the sealed plastic bag containing the clothes that Professor Phil Pagel, the senior state pathologist, had put in it. Vusi didn't look at the body. He didn't like any of this. He kept his gaze on the always elegant and well-spoken Pagel, who pulled the bright light hanging above the table down closer to the body.

'So he went missing on the 26 November, Vusi?' asked Pagel as he bent to inspect Richter's neck close up.

'Yes, Professor.'

Pagel was silent for a moment while he made his calculations.

'That's twenty-two days ago.'

'Yes, sir.'

'Lot of sand on the body. Could you tell me about the crime scene, Vusi?'

Ndabeni explained that he hadn't been there himself, but according to the briefing this morning – and the documents that Vaughn Cupido shared with them – it seemed that the body had been buried in the sand, rolled up in plastic. And then the big storm exposed it yesterday morning.

'I see,' said Pagel and reached over to pick up a few instruments. He forced the corpse's mouth open with them, took a torch and lit up the dark hollow inside.

'Want to hear something interesting, Vusi?'

'Yes, Prof.'

'In 2008, the Dutch authorities found a body in the western part of the Netherlands,' said Pagel, without looking up from his work, 'that had been buried under about a hundred-and-forty centimetres of sea sand. When the pathologists examined the deceased, they saw pretty limited decomposition and estimated the PMI – that's the initial Post Mortem Interval – to be about two weeks. But when the body was identified, they were told that the man had been missing for three months.'

Now Pagel looked up at Ndabeni. 'I think we might have a similar case here, my dear Watson.'

Vusi just grinned, and nodded.

'The late Mr Ernst Richter has been missing for more than three weeks, but a cursory examination of the decomposition indicates a much shorter period since death, don't you think?'

'Yes, sir.'

'Bit of a conundrum, Vusi, bit of a conundrum. But fear not, for I stand before you fully armed with the weapons of Dutch scientific research. Would you like me to elaborate?'

33

Francois du Toit began to talk about his mother for the first time, and Advocate Susan Peires noticed how his tone of voice and expression softened – so much more compassion.

And the more he spoke about her, the more Peires began to wonder whether he was indeed the one responsible for Ernst Richter's death.

Firstly there was the fact that twenty-seven-year-old wine farmer Francois du Toit was a relatively recently married man, and had himself just become a father. He spoke positively about his wife. Not the kind of person who would necessarily get involved in the murky world of Richter's alibi service.

Secondly, the long run-up, the in-depth history that he insisted on sharing with her. And thirdly, the picture that he attempted to create of his father with so much effort and detail. As though it served as mitigating circumstances. *See what a hard time my father had.*

He spoke of his father in the past tense. A few times he had said he wished he could have discussed this or that with his father. She assumed Guillaume had already passed away, but now she realised it had never been explicitly said. Perhaps they were just estranged. Was he not perhaps trying to build a defence for his father?

Every morning Peires read the *Cape Times* and *Die Burger* in her office. Over the past week she had followed the hysterical reporting of the murder investigation, the juicy revelations of all the moths attracted to the red-hot, all-consuming flame of Richter. She had listened to her friends' and colleagues' speculations, even participated in discussions about the case. The role of technology in the destruction of values; the country and the media once again focused on all the wrong places – like the crime stats and the effectiveness of the SAPD – while it was really about the moral state of South African society.

What did it say about the country if a business like Alibi could prosper? The general view of her circle: the nation saw ever more clearly the writing on the political wall, and everyone scurried like rats to enjoy the last hedonistic pleasures before The Good Ship South Africa was scuppered and sank completely. She wasn't entirely in agreement with this view.

The public consensus about the case was that Ernst Richter had got what he deserved. Nobody had actually vocalised this *ipsissima verba*, but it was fairly clearly implied in the newspaper letters pages and radio phone-in programmes. The old story of 'if you play with fire . . .'. She shook her head at it all, with a degree of wonder that humanity could judge others so easily. Although she knew where it came from: as advocate she had thought it through many times before – this obsession with murder, with crime and justice, was not just a fear of death or damage, it was an impulse to maintain order. Above all, people were creatures that wanted to be part of the herd at any price. So much time, so much money, so much energy was devoted to nurturing the herd, maintaining it and fitting in with it, that the herd *had* to be orderly. All that investment could not be made in vain.

Murder was the greatest disturbance of that order. Consequently it produced fear. Any act of murder was anxiously analysed for signs, inclinations, tendencies, so that the herd could avoid it in future. The Oscar Pistorius affair was the perfect example; the endless column inches, the hours of analysis on TV and radio, the digital articles and blog discussions, and the books when the case was concluded, all so that the herd could try to understand why a Golden Boy, an icon of the struggles of the herd, could do the unmentionable.

With Richter, the general approach was to demonstrate that he was never part of the herd in the first place. An outsider, outcast, tainted, scum. Not one of the ducks on our dam. Not one of us.

Susan Peires had to keep herself from falling into this trap. But even so, she could not see Francois du Toit as a patron of Ernst Richter's services. And he spoke so much of his father's rotten stars, and now, there was this much gentler approach when he spoke of his mother . . .

'My mother . . .' he began, and took a deep breath, stroking his right cheek with his fingertips, as if comforting himself. 'Helena. She was a Cronjé, a descendant of an original Huguenot family. They came to the country as Cronier, in 1688, if I remember correctly. She is the youngest daughter of Oupa Pierre and Ouma Elizabeth. They own

Chevalier, between Paarl and Franschhoek, the wine estate . . . My Oupa Pierre . . . people said that was the closest you could get to Afrikaner aristocracy.'

Du Toit looked towards the window. He paused, brought his hands slowly together, right palm stroking the fingers of his left hand. Susan Peires took note of the action, unsure of what the gesture meant.

'But things are not always as they seem,' the young wine farmer said. 'I find it so terribly interesting, the faces we choose to show to the world.'

34

Benny Griessel felt light.

He walked at the rear of the group of four, on the way to Desiree Coetzee's office: the programmer Rick Grobler in front, then Cupido, Liebenberg and himself.

It was the booze, thought Griessel. The lunchtime *dop* had lifted the yoke off his shoulders, yes, also the knowledge that he could get more again tonight. But the biggest reason was that he didn't have to contend with the thirst, that he no longer had to fight that endless, draining, depressing battle. That was what made him feel so good right now.

That was what made him feel engaged, *present*, once more, so that he knew the coming interrogation would be a distraction, comic relief in this slow-dragging day, which had produced nothing of any use so far. At the foot of the stairs he and Vaughn and Mooiwillem had exchanged a look, eyes saying: this is a *haas*, a civilian, that we can have some fun with. An *ou* who believes he has done something important enough to be a part of the investigation.

They saw it often, this mixture of sympathy and self-importance that caused people to project and insinuate themselves into an investigation. Most often it was a frustration to the investigators, but sometimes it was fun.

In the office Grobler sat down and leaned back comfortably, his tall gangly body filling the guest chair. He was athletic for his mid-thirties and the arms that protruded from the light yellow T-shirt showed a network of bulging blue veins. His hands and his Adam's apple were surprisingly big. But there was something nerdy about the bowed back, the slumped shoulders.

Mooiwillem Liebenberg leaned against the glass wall, Cupido chose Coetzee's high work chair, Griessel closed the door behind him and took his place in the other guest chair.

'Okay,' said Cupido. 'Full name and surname?'

'Ricardo Grobler. Rick.'

'So you threatened Richter in an email.'

'Yes.'

'What did you write in the email?'

'He had a week to repay the money or I was going to beat him up.'

'And then, what did he say to that?'

'He didn't say anything. It was the day he disappeared.'

'You threatened him on that very day?'

'*Jip.*'

'So that's why you are so worried.'

'I'm not worried. I didn't do anything to him. I just wanted to save you the trouble, for when you find the email.'

'You're a *lekker* cool customer, *nè*,' said Cupido.

'I'm an innocent customer. Tell me if I'm going to need a lawyer.'

'Because you've already got one?'

'No, but I know where to get one.'

'Why would you need a lawyer?'

Patiently, as if he had to explain to children, 'Because when you see the email, you will wonder about it. It gives me a motive.'

'You're very well informed about crime detection. Motive, *nogal*,' said Cupido.

'I read a lot of crime fiction.'

'And you think that's related to reality?'

Rick Grobler merely shrugged.

'Why would Ernst Richter borrow money from *you*? That dude was loaded.'

Again the shrug of the bony shoulders. 'Apparently not as loaded as everyone thought.'

'How much did he borrow?' Griessel asked.

'A hundred and fifty thousand.'

'*Jissis*,' said Cupido. Then, suspiciously: 'You're not messing with us?'

'No. That was what he borrowed.'

'When?'

'End of October. He said it was for a week, maximum, then he would pay me back.'

'What did he want the money for?' asked Mooiwillem Liebenberg.

'He said he just wanted to boost the books a bit. That was his word, boost. He said the VC partners were giving him grief . . .'

'What are VC partners?'

'The venture capital companies who have shares in Alibi. Ernst was extremely chummy-chummy. He said I was the only guy who would understand start-ups, and how the VC partners could be vultures. He said he would pay it back straight away, as soon as they had finished inspecting the books, and he would cover the bank fees, I didn't have to worry. And then he didn't do it. I went to see him in his office, nine days later, and I said I want my money. Then he said, sure, he would arrange it immediately; he'd just had his hands full. Three days later, still nothing. I went to see him again. Then he said he had signed off on the payment, it would go through in a day or two. When I went to talk to him three days after that, he avoided me. When I came to his office, he pretended to be on the phone. So I sent him emails. A few times, but he just ignored them. Until the twenty-sixth, when I sent the threatening letter.'

'Do you have proof that you lent the money to him?'

Grobler shifted in the seat so he could push his hand into the back pocket of his jeans. He took out some folded papers, selected one and handed it to Cupido.

'Of course. Here is the IOU that he signed. And it's all in my bank statements: the transfer . . .'

Cupido looked at it briefly, nodded and asked: 'You're a programmer?'

Grobler gripped the remaining folded paper in his large hand. 'Kind of. I am the head of data security.'

'So where do you get the one fifty K to just loan out like that?'

'In my free time I'm a freelance cyber-intrusions expert. I hunt zero-day vulnerabilities.'

'You hunt *what*?'

Standing next to the dissection table in the state mortuary in Salt River, Professor Phil Pagel told Detective Lieutenant Vusi Ndabeni that the Dutch pathologists were fascinated by the fact that the body they were examining had apparently been dead much longer than the degree of decomposition indicated.

'So they came up with an interesting experiment. They ordered almost two hundred fresh pigs' legs from an abattoir. They buried them in sand – sea sand, woodlands sand, dry and wet. Ten pigs' legs were used as a control, to decompose without burial. The results were very interesting. I'll spare you the details, but here's the conclusion: A body buried in wet sand decomposes much more slowly than previously anticipated. Now remember, the Dutch body in question showed about two weeks of decomposition, but the man had been missing for almost three months. After the pig leg experiment, they found he could easily have been dead for the full three months.'

'Wow,' said Ndabeni.

'Wow, indeed,' said Pagel. 'The study showed that even when a body is buried in dry sand, decomposition is significantly delayed. Now, to give you a more specific PMI, I'll have to go study the meteorological data for the past three weeks, and we will have to get Forensics to analyse the temperature and composition of the sand in which Richter was found. And even then it would be an estimate, kind of give or take a day or three. But I'm willing to bet my opera season tickets on the fact that Blouberg has had rain between 26 November and 17 December. Our man Richter here could well have been dead for three weeks.'

The programmer Rick Grobler explained to the detectives in layman's terms, expansively and at length, that accidental faults creep in with every application or operating system that is developed for computers – from Windows to web readers, email programs to Java and Flash. And when these programs are installed on millions of computers, some of the errors serve as hidden backdoors that cyber hackers can use to gain access to a computer and hijack its data.

'That's what you call a vulnerability.'

'Okay,' said Vaughn Cupido.

'A zero-day vulnerability is when you are the very first guy to discover that vulnerability. On day zero, when you report it.'

'Okay.'

'There is a very good market for reporting zero-day vulnerabilities; many people want them. Apparently the Chinese spies pay the most, America's NSA want them, the software companies buy them so they

can plug the gaps, and then there are your hackers, and the guys who
want to steal your money.'

'Who do you sell to?' asked Willem Liebenberg.

'To the good guys. There are a whole bunch of companies who buy
them. I am a freelancer. If I find something, I offer it to all of them.'

'Who are the "good guys"?'

'They are companies who take the vulnerabilities back to the software developers, so they can fix the bugs. For a price, of course. Or
they sell them to the antivirus companies . . .'

'What do you get for a zero-day?' asked Cupido.

'It depends . . .'

'Ballpark.'

'Anything from ten thousand to a hundred thousand.'

'*Lekker*,' said Vaughn Cupido.

'Dollars,' said Rick Grobler.

'*Fok*,' said Benny Griessel.

'How many have you found?' asked Willem Liebenberg.

'It's not as though they just lie around waiting for you to pick them
up. It's months and months of work. And if you offer a zero-day, you
have to point it out and exploit it too. As proof that someone could
exploit the vulnerability.'

'How many?'

'About two or three a year.'

'So what is your income, on average?'

'That's private information.'

'In a murder investigation, in which you are a prime suspect;
nothing is private,' said Cupido.

Grobler shifted uncomfortably in his chair. He hesitated before he
said: 'About two million. Per year.'

'Dollar?' asked Cupido incredulous.

'No, rand.'

'So why are you working in this place, if you're that loaded?'

'I . . . It's not good for me to sit alone at home . . . I have socialisa-
tion problems. My shrink says it's very important for me to be among
people.'

'Where were you on the evening of 26 November?'

'At home.'

'Alone?'

'Yes.'

'No alibi?' asked Cupido ironically.

'Looks like it.'

'Do you still have the email?' asked Griessel.

Grobler looked at the detective for a long time. Then he opened his hand, revealing the other folded document. 'I printed it out for you.'

He handed it to Griessel, who opened it out.

Griessel began to read out loud. Halfway through, the atmosphere changed suddenly and dramatically. Griessel said: '*Jissis.*' All three detectives looked at Grobler. The room hummed with tension.

35

'My mother was seventeen when she took on Oupa Pierre. Seventeen. In Grade Eleven,' said Francois du Toit with a sense of satisfaction. And admiration.

He sketched the scene for Susan Peires. His Oupa Pierre Cronjé, barrel-chested, big of stature and of ego, of high social standing, the archetypal Afrikaans alpha male, Great Patriarch, ruler of the grand Chevalier Estate. Respected. A Broederbonder. Member of the Board of Directors of KWV, staunch supporter of the National Party, member of the church council, committed Christian who made his whole family sit around the table every evening for family Bible study and prayers. *Boekevat*, they called it.

His mother, Helena: the youngest of three children, with her deceptively fragile body, because actually she had so much strength. Pretty, in a boisterous elfin way, with a bushy head of red-blonde hair that resisted ponytail or plait, loose tendrils always escaping from captivity; lively green eyes. A natural aptitude for Science and Biology; always off-beat in her opinions, her reading, her clothes. In a house where chauvinism reigned, she was regarded as a harmless eccentric, with a philosophy of 'give her time, she'll grow out of it'.

The night of the confrontation was some time in 1970. The country was in upheaval again. Winnie Mandela was under house arrest. South Africa was officially banned from the Olympic Movement. On the farm Oupa Pierre still used the dreadful *dop* system of giving his labourers some of the inferior excess wine as part of their pay.

Pierre Cronjé and his children sat around the big yellowwood table in Chevalier's impressive dining room. Everyone held hands, heads bowed, as he prayed with the bulky Family Bible open in front of him. In his solemn church voice he followed his usual recipe for prayer, from thanks for the abundance and prosperity, to a plea for blessing on his loved ones, the farm, and the harvest.

But tonight, mid-prayer, the voice of his daughter Helena Cronjé broke in, crystal clear, inappropriately lively and decisive.

'No, Lord,' she said.

Dumbstruck silence followed.

'No, Lord,' she said again, filling the silence. 'Don't do it. Don't bless a farm where the workers are on the *dop* system. Don't bless a farm where the workers are oppressed like slaves. Don't bless the harvest that has to be picked by drunk, alcoholic workers. Punish the owner, Lord, because he deserves it.'

All this with her eyes shut, her face screwed up in righteous sincerity.

Oupa Pierre recovered himself. He let go the hands of his wife and oldest son. His voice thundered across the table. He called Helena a Blasphemer and a Communist. He ordered her to get up and go to her room. He would deal with her later.

She nodded, as if that was precisely what she had expected, and left. Her mother Elizabeth, later known as Ouma Lizzie, was normally a subservient, dutiful wife. But now she ignored her husband's command to leave the child and followed her.

In the bedroom Ouma Lizzie tried to talk Helena round, begging her to tell her father she was sorry.

Helena shook her head, more of those rebellious strands escaping, took her suitcase from the top of the wardrobe and began to pack her clothes.

'What are you doing?' asked Ouma Lizzie.

Helena said she was going to move in with the Genants – one of the labourer families on the estate. She would work and harvest alongside them, and her father could pay her with the daily *dop* too.

Ouma pleaded. Helena packed. Until Pierre Cronjé walked in and threatened her with the heavy ordinance of the father-despot: disinheritance, banishment, reformatory school.

Helena said, do as you wish, I am going to move in with the Genants until the *dop* system ends.

Pierre played his penultimate parental ace: he would phone the police.

'Go on, phone them!' said Helena.

The camel's back broke, Pierre lost control. He grabbed his daughter's slender arm and shouted, spit spraying, with a rage-twisted face, that he would beat her. His wife Lizzie cowered moaning and praying in the doorway.

'Hit me,' said Helena. 'But make sure you don't stop till I'm dead, because if I get up, I'm still going to move in with the Genants.'

Pierre struck out, but at the oak door of the hundred-year-old *jonkmanskas*. The wardrobe door splintered under the attack, the wood slicing deep into his hand. He stormed out, chased the kitchen staff away, locked every door of the homestead and shoved the keys into his pocket.

Helena took her suitcase and sat down at the front door. She called down the passage, calm and determined: 'It's okay, the door will open in the morning, and then I will go.'

Pierre allowed his wife to bandage his bleeding hand and fled to his enormous study, where behind a closed door, with a bottle of ten-year-old KWV brandy, he brooded over his humiliation. In the depths of the night he came to the realisation that his daughter had planned it all carefully beforehand. She had anticipated her father's reaction, completely accurately. She knew him well. He had no choice. If he didn't capitulate, his daughter was going to cause a scandal; a scandal that he could ill afford socially, politically or religiously.

The next morning at six a.m. he found Helena slumped asleep beside the suitcase at the front door.

'I will stop the *dop* system,' he said.

Helena merely nodded, stood up and began walking, suitcase in hand, back to her room.

'You know it can't happen overnight,' Pierre growled after her.

'Two years,' said Helena without looking back. 'To phase it out. That's a realistic time frame.' She had worked it all out for herself already.

'She was seventeen,' said Francois du Toit again, and grinned in admiration. 'In Grade Eleven.'

36

At 16.23 the station commander of the SAPS in Stellenbosch phoned Frankie Fillander of the Hawks, to tell him they were paying serious attention to Ernst Richter's laptop which had apparently been 'mislaid'.

Captain Fillander had to swallow back his indignation, because the station commander was a colonel. So he merely said: 'It's a key piece of evidence, Colonel, we would appreciate it very much if you could track it down.'

Then Fillander went to Major Mbali Kaleni's office to hear whether she could ask the big Hawks boss, Brigadier Musad Manie, to exert some pressure.

That was how it worked. As a hierarchy.

Even though he was already convinced that the laptop was stolen.

At 16.34 he was bemoaning his lot to Lithpel Davids.

'We can track down that MacBook, Cappie. Apple has a thing they call "Find my Mac". If that laptop is on a Wi-Fi network, we can pinpoint it. But then we must get Richter's password for his Apple ID.'

'How do we do that?'

'You go out and detect, Cappie. That's what detectives do.'

'I have a sneaking suspicion you don't want to be here when I start cutting, Vusi,' said Phil Pagel, who was fiddling through his instruments to select the right one.

'No, sir,' said Ndabeni, relieved. 'I'd like to get the clothing over to Forensics.'

The state pathologist smiled. 'Of course. But I might have something else you can take to them.'

'Yes, Prof?'

'You see, Vusi, what we have here is almost certainly death by strangulation. We have the petechiae on the skin and the conjunctiva of the eyes – that's the tiny pinpoint haemorrhages you can see here . . .' and he pointed at the skin on Richter's face. 'And, of course, the very deep ligature abrasion around the neck. Now, you only see that kind of abrasion when the ligature was not removed immediately after he was killed. If the strangler just did the evil deed and removed the ligature, there would have been very little bruising. Come, look closer.'

Vusi had no desire to take a closer look, but he had too much respect for the legendary pathologist. He moved closer, reluctantly. Pagel slipped his right hand under the corpse's right shoulder and tilted the body. He pointed with the tip of his scalpel: 'Do you see that?'

Ndabeni drew in a deep breath and held it. He bent down and saw the tip of a piece of red twine in the back of the neck, as if it was growing out of the skin.

Vusi stood up quickly, blew out his breath. 'I see.'

'I think that is the actual ligature. Thin rope. Twine, almost. I think it has cut deep, and the post-mortem swelling is now obscuring it, or part of it. But some of it is still there.'

Vusi saw that it was the same baling twine that Forensics had so enthusiastically told him about. He didn't want to dampen the professor's pleasure at his discovery, so he just said, 'That's great, Prof.'

'You want to go wait outside while I get it out?'

'Please, Prof.'

From: *Rick Grobler* rickgrobler@alibi.co.za
Subject: *my money*
Date: *26 November 2014 at 09:33*
To: *Ernst Richter* ernst@alibi.co.za

ernst, you doos. You're a fokken wannabe hacker with your pathietic t-shirts, you will never be a genuine geek or a nerd, just a glorified graphic designer who can't even run a business. Fokken pathietic. You can try and avoid me at the office, but I know where you live, you doos. I'm not going to waste money suing you to get my money back. You have exactly one week to get the money into my account. The whole amount. If you can't do that I'm going to grab you by the throat and choke it out of you, I hope you understand me . . .

That was when Benny Griessel looked up and said: '*Jissis*.'

Grobler realised the atmosphere had changed. 'What?' he asked. 'I *mos* told you.'

'You know where to find a lawyer?' asked Cupido.

'Yes.'

'Then you'd better go and find that number, just now, 'cause you're going to need one.'

'There's more,' said Griessel, and he read: 'I'm going to beat you to death, then we'll see if the girls are still so crazy about your fucked-up little face. One week, you *doos*.'

'You don't think there's a slight over-use of the word "*doos*"?' asked Willem Liebenberg.

'And your spelling . . .' said Griessel. 'It's pa-thie-tic.'

'I was bloody angry when I wrote that.'

'And when you strangled him, were you also "bloody angry" then?' Cupido made quotation marks around the phrase with his fingers.

'I never touched him.'

'What did you strangle him with?' asked Cupido.

'He wasn't str— Was he strangled?'

'Damn straight.'

'Christ.' Rick Grobler sat up straight in the chair, and then leaned forward, like a man with a great weight on his shoulders.

'You're going to need some help, Rick, 'cause you are in very deep shit now.'

'Where were you on the afternoon and evening of 26 November?' asked Griessel. He looked at Grobler with renewed attention. The blue-veined arms looked more powerful now, the sinewy body surely capable of overwhelming Richter.

'I have the right to talk to a lawyer,' said Grobler and stood up.

'Sit,' said Griessel.

'But I have the right to make a phone call . . .'

'Sit,' said Cupido with a note of threat in his voice.

Grobler sat down. Reluctantly. 'I have rights,' he said with considerably less confidence.

'Listen, Tricky Ricky,' said Cupido. 'Where do you find all these rights?'

'The law says so.'

'But what law?'

'I don't know. That's why I have to get a lawyer.'

'Let me enlighten you, Tricks.' Vaughn Cupido stood up from his chair, leaned over the desk. 'Our constitution has a Bill of Rights. Chapter Two, to be exact. Article Thirty-Five. And it says you have the right to remain silent. And we have to tell you, if you are going to give us the silent treatment, there will be consequences. Such as, we will arrest your *gat*, and throw you in jail, where you can hang around for forty-eight hours with rapists and gangstas, killers and sodomists. Forty-eight hours, Tricks. That's a long time. But you got that right to legal representation and the phone call from the TV. American TV. So let me explain to you how it works at home here. Article Thirty-Five says you have the right to choose, and consult with, a legal representative. But here's your problem, Tricks. That Article Thirty-Five says *fokkol* about when. Not a single thing. Except that we must promptly inform you of your right to consult. So don't sit there and throw laws at us. We know those laws from back to front. And those laws say premeditated murder is a Schedule Six offence, and for the rest of your life the only zero-day vulnerability you're going to see is your own. You understand me now *mooi*?'

'I didn't do anything,' said Tricky Ricky Grobler, crossing his arms in front of him as if he wanted to cut himself off from them, from all of this.

'Where were you that night?' Griessel asked again.

'At home. And I was alone, and I don't have an alibi.' Trying to regain his equilibrium.

'You're *lekker hardegat*, Tricks. What time did you go home?'

'About six o'clock.'

'Straight home?'

'I went from work to the gym, and from the gym home. Six o'clock, close to six o'clock.'

'Where do you live?'

'Here in Paradyskloof.'

'Exact address.'

'Thirty Pison Street.'

'Piss on? What sort of *fokken* street name is that?'

'I don't know . . .'

'Spell it for me.'

Grobler spelled it.

'Okay. And where was your wife?'

'I don't have a wife.'

'*Stoksielalleen* then, all on your lonesome?'

'Yes.'

'And then what time did you go and ambush Richter?'

'I didn't . . .' Grobler's voice grew stubborn and uncooperative. 'I'm telling you now, I didn't see him again . . . I saw him that day at work, in his office. That was the last time. I went to the gym, and I went home, and I cooked a meal and ate it. Then I watched TV for about an hour, and then I sat down to work, on my laptop.'

'Looking for vulnerabilities.'

'That's right.'

'And there's not a soul in the fucking world who can substantiate that.'

'No.'

'You know we are going to find forensic evidence to prove you were the murderer, Tricks.'

'That's impossible. I wasn't near him.'

'We *hoeka* have a set of fingerprints in his car that we haven't identified yet.'

'You can take my fingerprints. Now.'

'And DNA samples?'

He made a gesture that said, do what you will.

'And cellphone records.'

He shrugged. He didn't care, he had lost interest.

'Then that's what we will do,' said Cupido and took out his cellphone.

37

Francois du Toit counted silently on his fingers, and then said that his mother Helena Cronjé would have been twenty-six years old in 1979, just finished with her Masters degree in organic chemistry. As a junior lecturer at the University of Stellenbosch she was working on her doctoral thesis.

Her relationship with her father Pierre had deteriorated so much due to her strong political, social and religious views that she no longer went to Chevalier. She met her mother for coffee once a week in Stellenbosch. She had had a few relationships during and after her student years, but all the men had beaten a retreat, apparently because they realised they would never live up to her high expectations.

Helena went walking and mountain climbing with the *Berg en Toerklub*, she was a member of the film club, she attended lunch hour music concerts. And in the winter of 1979, with an eye to travel ahead, she joined the Alliance Française.

That was where she met Guillaume du Toit.

He had been a member for a long time, to keep his French fluent. He was standing in a group of a few members, quiet, listening, when she entered. He could not keep his eyes off her. And as the evening wore on, he became all the more aware of this lightning bolt of truth: this woman was his future wife.

Two days later when she received a call from him in her tiny office, she could scarcely remember that he had been at the Alliance Française. But something about his quiet voice made her agree to a date. Later she would say it was the certainty, the sense of inevitability in his tone of voice, as if he was already sure that it was fated.

On that first date – dinner at the Volkskombuis – they realised Guillaume knew her father. He occasionally had to do quota inspections and wine tank measurements there. She told him of the rift between her and Pierre. And he revealed his troubled relationship with his own father, the first time that he had talked about it to anyone outside his family.

Two family exiles finding each other, and in each other, the characteristic that they believed they lacked in themselves: her fire, outspokenness and dynamism, his gentleness and quiet determination.

38

When detectives with enough experience work together, they develop an intuitive feel for each other.

Benny Griessel sat and listened to Cupido calling the Forensic Science Laboratory in Plattekloof and asking them to send people to Stellenbosch for fingerprints 'Because we have a suspect in the Richter case.' The last sentence said with great emphasis.

Griessel stood up, still with the vague euphoria of booze enveloping him, took the handcuffs out of his jacket pocket and pulled Rick Grobler up by his T-shirt, rough enough to confirm the seriousness of his intentions.

'Come, Ricky,' he said and twisted Grobler's right arm behind his back.

Cupido, who usually played the role of the bad cop, caught on immediately. 'Let's just think about this, Benna. It's not that simple . . .' he said.

Griessel clicked the cuffs around Grobler's right wrist.

Neither Griessel, Cupido nor Liebenberg believed with any conviction that Rick Grobler was the guilty one. The evidence in hand was just too flimsy. It just didn't chime with their instincts, honed through thousands of interrogations. Grobler had been just too shocked when he heard that Richter had been strangled.

But all three Hawks men knew, when you worked with members of the public as suspects – in contrast with hardened criminals – intimidation was a very handy instrument. Act fast, decisively and just a little bit roughly. Establish the Power of the Law, create a dynamic of inevitability, as though this were an irreversible process with only one endpoint, and a very unpleasant one at that. Now and then you got a practically instant frightened confession. Often it would at least provide a better indication of guilt. But mostly it kicked off a process of negotiation where the detectives had the upper hand.

But they must decide if he was worth the trouble and time to arrest and focus on. A mistake either way could at best be a waste of time and at worst a total disaster for the investigation.

'Will we take him out the front or the back?' asked Cupido.

'The front,' said Willem Liebenberg, promptly playing along, so that Cupido would be the only voice of sympathy.

'Let the press get their pictures,' said Griessel.

'No,' said Rick Grobler, his voice hoarse, while Griessel bent his left arm behind his back and cuffed that one too.

'Think about his mother, Benna,' said Cupido. 'What if she sees his face on TV, the poor aunty . . .'

'It was him, Vaughn,' Griessel said. 'We've got enough.' He began to push Grobler towards the door.

'Please,' said Grobler, his face waxen.

Griessel hesitated, deliberately. Grobler saw it as an opportunity. He talked fast, his voice filled with fear now: 'It wasn't me. Take my DNA, take my fingerprints, take anything. My phone is at my PC; I know you can trace it, where I was that day. Take it, please. Please.'

Still they just stood there. Give him space.

'I was stupid, I should never have threatened him, I know. Stupid, stupid, I should never have got so angry. Look, I've got social interaction issues, I'm working on that, but I swear, I swear . . .'

'Slow down with the swearing, Tricks. We've heard it all before.'

Grobler stood awkwardly with his hands behind his back. 'What can I say? What do you want . . . ? What can I do? It wasn't me, please, don't take me out of here like this . . .'

'What social interaction issues do you have?' asked Cupido, his voice sympathetic.

'Vaughn, we're wasting time,' said Griessel.

'It's nothing that . . . I struggle socially, that's all,' said Grobler quickly. 'I . . . my psychologist says I don't mirror well.'

'What does that mean?'

'I . . . struggle to read people, their reactions . . . I say things that . . . I talk too much, about my work, that's all that I . . . I don't understand that they don't know anything, and then they don't want to . . . It has nothing to do with Ernst Richter. It doesn't make me dangerous, it just makes everyone dislike me.'

Grobler dropped his head in humiliation, shoulders slumped.

'Sit, Rick,' said Cupido.

Grobler sat down again, but Griessel remained standing, a menacing presence.

'What have you got to give us, Tricks? How are you going to save your arse?'

Grobler made a sound of despair.

'It's your last chance, Tricks.'

Grobler looked up, but only at Cupido. He began to talk.

Arnold and Jimmy from Forensics were not so cheerful when Ndabeni walked into the laboratory with his plastic evidence bags.

'You could just have asked, Vusi,' said fat Arnold. He and his partner were frenetically busy sorting documents and stapling them together.

'We always do our best for you guys,' said tall, skinny Jimmy with reproach in his voice.

'Priority service for priority crimes, that's the policy – official, and our personal commitment. I mean, have we ever let you down?' asked Arnold.

'No, we haven't,' answered Jimmy. 'Never. So why, Vusi? *Why*?'

'Guys, I don't know what you're talking about,' said Ndabeni.

'It's okay, Vusi. We know you guys are feeling the pressure. But just keep in mind, we're only human,' said Jimmy.

'Maybe a little more than human, but . . .' said Arnold. He held two hands up in the air for Ndabeni to see. 'Two hands. Still only two hands.'

'You guys are kidding me, right?' said Vusi.

'Not this time.'

'You sure?'

'You ran to Major Kaleni. While we're working at the speed of light, you went and complained to The Great Cactus Flower.' Mbali Kaleni's first name meant 'flower' in Zulu. A host of unflattering nicknames had blossomed from it.

'I did not,' said Vusi indignantly.

'It's okay, Vusi. We forgive you.'

'I did not call the major, guys.'

They heard the honesty in his voice and looked up from their work. 'You didn't?' asked Arnold.

'No. I've been busy at the morgue. Why would I call her?'

'So she can call our CO. And tell him we're too slow.'

'I would never do that.'

'So why did she call our CO? Here we are, slaving away for you guys. We never get the credit, we never get the spotlight, it's all about the Hawks; but we do it anyway. And the thanks we get, is that our CO walks in here and says Major Cactus Flower is very unhappy about the pace of our work.'

'*Stank vir dank*,' said Jimmy. And because he suspected that Ndabeni would not understand the phrase, he added: 'It stinks.'

'I'm sorry, guys, but it wasn't me.'

They wanted to blame someone, and their body language showed they were reluctant to believe he wasn't the guilty one.

Jimmy stapled the last set of documents firmly and held them out to Vusi. 'Your GC-MS results.'

Vusi put the evidence bags on the table and took the document. He looked at it.

'I have no idea what this means,' he said as he studied the chemical tables.

'The report for ordinary human beings is on the last page,' said Arnold.

'Hastily compiled,' said Jimmy.

'But very accurate,' said Arnold.

'And to save you time, because you are such a busy Hawk, we'll tell you what we found.'

'Your baling twine and your plastic sheet show very high traces of Triazole.'

'You will also find electron microscope photographs in there of the Triazole powder granules.'

'Irrefutable proof.'

'Produced at the speed of light.'

'For the oh-so-busy Hawks.'

He waited for them to say more, but they just leaned back smugly in their chairs.

'What does that mean?' asked Vusi.

'We knew you would ask that question.'

'But we waited, to prove a point. You guys can't do all that busy, important Hawks stuff without us. Go on, admit it.'

'Of course we can't. You guys are geniuses.'

'Are you messing with us?'

'No, guys. I hold you and your work in the highest regard. And I'm very grateful for what you've done. And the speed . . .'

'You're a Hawk with a heart, Vusi.'

'One of the few.'

'Triazole is a fungicide, Vusi.'

'For agricultural use.'

'Farmers spray it on their wheat to kill fungi.'

'And on their vegetables, and their fruit.'

'Your problem here though, is that the Western Cape has all three, in abundance.'

'Wheat, vegetables and fruit.'

'The Swartland and the Overberg for wheat, Philippi and Joostenberg for vegetables . . .'

'Apples and pears in the Grabouw area, and of course grapes all over the place.'

'The concentration of Triazole is pretty high. Industrial strength.'

'Okay,' said Vusi.

'So if you ask us, Ernst Richter was killed on a farm. The Triazole, the baling twine, the very long plastic sheet, it all points to agriculture.'

'So if we were Hawks, we would look at the Alibi database, and get a list of all their wheat, fruit and vegetable farmer clients . . .'

'But that's just us.'

'The slowcoach scientists.'

'The tortoises to the Hawks' hares.'

'What we've also done, Vusi, just because we care, we've called three big agricultural companies in the Peninsula.'

'We didn't have to . . .'

'Exactly. But we did. And these guys tell us that more than 80 per cent of the Triazole is sold to wine farmers.'

'Which is statistically tricky, because more than 80 per cent of the Peninisula's agriculture, measured in earnings per hectare, is viticulture.'

'Or viniculture, if you want to be precise.'

'And we, thorough as we are, *do.*'

'A pair of very precise tortoises.'

39

**Transcript of interview: Advocate Susan
Peires with Mr Francois du Toit**

*Wednesday, 24 December; 1604 Huguenot Chambers,
40 Queen Victoria Street, Cape Town*

FdT: Ma is the most pragmatic, systematic, organised person I know. She thinks ahead. Not just a week or a month . . . That story about my mother taking on Oupa Pierre over the *dop* system only after working out how long it would take – that's the way she is.

Pa asked her to marry him, two years after they met. She said yes, but only in another four years' time. She had already planned her life for those years. First she wanted to get her doctorate, then she wanted to travel, for a year at least – Europe, India, America – before she married and started a family.

Pa had to wait. And he did. I think it was very hard for him, that year she was overseas. He flew over once to spend two weeks with her, but for the rest he had to be satisfied with postcards and letters . . .

He was already thirty-one when they married in 1985. She was just a year younger. They bought a house in Onder-Papegaaiberg in Stellenbosch, and Ma went back to work at the university as a senior lecturer.

Ten months later my brother was born. My parents christened him Paul. It's not a family name, just one they liked; they didn't want to honour Oupa Jean or Oupa Pierre with a namesake.

But Pa's relationship with the stars . . . The gods have a sense of irony, I think. Because Paul didn't inherit Oupa Jean's name, just his genes – almost all of them.

40

Rick Grobler's 'social interaction issues' were working against him now. He knew he had to be careful, because if he expressed his dislike for the late Ernst Richter too strongly it would complicate his case. But the pathology of his condition included the practically irrepressible urge to vocalise his feelings – whatever was on his mind came out of his mouth, inevitably and at length.

To add to that, if he did not explain how unpopular Richter was, he would remain the only suspect.

So he began slowly and carefully. He told the investigators that Alibi.co.za was really just smoke and mirrors. Not because the products did not work, but that almost everything that had appeared in the media and advertising was untrue.

'Take the story that each alibi is crafted for the client's specific needs. That's . . . nonsense. They . . .' and he gestured in the general direction of the client services department '. . . use the same stuff over and over. The same graphics. There are often complaints from people who say that's not what they asked for, and then client services say, go read the fine print . . . The clients have to take it, what are they going to do, sue us? Ask client services to show you the emails from all the clients swearing and bitching about the service . . .'

Grobler was gradually building up steam. He said the wonderful data security that Ernst Richter had described to the press was a myth. Any of the programmers could scratch around in the database as they liked. Just about the whole company knew that Ernst Richter regularly went through client details, looking for prominent people. Desiree Coetzee, the operational manager, had tackled him at least twice about it. But Richter said it was his company, he owned the data, he could look at what he wished. So the privacy he boasted of was nonsense. Everyone knew it, but no one had the courage to speak up about it.

'What did he do with the famous names?' asked Cupido.

'Nothing. It was an ego trip, that's all.'

'I thought everyone was so happy here?' said Benny Griessel.

'That's a load of *kak*,' said Grobler vehemently. And then, regretting the outburst: 'Sorry. But it's not true. After the downsizing everyone has been working harder and longer, and there are all these rumours that there are more retrenchments to come, because things aren't going too well for the company. Except for Ernst. He drives around in a TT and dates all the chicks in the town left, right and centre; every lunchtime he is out for two or three hours and then he comes back to the office half-pissed and high and then he wants to be chummy with IT and graphics . . .'

Finally his urge got the upper hand: 'I'm not the only one who thinks he's a *drol*. Everyone thinks so. And there they sit, too scared to say so. Just ask the other programmers. Behind his back they all said he's a wannabe hacker, with all those T-shirts of his, but he can barely code HTML. When we built the site, we realised he got stuck on HTML 4. He's a fucking fraud, I'm telling you. He's all false front, nothing about his image is the truth. Nothing. *Bo blink en onder stink*: all that glitters is not gold, my friend. And there are some people they fired who are much angrier than I am . . .'

'Such as who?'

'I can't remember all the names. There were two downsizings . . . But you should have heard them, when they came out of the admin offices . . . they all wanted to bliksem Ernst, because the newspapers were saying the company was booming; in the meantime they were firing people all over the place.'

'Did anyone threaten him? Say anything about—'

Cupido's phone rang. Vusi's name on the screen. He held up a hand in apology and answered it. He listened, said a few quiet words and then said goodbye. He looked at Rick Grobler. 'Tricks,' he said, 'how often do you go to wine farms?'

'Wine farms?' Completely taken aback at this new line of interrogation.

'What part of the question don't you understand?'

'Wine farms? What has that . . . ? I never go to a wine farm. I drink beer.'

'Where's your car?'

'Here in the parking area.'

There was a knock on the door. All four looked up. Desiree Coetzee stood there, a frown on her face.

Cupido stood up. 'We have very interesting chemical evidence, Tricks,' he said. 'We are going to take your car and analyse it, six ways till Sunday. And if we find you were near a wine farm, your mother is definitely going to see you on TV.'

A wave of relief seemed to wash over Rick Grobler. He let out a long and slow breath. 'Okay,' he said. 'Sure.'

Cupido hid his disappointment at this reaction and began to walk towards the door. 'Go with Captain Liebenberg, give him your ID number, your cellphone details and your car keys. We are going to take the car to Forensics, let it tell us its story.'

'How will I get home?'

'He will take you. And you stay there, Tricks. Don't you move without letting us know.'

'How long will my car . . .'

'When we're done with it.'

Cupido opened the door.

'The dayshift people want to know if they can go home.'

Cupido looked at his watch and saw it was already past five. 'Okay,' he said. 'Where can I reach you, if necessary?'

'I'll still be here for a while . . .'

Frank Fillander realised early on in his career as a policeman that he had many colleagues who worked faster than he did, and who were more intelligent. He had always had just two great assets: his unlimited patience and his insight into people. Handy characteristics when it came to detective work. It was because of these qualities that he slowly but surely advanced to Captain in the Hawks. Not bad for a fifty-one-year-old coloured man from Pniel, with only Standard Eight to his name.

At 17.24 he walked to his desk. First he called his wife, Vera, in Paarl and said to her: 'My darling, it's going to be a long night.' He listened to her complain that their youngest, their nineteen-year-old son, had broken up with his girlfriend again, because 'That child just doesn't know when he's on to a good thing, Frankie'. He consoled Vera with 'Give him time, my darling, he's still very young', said goodbye, and rolled up the sleeves of his white shirt above the elbows. Then he spread out the printouts of Ernst Richter's digital life on his desk.

Sergeant Lithpel Davids had explained in broad terms where each piece of information came from: first the SMS, WhatsApp and iMessages, then the Tinder interactions, the Twitter messages, personal and general, the Facebook conversations and all the dates in his calendar over the last three months. After that, the call register, which Davids said only represented the last two weeks before his death – calls received and calls made.

Fillander pulled open his drawer, took out the packet of chilli-flavoured biltong sticks, chose one and put the end in his mouth. He sat down, reached for the SMSes and began to read. He stroked his fingertips over the scar from behind his ear to his crown, where the hair traced the straight line in a grey strip. He was unaware of this mannerism, which he only displayed when deep in thought.

It took him over an hour to work through everything for the first time.

John Cloete, press liaison for the Hawks, received seventeen phone calls from the media after 16.00, as they prepared for evening news broadcasts, morning editions or the updating of websites. The reporter for the tabloid *Son* called him at 17.32 and asked if the post-mortem was completed.

'All I have at the moment is that Richter died by strangulation, Maahir. And you are the first one to know; that's your scoop.'

'When will you release it for the rest?'

'Later tonight.'

'That won't help me at all, John. The other papers will have it too tomorrow.'

'But you've got a Twitter feed and a website.'

'How about time of death?'

'I still don't have confirmation. The pathologist said the final report will take another couple of days.'

'Then I'm going with what I've got.'

'The rumour that he has only been dead a week?'

'Right.'

'Maahir, that's speculation.'

'So be it,' said the reporter and rang off.

Cloete sighed, lit a cigarette and leaned back in his chair.

When they were alone again in Desiree Coetzee's office, Cupido sat down opposite Griessel with a sigh. Then silence between them, as though they both needed to gather their thoughts again. The whisper of the air conditioner was the only sound, and a phone ringing somewhere.

'I will have to report to *Major* Mbali, Benna . . .' Thoughtful, grave, there was much less venom in the 'major' now.

Griessel could see that the responsibility of being JOC leader was resting ever more heavily on Vaughn's shoulders. Especially since they had made so little progress.

Another sigh from Cupido, then he told Griessel in careful point form about the call he had received from Vusi Ndabeni, about the pathologist's suspicion regarding the time of death, and Forensics' chemical analysis. He ended with, 'So where's your head with this thing, Benna?'

Griessel reflected. The healing glow of the lunch time *regmakertjie* had waned; he felt the fatigue in his body and brain. The best that he could do was: 'I don't believe it was Rick Grobler.'

'My sentiments exactly. We actually have *fokkol*. No suspect, except for the faint possibility of a few thousand Alibi clients, all the people who were fired, and half of the staff who didn't like Richter.'

Griessel nodded in agreement.

'I scheme we should bring Bones in, 'cause just about all that's left is the money,' said Cupido without enthusiasm. Major Benedict 'Bones' Boshigo was a member of the Statutory Crimes Group of the Hawks Commercial Crimes branch. When it came to complex figures, he was the man to go to.

'That's good, Vaughn.'

'What we *don't* need is one of those opportunistic crimes. Richter stops that fancy car in the wrong place at the wrong time, they hijack him, wrap him up, somewhere on a wine farm . . . and then they get cold feet, and they don't steal anything . . . No, that's flight of fancy . . .'

They resorted to silence again.

'I don't think Desiree Coetzee has told us everything,' said Griessel.

Cupido sat up. 'You reckon?' he asked in surprise and with a little bit of reproach, as though Griessel had committed a faux pas.

'Just a feeling.'

'I didn't pick that up.' Cupido considered the implications, and saw new possibilities. 'Benna, we must make a start at Richter's house. If you don't mind. I'll ask Willem and Vusi to give you a hand. I'll call the major so long, and then I will chat with Coetzee again.'

The tweet appeared at 18.08 on Twitter:

NoMoreAlibis @NoMoreAlibis
Will publish full alibi.co.za client database on the web in 18 hours.
URL to follow soon. #ErnstRichter #WhoKilledErnst #NoAlibi

The @*NoMoreAlibis* Twitter page didn't show the usual profile pic – just a black A in a fat font against a white background, with a red stripe slashed through it, like a no-entry sign.

It took thirty-one minutes before it went viral, and Captain John Cloete's phone began ringing off the hook.

41

Francois du Toit delved deep into his childhood.

He was thirteen months younger than his brother Paul. He could remember the house in Onder-Papegaaiberg, because that was where he spent his first six, nearly seven years with his father Guillaume, mother Helena and brother Paul. Happy, carefree memories, free from the sins of the father, unaware of the familial undercurrents.

He had darker features, inherited from his Ouma Hettie's Malherbe side of the family. Paul's hair was flaxen-white. Both boys had long locks on photos from that time, living evidence of their mother's unconventional views and ways.

Francois couldn't really differentiate between memories of Klein Zegen before and after they went to live there. He knew they visited the farm, sometimes when Oupa Jean was away. He could clearly remember Ouma Hettie on the veranda of the lovely homestead where she sat preparing beetroot, her hands scarlet, her voice gentle.

Years of political change that he as a child vaguely registered – among others his mother's joy in 1990 when F.W. de Klerk made a groundbreaking speech to parliament. And at the same time his father's concern about tension at work, a row between him and Dietrich Venske, apparently related to the new dispensation in the country.

The recollections of the first seven years all intertwined together, except the day of Oupa Jean's death.

Francois only remembered the consequences, the rest he would hear from the recollections of his mother and grandmother. 1994. A time of renewal and optimism and hope after the darkness of apartheid. International wine markets opening up, the KWV facing big changes. On a chilly Saturday morning in the autumn young Paul was playing in his first rugby match for Eikestad Primary School's Under-Nine team. The little blond boy, his hair now cut short in accordance with school regulations, stood out, by virtue of his astonishing talent.

Pa Guillaume stood beside the field, poker-faced. He hid his emotions over this prodigy, this sporting phenomenon sprung from his own loins, because he was uncomfortable. Upset, even. Partly out of surprise, partly due to his recognition of the origin of these sporting genes, and their potentially wider implications. But most of all because he could swear he saw his own father standing on the other side of the field between the screaming parents, slyly ducking out of sight now and then. At sixty-eight, Jean's walk was limping and slow: he was a man old before his time.

After the match, Guillaume's discomfort evaporated in the flood of congratulations from the spectators. They went out to celebrate Paul's achievements at the child's restaurant of choice – burgers and milk-shakes at the Arizona Spur. The family went home. Guillaume told his wife about Jean's presence at the match – the first interest he had shown in his grandchild.

Some time after three, the phone rang. It was Hettie du Toit with the news. Jean had been found on the Blaauwklippen road. He was sitting in his *bakkie*, beside the road, as if he had parked the vehicle there, upright, his arm still resting on the open window. Only his head bowed in death, like a man finally feeling remorse.

They suspected a cardiac infarction.

And Guillaume du Toit, whose life could truly begin on that day, who had wrestled for so many years between rage and hatred, wept uncontrollably. Nobody would ever know precisely what he shed those tears for.

42

Fillander read once through everything on his desk, and then leaned back in his chair and thought, this Ernst Richter wasn't a bad *laaitie*.

He knew bad. He had seen it in every possible shape and size. But this *outjie* didn't fit in with any of those categories.

He wasn't flawless though. There were a few things you couldn't help noticing.

Number one flaw: People Pleaser. Richter wanted to be nice to everyone. On the Tinder online dating site he'd chatted up sixteen, seventeen chicks, with a particular liking for blondes with long straight hair and a kind of innocence in their pictures, fake or not, eyes glancing shyly sideways like virgins. The same with the SMSes and WhatsApp and the Facebook stuff: nice to everyone who lived and breathed, even the fanatics who cursed and threatened him.

Case in point. Someone who called himself 'Jesus-is-Lord!!!' on Facebook posted a message for Richter that said, 'The lake of fire waits for you. You will burn. I will watch and laugh at you from the arms of the Lord. Revelation 21: But the cowardly, unbelieving, abominable, murderers, sexually immoral (!!!!!), sorcerers, idolaters, and all liars shall have their part in the lake which burns with fire and brimstone, which is the second death.'

And Ernst Richter wrote back to him: 'I respect your view. We all have the right to believe what we like.'

Just that. Very *nice*.

This chappie wanted people to like him.

Number two flaw: Player. Note the seventeen chicks chatted up until October. And even though he was so nice with all the girls, you could clearly see he had an agenda. He wanted to get them into bed eventually. Nothing vulgar, nothing direct – all slow and smooth and subtle, yes – but heading inevitably in that direction, as you would expect from a man of his age and means and disposition.

Vaughn Cupido said this morning that Richter and the girlfriend, Cindy Senekal, had been an item since early October. Since then there was considerably less chaffing about. Only three girls got serious attention. But until early November he was still having an affair with one, if you looked at the WhatsApp messages – what looked like three lunch hour *njapse* at his house in Paradyskloof, Stellenbosch.

But what's really interesting was that it was with an older woman, at least by Richter's standards. Sarah Woodruff, forty-one, with a mysterious Tinder profile photo, just a glancing camera shot, her face half concealed behind a hoody. She didn't look like his usual blonde babe, there was a hint of brunette there.

Which meant they would have to find her and talk to her. Fillander made a careful note.

Number three flaw: bit of a show-off. It began with his profiles on Facebook and Twitter and Tinder. 'Chief Executive Officer, Founding Father and Majority Owner of Alibi.co.za. Serial entrepreneur, serious businessman, supports an open society, open internet, freedom of speech and choice. Love my job, love my life. Wealthy, healthy, happy.' (And you could believe it, thought Fillander, because Richter's photo beamed out such a big happy-go-lucky smile.)

But it was the 'wealthy' that was a bridge too far, because any blonde chick could figure out for herself that he was a rich shit if she read all the other stuff.

Unsubtle show-off.

And then there was the 'humble bragging', what Frankie Fillander's pa called '*fyn brag*'. Every second photo that Richter posted or tweeted was designed to show how rich or cute he was. The car, the Audi TT, was often in the background. In June, a couple of Facebook photos of him in the Kruger National Park, with the words: 'Quick getaway to The Outpost in Kruger for a breather.' The expensive luxury of the resort was obvious. In August he tweeted a photo of a bottle of Alto M.P.H.S. on a beautifully set restaurant table, beside a half empty glass, a bread roll and butter dish, with the comment 'R1,000 a bottle. Wonderful wine, would pay double the price.'

An avalanche of *fyn brag*.

Richter wanted everyone to believe he was rich and successful but nice, Frank Fillander thought. That's what he was going for.

He took another stick of biltong, pushed it in his mouth and started from the beginning again. To make sure he hadn't missed anything.

'I'm not going to let the media determine how we investigate this case,' said Mbali Kaleni with an expression of total disgust on her face.

'That's not what I'm saying, Major,' said the ever-calm John Cloete. 'But I have to give them some sort of answer.'

'I don't understand the question.'

'The question is,' he said with a great deal of patience, 'whether we are going to investigate the apparent attempt by someone to publish the full Alibi client database on the internet.'

'Why would we investigate that, Captain? It's not our problem.'

'Major, with all due respect, if we give them that answer, the SAPS will not look good.'

'Why not? We are investigating the murder of that man. We did not use those alibi services. We're not here to protect philanderers and cheats.'

Cloete sighed inside. 'Shall I say that we are looking at all the matters pertaining to the murder investigation?'

'Will that help?'

'For a while.'

'Then you can say that.'

'Can I add that, should we find a link between the attempt to make the database public and the murder, we will be investigating?'

Kaleni considered. 'Okay.'

'Thank you, Major.'

'Does Vaughn know about these shenanigans?'

'I . . . I don't know. I came straight to you.'

She nodded. 'Then I had better call him.'

Cupido stood anxiously waiting for Desiree Coetzee in front of a restaurant in Drostdy Street called The Birdcage.

He'd seen how tired and upset she seemed after the stresses of the day. And he spotted an opportunity. He apologised for needing to talk to her again and said 'It doesn't have to be here'.

'Thank God,' was her reaction.

'Can I buy you coffee?'

'And lemon meringue pie?'

'Of course.'

She suggested The Birdcage and he agreed to meet her there. He drove there, pleased with himself. But the place was shut. The sign on the door said *Monday–Friday: 09.00–17.00. Saturdays: 09.00–13.00. Sundays: Closed*. Now, at 18.42, he was left wondering whether she had known this all along. Was she trying to avoid him?

Why? Didn't she like him or was Benna right, that she had something to hide?

His cellphone rang. It was the DPCI number. He answered.

Griessel tried to hide the tremor in his fingers when he and Mooiwillem Liebenberg pulled on their rubber gloves in front of Ernst Richter's house. It was a big, modern double-storey in Mont Blanc, a secure development in Paradyskloof, high up on the slope of the mountain. Three garages, grey tiled roof.

'He lived here alone?' asked Liebenberg.

'That's what they say.'

Griessel unlocked the door.

'Three garages,' said Liebenberg philosophically.

They went inside. The alarm warning beeped. Inside it was warm and smelled a bit musty, because the house had been closed for three weeks. Griessel walked quickly to the alarm panel and tapped in the code that the station commander had given him, along with the key. Then he and Mooiwillem fetched their murder cases and brought them inside.

Liebenberg opened the door to the left to have a look at the garages.

The space was almost empty. On one of the shelves against the back wall were a few bottles, aerosol cans and tins for cleaning cars, and a pile of cloths.

'Three garages and you only use one . . .' said Liebenberg.

Griessel wasn't feeling well: a faint nausea, the first signs that the headache was returning, a buzzing in his head like a distant swarm of bees. The hands trembling, *jissis*, it was the first time in three years that his *fokken* hands were shaking. And fatigue, a strong urge to lie down. It was rubbish; he could handle his drink, always could, but now his middle-aged body was betraying him. He shook his head to deny it all. 'I'll take the . . .' he said, but then Liebenberg's phone rang.

Mooiwillem answered. He listened for a long time, said 'At his house' once, repeated 'Okay' a few times, and rang off again. He grimaced and said to Griessel: 'Vaughn thinks Rick Grobler is threatening to put the names of Alibi's clients on the internet. He wants me to go and talk to him. He lives just down here . . .'

Liebenberg walked to the door.

They knew it was policy that at least two detectives searched a house together. A lawyer for the defence would be quick to ask, 'Is there a witness that you found this piece of evidence? Or did you plant it?'

But Benny Griessel knew that if Liebenberg slipped out quickly, it gave him the chance to find a bottle. And relieve the worst of the pain.

'Vusi will be here just now,' he said.

'Okay, partner, I'll be back soon.' And Liebenberg was gone and Griessel was alone in the big, empty house.

To his great relief Cupido saw Desiree Coetzee crossing the street towards him. She had an athletic stride, and walked with the carefree, unconscious self-confidence of a slender, attractive young woman.

His gut contracted. Surely this lady was out of his league?

'I'm very sorry,' she called out as she approached. 'I was held up.'

'It's okay,' he said. 'But the place is closed.'

'Oh.' Only slightly caught off balance. 'Of course. I forgot. Sorry . . .'

In that moment he seemed to catch a glimpse of the other side, the private Desiree Coetzee when she wasn't operational manager of Alibi. Softer, a little absent-minded, vulnerable. It melted his heart and gave him a great big dose of courage.

'There must be other coffee shops?'

'Yes. Of course. There, down Church Street . . .' They walked together in silence, and for the first time Vaughn Cupido wished he wasn't wearing his flamboyant rebel clothes.

'Do you have children?' she asked him when they turned the corner and headed towards the early evening bustle of street cafés, people, cars.

The question was so unexpected that he stammered. 'I, uh . . . No, I'm not . . .'

His intention was to tell her he was single, a respectable man. 'I have never been married.'

'I haven't either, but I do have a son,' she said. 'That's why I was late.'

He wanted to bite off his tongue.

At 19.11 on Twitter

NoMoreAlibis @NoMoreAlibis
17 Hours and counting. Alibi.co.za client database on the web. Sample data in 30 minutes. #ErnstRichter #WhoKilledErnst #NoAlibi

@NoMoreAlibis followers had jumped to 2,467.

43

**Transcript of interview: Advocate Susan
Peires with Mr Francois du Toit**

*Wednesday, 24 December; 1604 Huguenot Chambers,
40 Queen Victoria Street, Cape Town*

FdT: Oupa Jean's will was meant to nail Pa. Pa inherited the farm,
but not a red cent with it. There was a life insurance policy and a
few investments, not exactly a fortune, and it all went into a family
trust. Ouma Hettie had usufruct, a monthly income. And when she
died, Pa's sisters would inherit it all.

So at forty-two Pa got Klein Zegen, a farm that had been produc-
ing fair to poor quality grapes for KWV for half a century – mostly
Chenin Blanc and Pinotage. Oom Dietrich Venske joked that the
Pinotage that Pa pulled up systematically was so old that it might be
Sakkie Perold's hermitage-pinot-hybrids from 1925. That vineyard
was kind of symbolic of everything on the farm: anachronistic. Old
and old fashioned. Run-down . . .

Three months after Oupa Jean's death we moved to the farm.

Ouma Hettie wanted to move to town, but Pa talked her out of it.
He said he wanted her nearby after all the years of separation. And
she was the one who knew the vineyards and the farm accounts the
best. She moved to the cottage, about a hundred metres from the
homestead. Sixty-four years old, but still young at heart and in her
head. She had such a big influence on me . . .

In any case . . . I was still too small to see it really, but everyone
said it was as though Pa had woken up, begun to live – for the first
time. He threw himself heart and soul into the farm; he worked
from five in the morning to late at night, as though he knew there
weren't many years left to realise the dream that he had for Klein

Zegen. For the first time he believed his stars had aligned, because it was 1994, the Year of Democracy. The international wine markets opened up for South Africa, because we were the new, popular, exotic producer and everyone wanted to give our winemakers a chance.

And Ma stood shoulder to shoulder with Pa. She couldn't resign from her job as lecturer at the university yet; they were too dependent on the income. But she was behind Pa, with every fibre of her being. Of course from the beginning she said one of their biggest priorities was to look after the labourers. She handled that side. She was counsellor and social worker, nurse and minister, mother hen and magistrate, all in one. She began projects to improve their houses, to make pension plans for them, to create bursaries for their children. And when Pa started to slowly pay off the money he was forced to borrow, she convinced him to give them a share in the farm business.

They were happy, I think, in the first ten or twelve years.

And I think of everyone, I was the happiest. I enjoyed the farm the most. It was . . . I don't have anything to compare it with, it's all I know, but to me it was a paradise. The whole thing of . . . nature, the soil, the weather – rain and wind, heat and cold – the seasons, everything that worked together to make the wine . . . Pa wasn't a talker, I think he wanted me and Paul to learn to love wine as he did, through assimilation, experience, by seeing and feeling and smelling, by working and being with the labourers, by growing up between those vines ourselves, pruning and picking . . .

And I did. But not Paul.

I just didn't know how much that upset Pa.

44

Griessel fought against the urge to search for booze immediately.

Jissis, he wasn't *that* desperate.

But Vusi would be there soon. No time to waste.

He walked past the kitchen. The large stove looked new and unused, gleaming stainless steel. Double door fridge. Expensive coffee machine. Food spatter on the microwave glass door showed that that at least was in use. No dining-room table in the open-plan space. There was a sitting room on the other side. Gigantic flatscreen television, a narrow table under it with a DSTV decoder, a PlayStation 4 and an Xbox 360. Two easy chairs. A wooden cabinet, chunky and modern, against the other wall.

Liquor cabinet?

He tore himself away, went to the back. Two bedrooms and one bathroom were also on this level, both rooms unfurnished. He opened built-in cupboards. All he found was a vacuum cleaner.

He wavered at the foot of the stairs. Vusi would be arriving any moment now.

He walked quickly back to the cabinet in the sitting room and opened the little door. Wine, whisky, brandy, vodka, liqueurs. Most of the bottles were still sealed, as if Richter had been prepared for a party that never happened. A wide assortment of glasses. A corkscrew and beer bottle opener. Half a packet of salted peanuts.

He spotted the Jack Daniel's, half-hidden behind a few bottles of wine: Klein Zegen Fire Opal. He bent down, took out the Jack, and put it on top of the cupboard.

Have a slug from the bottle, he thought, don't dirty a glass now.

He grabbed the bottle by the neck, bent thumb and forefinger around the lid so that he could break the seal, and then he saw himself – for the first time that day he saw his desperation and his weakness, his thirst and his disease. And he remembered how it had been, the darkest years; he remembered the total dependence, the powerlessness, the consuming desire. His head whirled with the excuses of last night – he wanted to bring them back, make them new and strong – but in the moment they failed him. Doc Barkhuizen's phone calls, Alexa's SMSes, his children's disappointment if they knew . . .

So much emotion, his heart was full, his eyes damp, Lord, did he want to walk *that* path again, lose everything all over again? Why was he like this? So weak and dependent.

But you don't have much to lose, a voice in his head told him.

Just a sip. Think about all these things later.

He had to phone Doc now. He took his phone out of his pocket.

A car door slammed. Vusi was here.

Hastily he shoved the bottle back in the cabinet, closed the door.

They sat down at an outside table of the Basic Bistro on Church Street.

Cupido desperately wanted to break the uncomfortable silence of the last five minutes. And compensate for his slip-up. 'So, how old is your little boy?'

'Eleven,' she said.

A waiter brought them menus. 'Would you like to eat something?' he asked.

She gave him a long steady look, as if trying to judge his motives. 'Are you going to eat?'

'Yes, if you want . . .'

'Okay,' she said, with a little shake of the head that he couldn't fathom.

They studied their menus.

She put hers down. 'I was eighteen when I fell pregnant. Here, in my first year at varsity. It was complicated. The father is white – a sort of one-night stand. We were both still kids. Terrified.' She spoke without embarrassment, in a do-with-it-what-you-will way. 'Our parents on both sides were furious with us. His because he'd had sex with a coloured girl, mine because they had to sacrifice so much to get me into university. Opportunities squandered, that sort of thing.'

'Where do you come from?'

'Robertson. Small-town girl. You?'

'Mitchells Plain.'

She nodded, as if that explained something to her, and Cupido burned to ask what that might be.

The waiter took their order. Cupido said: 'I may have to take a few calls . . .'

'That's okay, it's not a date.' He wasn't good at hiding his feelings. She saw the discomfort written on his face and added, 'I know you're working.'

He wanted to ask her how she had ended up at Alibi, a girl like her; if she had a boyfriend. But he knew that would betray him.

'Did you hear someone wants to put your client database on the internet?'

'Yes. It's going to destroy us. If it happens.'

'But this morning you said you were doomed in any case, because of the overdraft.'

She picked up a fork, twirled it in her fingers. 'You want to know something weird? When Ernst went missing, with all the media coverage, our registration stats rose by 32 per cent. There's no such thing as bad publicity. *Die een se dood is die ander se brood.* One door closes, another one opens, don't they say? It's sad, I know, but that's how the world works. And today again. I check the stats every day before I leave. There was a big spike this morning: new registrations. But this thing about the database, it's going to scare people off. Even if it is just a scam.'

'You think it's a scam?'

She shrugged.

'Who would want to do this? And who can? Any suspects?'

'Too many. All the IT people who were downsized . . .'

'What about Rick Grobler?'

She considered the idea with downcast eyes, lips pressed together. 'I don't think so.'

'Why?'

'Why would he do that? What's to gain?'

'He's one angry *ou* . . .'

'He was very angry about the money, but the data . . . that's his baby. He's old school. Data security is holy. He takes great pride in his work . . . And . . . I think he likes me, to be honest. Sort of a schoolboy crush . . .'

She knows she's beautiful, thought Cupido. And it's not a bad thing. He himself was a great believer in having a healthy self-image.

'So you know about the money that Richter borrowed from him?'

'Rick came and told me when Ernst missed the first payment. Me and Vernon Visser.'

'Vernon Visser?'

'The chief financial officer.'

'Oh, *ja*.'

'We went to talk to Ernst. We were very worried. But Ernst said it's all okay, just wait until the VC partners have had a look at the books.'

'And the email about how Grobler is going to strangle Richter?'

'I didn't see that. Is that why Rick is a suspect now? Because of an email?'

'Yes.'

Again the thoughtfully compressed lips. 'I don't think . . . No, it wasn't him. Rick . . . He's a lamb.'

'A lamb doesn't write that kind of email. There's a lot of violence in it, and lots of anger.'

'Genuine?' With real surprise.

He nodded.

She processed that. 'But you're not sure it's him.'

'Why do you say that?'

'Because you're here, and you're not just asking about Rick.'

She was a clever woman, he thought. 'How many people can get at the database? To put it on the internet?'

'The data is very secure from outside hacking. But inside the firewall . . . All the techies, basically. They have to have access to do their work.'

'And you think it's someone who was fired?'

Again the shrug, that it's-not-my-problem air.

'You don't care?'

'I care, about everyone who works there. But the ship has been sinking for a while, and when Ernst disappeared . . . I just don't see a future without him. The VC companies are embarrassed about us already, and if the truth about the finances comes out, if the bank recalls the overdraft . . . It's just a matter of time . . .'

'What will you do?'

'I've had my CV out for a few weeks now already ...'

They sat a while in silence.

'My colleague believes you haven't told us everything,' said Cupido, knowing he had to broach the uncomfortable subject some time or other.

'The one who looks like a Russian politician, with manners to match?'

Cupido smiled. No one had ever described Griessel quite like that. 'One and the same. But he's not always like that; he's been through a tough time this week.'

She pulled up her shoulders. 'I've answered all your questions.'

'What else should I have asked?'

Desiree Coetzee put down the fork and looked at Cupido with those dark eyes, for a long time. Just when she was about to speak, the gourmet burgers arrived.

On Twitter, at 19.32:

NoMoreAlibis @NoMoreAlibis
Alibi client: Userid: DoubleB. Paid by Basil Simphiwe Bhanga. FNB:
62366255282. Nine alibis. #ErnstRichter #WhoKilledErnst #NoAlibi

There were now more than four thousand followers. But only four of them – all journalists – were sufficiently well informed to wonder whether this Basil Simphiwe Bhanga was Basil Simphiwe Bhanga, Member of Parliament for the African National Congress.

Just before eight that night Fillander called the number he had for Sarah Woodruff, the older woman that Richter had seen three times for a lunch hour *njaps*.

It rang for a relatively long time before the 'Hello?'

A young voice? 'Who's speaking?' asked Fillander.

'It's Soretha,' with an uncertain questioning tone, making Fillander suspect it was a child. He could hear the sound of a television in the background.

'Is this your phone, Soretha?'

'No, it's my mother's, she's in the toi ... in the bathroom.'

'Can I speak to her?'

'Just hold on . . .' He heard her call. 'Mamma! Telephone . . .'

Fillander heard a man's voice, impatient: 'Who's looking for her?'

'I don't know, Pappa . . .'

He had a strong suspicion about what was going on here. Sarah Woodruff was a married woman. He tried to think of some excuse, a white lie to protect her, but the day had been too long already, so he just said: 'Never mind, I think this is the wrong number,' and cut the call.

He would try again tomorrow morning.

He phoned Cupido to hear where else he could help now.

45

Francois du Toit had come into her office an extremely tense man, but the talking had gradually calmed him down. Now, when he reached his own part in the story, when he spoke about his own brother, Advocate Susan Peires saw the tension returning. As if he was in the final straight and racing towards a conclusion.

She had to make more and more of an effort to concentrate, because her blood sugar was dropping. It was an hour after lunch time. She waited for a pause from him and then said she was accustomed to routine and so was her metabolism, would he mind if she ordered something to eat. There was a sandwich service; what did he like?

She saw his return to reality, how the focus in his eyes shifted, and the frown of his concentration turned to one of discomfort and apology. He was so sorry, he said. The time, he had lost track, yes, of course, of course, go ahead.

She smiled and waved his apology away. It was nothing, she understood, and asked what he liked.

Anything.

She knew in his embarrassment he would try to choose whatever was the least trouble, and she didn't want to delay longer than was necessary. She suggested the chicken and bacon, and he said, yes, thanks. Wholegrain? Yes, fine. Tea? Cold drink?

Tea, please.

She rang her secretary, placed the order, and asked him to please, continue.

'My brother . . .' he said, and paused for a long time, picking up the thread of his story again.

So it was the brother, she thought, her latest guess at who had murdered Richter – the brother Paul, who had inherited Oupa Jean's violent genes.

46

Late that night they sat outside Richter's house.

Benny Griessel looked up, at the mountain's dark jagged outline etched against the starlight and the paper-thin crescent moon that drifted ominously above the peak. Then down, at his four colleagues. He sat with Vusi and Liebenberg on the garden wall, Cupido leaning against the engine bonnet of the Hawks' BMW. Fillander sat cross-legged on the paving stones. Each of them busy with a can of Coke and a sandwich that Mooiwillem had bought at the Woolies food kiosk at the Engen filling station down the road. They were hungry and thirsty, and cheerful, despite the fact that the search of the house had produced nothing. The conversation darted back and forth, from speculation about the case to general banter and good-natured teasing.

Griessel was still emotional, an unwelcome cloak that he could not shrug off. Part exhaustion, part alcohol withdrawal. Doc Barkhuizen had explained all these things well enough to him, so he knew that the alcohol was messing with the chemistry of his brain. Insuperable and real, these effects were active now, exaggerating emotions, like his sense of incredible gratitude that he could be there among them – his comrades in arms, his friends, the people who accepted him without judgement. And the bond between them, forged by the mutual experience of the dark side of this community: Members of the Service, forming that oh-so-thin line, the fragile barrier between the devil and the deep blue sea, a solitary – now even rejected – group. A band of outcasts, they truly only had each other.

The feelings threatened to overwhelm Griessel. He disguised the wave of emotion with a last big gulp of Coke, and lit a cigarette.

'I don't want to offend, but really, white people will always be an enigma to me,' said Vusi.

Frankie Fillander said coloured people like him didn't even know what 'enigma' meant.

The detectives laughed, quietly, out of consideration for the people in the nearby homes.

'How can one guy live in such a huge house, all on his own?' asked Vusi and shook his head in disbelief. 'Such a waste.'

'If he was a darkie,' said Cupido, 'at least twenty-eight people would have moved in here.'

'Exactly,' said Ndabeni, his smile gleaming in the glow of the street lamp.

'I have a theory,' said Fillander.

'About darkies?' Cupido wanted to know. 'Too late. Steve Hofmeyr has already formulated them all . . .'

Vusi clicked his tongue. 'That guy, he's bad news for this country.'

'Amen,' said Cupido.

Fillander said no, he had a theory about Richter. He had listened to Liebenberg's report about his conversation with his mother. He had listened to Cupido's feedback on their day at the Alibi offices, and his insights after the date with Desiree Coetzee . . .

Cupido said, it wasn't a *fokken* date, Uncle Frankie. And Fillander said, so why do your eyes shine like that, Vaughn, when you talk about that chick? 'Every time you say "Desiree", rose petals fall from your tongue. Not to mention the candle-lit dinner for two . . .'

Cupido said there were no damn candles . . .

Fillander said, *ja*, sure. He said he had also thought about all Richter's social media stuff, everything he had read through this afternoon. He jerked a thumb in the direction of the house behind them, said he had taken a good look at the place. That big bedroom up there had to be put to one side, in the correct compartment, because Ernst Richter was a man of three parts.

'The bedroom belongs to Richter The Player; let's call it this guy's Part One. Look at that extra-large king-size bed, fancy duvet cover and all the pillows; that antique chest of drawers; the tasteful nude painting on the wall. It's like he called in an interior decorator. Look how different the bedroom is compared to the rest of the house, fancied up so nice. It's a love pad, for all the chicks that Richter Tindered and chatted up on his phone. One of which seems to be a married woman, and that's significant, but I will get back to her just now.

'Part Two is Richter The Kid. Check it out down there, by the flat screen. Two games machines, and those game controllers are well worn; he spent a lot of time there. And all the games on the iPhone, and that thing they told us, him sitting with all the people who have to fake the alibi documents. That chap was still just a *laaitie* at heart. Maybe because he couldn't be a child when he was meant to be. I kind of got the impression that everything was a game to him, and that's also significant, because those sorts of guys don't think properly about consequences.

'And then there's Part Three. And I keep trying to remember the name of that chappie who made himself wings of candle wax and chicken feathers, and then tried to fly . . .'

'That sounds like Billy April from Bishop Lavis,' Vaughn Cupido said. 'You know, that crazy crackhead who jumped stark naked from the . . .'

'No, no, no, that *outjie* in Greek mythology,' Frank Fillander interrupted him.

'Not my jurisdiction,' said Cupido.

'Icarus,' said Vusumuzi Ndabeni.

'Icarus!' Fillander snapped his fingers as if it had been on the tip of his tongue all along.

'Not bad for a darky from Gugs, Vusi,' said Cupido. 'Greek mythology, *nogal*. But please keep it to yourself. I can just see some Mitchells Plain mama calling her son Icarus Fortuin when that gets out.'

They laughed, louder than they meant to, and Fillander said: '*Kêrels*, quietly, the neighbours will complain. Anyway, Icarus, that's the *kêrel*. And then he flew too high, and the sun melted the candle wax, and he crashed and burned in his *moer in*. Now that's Part Three of Richter. Look at the house. It's rented to impress. Look at the car; it's on nearly every Facebook photo. Look at the company, Richter just pumped money in; let's keep up appearances, at all costs. And now Vaughn says the Coetzee chick said it's because Richter's own money ran out that he had to go and borrow. But according to her arithmetic, he put in way more cash than she thought he had in the first place.'

'So, what is your theory, Uncle Frankie?' Mooiwillem asked.

Fillander got up stiffly from the paving. 'These old legs,' he groaned. 'I'm getting to that, Willem. This morning I read the piece that the *Rapport* wrote about Richter. How he explained that his father had died when he was fourteen years old. What a hard time his mother had. Now, when I listen to all that, I think it was a whole lot worse than he let on. I think that mother of his was devastated. Husband dead, finances in chaos, child to care for, and maybe genuine poverty, for a while at least. Now, a *laaitie* of fourteen who sees his mother struggling desperately, he's going to feel responsible, and powerless. He's the man of the house, but he can't help; he has to watch his mommy suffer. You see it a lot in the coloured community.

'But young Ernst, he has more troubles, because he's in school with the rich kids; he's going to feel inferior when she drops him off in their old *skedonk* of a car. He can't take pals home, because there's no Coke in the fridge or snacks in the cupboard. He's going to get damage, that *laaitie*. The sort of damage that will shape his love life and his financial life, for the rest of his life . . .'

'That's deep, Uncle Frankie,' said Vaughn Cupido.

'But it's true,' Vusi agreed. He knew real poverty.

Fillander nodded and continued. 'Now, I've seen that a lot, people who grow up in hard times, and make something of themselves. They compensate for the rest of their lives, 'cause why, they don't want to go back to the tough times, by hook or by crook. They do stupid stuff . . .'

'True story,' said Cupido.

'Now what are the three most common motives for murder?' asked Fillander.

'Domestic squabbles, money and revenge,' said Vusi.

'That's right,' said Fillander. 'And we've just ruled out domestic, 'cause there is no . . .' – and he pointed at the house again – 'domestic life to speak of. So my theory is, revenge, or money. That revenge could come in the form of a jealous husband, and I'll follow up on that tomorrow. But I'm sort of leaning in the direction of money, because it sounds to me as if there were all sorts of financial shenanigans going on with this *kêreltjie*.'

Liebenberg nodded thoughtfully. Ndabeni stroked his perfectly manicured goatee. Cupido softly let out a fizzy-drink burp and said: 'There's another financial shenanigan . . . maybe . . .'

Everyone looked at him.

'During my interview with Miss Coetzee'–Vaughn emphasised the word 'interview' and '*Miss* Coetzee' emphatically while looking at Fillander – 'she told me a very weird thing happened in November of last year. She said she was working a bit late one night, and when she left at *tjaila* time and was walking to her car, this dude got out of his car. Grand car – Mercedes S-Class by the sound of it, those things retail for a million and a half. Dude was fifty-something, whitey, but smart: classy suit, designer rimless glasses, hair manicured all professional-like. And he comes over to her and asks in fancy English, do you work at Alibi? And she says yes. And he says, you're the operational manager, Desiree Coetzee. And she says yes, but she's rattled, 'cause it's not exactly common knowledge, Richter is the only public face of the company. So the classy dude says, Someone's trying to blackmail me, here from Alibi, and let me tell you, I will go public, but pay I will not. If I go down, you go down. I will give you a fight you will not survive. And the dude turns around and gets in his Merc and drives away.'

'*Bliksem*,' said Mooiwillem Liebenberg.

'Wow,' said Vusi.

'That's right,' said Cupido. 'She says she's completely shocked, and she stands there thinking for a long time, and then she phones Ernst, there from the parking lot, and she tells him about this dude. She said he went all quiet, for so long she thought the line was dead, 'cause why, MTN's cellular service sucks here in the Stellenbosch. And then he came back and he says Des, we have to check this out, this is very bad. Let's talk tomorrow. So she worries all night long, next morning first thing she pops in to see Richter. And he says, What can we do? It could be anybody; we can't just throw out a general staff memo that says "Please don't blackmail the clients". But he would check the computer logs; he would reconsider whether all the programmers really needed access to the database. And they left it there, never to be spoken of again. Only a few days later, when she was lying in bed, 'cause the thing worried her *kwaai*, and she thought, wait a minute, Ernst is the one who looks through the database to see who all the rich and famous clients are. She caught him one time: two of the techies had come and whispered in her ear. He's the one who's so worried about the finances; he's the one pumping money in. Could it be *him*? But she had no proof, and the thing blew over.'

'Well, I never,' said Frank Fillander.

'She said about four months later, sort of half by accident she saw a photo on a news site, a guy that got a Chamber of Commerce achievement award, and she thought, but this is the dude with the Merc. Not absolutely sure, 'cause it had been quite dark in the parking lot, and a few months had passed, but it looked like the dude – fancy haircut, fancy glasses, his name and all, there by the photo. Turns out he's a captain of industry, chairman of the board of a company that does marine cargo insurance, ShipSure, here in the Cape. So she does a little detective work herself, slips into the database, and sure enough, a guy with the right initials and surname made a few big payments for an extensive alibi, September of 2013 – fake airline ticket to London, fake hotel bills, that sort of thing.'

'So, what did she do?' asked Vusi.

'Nothing. Sort of filed the info away in her head. She couldn't remember the guy's first name, surname is Habenewt or something, she's going to SMS the details tomorrow.'

They all chewed over the information, until Cupido looked up at where Griessel sat on the wall, head down. 'What do you think, Benna?'

At that moment, his only thought was one of shame. Because his colleagues had been thinking about the case, the whole day long. And he, Griessel, had been mainly concerned about his next *dop* – and how he could get away with it – and, while he had helped to search Richter's house, about Alexa and whether he should go home or not. Because he didn't know what kind of welcome, if any, he would get from her, and he didn't have the strength for a confrontation or tears. Shame, because they looked at him with so much expectation and respect, they thought something meaningful and intelligent was going to come out of his mouth.

From somewhere – he didn't know where – something leapt from the back of his mind. He said: 'I think . . . it matters that he was buried other side Blouberg. It . . . says something, Vaughn. His house, his

office, everything is here in Stellenbosch. His car was found two kilometres from Alibi, but the body in Blouberg. The problem is, I don't
know what it says.'

They all nodded, agreeing.

He wanted to tell them not to be so impressed by the statement; he
didn't deserve it.

47

The brother Paul, the firstborn son who would inherit the Du Toit's family farm, was always a wild, unfathomable creature.

He was a beautiful child, with his pale blond hair, his fine features and the supple body with its athletic promise, which later exceeded all expectations.

His sporting prowess was astonishing, the natural talent so blindingly obvious. His light burned so much brighter than his peers that Guillaume received calls from as far as Pretoria about the child's possible rugby future. Large sports bursaries were mentioned while the boy was still in primary school.

The combination of appearance and ability enchanted everyone, from schoolmates to teachers, so that they dismissed other signs, the less positive characteristics, as the idiosyncrasies of the genius, the future superstar in the making. In general there was an unspoken feeling of privilege for them to be able to see this success unfolding in front of their very eyes. *One day I will be able to say I knew him in primary school.*

Young Paul du Toit paid no attention to instructions on the rugby field; he had no feeling for the team or his role in it. Every match was an exhibition of his personal brilliance; his game was always selfish and narcissistic. And as long as it helped them win, the coach didn't criticise him for it.

In the classroom there were acts of disobedience, defiance of authority. When Paul was thirteen and in Grade Seven, his new teacher – an experienced teacher, and no worshipper of the Great God Rugby – objected to this kid glove treatment, and called Helena to arrange a meeting. Helena came to listen, with an open mind. But when she went home, she chose not to discuss it with her son or husband.

Partly because Guillaume was so terribly busy rebuilding Klein Zegen, and so was she.

Partly because she was aware that her own rebellious genes were also part of Paul: in opposition to her conservative father's one-dimensional views, her philosophy was that Paul's individuality must be protected. They could shape and direct it later. Her suspicion of any official system, and the one-size-fits-all approach of all primary schools, made her reluctant to take the teacher's feedback seriously. Children must be allowed to be children – a bit wild, a bit free. Goodness knew, more than enough years of restrictive adulthood lay ahead.

Helena had also previously pondered the complexity of the psychology her wonderchild was caught up in. The glorification of his rugby talent in this country, and especially in this town, at such a young age, would invariably have a huge influence. They – the school and all the staff – couldn't expect to enjoy only the benefits.

She tried her best to keep Paul's feet on the ground, to expose him to activities and interests that lay outside his natural abilities. Without success.

Perhaps the sheer normality of the younger brother Francois also had an influence on how the parents reacted. Francois was the stabilising counterweight to Paul's tempestuous nature. He was the one who was interested in the farm, the vineyards and the wine, who was academically stronger, who read, who barely made the second team in rugby and cricket. And he was humble in the face of his brother's astronomical ascent, merely content to bask in reflected glory.

48

At 22.52 Major Mbali Kaleni's cellphone rang.

'I'm sorry to call you at home, Mbali,' said Brigadier Musad Manie, commander of the Hawks in the Western Cape.

'I'm at the office, sir,' she said with a touch of reproof in her tone.

Manie understood his commander of the Serious and Violent Crimes group well. He knew better than to let this bother him. 'Anything I should know?'

'No, sir. I'm waiting for my team to get back. They've just left Stellenbosch.'

'Any progress?'

'Captain Cupido should give me a full report within an hour, sir. They have put in a lot of work, but I don't think there is a solid suspect yet.'

'Okay, Mbali . . . I've had a call from our National Commissioner. Now, I just want to let you know, I'll manage it from my side, but . . . This thing about the database, you know, the clients of that company, the guy on Twitter making the names public . . .'

'Yes, sir, Captain Cloete has been keeping me posted.'

'Okay. The Commissioner says she is getting a lot of pressure from . . . well, from higher up, if you know what I mean.' He broached the topic warily: he had a strong suspicion what Kaleni's reaction was going to be. 'Now, I'm not—'

'Sir, I will not have my team distracted by—'

'Major, please, let me finish. I'm not saying you should do anything about it. I will manage it from my side, as I said. I just wanted to let you know, there is pressure, and there is concern. The word is that there is a member of parliament who has been contacted by the press in this regard: a very respected member of parliament, a husband and a father. And apparently, this member of parliament is completely innocent, and is being implicated as part of a smear campaign by the oppo—'

'Sir, I do not believe that . . .'

'Me neither. But that's not the point. I have to report back in the morning, and all I'm asking is, if there is any information pertaining to this leak of the database, please let me know.'

'Yes, sir.'

'Thank you, Mbali.'

Griessel drove back with Cupido. The Bottelary road was quiet at this time of night.

Cupido prepared his speech. Only beyond Devonvale was he ready to talk to Griessel.

'You know I'm your friend, Benna?'

Griessel sighed; he could guess where this was leading. 'Vaughn, I don't want to talk about the booze.'

'You don't have to. I just want to make a speech; use it, don't use it, your choice, it's a free country. But if I'm your friend, it's my duty, *wraggies*, Benna. Friendship is not saying the things you *want* to hear, but the things you *need* to hear. I understand this thing with Vollie Fish, Benna. And man, I understand the thing about Colonel Nyathi getting killed. These things stick to a man's clothes. Remember Barry Brezinsky of Narcotics? Barry the Whole Pole? Gunned down in his driveway just before he could testify? I was on that same case with him, Benna; he was the lead investigator, big drug syndicate. That morning I was standing next to his car, Barry dead there inside, blood everywhere, and his wife and children standing in the doorway and they didn't cry, Benna, they just stared, with that look that says we don't know what the *fok* we're going to do now. The future had just evaporated, there was just desolation stretching out in front of them. Took me two years to get over it, he was like a bru' to me; he was my mentor, Benna. From a wet-behind-the-ears constable, he made me the detective that I am. Lots of anger after Barry, I'm telling you now. A hell of a lot of anger. I wanted to go out and round up all the dealers and suppliers and beat each and every one to death with a blunt instrument. So I know the feeling. But I went to see a shrink, and he helped me a lot, Benna. There's no shame—'

'I did see a shrink, Vaughn.'

'Go back, Benna.'

'She can't help me.'

'But do you want to be helped, Benna?'

'Fuck you, Vaughn.'

'That's okay. Let the anger come out. I can handle it. But let me say a few things you really don't want to hear, *ek sê dit* in friendship, Benna, *een dag sal jy versta*. Do you really want to be helped? Really? 'Cause why, I scheme it's a handy excuse. Shrink can't help, so I drink. Fact is—'

'An excuse, Vaughn? An excuse? You have no *fokken* idea . . .'

'Fact is, the shrink can help . . .'

'How, Vaughn? How? How the *fok* can the shrink help? Is she just going to whip out a magic wand . . . ? Did you . . . Why did Vollie Fish shoot his wife and children? Do you know why? Because I know, Vaughn. I know exactly. I know what he knew. And he knew he couldn't hold it back any more. It was coming closer, growing bigger. More and more. When Frank asked tonight what are the big motives for murder, didn't it make you think, Vaughn? Take the money motive, just the money motive. The house robberies and street robberies and farm robberies and cash-in-transit robberies and shopping centre robberies and autobank robberies – more and more and more of them, and all of them more violent. It's a cycle, Vaughn, the children seeing violence and experiencing violence since they were only this high, it's what they know, it's what they become. It's not their fault; it's their world.

'How are we going to save them? How are we going to turn this around? There are people streaming in over our borders, Vaughn, to come and rob us, because there's money here, there's progress here. We can't stop the tide, it's not ever going to draw back. You know how the world looks. And everything is on the rise, not just robbery. Domestic violence, revenge, everything just gets worse. The disease, the serial killers, more, every day there are more of them, and they are getting sicker, Vaughn. It's like a . . . I don't know, this *moerse* train that's just picking up speed. The brakes are fucked, Vaughn – *we* are the brakes, and *we* are fucked . . .'

'How can you say that?' Cupido forgot about his carefully prepared speech; he was angry now. 'You're taking on my pride now. How many *ouens* have you and I put in *tjoekie*, this past year? How many? The SAPS, every day? Why are the courts so full, Benna, if we're fucked? And the jails? That's bullshit, Benna, we are a long way from being fucked . . .'

'How many dockets . . .'

'No, now you have to give me a chance, 'cause that argument of yours won't fly. 'Cause crime is increasing we all have to sit and drink? That's your solution? You think it's an—'

'That's not what I'm saying . . .'

'Now what are you saying, Benna? That just you can sit and *suip*, and the rest of us must struggle against crime? You think this is a unique situation here with us? Look at all the mighty First World countries, Benna. Take America. War on drugs, for decades, and they are losing it, in their *moer in*. Must they just sit back and *suip*, hey? D'you know how many boatloads of poor immigrants arrive there with them, in all those European countries? You think their crime is dropping? It's the state of the world. If this job was easy, then anyone could do it. But no, anyone can't do it. We can. We are the Hawks, *pappie*, the cream of the crop, best of the best. And you, Benny Griessel, you're the best cop I know. By a long shot. When you're sober. But now your head is full of all sorts of shit, and you like it, 'cause it's a *lekker* excuse for a *dop*. So, as your pal, as the *ou* who likes and respects you, I'm telling you tonight, man up, Benna. Grow a pair. Go back to that shrink and tell her you're not giving up therapy until your head is clean.'

Griessel said nothing.

Cupido tried to get his feelings back under control. When he spoke again, his voice was quieter, calmer: 'Where's the booze going to take you, Benna?'

Still Griessel was silent.

'Just think about it. Where's the booze going to take you?'

At half past eleven Griessel found a place in Long Street that was still open. He quickly drank one double Jack at the counter, then he drove home. His body told him he should have had another one, but he controlled the thirst – he kept to the agreement he had made with himself, there beside Cupido.

He parked in the street in front of Alexa's house. The lights were still on. He had expected that. He remained sitting. How was he going to handle it? After being so totally pissed last night, after he had ignored her calls and SMSes the whole day?

It depended on which Alexa he was going to find inside.

He got out, locked the car and went in.

Alexa sat waiting for him in the sitting room.

'Hello, Benny,' she said. There was relief in her voice. He could see the tension in her body and mouth, but also the control, and he was grateful for it. He was suddenly, overwhelmingly aware of his love for her. He stood in no-man's-land between the door and where she sat. He knew she would smell the alcohol if he kissed her, but he badly wanted to. They both needed it.

Her eyes were on him. He went to her, bent, kissed her. Her hands were behind his head, she pressed his lips hard against hers and kissed him for a long time.

'Your mouth tastes like paradise,' she said. She gave him a crooked smile, her eyes moist. 'Thank God you're not drunk.'

It was not at all what he had expected. Suddenly he was emotional again, because he didn't deserve *this* mercy. Until he realised it might be a strategy, agreed between her and Doc Barkhuizen. Let him say what he wanted to say. He straightened up again. 'I'm going back to the psychiatrist, when this case is over.'

'Okay.' She said it so quietly that he could barely hear her. 'I'm glad.'

'Until then I will drink, but I won't get so drunk again.'

She didn't react. He knew it was because she was also an alcoholic. Any prediction about how you were going to handle alcohol was ridiculous. That was the first of the Alcoholics Anonymous Twelve Steps, the recognition that you were powerless against drink; that your life was out of control. But tonight he had only drunk one double. He could do it again.

'Then rather come and drink at home. Just don't leave the booze here. Keep it in your car.'

He thought about it. For a moment it seemed like a wonderful possibility, a solution. But then he realised that it would be incredibly selfish of him. To sit and drink in front of her, knowing she also longed for the same release.

He just nodded. He wanted to change the subject; he wanted the normality of their before-booze-life back. He wanted to ask 'How was your day?' but he couldn't, because he knew her day had been hell.

'Have you eaten?' she asked and got up out of her chair slowly.

49

Francois du Toit's narrative sped up. The words flowed from his mouth, the emotions passing across his face like the shadows of clouds, his hands and body expressive too. Sometimes he got up and moved around, or he sat still, his gaze distant, remembering.

His brother Paul's first big scandal at school, age sixteen, in Grade Ten in Paul Roos Gymnasium. Ma Helena received the phone call from the principal; he would like to see both parents. Yes, it was urgent; he preferred not to discuss it over the phone.

Guillaume and Helena went straight away. On the way they speculated. Paul wasn't strong academically, but he was passing. What could it be?

The principal invited them into his office, his manner awkward, voice muted, eyes evasive. There had been an incident. The young teacher who taught geography, an attractive woman . . . Paul waited until his friends left the classroom, then he walked up to her and made an improper suggestion. *Nou ja*, sometimes at this age . . . the boys . . . they didn't always have a sense of the acceptable: their hormones, the talk among them during breaks. And it was a boys' school, Paul had no sisters, it happened . . . But the teacher was terribly upset, especially about the way he'd spoken, what she called the 'brute vulgarity and arrogance' . . .

'What suggestion did Paul make?' asked Helena.

'An improper suggestion.'

'That we have already determined. I want to know exactly what he said,' said Helena as Guillaume put a soothing hand on her shoulder, which she ignored.

The principal seemed to shrink back in his seat, reluctant to utter the reported words.

'Helena . . .' pleaded Guillaume.

'No,' she said. 'I can't talk to him unless I know precisely what he said.'

The principal marshalled his courage and dignity, and said: 'Paul apparently said that he'd heard that she was sexually active at university, and he would like to have sex with her.'

'Are those the words that he used?' Helena asked in disbelief. 'The "brute vulgarity and arrogance"?'

'No, not entirely.'

'Helena,' said Guillaume, this time louder and more urgently.

Helena stood up. 'If you can't tell me precisely what my child said, I will go and ask the teacher herself.'

'He said he heard she had fucked around at varsity, and he wanted to fuck her,' said the principal with barely-suppressed revulsion. 'Up the . . .'

'Up the what?'

Guillaume just sighed.

'I'm not going to say it in front of you.'

'Then say it to my husband,' she said and stormed out.

When Guillaume came out later alone, she was waiting for him in the car.

'Up the what?' she asked.

'Up the arse,' said her husband.

A strange, complex sound escaped from her lips.

They talked to Paul, that afternoon. Paul said the teacher was lying. It was she who told him that's how she wanted to be fucked. He used the word bluntly in front of his parents, like a status symbol.

That was the first time that both parents realised their son had a serious problem. They remained calm and threatened to call the teacher. He scoffed, remorseless: 'Everyone knows she's a slut.'

Helena insisted that he was going to apologise to her. Paul refused. She said they would ban him from all sports. He said they couldn't stop him playing rugby.

Guillaume said they could. It would only take one call to the school principal.

Paul shouted at them, called them '*fokken* stupid'. They sat in the Klein Zegen sitting room, shocked and overwhelmed by the day's revelations and this crazy tirade from their son. It was as if he was a stranger standing there, observing their stunned silence with absolute arrogance.

Guillaume recovered first. He stood up and walked to the telephone. 'I'll phone the principal then.'

'OK, I'll apologise to the bitch,' Paul spat and stormed out.

Helena drove over to see the teacher that very night. The young woman was traumatised. She told Helena about other disturbing behaviours – the manipulations, lies, cheating on a test paper. She said it was so difficult because it was her first teaching post, she didn't want to 'make waves' so soon. And then there was Paul's status as sports icon, in this sports mad boys' school . . . But there was something wrong with that boy, something wasn't right.

Helena rang a friend and colleague at the university Psychology Department. She and Guillaume went to talk to him the following afternoon. He agreed to see Paul. They had to use the sports ban as blackmail again to get their son there.

The psychology professor spent five hours, in four separate sessions, with Paul. Then gave his report to the parents. That was the conversation where the word 'psychopath' was mentioned for the first time.

50

Cupido only got away from the office after midnight.

He drove home, to his house in Caledon Street, Bellville-South. At this time of night it was only a ten-minute drive.

He got out, opened the gate. He looked at his house, lit up in the car headlights. It was as if he saw it with new eyes, this little place he had bought eighteen months ago. The first property in his name. Here, because he wanted to be close to work, and amongst his people. He could have afforded a townhouse in Bellville, he could have gone to live with the whiteys like so many upwardly mobile coloureds did, but he didn't want to.

He unlocked the single garage door, pulled it up.

This was his pride and joy: three bedrooms, about twice as big as the house that he and his brothers grew up in with Daddy and Mommy in Mitchells Plain.

Progress. For him. But what would a woman like Desiree Coetzee make of it? A girl with an MBA degree, those were *kwaai* qualifications; she lives in another world. How would she look at it? Because if you put this house down anywhere in the white suburbs of Stellenbosch, it suddenly looked heavy common. The low concrete wall with ornate little pillars – he still wanted to break that down, build something nice. The yellow walls were just a shade too shrill, he wanted to repaint them, something classy, off-white, cream. But when? All his time and money so far had gone into the bathroom renovation.

Don't think like that. If she was a woman of substance, she would look at the man, not the house.

Was he ready to have a *laaitie* in his life? Another man's child. A whitey's child.

He turned around, walked back to his car, grinning at himself. Slow down, Cyril, you haven't even had a proper date with the dolly, never mind what Uncle Frank insinuated.

He pulled in, closed the door, went into the house, put on the lights, and the TV. Opened the fridge, wanting a beer, but if he drank one now, he would want to pee at four tomorrow morning. He weighed up the implications, took out the beer, pulled the tab, sat down in front of the TV.

Some talk show. He turned down the sound, put his feet up on the coffee table.

Crazy day. Full of surprises, of which Desiree Coetzee was the biggest. He just couldn't get her out of his head. But you need to focus, *pappie*, 'cause why, surprise number two is JOC leader, *Major* Mbali had appointed him, *nogal*, and he was *kwaai* suspicious. Tonight, when he went to report, it was like the Giraffe reincarnated. She was still there waiting for him, at this time of night. She was supportive, empathetic. She talked the whole thing through with him and said: 'Good job, Captain. Thank you.'

No sarcasm.

Mbali. She said that to him. *Good job*. Go figure.

She told him about the pressure from above. She said the dude doing the database reveal had already exposed one ANC politician, one TV newsreader and a whitey former soapie star. Cloete said the media were having a field day. Or night. Twitter was all abuzz.

She asked if it could be the suspect, Rick Grobler, and he said Mooiwillem had gone to investigate, Grobler denied, denied, denied, but it was impossible to say for sure. Personally he, Cupido, didn't think Grobler would want to publish the database, there was just no upside for the guy.

She said she was pushing Forensics very hard for the analysis of Grobler's car.

He said they needed Lithpel Davids and Bones Boshigo, 'cause this thing is all about money and technology. Could she help with a search warrant for the bank, so they could investigate Richter's financial affairs?

And she said, first thing tomorrow morning. Go get some sleep, Captain, I'll get you everything you want tomorrow. Just like The Giraffe – the late Colonel Zola Nyathi – always did. Nyathi, who had been shot dead in front of Benna. Which made Cupido think of Griessel and his speech that got so out of hand, he was very sorry afterwards. He said things he shouldn't have, Benna got him going with that '*We* are the brakes and *we* are fucked'. The Hawks were Cupido's greatest pride and joy. He would die for that unit, and if Benna or anyone else dissed the Hawks, then he really lost it.

Maybe it was because he didn't have a wife and children, maybe that's why he couldn't understand what was going on with Benna.

But maybe that could change.

NoMoreAlibis @NoMoreAlibis
Twelve hours to go. Lots to reveal. Big men will fall. A few women too.
#ErnstRichter #WhoKilledErnst #NoAlibi

Three men, in three different cities, woke their wives between midnight and one a.m. to confess their Alibi sins. Two of the three began their speeches with 'I did a very stupid thing'. The third, the Dutch Reformed minister of a well-off congregation in Pretoria tried a different tack: 'Come pray with me.'

51

**Transcript of interview: Advocate Susan
Peires with Mr Francois du Toit**

*Wednesday, 24 December; 1604 Huguenot Chambers,
40 Queen Victoria Street, Cape Town*

FdT: Because I was one year younger than Paul, it was like I saw him
from a distance . . .

    When I got to the high school, no one would believe I was his
brother. He was just so much more . . . I was never jealous of his
rugby talent. I admired him for it. But I was jealous of his . . . He
had a way with people, even after things began to unravel.
They . . . You couldn't help liking Paul, and you wanted him to like
you. He was so extraordinarily handsome, like a figure from a
Michelangelo painting . . . And he was a real livewire, always on the
go, not still for a minute; he was always taking the lead, tackling
something. And he was so incredibly charming. If he noticed that
someone didn't like him, he would set out to . . . Later I realised he
was a master manipulator, but in those days, when I was in Grades
Eight and Nine, I just thought it was phenomenal. It was so cool to
be his brother. When I went to Paul Roos in Grade Eight all the
seniors came over to take a look at me, to see this second-rate Du
Toit boy. There was a sort of fascination and . . . a relief, I think, that
the blinding lightning that was Paul hadn't struck twice in the same
family. It was fair, it made sense; it chimed with their understanding
of the balance in the universe . . .

    The only thing about Paul that . . . I felt guilty about it, in a way
I knew it didn't help to feel like this, but when he told people he was
going to be a wine farmer one day, that he was going to inherit
Klein Zegen . . . and he said that a lot, to anyone who would listen.

It sat here in my chest, an unease, a feeling that it wasn't right, because he wasn't interested. He didn't love the farm and the vineyards and wine like I did. Why should he get everything? Why couldn't he just get the sporting prowess and the personality? Why must he get the farm as well?

But somehow I learned to cope with it, learned to make peace with it.

The business with the teacher . . . Actually I knew very little about that. You can imagine, the school and my parents kept it hushed up. The first time that I was really shocked, when I realised he had a big screw loose, was in the Christmas holidays that same year. He had finished Grade Ten, he had played his first match for the first team. Remember, he was only sixteen, it was in the newspaper, *Eikestad News* . . .

In any case, that holiday . . . My father's new wine cellar was almost finished. I took great pleasure in it, sitting there in the cool darkness, looking around me at everything, smelling the smells, thinking of the wine we would make. Anyway, I came out of the cellar one afternoon in the middle of December . . . Behind the cellar there were heaps of sand and stone and bricks that hadn't been cleared away, and I heard someone crying softly. When I went round to see who it was, I found Paul, with two of the labourers' children. Abie, he was about nine, and his sister Miranda, about fourteen. And . . . Paul was busy . . . We don't need to go into detail, Paul was busy forcing them to . . . with each other. They both stood there naked, those skinny bodies. It was Miranda who was crying and pleading. It made me . . . Little Abie's nose was bleeding. I think Paul must have hit him or something. It was a huge shock, and it was Paul who scared me the most. Before they saw me . . . there was this look on his face, this expression, it frightened me. I can't describe it, I just knew it was . . . sick. That was the first time that I knew there was something seriously wrong with him.

When he saw me, he wasn't even startled, I remembered that later . . . He just began lying, so glibly, said he found them there like that, they were *hotnots* who do dirty things, but Miranda said through her sobs that it wasn't so and, please, I must help them.

Then Paul swore and told them to *fokkof*, take their clothes and just *fokkof*, and then he began to threaten me. He said if I said a word, he would tell Ma and Pa that I did this and that – wild, horrible things. I didn't know what ... I had never seen him this way before ... He reminded me of a cornered dog, his lips drawn back, threatening, growling at me ... I said nothing, I was so totally dumbstruck and disappointed. Paul was my absolute hero ... and in an instant he was ... He laughed, and asked if I had seen the expression on Miranda's face. Then he changed back into his usual charming self.

For two days I walked around with this weighing on me. Then Pa sent me to call one of the labourers. I came across Miranda, at the stream, she just sat there staring and crying. When she saw me, she ran away. Then I knew she thought I was like that too. It was ... It probably says something about me, my psychology, but I didn't want her to think I was also like that. So I went to talk to my mother. I don't know why I didn't talk to Pa. But today I know it was better that I talked to Ma first.

52

Friday 19 December. Six days before Christmas.

Captain John Cloete was the first in the office, just after 06.30. He made himself a cup of instant coffee and sat down at his desk, with the Tupperware tub full of rusks that his wife packed in for him every morning. He put the day's papers down in a stack on his right and picked up the first one.

The *Son* headline screamed across a two-page spread: *ERNST ABDUCTED*. And below that: *Did vigilantes torture Richter for names?*

Cloete reached for his pack of cigarettes and lit one while he read. Every now and then he dipped the rusk in the coffee.

The story began, as he had expected, with the 'exclusive exposé that a source close to the investigation' said Richter's body was in too good a condition for the length of time since his disappearance. It was possible that he had been kept captive for a week or longer before being murdered ('The Hawks spokesman did not deny it.') – perhaps so the code words for the Alibi database could be obtained. And then the article began to speculate that @NoMoreAlibis was not just one person, but a group of religious extremists, who might be behind the abduction and murder. The newspaper quoted a Facebook comment, more than a year old, which was posted on Richter's timeline: 'We will fight you in the Name of the Lord. We will expose you and all the sinners who flock to your website. Your day will come soon.' The name of the author(s) was simply 'Revelations'.

Reports about the exposed alibi customers – TV news reader, the ANC Member of Parliament and the soapie actor – featured on page three.

The Hawks liaison officer sighed deeply, put the *Son* aside and pulled *Die Burger* closer. The main article was about the former Afrikaans soap star who in a statement, released by his agent, asked the country and his wife for forgiveness for his 'mistake', which had been short-lived and 'foolish'. The Member of Parliament's reaction to the exposure was also quoted: 'This is the latest attempt by the opposition party to blacken the name of the government.' A Democratic Alliance spokesperson said *this* statement was far-fetched and the ANC member's unfaithfulness was just another sign of the party's moral decline.

ALIBI MURDER: EMPLOYEE IS A SUSPECT was the *Cape Times*'s headline, above a photo of Vaughn Cupido and Benny Griessel arriving at the offices in Stellenbosch. Cloete guessed that the source of the information was a member of the police station at Stellenbosch, because the report mentioned that the car of an Alibi employee was there being investigated by Forensics.

He was still reading the rest of the story when his cellphone began to ring. He knew it would be journalists testing the media's rival theories.

He drank the last of his coffee before answering.

It was going to be a long day.

The 'source close to the investigation' who had been quoted by the *Son*, was Detective Adjutant Jamie Keyter.

Just after seven he sat, with four other detectives of the SAPS in Table View, looking through the newspapers with a degree of satisfaction that 'his' story had made the front page. He eyed the photograph on the front page of the Cape Times with envy, the two Hawks crossing the street with such purpose. This had been *his* case. His photo should have been on the front page.

He recalled how Cupido had scolded him at the mortuary over his handling of Ernst Richter's mother. That *windgat* Captain thought he was the *kat se gat*, the bee's knees.

Then he spotted the mark on the cheek of the other detective, Benny Griessel.

He knew Griessel, had worked with him a few years ago on the Artemis murders. He didn't remember him having a birthmark.

And then he recalled the conversation Cupido had had over his cellphone, there in Salt River. He couldn't catch all of it. '*Jissis*, Arrie, *baie dankie*. Just keep him there, just don't book him, please. He's had a very bad day. I'm on my way, give me ten.' And: 'Assault? Benny?'

Benny Griessel, the legendary detective and alcoholic – everyone in the Cape police knew about him, and his drinking habits.

Keyter studied the photo. It was a bruise. Assault? Had Griessel been involved in an assault?

If he had been drunk again, the chances were good.

And 'Arrie'. You didn't have to be a mastermind to work out that 'Arrie' was a policeman, because Cupido had said 'just don't book him'. 'I'm on my way, give me ten' meant Arrie was at a station reasonably close to the Salt River morgue. Could it be Colonel Arrie September, station commander of Cape Town Central?

Yes, a very good chance.

Griessel was unaware of the mark on his cheek that had begun to take on a purple shade this morning, though the slight swelling had subsided. He stopped in the basement parking garage of the Directorate of Priority Crimes Investigation building in Bellville, his thoughts on the uneasiness at home this morning. He could see Alexa was unhappy. He knew why. And there was nothing he could do to make it better. She smiled a small, tight, brave smile, and hugged him often, tentative little gestures that he couldn't quite read.

He still suspected it was a strategy, born out of discussions between her and Doc Barkhuizen.

He knew he had to phone Doc. He didn't want to. What was the point? He knew exactly what Doc would say to him, and he knew he wasn't going to listen.

His drinking agenda was drawn up for the day. He had to get Fisherman's Friend for his breath, and a bottle for his car. Then he would be okay.

He got out of the car. The dull pain from the gunshot wound to his arm had come back. How long before that left his body and his mind? It had been six months since the day he and Colonel Zola Nyathi were attacked on the N1 highway. He survived. Nyathi died.

From the far side of the parking garage he could hear Vaughn's voice calling him.

Cupido walked over to him. He greeted him and said: 'Benna, I want to apologise for last night. I thought, I have no right. I don't have children, I don't know what it's like. I was out of line. So I'm saying sorry, Benna.' He put out his hand.

Griessel took it, surprised, because Vaughn Cupido wasn't known as a man who said sorry. And he had a good look at his colleague, saw the seriousness, and something else – was it the shoulders, the eyes, the determination around the mouth? Then he noticed the clothes. This morning Cupido fulfilled Mbali's requirements, dressed up in black trousers and jacket, light blue shirt and black leather shoes. But that wasn't all. There was an attitude, an air of something different. A calmness, a . . . it was as though Cupido had . . . grown up in the course of one day. Those were the words that came to mind. As if he was embracing the responsibility of JOC, as if it sat easily on him now. And he felt a pride and a loss; he hoped the mischievous Vaughn, the free spirit, the rebel, was not gone for good. And he felt a measure of shame, because Cupido was moving forward and he had slid back.

'I'm going back to the shrink when this thing is over,' he said quietly, reluctantly. He had wanted to do it on the quiet, because he didn't want Cupido to see the effect that last night's lecture had had on him.

Cupido put his arm around Griessel's shoulders. 'That's great, Benna.'

Then both of them felt awkward, and they walked side by side to the entrance.

Cupido's phone rang. He answered, listened, then said: 'What sort of statement?'

'Just had a call from a big-firm lawyer,' said Cupido to the meeting. 'He says he has a client who wants to make a statement to us. The client is the regional manager of Premier Bank. He was using the Alibi services, and he says Ernst Richter tried to blackmail him into providing a big overdraft for the company.'

'Well, well, everything's coming out of the woodwork now,' said Frank Fillander.

'When?' asked Mbali Kaleni.

'He didn't say. He asked if we could come through for a meeting, so I said he'd better get himself and his client over here – we're in the middle of an investigation, in case he hadn't noticed. But the big question is, how many people did Richter blackmail?'

'And how do we find them,' said Vusi Ndabeni.

'That's why we need Bones,' said Cupido. 'Urgently.'

'Bones might be testifying this morning, I'm still waiting to hear from his commander. But he will be available this afternoon.'

'Thank you, Major. Uncle Frankie will be looking at the jealous husband angle, and we're waiting for the forensics on Grobler's car, and the cellular spider web from IMC. That's about all we have, until Bones starts looking at the financials. I'm also taking Lithpel to Alibi this morning, to look at the database and stuff.'

Kaleni nodded her approval. 'Anything else?'

'Forensics called,' said Ndabeni. 'They analysed Richter's clothing last night. They say they've found something.'

Everyone looked at him.

'The clothes – the jeans and the T-shirt – show residue of . . .' Vusi consulted an exam pad on which he had written some notes, 'Triazole. The same fungicide that's on the plastic. They also found dirt in the back pockets of his jeans, but nothing in the front pockets. They say the dirt is inconsistent with the Blouberg sand, and there are also traces of the same dirt on the back of his T-shirt. Their theory is that the body was dragged through this dirt, on his back, before it was wrapped in the plastic, so it might come from the scene of the crime.'

'Okay,' said Cupido hopefully.

'They're still analysing the pocket dirt, but the interesting thing is, they've found an unusually high number of flower petals and thin twigs of a zigzag shape in the pocket dirt. The petals and the twigs are from a jacaranda tree. They think that's a pretty good indication that the murder scene was under, or very near, a jacaranda.'

'That's not going to help much,' said Mooiwillem Liebenberg. 'Do you know how many jacarandas there are in Stellenbosch? Hundreds.'

Vusi wouldn't let himself be put off stride. 'I know. I got hold of the director of the Botanical Gardens in Stellenbosch about fifteen minutes ago. He says there are probably around a hundred to two hundred jacaranda trees in Stellenbosch, and they are all of the Blue Jacaranda species, or Jacaranda mimosifolia. These jacarandas flower in November and early December, which is consistent with Richter's time of death. Now, Forensics say the fungicide and the plastic indicate fruit or vegetable farming, so I asked the guy from the Botanical

Gardens about jacaranda trees on the farms around Stellenbosch. And he told me a pretty interesting thing. He said most of those wine estates are very eco-aware, because they are competing on the international market, where these things count. Jacaranda trees are originally from South America, and the government has listed the jacaranda as an invasive species. So the wine farmers have been pulling out a lot of jacarandas. There aren't many of them left on the farms . . .'

53

December of 2002 was the beginning of nine years of hell for Helena du Toit.

That was the month that her greatest fear was realised: her firstborn son was very sick. After the incident with the teacher she had kept hoping that Paul's social personality disorder wasn't so extreme. The psychologists told her there were psychopaths who functioned in the community, whose symptoms were less destructive, with the right supervision they could lead a relatively harmless life.

But the incident with the labourer's children struck that hope a fatal blow.

Initially she said nothing to her husband. First she arranged counselling for little Abie and Miranda and personally went to apologise to their parents. Then, in her characteristic intense way she consulted the experts, and studied the literature herself until she was absolutely certain, convinced that no therapy or medication would make a difference. Psychopaths were incurable.

For a long time she fretted over how to handle it all. After seven years of blood, sweat and tears, Guillaume was set to make Klein Zegen's first high-quality wine of its own. He was burdened by substantial and worrying debt. The establishment of new vineyards of Cabernet Sauvignon, Merlot, Petit Verdot, Malbec and Cabernet Franc was a long and expensive process; the new cellar had cost much more than they had expected.

The next three to five years were crucial for their future. The wine had to be made, bottled, marketed and distributed, locally and internationally. Guillaume had his hands very full; she would have to take responsibility for her son's condition.

Only in early January 2003, when she had a plan of action, did she sit down with her husband and break the news to him. They wept together, and then she told him what she was going to do. Afterwards they explained the situation together to their younger son, Francois. Eventually she asked Paul to join them.

You can't help it that you are like this, she said to her elder son. Your brain is simply wired differently; you can't feel remorse, or empathy. They say it's a birth defect and you will always be like this. We love you, even though you will never understand what that means. But you are a danger to everyone. You are capable of very evil things, and it is our duty as parents to do everything in our power to keep you from this. Psychopaths don't respond to punishment, but there is one form of treatment that yields positive results: reward. So from today you are forbidden everything. Everything. But every week that you do no one any harm, we will reward you: with the right to play rugby; with the right to go to school; with the right to be part of this farm and this family.

She explained the rules and conditions. Outwardly she was the picture of self-confidence, but inwardly her fear was great and her hope faint.

Because everything that she had heard and read underlined one single fact again and again: Paul was a time bomb. The only question was when he would explode.

54

At 08.08 @NoMoreAlibis tweeted: *4 hours to go. Alibi client: Userid: John Two. Paid by Johannes Frederickus Nel. Author? ABSA:4155791155. 19 alibis.#WhoKilledErnst*

Within three minutes the first journalist called the head office of Ad Altare Dei, the publisher of religious books in Cape Town's Foreshore area, to hear whether Johann Nel, author of *One Day at a Time* and fourteen other bestsellers, wished to make any comment.

The regional manager of Premier Bank and his lawyer were like peas in a pod – both fat, middle-aged, balding and bespectacled. The only difference was that the regional manager was scared and the lawyer indignant.

Griessel had no idea why lawyers were so often indignant when talking to detectives. He suspected it was part of a defence strategy, and partly influenced by their habit of jumping up in court and saying: 'Your Honour, I object . . .'

He and Mooiwillem talked to the pair in one of the Hawks' small meeting rooms. The room was too hot. Someone had forgotten to turn on the air conditioning at the Directorate for Priority Crime Investigations – the DPCI – after Eskom's customary load-shedding power cut yesterday. The two fat men perspired heavily, the regional manager mopping his forehead and the back of his neck with a handkerchief.

The lawyer's sweat dripped onto the table in front of him. 'It was in May. Early in May,' said the regional manager, his voice surprisingly shrill for such a large man. Stress, perhaps.

'Of this year?' asked Griessel.

'That's right. The eighth of May.'

'Your memory is good.'

'I wrote it down.'

'How did he contact you?'

'On my cellphone.' And then he wiped his forehead with his hand-kerchief and was silent.

'Could you see his number?'

'No, it was one of those No Caller IDs. But when he SMSed, I saw the number.'

'Go on, tell us the story,' Liebenberg prodded.

'Oh. Okay. He phoned me, it was three o'clock in the afternoon, just a few minutes after three. When he asked if I was alone, I said yes. Then he asked me, did my wife know I had a *skelmpie*? Then I asked who's talking? He said it didn't matter, did my wife know I had a bit on the side? I put the phone down. Then he sent me an SMS, and he said if I didn't want my wife to know where I was on Friday 11 April, I better pick up when he phoned again. And he phoned again. He said it wouldn't help to put the phone down, I would just make things diffi-cult for myself. I said what do you want? He said an overdraft of a million. And I said no. Then he said he would call my wife. I said he should go ahead. Then he put the phone down.'

The regional manager dabbed the handkerchief against his fore-head, and then against his upper lip.

'That's all?' asked Liebenberg.

'Yes, that was the last time that . . . but I wanted to know who it was. Then I thought, that night, who could have known. And I thought there could be no one, because . . . The circumstances . . .'

The lawyer lifted his hand to caution his client. The regional manager nodded. 'I . . . we were very . . . discreet. Nobody could have known the date or time, except the people at Alibi. That was the only possibility. The next day I phoned them, because I wanted to tell someone there that one of their people was blackmailing clients. I phoned and asked to speak to the boss. They wouldn't put me through. Then I googled the company, I wanted to know who the managing director was. I found out it was this Ernst Richter. So I googled him and there was a video on YouTube from a news website, about this Ernst Richter, when he launched Alibi. I watched it and then I recognised the voice. That's all.'

'You did nothing further?'

'No. Yes . . . I tried to delete my profile at Alibi, but it's nearly impos-sible. I could only cancel the service.'

'You never contacted him?'

'No.'

'You did nothing more?'

'No.'

'Why are you here?' asked Griessel.

The lawyer said: 'We are here in the spirit of full disclosure.'

'What for?' asked Griessel.

'Because you . . .' the regional manager began, but the lawyer lifted his warning hand again.

The regional manager wiped the handkerchief nervously across the back of his neck and shook his head. 'I don't think it will do harm to tell them that I know they can see nowadays everyone who Ernst Richter phoned on his cellphone.' He looked at Griessel. 'I don't want you turning up at my house one night with a lot of questions, Captain. I'm sure you will understand. That's why I'm here.'

'You said he could phone your wife?' Griessel didn't believe this part of the story.

'Yes.'

'But you don't want us to come to your house?'

'Captain,' and the regional manager sighed long and deep. 'I . . . if I allowed him to blackmail me, if I began to sacrifice my professional integrity . . . What do I have left, as a banker? Where does it end? My marriage . . .'

The lawyer put a hand on the regional manager's arm.

The regional manager pulled his arm away. He said: 'For twelve or thirteen years now, my marriage hasn't been what it should be. If I have to, I can do without it. My children are out of the house, they will be able to cope. I don't want to hurt anyone, but if there is no other way . . . My job, I can't be without my job. That is who I am.'

At 08.47 Vaughn Cupido received an SMS from Desiree Coetzee:

The man's name is Werner Habenicht. He's the chairman of ShipSure. www.shipsure.com *Cell 093 448 9091 thank you for last night, it was quite lekker.*

Cupido read the last nine words over and over. Repeated them, analysed them.

She needn't have said them. But she wanted to. Because she thought, let me encourage this guy, I like him. *Was quite lekker.* As if she was a little surprised over how *lekker* it was. Or the '*quite*' could also say, it was very *lekker*, but I don't want to say it quite so strongly . . .

Of course it was *lekker*, Desiree Coetzee. I am Vaughn Cupido, pride of the Hawks.

He got up to go and fetch Lithpel and give Griessel the details about Habenicht.

It was already after nine when Frank Fillander phoned Sarah Woodruff.

She answered with: 'Louise, hello?' The question in the melodic voice was playful, *who might this be?*

After a moment of uncertainty about the name that didn't fit, the penny dropped – Sarah Woodruff was an alias.

'Can I speak to Sarah, please?' he said deliberately, because if she wasn't alone, it would give her the chance to say it was the wrong number. 'Sarah Woodruff.'

The long silence on the line had a meaning he could not yet fathom. 'Who is this?' she said, barely more than a whisper.

'Louise, my name is Captain Frank Fillander of the police Directorate for Priority Crimes Investigation. I would like to talk to you about Ernst Richter.'

She didn't reply. He went on: 'I think I understand the circumstances. Can I meet you somewhere? In the next few hours?'

It took her a while to process it all. 'Can I . . . is your office private?'

Jimmy, the tall, thin member of the Thick and Thin team, phoned Ndabeni just before nine.

'We have solved one of the great mysteries of the case, Vusi.'

Ndabeni couldn't tell if Jimmy was playing with him again. 'That's nice,' he said.

'I'm not kidding you this time. We're going to save you guys a lot of work.'

'That's nice, Jimmy.'

'That's nice, Jimmy? That's the best you can do?'

'I can do better, once I know what mystery has been solved.'

'Okay, Vusi, that's fair enough. So, here it is. You can forget about vegetable farmers and apple farmers. We think you should start concentrating on grapes, because we have now completed our analysis of the pocket dirt, and we've found a significant percentage of decomposed vine leaf matter. We can't tell you what kind of vines, we will have to get DNA analysis done, and that's going to take weeks. But we are talking Stellenbosch, and that's pure wine country.'

'That's great, Jimmy.'

'At last we get a "great".'

At 09.08 @NoMoreAlibis tweeted: *Every date of every alibi of every client coming in three hours. URL to follow soon. #ErnstRichter #WhoKilledErnst #NoAlibi*

His followers now numbered 31,714.

Transcript of interview: Advocate Susan
Peires with Mr Francois du Toit

Wednesday, 24 December; 1604 Huguenot Chambers,
40 Queen Victoria Street, Cape Town

Sound file 9

FdT: One per cent of any population are psychopaths. That means
there are over half a million of them in South Africa. Half a million.
That's a lot. And one of them was my brother. They are fascinat-
ing, and impossible to understand, for normal people. You can't
put yourself in the shoes of someone who has no conscience.
Absolutely none. Zero. There was this interesting research a few
years ago on a psychopath's language use and patterns. All of us,
when we speak, use filler words. Hesitations like 'um' and 'ah',
when we have to think before we say something. They found that
psychopaths use more fillers than ordinary people. Because they
have to think hard what will sound normal, so they can hide their
sickness. That's the theory.

Psychopaths talk twice as much about basic needs as we do.
Things like eating and drinking, and money . . .

I can tell you thousands of facts about psychopaths. My mother
became an expert on them. She made it her life's task to protect the
world from Paul. She went to tell the principal her son was a
psychopath, and he had the choice of whether to admit Paul to the
school, or not.

I think that was an interesting moral dilemma. This fantastic
sporting talent . . . there was this former Springbok coach who said
then that Paul du Toit was the greatest genius player he had ever
seen in his life. His vision, his skills, hands, feet . . . How do you

keep a boy like that out of your school? And what cruel fate would dish up that combination?

The principal said Paul could stay, as long as he behaved. They made an agreement on feedback about Paul's behaviour at school. She went to see the rugby coach, explained the system to him. My mother was absolutely consistent and fair. If Paul hadn't exhibited any socially unacceptable behaviour on a Monday or Tuesday, he was rewarded with rugby practice, the same for Wednesday and Thursday. A whole week of good behaviour earned him a rugby match. And it worked.

Until the first term of matric. Then he couldn't help himself. He raped a girl.

It was on the spur of the moment. My mother was a few minutes late fetching him from rugby: the traffic in Stellenbosch . . . He saw the girl walking along the Eerste River, past Paul Roos rugby fields . . . Two guys heard her scream, they ran to help, but they were too late. My mother was standing beside her car waiting for him when she saw the police van stop. She knew then.

The trouble was, it was three weeks after his eighteenth birthday. He would be tried as an adult.

56

She was a beautiful woman, Sarah Woodruff. In a quiet, understated way. It was a beauty that whispered, that grew, with the ripening awareness of every dimension – appearance, voice, hand movements, shy smile, focus of the dark eyes.

Frank Fillander, with his knowledge of people, his ability to judge character, thought about her afterwards. His theory was that she was a late bloomer, maybe a brooding, gangly teenager, introverted, but with a desire for sensual things that were beyond her. Until, at seventeen or eighteen, her body and face gradually bloomed to beauty. She would have been surprised by the sudden windfall of young men's attentions. She would have enjoyed it as something possibly fleeting – in contrast to women who had been as pretty as a picture, ever since they were little, and viewed it as their right.

He speculated that she got serious with her future husband early on, that the first years of their marriage were intense, that her husband was captivated by her sensuality and appetite. But time and children and his career and the tedium of being a stay-at-home-mother made everything worn-out, pale, diluted. Only the dynamo inside her was still driving, energetic. So that at the age of forty-two she craved one last roll of the carnal dice. Before her looks – so she told herself – began to fade, before her transient allure evaporated.

She read about the phone app in a women's magazine. She downloaded Tinder, curious, and with just enough nervousness to heighten the excitement. Sarah Woodruff's real name was Louise Rousseau. She told Fillander she'd chosen the Woodruff alias from a book: *The French Lieutenant's Woman* by John Fowles, a literary reference of which the men on Tinder were completely ignorant, since not a single respondent ever referred to it.

She chose her profile photo carefully and started to use Tinder. She got a lot of attention, but only from younger men. Her hopes for, and fantasies about the older, wiser, cerebrally stimulating and sexually more experienced older men evaporated quickly. They – and her peers – were apparently active elsewhere online.

She responded to only one: Ernst Richter. The lowest common denominator on Tinder was really astonishingly low, and at least he was polite. He was cheerful, lively, interesting in his way, with a childish sense of humour. And he was patient, not intrusive.

She began a conversation with Richter that went on for two weeks. It made her solitary mornings fun. Entertaining. Sexy. The sound of an incoming message was a little thrill. Slowly she began to wonder: what would it be like with a young man? All that sexual energy, all that lust; for though he was never vulgar, he was honest about his desires.

She agreed to a meeting at his house, as it was very private. Her greatest fear was to be seen by a friend or acquaintance, to be confronted with awkward questions.

She took trouble with her appearance, her perfume, her clothes. When she picked up the car keys, her courage deserted her. She stopped in front of the mirror, feeling suddenly both relieved and disappointed, looked at herself, and decided to go after all.

He met her at the front door with a bunch of flowers and box of expensive chocolates. The thoughtfulness, the gesture stole her heart.

But even when he kissed her in his sitting room, she didn't know whether she was going to have sex with him. She let herself be led, minute by minute, by impulse, by what felt good. Eventually she rewarded Richter's patience with total abandon. And to her surprise he was skilful, gentle, and was blessed with the rare talent of endurance. So she met him at his house twice more in the following weeks.

Initially she suppressed her feelings of guilt. But it was as though her husband sensed her awakened sexuality and began to pay her attention again. She sent Ernst Richter one last message and removed the app from her phone. And that was it.

'Is there a chance that your husband knew?'

'No.'

'How can you be so sure?'

'I know him too well. He would have said something, he would have confronted me, he would have tried to access my . . . I have a code on my phone, there is no way he could have . . . Even if he suspected: I was incredibly careful, because the last thing I wanted to do was to hurt him.'

Fillander just looked at her. He wasn't entirely convinced: he knew people think they're so smart, so careful, but they make mistakes. Always.

Where was her husband on the night of Wednesday 26 November?

He observed her closely, because the body and eyes reveal the unease and lies. He saw nothing. She just said with quiet certainty it wasn't him. And she was practically certain that he had been at home, as usual. He almost never worked late, he didn't travel. He sat watching TV, every night.

She would have to make absolutely sure. Could she?

Yes, she could. Give her a day or two.

He asked her for her husband's cellphone number. She gave it to him.

He asked her about Richter's personality.

She said he was a boy. Nothing more, nothing less. A boy, a lovely boy in a man's body, with too much money and too many toys, who wanted to try it with an older woman, as a novelty. He was the sort who was nerdy at school, and now wanted to exploit the attraction that success brought before it disappeared.

She didn't know if it was her imagination, it could be . . . But there was a sense of urgency about him, an intensity. As if he knew the end was near.

Griessel slipped away from the DPCI building just after the bottle stores opened. Midmar, Home of Discount Liquor, was just around the corner, in Voortrekker Road.

They sold Jack Daniel's in miniature fifty millilitre bottles, in packs of ten; the kind you get on planes. He asked for a tin of Fisherman's Friend, paid for it all, and broke open the pack of mini-Jacks right there at the cash register. The cashier's eyes were on Griessel, knowing, as he divvied up the bottles between his jacket pockets. He ignored her. His big challenge would be to keep the bottles from clinking when he walked down the passage to his office.

Griessel adjusted the bottles in his pockets on the way back. He went to the toilets and swiftly downed one of them. Hesitated a moment, then drank another. Popped four of the peppermints into his mouth and stood sucking them, swishing the saliva around. Then he went to the rubbish bin and hid the two empty bottles under the used paper handtowels. He rearranged the remaining eight bottles so that there was less risk of noise.

He met Mooiwillem in the passage. 'I've been looking for you, Benny. We have to go and see the Habenicht guy.'

'I just need to go to the office first.'

So he could stash four bottles, and take four along with him.

Then he'd be ready for this day.

Nothing of note really happened until Bones Boshigo arrived at Alibi. co.za in the afternoon.

Cupido and Lithpel Davids drove through to the offices in Stellenbosch. Cupido said he had to pay a quick visit to the Premier Bank branch, he wanted to deliver the search warrant, so that they could see what was going on there.

'You know he banked at FNB too, Cappie?'

'How do you know that?'

'Because he had an FNB app in his phone, that's how.'

'And Premier's'

'That too.'

'Then we will have to go to FNB as well.'

Griessel and Liebenberg met Werner Habenicht, chairman of the board of ShipSure, in his luxury office in Loop Street, on the top floor of Triangle House. It had a magnificent view over Table Bay.

Habenicht was one of those trim middle-aged men – grey hair cut short and neat, tailored suit, subtle, stylish cufflinks on the pale blue shirt, and his figure still fit and athletic. The lawyer who was also seated at the conference table was younger, with thick black brows and an indignant attitude.

They could get nothing.

Yes, he was an Alibi client, said Habenicht. He sat completely still when he spoke; his words and sentences were just as careful and deliberate as the man himself. But his tone of voice was authoritarian, like someone who was accustomed to being in charge. And he talked down to them, with the sort of disdain they increasingly encountered, especially from the wealthy.

The reasons for his membership had nothing to do with them. Yes, someone tried to blackmail him. No, not over the phone, but via anonymous, untraceable email. The blackmailer wanted a hundred thousand rand. No, he no longer had the email. The case had been dealt with already.

How?

He had been to talk to them, and never heard from the blackmailer again.

Had he waited in the car park for Desiree Coetzee one evening?

He had been waiting for any of the three top people. She was merely the one who came out first.

How had he known who she was and what she looked like?

He did his research. All the information was available on CIPC. And all three were on Facebook. Richter, Coetzee and the financial director, Vernon Visser.

Did you have any contact with Richter?

No, none.

And because Griessel thought Habenicht was a *doos*, he asked: 'Where were you on the evening of Wednesday 26 November?'

Habenicht was not a man who sighed. He looked at Griessel with icy dislike, got up, walked to his desk, and pressed a button on his telephone. A woman's voice answered: 'Mr Habenicht?'

'Where was I on the twenty-sixth of November?'

'Just a moment, sir . . .' He waited impatiently until she said: 'London, sir. You were in London, for your meeting with Lloyds.'

Vusumuzi Ndabeni was there when Forensics fine-combed the blood red Volkswagen Golf GTI Cabriolet belonging to the programmer and seeker of zero-day vulnerabilities, 'Tricky' Rick Grobler.

Vusi could see the car was sparkling clean. And he thought there wasn't enough room in this vehicle to hide a corpse, especially not one wrapped in black plastic.

They took fingerprints inside and out, they vacuumed the seats and the carpets, they took samples of the carpet fibres, and they linked a computer to the car's GPS system so that they could see precisely where Grobler had driven.

This is not a murderer's car, thought Vusi. It was just too sexy. One day he would also have a car like this.

At precisely 12.08 @NoMoreAlibis said: *Full database of all former and current Alibi clients now available at pageeasy.com/nomorealibis/*

57

Advocate Susan Peires mentally totted up the sums while Du Toit was talking.

If Paul du Toit had been sentenced for rape as a youth, first offender, he would theoretically already have been released. And able to murder Ernst Richter.

She knew psychopaths. As a criminal defence lawyer she had dealt with her fair share. And the whole concept of Alibi – the ability to deceive others about your activities while you were up to no good – was one that would appeal to a violent criminal with a serious personality disorder.

Francois du Toit was here to ask her to represent his brother. For the sake of his parents who had suffered so much. This was the groundwork he was trying to lay.

She wouldn't accept the case. Without exception, her experience of psychopaths as clients had been upsetting and unpleasant. They lied, manipulated and in the end terrified you. She had also listened to enough forensic psychologists to know they must be removed from society for as long as possible, because they would simply wreak havoc again, every time, as soon as they were released.

Out of courtesy she would hear him out. But she had made up her mind.

58

Vaughn Cupido's day wasn't going quite as he had hoped.

He'd been in a hurry to get to Stellenbosch to see Desiree Coetzee again, but she wasn't at the office. According to her personal assistant she had gone to the city for negotiations with the two venture capital companies about the future of Alibi, along with the other member of the management team they needed to throw some light on the subject – the head of finance, Vernon Visser.

He could sense the tension among the staff over the outcome of the talks, and a vague antagonism towards the members of the Hawks, as if they were responsible for the possible dissolution of the business. It was only the ever-animated Lithpel Davids who quickly bonded with his digital brethren, the programmers, and began to immerse himself in the systems.

Cupido sat in Desiree Coetzee's office and struggled with the statements that he had received from the two banks. Richter had two accounts at Premier – a credit card and a cheque account. At FNB there was another personal cheque account. And besides ordinary expenses like house rental (an astronomical R38,000 per month), municipal services, petrol, groceries and restaurant meals, nothing really made sense. Amounts were transferred back and forth between accounts and there were quite a few totally inexplicable expenses and deposits.

He needed Bones Boshigo.

At lunchtime he crossed the street to the Pane e Vino restaurant alone. Intent on a computer screen Lithpel had said, 'I'm in the zone Cappie, *sommer* bring me back a takeaway.'

There were fewer reporters outside today, but he was greeted as usual with a chorus of questions. He just shrugged, holding up his empty hands: they knew they had to talk to Cloete.

He sat looking at the Alibi offices through the restaurant window.

He thought about Desiree and the fact that today she was fighting for her professional life.

That was the problem with crime. A detective came in and did his detecting and made his arrests and he stood in the witness stand and then he moved on. But the crime didn't stop there, it touched people's lives; it's like that little *klippie* in the water, the pebble dropped in the pool, the ripples don't stop when the accused is sentenced.

Desiree needn't worry, he would take care of her.

Cupido ordered pasta. It was the most delicious he had ever eaten, and he wished she were there to share it with him.

Before he had finished eating, his cellphone rang. An unfamiliar number, but he answered.

'Vaughn, this is Arrie September . . .' He sounded stressed.

Cupido's gut contracted instantly. There could be only one reason why the commander of Cape Town Central was phoning him directly.

'*Jis*, Arrie?'

'We have a bit of a problem. An *ou* from the *Son* called my press liaison. Wanted to know if Benny Griessel of the Hawks was involved in an assault on Wednesday night. My liaison knows nothing about it, Vaughn, 'cause there's nothing booked. But the *outjie* from the *Son* said he had it on good authority, and my liaison should check with me and call him back.'

'*Jissis*, Arrie,' said Cupido, putting his fork down, his pasta forgotten.

'I know, my bru'. Did you square things up at the Fireman's?'

'I did. They swore to the heavens, *hoog en lag*, that they would drop the thing.'

'Okay. All I can do is to say we have no record of such an incident, because that's true. But you and Griessel have to do something, Vaughn. Make this thing go away.'

'Arrie, thanks. I owe you big time.'

'Make it go away, Vaughn. You know how things are, nowadays. It's my *gat* on the line here.'

When Benny Griessel began working at the Hawks, the Information Management Centre – later known as IMC – had been an intimidating place for him. He was constantly afraid that someone would unmask him as the technophobe he was. But with the help of IMC Captain Philip van Wyk and Cupido the technophile, always flamboy-antly willing to share his knowledge, Griessel had learned a great deal over the past two years.

When Van Wyk and his team projected the phone spider web on the wall, he knew how it worked: the icon in the middle of the image represented Ernst Richter's cellphone. The lines that stretched out from it like a web represented, on the left, the calls he made and, on the right, the calls he received – within a certain time period. IMC could manipulate the program so that the spider web displayed any time period, from a specific hour to a year or more.

The thicker the lines, the more calls were made to a specific number or received from it.

'Here we are looking at calls over the past year,' said Philip van Wyk. 'There are seven people whom Richter phoned frequently. His moth-er's number is one. The rest are all colleagues. One of them is the guy you suspect . . . Ricardo Grobler.'

'How many calls to Rick Grobler in the week before Richter's death?' Mooiwillem Liebenberg asked.

Van Wyk waited for the technician to make the necessary adjust-ments to the program. The image changed on the screen. 'Not one,' he said. 'Give us the last month before the murder . . .'

The slide changed again. 'He only talked to Ricardo Grobler twice in that month, but if you look at this time period, things look slightly different. His mother is still number one, but there are two new numbers on the hit parade, in the second and third place. Both are landlines, to companies in the city: Marlin Investments and Cape Capital Partners . . .'

'Those are the guys who financed Alibi,' Griessel said.

'Show them the graph of total calls to those numbers over the past year,' Van Wyk requested. And then: 'It's a hockey stick pattern, as you can see. From January to September the total calls increase steadily, but in October and especially November there is a strong upward curve. I don't know if that means something to you.'

'We think their money began to run out,' said Griessel. 'He must have been asking for more financing.'

'That is the only anomaly we can pick up,' said Van Wyk.

'Did you RICA them all?' asked Griessel. Thanks to the RICA legislation, every cellphone number was linked to a personal identity with complete address details. IMC identified all the people who a victim had contact with, and then did a database comparison to determine whether any of them had a criminal record, used a stolen phone or evaded the RICA process.

'We did. There's nothing.'

Frank Fillander spoke up for the first time. 'I have the number of the husband of one of Richter's *skelmpies*. Can you run it through the system quickly?'

At 13.52, when Cupido was back at Alibi, Major Mbali Kaleni phoned. When he saw the number his unease grew. Had the media phoned Cloete too about Benny's assault?

'I have a toxicology report for you, Captain,' she said.

At first relief, then astonishment that she could have the toxicology report completed in only two days. The Department of Health usually took six months to process a victim's blood tests. That there was not even a trace of triumph in her voice was even more impressive.

'Major, that's incredible. Thank you,' he said in genuine admiration.

'They found low levels of active THC, but that's all.'

Cupido knew that meant that Richter had probably smoked *dagga* in the last seven days before his death, which they more or less already knew.

'Thank you, Major.'

'Any news?'

'We're waiting on Bones.'

Just after two the thirst began to gnaw at Griessel. With two little bottles in his pocket he walked to the bathroom, drank them down to the last drop, rinsed his mouth with water, then masked his breath.

He lingered so that the six peppermints could do their work, and his thoughts drifted to the conversation this morning with the regional bank manager, Habenicht, and the IMC. He'd been functional. No, more than that. He was a good detective, he hadn't missed anything.

This drinking routine could work. The monster was under control and he could keep his focus. He must just carry on like this. Then nobody could say anything.

Before he walked out, he blew into his palm and sniffed it. As long as he didn't get too close to anyone . . .

Outside in the passage, wondering what to do next, it occurred to him that he couldn't remember seeing the name of the regional bank manager on IMC's spider web. He remembered clearly that the man had said Richter had called him on his cellphone.

Had he just missed it?

Probably a good idea to go and make sure.

Major Benedict 'Bones' Boshigo was a member of the Statutory Crimes group of the Hawks Commercial Crimes unit in the Cape, and something of a legend. He was a Pedi from Limpopo; a clever man, who thanks to a bursary had earned his Bachelor's degree at the Metropolitan College of Boston University in the USA. His nickname was thanks to his reed-thin figure, the lean body of a long distance athlete – he had completed the Comrades marathon seventeen times and the Boston and New York marathons once each.

And, after Vaughn Cupido, he was also the detective with the best self-image in the DPCI. When he walked into Desiree Coetzee's office just after three, his first words to Vaughn were, 'Hey, relax. The cavalry is here . . .'

'The cavalry took its own sweet time. Married life slowing you down, Bones?' Boshigo hadn't been married a year yet and told every-one who would listen about the huge amount of *lobola* he'd had to pay 'for my special lady'.

'Married life is what speeds me up, brother . . .'

They were interrupted by Cupido's ringing cellphone. He saw that it was Major Mbali again.

If it was about Benny this time, then he was ready for her.

59

*Wednesday, 24 December; 1604 Huguenot Chambers,
40 Queen Victoria Street, Cape Town*

FdT: What I remember best about that time is my feeling of guilt.

It was a huge shock for the whole community. Few people knew about Paul's . . . problem. Most simply knew him as the phenomenal rugby player, so there was this . . . trauma, at the school, in the town, in the wine community.

My father, everyone loved Pa. I think it was because everyone knew what a hard time he'd had with Oupa Jean, and because he was so different, so gentle. He was good with people, he was very humble as a wine maker, this underdog who had worked so hard to . . . So, when Paul was arrested, there was huge sympathy for him and Ma. And there was this atmosphere of . . . as if someone had died, which wasn't very far from the truth.

But for me . . . I couldn't help it, I was sad, and shocked, but I also felt this intense joy. I thought now I can farm. If Paul is in jail, I can farm. And then I would feel so guilty for thinking like that, that I could be so glad about it. And I wondered if I was a psychopath too, and then I would try to rationalise it . . . I was sixteen, it's probably not abnormal for a sixteen-year-old to do that. I thought Paul wasn't interested in the farm, he didn't love it the way I did, so it was really the just right thing . . .

But then the guilt ate me up when I looked at my mother and father's grief.

No one wanted it to go to court. The girl's parents wanted justice done, but if they could avoid having her testify . . . My father hired the best legal people. Everyone tried to make a deal with the State prosecutor. The problem was, Paul . . . Psychopaths enjoy the lime-light; it's such a weird thing. Paul wanted people to notice him; he wanted to be the centre of attention, whether it was on the rugby field or in court.

So it went to trial. There was a lot of publicity. I don't know if you remember it, it was ten years ago . . . It cost my father a fortune, that case. A fortune that he didn't have. It broke him. In every way, I think . . .

It changed my life too. I was only one term away from Grade Eleven in Paul Roos. It was hard. I wasn't the brother of the aspir-ant Springbok Paul du Toit any more, I was the brother of the sick rapist.

In April of that year I went to boarding school, Boland Agricultural High School, in Paarl.

60

The computer specialist at IMC searched the database for the regional bank manager's number, without success.

'We imported the records for the past year,' he told Griessel. 'When was the call made?'

'In May, of this year,' said Griessel. 'The eighth.'

'You're sure of that?'

'Yes.'

'Then he didn't phone from this cellphone number.'

'Thanks,' said Griessel. He wanted to tell Vaughn, and as it so often and inexplicably happened, his phone rang at that instant and it was Cupido. 'I think Ernst Richter had another cellphone,' Griessel said when he answered.

Cupido was silent for a long time before he spoke. 'That's great, Benna, but we've got another little problem. Major Mbali has just phoned me. Trouble is, the *Son* has just phoned Cloete and asked if you were involved in an assault Wednesday night. So Cloete said, of course not, you were on the Richter case. So the guy from the *Son* asks, then where does the bruise on your cheek come from? 'Cause why he heard a little birdy singing . . .'

Griessel said nothing; he just touched the tender spot of the bruise as he walked out the door of IMC and headed for his office.

'Benna, are you there?'

'Yes.'

'So Cloete said we don't comment on that sort of personal stuff, and he went to see Mbali, and Mbali called me. To make sure we were together that night.'

Benny could see Mbali Kaleni, down the passage, at the door of his office. '*Fok*,' he said involuntarily and came to a stop.

'My sentiments too, Benna. You keep to the story. The Fireman's swore they wouldn't say anything, but now I want to know, the *ou* that you panel beat . . .'

'I didn't panel beat him.'

'Okay. But what are the chances that he's going to come out of the woodwork?'

'I don't know. And Mbali is waiting outside my office for me.'

'Stick to the story, Benna.'

'I will.'

'Okay. So, how do we know that Richter had another phone?'

His relationship with Major Mbali Kaleni was an odd one. Griessel had been her mentor back when he was still with the provincial detective branch and she was an inspector at Bellville SAPS. Just after he had stopped drinking. She only knew him sober and on the wagon, although she must have been told about his old drinking problem.

Then she had been shot during the kidnapping of a young American tourist, three years ago now, and he had been first on the scene. Afterwards she swore Griessel had saved her life.

From then on, in her eyes he could do no wrong. It made him uncomfortable, because he had a history of letting people down. But still, he liked the respect, and the relationship they had, because he admired her. She was everything that a SAPS member should be. Intelligent, principled, fair. Despite her somewhat quirky personality, and her obsession with food, she had risen in the almost exclusively male world of the Unit for Serious and Violent Crimes – no easy feat. And he liked her. Behind the sometimes clumsy and outspoken person he'd caught glimpses of a brittleness, an insecurity at times.

He didn't want her to find out what a weakling he really was.

'Hi, Benny,' she said and he could see it was hard for her.

'Major,' he greeted her in return.

'Can we talk in your office?'

'Of course.'

He allowed her to enter first, careful to keep his distance, because the peppermints were only effective up to a point. He wanted to close the door, but realised that would seem unnatural.

'Benny, I've just heard that there are malicious rumours about how you got that bruise. The media is out to get us again, but I want you to know I will not tolerate it. Our job is difficult enough.'

At her words, the truth pressed hard against his chest. He wanted to tell her everything, because if this cat got out the bag any other way, the damage to her and their relationship would be much greater. The only thing that stopped him was that telling her now would implicate Cupido too.

'What kind of rumours?' he asked and could hear the guilt in his tone.

'Stupid rumours; you don't have to worry about it. I just wanted to tell you.'

'Thank you, Major.' He saw her weariness, the weight she had lost. Was it just the diet, or was her job taking its toll?

'You're welcome . . .' She moved towards the door and he stood back, so that, please God, she wouldn't smell him.

'I think Richter had another cellphone,' he said to fill the silence, to change the subject.

'Oh?'

'I . . .' Now he was sorry he'd said it, because now he would have to explain, then she would praise him, which wouldn't feel right at all. 'Willem and I, we had his number checked against the bank's regional manager, the guy he wanted to blackmail. Richter didn't call from his regular cell number. So there might be another one . . .'

'That's great, Benny. It just might be . . . If anybody can crack this case, it's you.'

Cupido sat with Bones Boshigo, who was busy on his laptop trying to sort Richter's account statements, sent as electronic CSV files by the banks, into Excel. 'This is not the Stone Age, *nè*, Cupido,' he'd said. 'Doing it by hand will take a week.'

'And doing it this way?'

'A day or two.'

He didn't have 'a day or two', but what could you do? Now he sat staring through the glass of Desiree Coetzee's office at the Alibi staff down on the ground floor.

And there was Desiree, coming through the front door, wearing a white summer dress. She looked beautiful; Cupido's pulse quickened. She walked up to some of the employees, chatting here, lingering there. She had a way of moving her delicate hands – small, precise movements that captivated him.

There was reserve about her though, and as she approached the stairs, closer to him, he could see her facial expression: the smile was taut and forced.

She wasn't bringing good news back to her staff.

At the foot of the stairs he saw her suddenly stop and turn her head to the left. Someone had called her. He followed the direction of her gaze. Tricky Rick Grobler was approaching.

Cupido had not known the programmer was at the office today.

Grobler looked stressed, his expression intense. Just before he reached Coetzee he glanced furtively up to where Cupido was sitting, then quickly looked away again. He said something to Desiree. She made a soothing gesture with her hand.

Grobler spoke animatedly.

Desiree nodded. She put a hand on Grobler's shoulder, comforting, calming. He looked at her gratefully, and Cupido could see there was a certain dynamic. He felt jealousy surge up in him and he knew it was the wrong time for that. He couldn't allow it to show, professionally or personally.

Desiree Coetzee spoke and Grobler nodded, nodded again, She touched Grobler again on the shoulder, as if encouraging him. Then she turned, walked up the stairs and saw Cupido. She looked him right in the eyes, but he could read nothing in her expression.

He opened the door for her.

'They are going to close us down,' were her first words. Her shoulders slumped and she fought back the tears.

He wanted to reach out and comfort her, despite what he had just seen. She must have sensed the wish, because she squared her shoulders again and moved quickly around him to her desk. 'I'm getting everyone in – the night shift, everyone. I have to let them know . . .'

Bones looked up, took her in. Cupido knew he had an eye for a pretty woman. But he mustn't start with his tricks now, Desiree was very fragile.

He introduced Boshigo formally, adding, 'Bones is here to look at the books.'

She greeted him and sat down heavily, as if a great weight pressed her down into the chair. 'Vernon, the financial manager, will be here in a few minutes . . .'

'When do you have to close?' asked Cupido.

'It will take a month or two. There are a lot of legal implications. But they want us offline before Christmas.'

'Sorry,' he said.

She didn't respond, just brushed her hair out of her face.

'I see Rick Grobler is here,' said Cupido.

'Yes. He wants to get whoever leaked the database . . . He wants to find out who did it, who NoMoreAlibis is.'

'And how exactly is he going to do that?'

'Rick is clever with that kind of stuff. He said he's already started; he's going to follow the guy's digital footprints.'

'To do what with?'

'To clear his name with you,' she said, as if it was just all too much. 'He said he's done his research. It's a criminal act. Digital theft. And why aren't you lot more worried about it?'

61

He told her that his Ouma died in his final year at school. He said she was barely seventy-five, but you can only bear so much trouble in one lifetime. He often wondered how much she regretted that night when she danced with Oupa Jean for the first time. Her life could have been so different.

But let him move on, because the next seven years were relatively unremarkable, with Paul in jail.

He, Francois du Toit, completed his school education and began to study Viticulture.

His father, his poor father, saw his dream of making fine wines slowly swallowed up in the debts owed to the legal team that defended Paul.

He sold more and more of his new vineyards' harvest to Oom Dietrich Venske, the old colleague from KWV, who bought the neighbouring Blue Valley Estate in 1994.

Oom Dietrich said Pa was never the same again. It was as if he'd been emptied out. He was doing only the basics, while Venske's wines fared better and better, finding success first locally and then gradually internationally. It was proof to Francois that this valley, this soil, could produce wonderful wines.

He tried to talk to his father, in his final year at school and during his university studies, partly because he was deeply concerned about Guillaume – who sank deeply, ever more profoundly, into silence and depression – partly because of the farm. And because he wanted to know whether his father would allow him to take over. One day when he was ready, of course.

There was no reaction to speak of. All he got, once, was 'We will see.'

His mother Helena said 'Give him time.'

So after his studies he went to France. For three years. To get away from everything. To begin his own life somehow. To wait for news. He worked in the Gironde, he picked grapes and pressed them, swept out cellars and drove tractors, carried crates, waited on tables and worked in a butchery in Bordeaux. He stole with his eyes from the famous and less famous wine estates, asked for advice, always eager to learn. He kept his dream alive. His father's dream really, which he wanted to bring to fruition.

It was at that butchery in Bordeaux that he met Susanne Taljaard, simply called 'San' by friends and family.

Francois was busy cutting up a pig carcass at the back. The owner, Bernard Gaudin, fetched him to act as translator, because Bernard's English was poor, and there was someone at the counter who spoke only stilted French and was asking important questions.

He put down the knife, wiped his hands on his apron and went with Gaudin to the front. She was standing there. A tall girl, her eyes large and green, her blonde hair cut short, her mouth so luscious and full.

'Do you speak English?' she asked plaintively, and he heard her strong accent.

'I can do better than that,' he said in Afrikaans, surprising her with the language, enjoying surpassing her expectations..

'*Ek soen jou sommer!*' she said joyfully, but refrained from actually kissing him. But her smile rose like the sun, and he smiled back, basking in the glow of pleasure.

She had come to ask for the recipe for *gratton de Lormont*, she said. Bernard was famous for this genuine Bordelaise pork terrine, made to a traditional recipe, and *grenier médocain*, the local sausage, definitely the most delicious in the world – all of this spoken with the sound of Pretoria in her mouth.

'I'll have to tell him why you want it.'

'Because I want to make it and serve it in my restaurant.'

San, the chef. She had completed her studies the previous year and was on a culinary tour of Europe, with big dreams of opening her own, intimate little restaurant in the Cape.

'If you'll have dinner with me tonight, I'll ask him.'

'Cool,' she laughed.

She'd only meant to stay in Bordeaux for two weeks. Fourteen months later she went back home with him.

                              ★   ★   ★

The call came on the second of January, from his mother, Helena.

He and San were in Pau, in the South of France. She was searching for the 'recipe for the world's best foie gras' made by two brothers in the Pyrenees, a heavenly pâté that melted in the mouth.

'Pa's dead, Francois, Pa's dead.' That was all she could manage to get out before she broke down and had to pass the phone to Dietrich Venske.

Their neighbour, his voice heavy and sombre, told him Guillaume and Paul were both dead. He must come home right away.

62

The Hawks' Friday dragged on in seemingly endless tedium.

It was dull even for Captain John Cloete, because the media attention was on the published Alibi database, a goldmine that kept the journalists digging for ore, which they could refine into juicy stories for pages one and three.

Benny Griessel had to drive to the city so that the regional manager from Premier Bank could sign documents for a subpoena according to Article 205 of the Criminal Procedures Act. Then IMC could obtain his cellphone records and find out which number had been used to call him on the eighth of May.

It gave Griessel the opportunity to down another two mini-bottles of Jack. He drove the Hawks vehicle, so he made sure his hand hid the bottles while he swallowed first the one and then the other at two different traffic lights.

He wondered why his drinking pressed so uncomfortably on him this time. When he was drinking before, now more than six hundred and four days ago, it hadn't bothered him. And in those days he had a wife, a marriage, a family. Sort of – because when you drank, none of these things were really functional. And neither were you.

But nobody expected anything of him then. Anna, his ex, didn't expect him to be a model husband. His children did not expect their boozer dad to be a father figure, and to his colleagues he was simply the drunken passenger of the Detective Branch – *Dronkgat* Benny: a tragic case (because the same could happen to any of them), but at least a reliable source of tragicomic amusement.

It was his ex-colleague Mat Joubert, now a private detective in Pinelands, who got him on the wagon. And General John Afrika, then Provincial Commissioner, who believed in him. And Musad Manie and the late Zola Nyathi and Vaughn Cupido and Mbali Kaleni, the whole Hawks team, who had given him a second chance at life, and now he was busy pissing it all down his throat. It was because they had expectations of him, that was why he felt so uncomfortable.

He hadn't asked for it. He hadn't asked for their trust and friend-ship and expectations. He couldn't help it if they were going to be disappointed. That was their problem.

He thought all of this with the warm glow of alcohol soothing him, and the taste of Fisherman's Friend settling like metal in his mouth.

But he couldn't shake off the unease.

Vusi Ndabeni postponed his other responsibilities as long as possible, because he didn't want confrontation.

When the team from Forensics was completely finished with Rick Grobler's car, he knocked on the door of the station commander at Stellenbosch SAPD.

He introduced himself and said: 'I'm here about the lost laptop, sir.'

The SC frowned deeply. 'It is a very big embarrassment, Captain. I run a tight ship. This sort of thing does not happen here.'

'Yes, sir.'

'I've had my people turn the station upside down. I've had a look at the evidence registry myself. But it's gone. Disappeared into thin air. For which I unconditionally apologise. I will call Brigadier Manie before the end of the day and apologise to him too.'

'Thank you, sir,' said Ndabeni, because there was nothing else he could say.

Vernon Visser, the financial director of the dying Alibi.co.za was a coloured man with a short, soft body and a goatee to disguise his double chin. He spoke in rapid bursts, as if the words had been damming up and then broke out suddenly. In the intervals, he inhaled sharply and loudly through his nose. Vaughn Cupido and Bones Boshigo had to get used to these mannerisms first before they could properly concentrate on what he was saying.

The books were open, he assured them. It wasn't a pretty picture, but everything was there, 'warts and all'. And he would point out to them where he had been 'creative', in accordance with Ernst Richter's instructions.

'There's no illegal monkey business,' he said in one rapid-fire sentence. And then the next one, a heartbeat or two later: 'I mostly entered Ernst's contributions as alibis requested by clients.' Another pause. 'To appease the venture capital partners. Nothing else.' The words dammed up again: 'He wanted me to spread his payments, and also note them as new clients.' A deep breath through the nose. 'I said, no, that's too complicated. And it's borderline fraud.' Visser looked at Boshigo. 'Desiree will confirm it all. She knows everything.'

Cupido suspected the financial director was very nervous; he couldn't believe the man always talked like this. And he thought Visser and Desiree were of the few coloured employees, if you excluded the usual receptionists and personal assistants – probably Black Economic Empowerment concessions.

'Why are you so nervous, my bru'?' he asked.

'Wouldn't you be nervous?' Words dammed up again. 'The boss ordered me to cook the books legally, and now here's a man from the Commercial Branch sitting in front of me.' He pointed at Boshigo.

'I get that, *nè*,' said Boshigo. 'But not to worry. I'm not here to investigate you for fraud. I'm here to catch a killer.' Bones could be dramatic when he worked with the Serious and Violent Crimes team.

'Okay,' said Visser, tensely. He didn't seem reassured.

'So give us the bird's eye view,' said Cupido.

'The bird's eye view is that this company has never been profitable. And the way we were burning money, it was a stretch. I told Ernst a thousand times. You can ask Desiree.' He looked in the direction of her office in the hope that she would come to his rescue. 'These offices were too expensive. We had too many people. We paid them too much. And Ernst's money was going to run out. But he just said we'll get there. That's the bird's eye view.'

'How many people did he blackmail?' asked Cupido.

Visser shrank. 'I know nothing about that.'

'Did you ever receive strange payments, large sums?' asked Boshigo.

'Only from Ernst.'

Bones looked at Cupido. 'I think we should focus on Richter's personal finances, *nè*. That's where we should start.'

Cupido saw that Vernon Visser was visibly relieved.

★   ★   ★

As Vaughn drove back to the office he thought how he didn't trust the finance director. He didn't know exactly why, but that relief was just too great when he realised that the focus would not be on his books.

What is he hiding?

He also didn't trust that moment that Desiree Coetzee and Tricky Ricky had shared. Or was it just that he didn't *like* it?

Did she have a thing for whiteys?

Not a pleasant thought, but you couldn't just ignore the possibility.

The father of her *laaitie* was white.

You got coloured chicks like that, thought a white guy was a step up the social ladder, parading up and down Long Street, hanging onto their arms. Check me out, I caught myself a whitey. All those Germans and Scandinavians who came to the Cape to get themselves a *chlora* for the summer holidays, because they thought coloured and darkie chicks were wild in bed, and as a bonus it made them feel non-racist. He hated it all.

But maybe he was jumping the gun. It was his heart talking now. The little green monster of jealousy.

He was there when Desiree Coetzee addressed all the Alibi staff. He sat there listening to how beautifully she spoke. Compassion, real compassion. And eloquence. He would not have been able to make that speech, to tell people they would be unemployed in January, and this just before Christmas. But she pulled it off; many of them came over to thank her afterwards.

She had class, this lady. Real class. And that was what frightened him. Better not to think about these things. Let him rather get his docket up to date, and hear what Benny had to say.

Benna said the regional manager had signed the two-oh-five indemnity, and Cupido said: '*Jissis*, those peppermints help *net mooi fokkol*. I can smell you from this side of my desk.'

Griessel leaned back in the chair. His face betrayed his embarrassment.

Cupido sat dead still staring at him, and then threw his hands up in the air. He stood up, went over to shut the door and said: 'What are you going to do if Major Mbali smells you, Benna?'

'She hasn't smelled me yet, Vaughn.'

'Not yet, not over all that cauliflower in her office. But now you stink like a shebeen . . . How much have you drunk today?'

'I don't think that has anything to do with you.'

The frustrations of the day were piled high in Cupido, and his temper rose. 'But it has, Benna. It *fokken* has. 'Cause why, my *gat* is on the line here. I'm the damn fool who lied for you two nights ago, while you lay *poepdronk* in Cape Town Central cells. I am the one who told Major Mbali just this afternoon, that, no, Benna was with me, he banged his head against mine, it's a fucking media conspiracy. And now here you go on the booze again, and at work, while you're working on my case . . .'

'Your case, Vaughn? *Your* case?'

'*Ja*, Benna, my case. I didn't ask to be JOC leader, but here we are. And as your JOC leader I'm telling you now, get your *dronk gat* back home, 'cause you're going to sink the both of us.'

'You're sending me home?'

'Damn straight. And I'm going to take you myself, before you get your *gat* arrested for DUI.'

'I'm not drunk.' Griessel got up. 'I thought you were my friend.'

'But that's the *fokken* point. I am. And if you were sober, you would see it.'

Griessel shook his head and left.

'And when you get home, you better have another think. Where will the booze take you? And do you really want to go there?'

Fok Vaughn Cupido. The JOC leadership had gone straight to his head.

Griessel drove home, feeling thoroughly indignant. He wasn't drunk. He was busy doing his work, reporting on the work that he had done, the work that he had done according to the book.

He was the one who had found out that Ernst Richter had another cellphone.

He was the one who remembered that the blackmailer had sent an SMS. You could only do that from a cellphone, not from a landline. He, Benny, the former technophobe.

And now Vaughn was sending him home, as if he were the new commander?

There were a lot of detectives who drank a beer or a glass of wine over lunch and smelled of alcohol. But that was okay. Just because he had a reputation, a history, he was being discriminated against.

He seethed all the way into the city. There he looked for a drinking hole so he could show them all.

63

Susan Peires realised she was leaning forward in her chair, spellbound by Francois du Toit's narrative.

She had been so sure it was the brother, Paul. But now the young wine farmer said that his brother and father were dead, back in January 2012. Nearly three years ago.

'Could I have some water, please?' he said.

She realised she hadn't been paying attention, lost in her own thoughts. And she was disappointed that he had interrupted his story.

'Oh sorry. Of course.' She pressed the Stop button on the recorder, stood up, her legs cramping from sitting so long. She opened the door and asked her assistant for a carafe of water and two glasses.

When she came back, he was standing staring out of the window.

'That's a lot of heartache for one family farm,' she said.

'That's why I said there was some kind of curse on Klein Zegen. I have sometimes wondered whether I shouldn't get the name changed.' He smiled wanly.

She wanted to know how the father and son died, but she knew her assistant would bring the water in soon. Let her come and go first. So she went over and stood beside him, looking at the Company Gardens down below.

'There seem to be more holidaymakers this year,' he said.

'It's probably easier to cope with the load-shedding blackouts by the seaside.'

'Yes . . .'

The water arrived and he poured out two glasses for them and sat down. She did the same.

He took a deep breath.

She started the recorder and nodded to him.

'We are nearly there,' he said with a certain fatigue, as if this were a mountain he had to climb.

He was the only one left, she thought. He himself was involved with Ernst Richter. She quickly suppressed the vague sense of disappointment that she felt and smiled encouragingly at him.

'At New Year 2012 Paul was released on bail. Pa went to fetch Paul from jail, in the car.'

His voice changed; there was a deeper tone, the pressure of emotion.

'Eight o'clock that night they crashed into the back of a stationary truck between Three Sisters and Beaufort West. The truck was parked beside the road – quite a few metres from the road: a straight section of road. Wide. The driver had set out some of those warning triangles in front of and behind the truck. It had just become dark. Pa was driving very fast. The traffic police said it must have been around two hundred kilometres an hour.

'The official version was that Pa had fallen asleep. People said maybe they were fighting. As in they'd actually come to blows . . .

'But I don't think . . . When I put everything together, when I think about Pa's silences whenever I talked about my future, when I take into account all the circumstances of the accident, and Paul – the person that Paul was. And the life insurance policy had a suicide clause . . . I think Pa drove into the back of that truck on purpose. I think he realised he would never realise his dreams, and he didn't want Paul to do any more damage. Not to him, not to the farm or to me, but especially not to Ma.

'It was a murder and a suicide, all in one, in a way that would protect us. And allow the insurance to pay out. That's what I think. And that's what Ma suspected too.'

64

Saturday 20 December. Five days before Christmas.

Detectives don't like Saturdays, because no one is available when you need them. Support units were understaffed, magistrates were harder to reach for warrants, suspects were not at home or at work, businesses closed early, or did not open at all. Banks were full and busy and had no time to give attention to investigative requests.

It disrupted the rhythm of an investigation.

At 07.30 they sat in Major Mbali Kaleni's office – Cupido, Bones Boshigo, Vusi Ndabeni, Mooiwillem Liebenberg and Frank Fillander.

'Where's Benny?' asked Mbali.

'I've asked him to take a look at Richter's house and office again. He's the one who found evidence of a second cellphone. Maybe we missed the phone, or the SIM card or something. He's taking another look . . .'

She gave him such a long look that Cupido wondered how suspicious she was.

'Okay,' she said. 'What do we have?'

Cupido nodded at Bones, who was getting his papers together.

'Regarding the last twelve months' worth of bank statements, nothing but the odd suspicion here and there, I'm afraid. The main problem is that we only received the past year's statements from the bank . . .'

'That's all we requested yesterday, but we'll get everything this morning,' Cupido explained.

'Right. So the bad news is, there seems to have been no shady income, like from blackmail, during this time. As a matter of fact, there has been no income in the past year, except for interest on his balance. Which he kept in a money market account, by the way, at Premier Bank. But that interest dwindled month after month, because he was putting money into Alibi all the time, *nè*. Now here's the interesting part. This *boy'tjie* was basically flat broke in November. At the end of October, he didn't pay the water and electricity on his rented house. And he went to the limit of his credit card facility on Tuesday 25 November. For the first time, if you look at the statements. So my theory is, he was very desperate in November, because he knew time was running out. The Alibi overdraft was due to be paid back in December; the company was still not making enough money, and his personal funds had run out. And desperate times, *nè*, we all know what that means . . .'

'Desperate measures,' said Vusi.

'Exactly. So all you need to do is to find out what the desperate measures were that got him killed,' he said with a typical Boshigo wave of the hand, as though he had solved their case for them.

'A big shakedown, maybe,' said Cupido. 'Which went wrong. We now know he was a useless blackmailer. None of his schemes were working . . .'

'Not in the last twelve months, at least,' said Frank Fillander.

'Right,' said Bones.

'We need to find the other phone,' said Mbali Kaleni. 'I'm glad you've got Benny working on that.'

'There's one more thing,' said Bones Boshigo. 'It could be quite important.'

Everyone looked around hopefully at him.

'Last night in bed I was thinking . . .'

'So the honeymoon is over, Bones?' asked Cupido.

'*Hayi*,' said Mbali sternly, because she didn't tolerate sexual insinuations on her watch.

'Sorry, Major,' said Vaughn.

'Go ahead, Benedict.' Mbali was the only one, since her promotion, who didn't call him 'Bones'.

'I was thinking about his financial position. That Visser *boy'tjie* told me yesterday that Alibi.co.za was started with three point two million rand, *nè*. The two venture capital firms put in seven hundred and fifty thousand each, and Richter threw in one point seven million, because he wanted the majority ownership. This is going to get a little complicated, so I need you to stay with me on this . . .'

They all nodded.

'Okay. So Richter had one point seven million in cash. That's a lot of money for a guy his age. I asked Visser, where did Richter get that kind of dough, and he told me the story of the web hosting and development company that Richter co-owned, the one he sold his shares in, back in 2010.

'Now, concentrate, people, because this is important. He invested one point seven million in Alibi in June of 2013, which is eighteen months ago. But a year ago, he still had a bank balance of just over six hundred thousand rand. That's the money he has been paying into the Alibi deficit.

'When we add up those two figures, it gives us two point three million rand. And that's what kept me awake last night, because there is no way a web development company is worth almost seven million bucks.'

'Seven million? Where do you get the seven million from?' asked Willem Liebenberg.

'Good question, *nè*. I told you this can get complicated. And that is once again proof that the average IQ over at the Statutory Crimes Group is much higher than at Violent Crimes. Major Kaleni excluded, of course.'

'*Ja, ja*, I was smart enough to get you involved, so get to the point,' said Cupido.

'Fair enough,' said Bones. 'Let me explain. Richter co-owned the web development company with two other guys. There were three partners. He had at least two point three million at the beginning of 2013. So let's say he must have sold his share in the web design company for at least two point three million: one third of the total value. Which means the company was worth just under seven million. Three partners. Three times two point three. You getting it?'

They got it.

'And that's the problem. Web design companies are just not worth that much. It didn't make sense. I thought I missed something, somewhere. So last night, I called the Visser *boy'tjie*. Funny guy, that one. And I asked him what was the web company Richter co-owned. So he gave me the name: PixelPerfect. And I started to dig a little. First, I found that they weren't just a web design company. They started writing apps for iPhones pretty early on, and that was their main source of revenue by the time Richter left. But still, not a big operation, still not worth much more than maybe three million, give or take. And then I searched the Business Day archives, and I found a little news story about the actual deal. Turns out PixelPerfect was sold to an affiliate of Naspers in 2010, and Richter left, taking his share. The sale was for only three point one million. Richter's share was only about a million bucks.'

'A million?' asked Cupido.

'Indeed,' said Bones. 'That's a lot less than two point three.'

'Okay,' said Vusi, 'I'm with you.'

'So who's going to ask the question, *nè*?' Bones wanted to know.

'Where did he get the rest?' asked Frank Fillander.

'Bingo. Where did he get another one point three million? At the very least. I think it's a lot more, because he bought a fancy little car, he was renting an expensive house, and he was living a very expensive lifestyle. My guess is, he had another two million bucks that he got from somewhere.'

Vusi whistled softly. Cupido wanted to swear, but he couldn't do so in front of Mbali. He thought it all over. He said: 'It must have been between 2010 and 2013.'

'But he didn't work during that time,' said Mooiwillem Liebenberg. 'His mother said he travelled for . . . I think she said for about a year.'

'Where to?'

'She didn't say.'

'What did he do while travelling?'

'I don't know.'

'You will have to go see her again today,' said Cupido.

'Roger.'

'And that,' said Bones, 'is why I am going to be at Premier Bank this morning when they open, and I'm going to get his bank statements, all the way back to 2010.'

The thirst. The first thing that Griessel became aware of was the thirst, and then the pressure on his bladder.

He got up, walked to the bathroom, urinated. He was unsteady on his feet.

Lord, he was still drunk. He opened the tap at the hand basin, slurped greedily at the water. It splashed over his face, his bare chest.

He wiped his mouth with the back of his hand, stumbled back towards bed, stopped in the doorway. Where was Alexa? Her side of the bed was undisturbed.

He tried to recall the previous night. He had been at The Dubliner, the Irish bar in Long Street. He'd drunk a lot. But he hadn't made trouble, not as far as he knew.

But how did he get home? He couldn't remember at all. *Jissis*, he must have been extremely drunk. He looked at his watch. It was twenty past eight. He was horribly late.

Where was Alexa?

He walked out, down the passage and negotiated his way downstairs carefully. He didn't want to fall and break his neck now.

She wasn't in the kitchen, dining room or sitting room.

He went through the laundry room to the garage. Her car wasn't there.

What the fuck happened last night? Where was she?

He struggled back to the bedroom; maybe she had sent him an SMS. The hangover bloomed through him, and his head throbbed painfully.

He scrabbled around for his cellphone, and eventually found it in the pocket of his jacket, which was neatly hung up in the wardrobe.

Had *he* put it there last night?

On his phone there was only one SMS from Vaughn Cupido. *I'm covering for you again. You've got Richter's house keys. Go look for evidence of cellphone. If you are sober. If not, stay home.*

Short, sharp and cold.

Now Griessel remembered yesterday afternoon, how he had been sent home. He was suddenly overcome with nausea. He hurried to the bathroom, lifted the toilet lid and retched, but nothing came out, just raw sounds from his throat. His stomach contracted again and again.

The waves subsided, but the nausea remained. And the self-hatred. He was disgusting.

He rinsed his mouth out again, drank more water. Walked to the bedroom window to see if his car was down there in the street.

It wasn't there.

Where was his car? Where was Alexa. How the fuck was he going to get to Stellenbosch?

He picked up his phone, rang Alexa's number. It rang, then went over to voicemail. He left her a message. 'Alexa, I'm sorry.' A too-long silence before he added, awkwardly: 'Do you know where my car is?'

He swallowed a couple of headache pills and was on his way to the shower when he heard the beep of an SMS.

Your car is at The Dubliner.

Just that.

65

Transcript of interview: Advocate Susan Peires with Mr Francois du Toit

Wednesday, 24 December; 1604 Huguenot Chambers, 40 Queen Victoria Street, Cape Town

FdT: My mother . . . She'd always been strong. She was always the one who held everything together – like Ouma Hettie before her. But with Pa's death . . . The thing was, she was devoted to Pa. It was the sort of love that . . . I don't know, it's impossible to describe. She felt she had to protect Pa from the world. Her quiet, gentle husband who had had such a difficult life, for whom the stars . . . She . . . I know I'm speculating, but it seemed like Pa was the sort of man that she wanted all men to be. Loving and fair and . . . unchauvinistic. I can't think of another word now. She felt responsible for Pa, and she was angry that he'd said nothing to her, of his plan to take Paul . . . away. And she admired him for it, because she knew exactly why he did it.

It was a terribly difficult time for both of us. With the funeral, and the will, and the winding up of the estate.

Ma inherited everything.

But she was through with the farm. She didn't want to be there. She wanted to move to town. She was fifty-nine years old, she said she could still lecture or something. Or get involved with a charity.

She said we could sell the farm. It was the sensible thing to do. It was worth an enormous amount of money, which she didn't need – the life insurance and Pa's pension would take care of her until she died. But I was the one with the dream of making wine. I could take the money for the farm and start somewhere else, because the whole concept of a family farm was a medieval, feudal concept. Out of date.

But it was my choice. If I wanted the farm she would give it to me immediately.

I was very emotional. I said I wanted to make a success of Klein Zegen. For Pa's sake. For all the blood and sweat and tears of my ancestors.

They are all dead, she said. And there is no capital. Not a cent.

I said in two months we will get the money for the harvest from Oom Dietrich Venske. That was all I needed.

You're making a mistake, she said.

I still don't know whether she was right. But I do know that if we had sold the farm I wouldn't be sitting here now.

I asked her to transfer Klein Zegen into my name – actually to a family trust, because that was the best way to do it.

But I forgot about the curse. About the stars, about giddy Fortune's furious fickle wheel. I thought my life, our family's life, that farm, was a story, and I was the one who would give it a happy ending.

I was wrong.

66

Benny Griessel was familiar with this sweat, the product of three days of boozing, with last night's relapse as the final straw. It was a sour sweat; your whole body stank of stale booze. The more you perspired, the more you stank.

He walked in the scorching heat of Saturday morning, jacket over his shoulder, his tie loose. The headache pills weren't working and the hangover sweat flooded from his pores. He could smell himself, all the way from Alexa's house to Long Street. But he had no choice. He had called a taxi company, who'd wanted to charge him a ridiculous amount to take him just three kilometres. And his wallet was completely empty after last night.

His head as well. Empty. And hurting. Empty of the justifications and excuses. Empty of clever drinking plans.

He didn't want to think, or feel, he just wanted to walk and get his car.

It was down in Kloof Street, close to the crossing with Buitensingel, that it happened. It was pure chance, a freak of light, the incidental angle of the sun with the reflection in the window. The name of the shop was *o.live*. There was a mirror in their window display, ornate, gold-framed. When he walked past, he saw the movement in the mirror, a fleeting reflection of a pathetic figure, brightly lit. And he registered that it was himself. He halted, turned on his heel and walked back to take a better look.

Earlier, in Alexa's bathroom, the light had been soft and his thoughts elsewhere. But now in the merciless sunlight, he saw the wreck he was: the messy, greasy hair, sweat dripping from his face, sweat stains under his arms, dark shadows under his bloodshot, vacant eyes, the fine network of blue alcoholic veins over his nose and cheeks. His sloping shoulders, shirt hanging out on one side so that his navel and a small triangle of belly hair was visible.

Christ.

Where will the booze take you? Cupido had asked.

Now he could answer: Here, Vaughn. One Alexa-bought shirt and tie away from being a *bergie*, one drink away from destruction.

His empty head was suddenly crowded. Vaughn had sent him home. Vaughn Cupido, of all people. Vaughn, who continued to protect him, despite the fact that he had gone on a bender yesterday, despite the fact that he could damage his colleague's career.

Alexa was gone. She'd left him. Just like Anna before her. And there was a gaping hole inside him. He missed her, everything about her. Her exaggerated love and attention, her soft touch, her voice, her full body, her presence, her scent.

He saw the truth, in that moment in front of the mirror: if he had another drink today, he would never stop. His body wouldn't be able to handle it. He felt it in all the pain and nausea. His body telling him, now you're drinking to drink yourself to death. He saw that future, and he saw himself with no Alexa, no children, no car, no job. Anxiety overwhelmed him. His life was totally out of control. He was completely helpless in the face of alcohol. And *this* time it was final.

As though he had only one chance left.

He knew what he had to do, even if it seemed impossible now. He had to overcome the desire to drink. The thirst. That was the root of the evil. Get his head right, drive out the demons. He had to have Alexa in his life, he knew now he couldn't live without her. He had to try and keep his job, with or without the respect of his colleagues. He didn't want his children to know how he looked and where he was now.

But could he? Could he really?

Jissis, he was so fucking scared.

He would have to try. One last time.

He tore himself away from the mirror.

Stinking and sweating, he reached his car, and the first thing he did was to send Alexa an SMS. *Just tell me you're safe.* He couldn't ask her if she was okay, he knew what the answer to that was.

And then he phoned Doc Barkhuizen, his sponsor at Alcoholics Anonymous.

'Benny,' Doc greeted him as always, no judgement in his voice, because he was addicted to alcohol too, though he hadn't drunk for many years.

'Doc, I'm fucked.'

'Do you want me to book you in?'

'Not now.'

'What's wrong with now?'

'Work. I can't now. Genuine.'

'Do you want to come and talk?'

'First I have to fix things at work.'

'Come and get medicine then.'

'Okay.' He knew the Ativan would help with withdrawal, would calm his spirit and lessen his anxiety and the trembling of his hands. And it would help to see Doc.

'I'm on my way.'

He wanted to phone the psychologist, but at that moment his phone vibrated and beeped in his hand. Alexa: *I am safe.*

I phoned Doc, he wrote back. *I want to see the psychologist today.*

He waited for a few minutes, but she didn't reply. Then he called the shrink.

Just after nine Mooiwillem Liebenberg and Frank Fillander knocked on the door of Mrs Bernadette Richter's house in Schoongezicht, Durbanville.

It was only after the second knock that she came to the door. She was still in her dressing gown in spite of the day's heat, and she looked confused and neglected, unkempt. Liebenberg had to introduce himself before she remembered him. She kept looking nervously at Fillander. They didn't know if it was because of the knife scar or because he was coloured.

She led the way to the sitting room. Sit, she said, while I get ready. Liebenberg said it's really not necessary.

Sit, please, she said, with such an air of vulnerability that they felt guilty.

They waited twenty minutes before she emerged again. She looked better, hair brushed, lipstick on, wearing a dress and sandals. She offered them coffee. She said the doctor had given her tranquillisers so she could at least sleep a bit, but when she woke everything was so hazy. All in one long, rambling sentence.

They said no thanks to the coffee, and that they understood.

'Did you have anything . . . ?' She let the sentence hang.

'No, ma'am, but we think we're making progress at least. A case like this, it takes time to eliminate all the possibilities one by one. We're here because we just want to get your son's complete history, if that's all right with you, of course.'

Fillander heard the genuine compassion in Liebenberg's gentle voice, and he thought, here was the source of his reputation. It was his colleague's great talent.

'Of course,' she said, and stood still, looking about her as though she was lost. Then she seemed to realise where she was, and sat down. 'If I can help . . .'

'We want to talk about the time Ernst went travelling.'

She looked at Mooiwillem, and he could see how she remembered, how her eyes went out of focus. Tears welled. '*Ai*,' she said. 'Excuse me . . .'

'We understand, ma'am, and we are really sorry to have to bother you.'

'You're just doing your job. Let me just get some tissues,' she said. She stood up and disappeared down the passage. She stayed away so long that they exchanged meaningful glances. 'She's not well,' Liebenberg said. 'She was a lot better yesterday.' But then she was back, with a handkerchief under her watch strap and a bunch of tissues in her hand.

'Excuse me,' she repeated, 'did I offer you coffee?'

Again they said, thank you, but no thank you.

'Very well. Ernst's travels,' she said and wiped her nose. 'It was some time ago. I was . . . The child deserved it. He had worked so hard. It was difficult for me, you can imagine, the first time in my life truly alone; he was such a caring son, even when he lived in the city, he was here two, three times a week, phoned nearly every day. And then suddenly he was gone, overseas, it felt like an eternity. Of course I didn't say anything, I didn't begrudge him the chance . . .'

'What places did he visit?'

'Oh . . . He went to the East. He was crazy about the East, about their art. He always said the Eastern scripts are graphic design, they are so much lovelier than ours.'

'What countries in the East, ma'am?'

'Now you're asking me. So many of the Eastern countries: Thailand, China, that one where the Americans were given a hiding . . .'

'Vietnam?'

'That's right. Vietnam. Ernst was crazy about Vietnam. Such a simple lifestyle, he said. Friendly people. And beautiful art.'

'Was it just those three countries, ma'am? Thailand, China and Vietnam?'

'No, I'm not sure now. There might have been more. Korea? Was he in Korea? I don't really think so . . . What other countries are in that part of the world? Japan? I think . . . Yes, yes, he went to Japan as well. Tokyo, oh, he sent me a postcard from Tokyo, there's such a multitude of people there, I remember he wrote about the hordes of people . . .'

'You don't perhaps still have some of his letters?'

'No, Ernst wasn't one for letters. He phoned every other week, from the most exotic places. And sent postcards. And the SMSes. He always used to say that it was a disgrace that he owned a technology company but his mother couldn't use email. He bought me a computer, but I could never get my head around it.'

'Do you still have any of the postcards?'

'Yes, I have . . . But you won't take them away, will you?'

Liebenberg looked at Fillander and said: 'If we could just look at them here first?'

67

Wednesday, 24 December; 1604 Huguenot Chambers,
40 Queen Victoria Street, Cape Town

FdT: In that time immediately after Pa's death . . . Oom Dietrich
Venske, I don't know what we would have done without him. He
was very supportive. He offered to buy the entire crop, at a very
good price.

But nothing is ever straightforward. That year . . . 2012 was
an exceptional vintage; the entire wine industry was excited
about it, the weather was just perfect. It was a winemaker's dream
year. The temptation was so great to . . . to take those grapes,
and make a plan. Borrow money, anything to get that harvest
into a bottle.

I couldn't do it on Klein Zegen, the cellar that Pa had built years
back – it wasn't in decent working condition. I would have to renovate it first. Buy new vats, and see if I could get used vats. I had a
very specific idea for a Bordeaux blend, about 50 per cent Cabernet
Sauvignon, 40 per cent Merlot, and the rest just enough Petit
Verdot, Malbec and Cabernet Franc. We had all the grapes for it.

But I decided, no, I must do the right thing. I must sell the harvest
to Oom Dietrich. There would be other good years, I must think
long-term. And we wanted to use Oom Dietrich's money to set up
San's restaurant. We wanted to convert Ouma Hettie's little house:
nothing big, just ten tables or so, a bistro with traditional French
cuisine.

We did our sums. If she could also generate an income, we could
make this thing work . . .

In any case, we were on the point of talking business with Oom Dietrich. Then a man arrived on the farm with an offer. One that was so incredibly tempting.

68

Doc Barkhuizen's consulting rooms were in Bellville, in one of the old renovated Boston houses.

He didn't see patients on Saturdays, because he was seventy-two years old now and the only reason he was still practising was so that he wouldn't be idle. The devil makes work for idle hands.

'You stink,' he said to Griessel.

'I know.'

'And you look like a dog's breakfast,' he said as he counted out the pills and tipped them into the neck of the bottle with a sweep of his hand.

'I know.'

'I hear it was that thing Wednesday, with your colleague . . . the family murder.'

Griessel did not respond.

'I told you I could see a booze-up coming. But you don't listen.'

He shoved the pills across to Benny. 'You know you can't drink and take these pills.'

'I know.'

'Tell me what you're going to do.'

'I'm seeing the shrink this afternoon.'

'That's good.'

'And I want Alexa back.'

'How do you plan to achieve that?'

'I don't know.'

'If you can stay sober till tomorrow, I will try to help. It will be tough; you've done a great deal of damage . . . but you leave her alone until I tell you. You hear?'

'Thanks, Doc.'

'"Thanks, Doc." It's no good thanking me. You should have phoned me before you went off on a bender. What use is a sponsor if you don't use him? You're a rotter and a *bliksem*. And if I were Alexa Barnard I would tell you to go to hell. You hear?'

He only nodded.

'You can't go to work with that smelly body. Do you want to shower?'

'Please, Doc.'

'I hope it helps.'

It was difficult for Liebenberg and Fillander to track the long-ago travels of Ernst Richter. His heavily medicated mother took out the postcards one by one, and was overcome with emotion as she read them. She wanted to tell them stories, sometimes disjointed, of her late son and his wanderings, and she was reluctant to hand the postcards over to them.

Fillander sat with notebook and pen trying to catalogue Richter's movements back then. Liebenberg studied dates and postage stamps so that they could arrange them according to time and country. It took more than two hours to put it all together:

Richter arrived in Bali, Indonesia late in February 2011, where he stayed for approximately three weeks. After that he was in Bangkok, Thailand for more than a month. Early in April he visited a number of other destinations in that country, before he went to Vietnam in May, for six weeks. After that Hong Kong. In September he travelled in China, and in October he began his return journey – Bangkok again, then Kathmandu in Nepal, then Kolkata. New Delhi and Mumbai in India, before he came back home via Mauritius in November.

Ernst Richter's correspondence was clearly focused on letting his mother know he was doing well. Short, hurried messages that said the places and people and food and art and the natural beauty were 'awesome' and 'cool' and '*lekker*' and 'cute'. Sometimes he complained about the weather. 'Raining constantly' or 'The humidity is so high' or 'Scorching hot'. And he hoped everything was fine with his mother, and 'Will phone next week from . . .' and '*Lekker* to hear your voice, Ma'.

All pretty meaningless, as far as their investigation went.

They asked her if he ever worked overseas.

She said no, Oh goodness me, the child was taking a break, he needed it so much after all the years of terribly hard work, day and night.

Did he ever say anything over the phone about money matters?

No, never.

Did he go to investigate business opportunities in the East?

Not that she knew of. He must have looked at things through his entrepreneurial eyes; he was such an entrepreneur, such a natural businessman.

But he never said anything?

No.

Apart from the payment he got for the web design company, did he ever inherit or win money, come into a windfall somehow?

Now where would the poor child inherit money from? 'I am the only family he has,' she said, as though he were still alive.

On the N1 on the way to Stellenbosch, Griessel remembered a few things about the previous night.

Alexa had been there. He could remember that much. He was very drunk, but she was standing beside him. She said very little. Just that she would be there until he was finished.

Had she taken him home?

Had he phoned her from The Dubliner?

He took out his phone, while he drove, and checked his call register.

No, no calls after he left work.

How had she known he was in The Dubliner? He'd never been there in his life before.

Surely she hadn't followed him?

'It's drugs,' said Frankie Fillander as they took on the Christmas shopping traffic in Durban Road on the way back to the office.

'*Yip*,' said Liebenberg. 'Even the time period makes sense.' Because they both knew that was the only way you could make more than two million rand in ten months.

And South East Asia was back on the international drug dealing hit parade. Thailand – part of the so-called Golden Triangle of drugs in that region – was the Mecca of the heroin black market, but international cooperation and the attempts of the Thai government had largely forced it to a standstill, for nearly a decade.

But from around 2007 the cultivation of poppies in Myanmar began to increase. And in 2010 and 2011 they became the world's biggest suppliers of methamphetamine – the key ingredient of *tik* – thanks to the inhospitability of Myanmar's northern regions and *tik*'s growing popularity in Asia.

Ernst Richter's travels followed all the main smuggling routes, more or less – Thailand, Vietnam, China and India.

'Bad news,' said Fillander. 'Bones won't find anything. It's a cash business that. They don't work through banks.'

It was no easy task, getting three years' statements in printouts and digital files from Premier Bank, with a search warrant that was pretty light on detail.

Cupido, Boshigo and Ndabeni went together to the Stellenbosch branch, because the more Hawks people, the greater the pressure, the more official and serious it seemed.

First they were kept waiting to see the branch manager, because it was 'a very difficult time of year, he's busy with clients'. And then the manager wanted to call his head office before he handed over the Richter statements – on a Saturday morning, when the head office staff of Premier Bank were all on their weekends. Finally he reached a senior general manager on his cellphone on the golf course, and the man said he must cooperate. A whole hour later.

Then there was a problem with the system, which necessitated more calls to Johannesburg, and pushed Cupido's patience past breaking point.

'I'm telling you now, you are going to get those archived statements for me this morning,' he told the bank manager, wagging a threatening finger, 'or I will charge you and your bank with obstruction. This is a murder investigation, not some disgruntled client you're dealing with. You don't mess with the Hawks, *pappie*. So tell those people on that phone they must get their backsides in gear. *Now*. Or I will bring down the full force of the SAPS on you.'

They emerged from the bank with the statements – printouts

and digital – only just a little before twelve, filled with renewed hope that Bones would be able to decode it all. Until Frank Fillander phoned and said it was drugs, because it was Southeast Asia. And that meant cash.

Vaughn Cupido had cut his eye teeth at the Narcotics branch. He knew that industry. He knew Fillander was right. He stood in the hot sun of Stellenbosch's busy Plein Street, beside the Hawks car, and threw up his hands in the air. '*Jissis, fok!*'

A coloured aunty walking past, all dressed up in her Saturday best, paused to admonish him: '*Haai nee, boetie.* Your mother would cry herself to sleep if she heard you talking like that.'

69

Transcript of interview: Advocate Susan
Peires with Mr Francois du Toit

Wednesday, 24 December; 1604 Huguenot Chambers,
40 Queen Victoria Street, Cape Town

FdT: Did you ever hear of Gary Boom?

SP: No ...

FdT: The Bordeaux Index?

SP: No ...

FdT: Gary Boom is a South African. He was born here, in Cape
Town, in the fifties. He was a beer drinker in his younger days. Then
a friend took him out for dinner one night and let him taste some
good wines, and he fell in love then and there. But he could only
really afford to drink fine wines when he moved to London and
made a fortune in the City.

In the nineties, he grew more and more dissatisfied with the lack
of transparency and the shoddy service in the London wine trade.
They say he once ordered a whole case of Château Pétrus, and
when they delivered it, he wasn't at home. The guy just left it at the
back door. Château Pétrus! It's like ... that's thousands of pounds
of wine. That was the last straw, and Boom decided to do something about it.

He went and worked for a year at a wine dealer's to learn about
the industry, and then he started his own company. The Bordeaux
Index. But he approached it completely differently. The Bordeaux
Index is like a stock exchange for wines. Boom decided everything
should be open, transparent; everyone must be able to see what
wines were selling for. And his clients could buy and resell, because
after all wine is really an investment.

And it's a good investment. The wine index has been doing better than the stock exchange since 1982, and up until the early 2000s it grew at a fairly constant rate.

But then something very big happened in the international wine market: China.

There are many theories, but it really comes down to one thing: Chinese economic growth had produced a new generation of the nouveau riche. Since 2000 they had developed an ever-increasing taste for Western luxuries, ways of flaunting their status. And red wine – expensive, good French red wine – is one of the most cultivated luxuries and status symbols you can get.

By 2011 China was the fifth largest importer of French wine. In two years, they say, it will be the biggest wine consumer in the world.

The next big thing came along in the form of the vintage years 2005, 2009 and 2010 in Bordeaux. Phenomenal years. With the Chinese splashing out, and the limited volume of wine, prices began to rise sharply. And they kept rising. In 2011 Château Lafite Rothschild sold for five hundred euro a bottle. That's more than five thousand rand. For one bottle. In 2012 the price was around eight thousand rand per bottle. And now, this year, this December, a bottle sells for eleven thousand rand.

And most of them are bought by the Chinese. For decades London and New York were the cities that hosted the biggest wine auctions. In 2011 Hong Kong took over that title.

All of this is important to understand.

And then you must also remember, my dream was always to make a Bordelaise blend, something like the wine of Château Lafite Rothschild.

70

Benny Griessel knew he had to do a meticulous job of searching Ernst Richter's house again. If he could find the missing, hidden cellphone – or anything that would make a difference in the case – he could at least begin to deserve Vaughn Cupido's loyalty. And perhaps begin to win back his friendship.

So he worked slowly and thoroughly, despite his body's complaints. He carefully considered every room, thought of all the hiding places that he had discovered in his life, put himself in Richter's shoes – where would he have hidden something in this house?

He began with the garage, but there were practically no possibilities there.

He spent an hour on the kitchen. He unpacked every cupboard, looked in every pot, poked a pencil into the instant coffee tin and the sugar packet, fiddled with the De'Longhi Prima Donna coffee machine until the little front door swung open, and the water container came out.

He searched the stove, fridge and freezer, he moved the appliances away from the wall so he could look behind them. He did the same with the washing machine and dishwasher. He lay on his back under the sink and realised the Ativan was making him drowsy – he hadn't slept very much either and the hangover was still very much with him. His head felt very thick. He swore out loud and his words echoed through the silent house.

He found nothing in the kitchen or the laundry room.

In the sitting room he gave the drinks cabinet a wide berth at first. He was busy squeezing the chair cushions one by one when his cellphone rang. Cupido.

'Hello, Vaughn.'

'Where are you, Benna?'

'Richter's house.'

'Praise the Lord.'

Griessel said nothing.

'Benna, can you have a look around for Richter's passport? And drugs?' And Cupido filled him in on the new theory about the victim's travels through South East Asia, the two or three million rand of unexplained income.

Griessel said he would see what he could find.

'But nothing so far?'

'Nothing yet.'

Vaughn's voice dropped to a whisper: 'And are you sober, Benna?'

'Yes.'

He spoke again normally: 'We are at Alibi. Vusi and I are going through his office again. Bones is sitting here with the bank statements. When you are finished, come round here . . .'

To see if he was really sober, thought Griessel. He rang off and finished patting the seat cushions and checking the undersides of the chairs. He searched inside the TV cabinet, opened every computer game DVD case, looked behind the decoder and game consoles, felt for a possible false bottom in the two drawers where remote controls and manuals were stored.

Nothing.

Time to do the drinks cabinet now.

He went outside first, smoked a cigarette, looked up at the mountain behind the house.

He had a gnawing feeling that he had already missed something. A sum that didn't add up. He must gather all his strength, concentrate, what could it be?

He didn't know. But the feeling wouldn't go away.

He took a deep breath, walked back in and began to search the liquor cabinet. He unpacked everything. Thirteen bottles of red wine. Five were French. Château Lafite Rothschild. Never heard of it. The rest were local. Two cylindrical tins for expensive whisky made him pause, but the bottles were still inside, the seals unbroken.

When the cupboard was empty, he inspected it slowly and thoroughly. There were no hidden cavities. With some difficulty, he lifted the cabinet and looked underneath it.

Nothing. Zilch.

He packed everything back, carefully, methodically, with trembling hands and his brain in neutral. A bottle of Jack Daniel's rested cool and heavy in his hands. He put it back. Closed the door.

He went out to smoke another cigarette.

It felt like a victory. Even though the perspiration was clammy on his skin.

At sixteen minutes past one Cupido SMSed him. *Passport found here.*

By half past one Griessel was famished, and remembered he had skipped breakfast. He drove to the Engen garage on the R44, withdrew cash and bought a litre of Coke and two sandwiches. He ate one on the way back to Richter's house, and sat at the kitchen counter to eat the other.

He thought through the search. He still had to look in the ceiling above the first floor, and comb through the garden.

He had done the bathrooms, the toilet water tanks, the bedroom, every corner of every cupboard, every single pillow, every mattress. He'd taken down every painting, hung them all back again. And found nothing.

But still he had the feeling he had missed something.

He munched on the sandwich and drank Coke straight from the bottle and tried to puzzle it out. There was something about this house that did not fit Richter.

Did he perhaps have another place?

Surely Bones would have picked up on something like that from the statements.

What was it that bothered him about the house?

He looked over the kitchen and sitting room. He thought about the bedrooms upstairs. And then the feeling slowly took on a vague shape, and he thought: Richter lived in and with and through technology. It was his life.

But here in this house there was practically none: just the two game consoles and the coffee machine. He got up, looked for the power button on the coffee machine, switched it on.

A small screen lit up. The machine went through a cycle, made noises, sprayed out a little steaming water.

It worked. There couldn't be anything hidden in some electronic nook or cranny, as far as he knew.

He sat down again, drank more Coke.

Richter lived his life through technology.

Cellphone. More than one. And a laptop that had disappeared.

Portable technology. That you could take from work to home to continue with your life.

One cellphone gone. Laptop gone.

No, he didn't know what it meant. And his brain was woolly from the medication, the lack of sleep, the alcohol withdrawal.

He gulped the last mouthful of Coke, got up, took a torch from his murder case and went to look for the access panel to the ceiling.

Only dust, that was all he found. And sweltering heat under the roof, so that the perspiration streamed off him. Two hot water geysers, which he inspected from top to bottom. No trace that anyone had been up there in months.

He climbed out again, walked down the stairs, outside, and started from the far end of the garden. A long, alluring blue swimming pool. He fiddled with the outflow filter and examined the Kreepy Krauly, then the whole pump and filter housing. Walked through the garden, looked at places where the ground might have been disturbed.

At half past two he took a shower in Ernst's third bathroom to wash off the dust and sweat of the attic and the garden. He wanted to be clean, tidy and as fresh smelling as possible when he arrived at Alibi's offices. Hopefully it would compensate for how bad he looked.

Under the running water he played the whole case through mentally. The body found beyond Blouberg, the car in the industrial area here. The forensic investigation showed that he had been strangled some-where in the area, under a jacaranda, near a vineyard. Cupido said it looked as though Richter had made large amounts from something to do with drugs.

Drugs.

Big money. The long tentacles of the drug networks. And an industry that did not hesitate to eliminate useless links in the chain.

Richter had had a public cellphone, and one for blackmail and perhaps other monkey business.

The laptop had disappeared.

That's all they had.

He turned off the water, dried himself, dressed. Then he locked up carefully and drove away.

In the bottleneck of the R44, on the way to the Alibi offices, his brain was in neutral.

And then it came to him, from somewhere in his subconscious, the back of his mind, from wherever.

This wasn't new to him. He had experienced it often. You put in the information, collected all the facts, sifted through them all and then you left it all there inside, to mix and marinate, to sink in. And sometimes, in the night, on the edge of sleep, or in the early morning, in the shower, or from the weary haze of a hangover – somewhere where your thoughts are unfocused and loose – then it jumped out.

The memory of yesterday's hangover floated into his mind: him and Cupido, on the road from Bellville to Stellenbosch, Thursday morning. How he was trying to explain to Cupido that if Vollie Fish had also been a drinker, he wouldn't have committed suicide. How Vaughn had just snorted, and said read the stuff on the back seat. And so Griessel had read the docket from the Stellenbosch detectives.

And it gave him the idea now.

It wasn't the kind of idea to make him turn on the siren and speed off, or reach for his cellphone to call Vaughn. It was just a possibility, something that required attention and further inspection.

A thing that would show Cupido that his heart and mind were in his work after all. And just maybe it would produce something useful?

He didn't drive straight over to Alibi. He headed for the SAPS Stellenbosch charge office first.

Griessel joined his colleagues in Desiree Coetzee's office. She wasn't there, but Vusi and Bones and Vaughn were, all of them around the desk, their eyes on Boshigo's laptop screen.

They greeted him, but barely looked up.

'You didn't find anything,' said Cupido, resigned.

'No. You?'

'We'll know in fifteen minutes,' said Bones, his hand on the computer mouse, eyes on the Excel spreadsheet.

'Can you come with me quickly?' Griessel asked Cupido.
Vaughn looked at him. Questioning, measuring.
He just waited.
'Sure, Benna.'
'We'll be back soon,' he said to the other two.

71

Francois du Toit told her how a man had arrived at the homestead in late January 2012, pulled up in a white Toyota Corolla, at about eleven in the morning.

In his hand he held a paper bag containing a bottle. He was charming and friendly, but in an appropriately quiet way, out of consideration for their recent loss. He offered his condolences immediately, apparently with genuine sympathy. He had an easy manner, with a tone that was professional yet informal. Impressive: so young and yet so self-assured. He introduced himself.

'I'm Ernst Richter. I'm an entrepreneur. I would like to talk to you about a business opportunity.'

What sort of business opportunity?

Is there somewhere we can talk?

Of course, come through to my office.

Francois du Toit suspected it was insurance – crop insurance, or life insurance. Perhaps chemical pest control; there had been enough reps for that on the farm back when he was still at school. And in those seconds he reasoned that he might as well get the information for future reference, even if he wasn't going to buy now.

It could do no harm.

Ernst Richter sat down in the office. In its contents and atmosphere, everything about it, it was still his late father Guillaume's office; he hadn't had time to change it yet.

Richter put the paper bag down on one side of the desk, and outlined his proposal in a calm, rational and well-prepared manner. He said that in the last few months he had done a great deal of research into the wine industry, as he had recently returned from the Far East, where he had identified incredible business opportunities. And now he was looking for someone to realise these opportunities with him.

He offered information on the Chinese wine market, statistics and figures of which Du Toit was generally aware. In the Gironde, in fact, in the whole French wine industry, the Chinese market was a hot topic.

The opportunities were precisely in that market, Richter said, especially this one specific and enormous opportunity.

First he named the figures, like a good salesman who had carefully done his homework about Francois du Toit and the situation on Klein Zegen: I can guarantee you two million rand. Two million profit. The first half million within the next week – that's a deposit. The second half million within six months. And when you deliver, another full million.

And what do I have to do?

You must invest your crop in the transaction. And you must make wine for me.

What kind of wine?

Ernst Richter nodded, reached for the paper bag, put his hand inside and pulled out the bottle. He put it down between them.

It was a bottle of 2010 Château Lafite Rothschild.

This wine, Ernst Richter said.

72

Griessel led Cupido to his car.

'We're going somewhere?'

'Yes. To Jonkershoek.'

Another curious look, but Vaughn got into the car. They drove away.

'The only appointment I could get with the shrink today was this afternoon at six o'clock,' said Griessel. 'Just so you know where I am.'

Cupido looked at him. 'That's good, Benna. Proud of you.' But without total conviction, as if he was hesitant to believe too soon.

As they passed through the town centre Cupido asked: 'What's in Jonkershoek?'

'Stellenbosch's station commander. They have a Christmas *braai* for the station staff.'

'Are you going to tell me what it is that we want there?'

'We're going to . . . Let me tell you what bothers me. The Stellenbosch detectives' docket on Richter's disappearance, what does the quality of that docket say to you?'

'Solid policing. Everything by the book.'

'That's right. It's good work. The whole investigation back when he was reported missing, it was good work. Richter's car was brought in, kept under lock and key. When Vusi and Forensics wanted to look at it, everything was available and in good order. The detectives searched Richter's house, and left everything neat and tidy. The house keys – I went to collect them from them. No problem, they knew where they were. Everything "by the book". And you know where good work begins.'

'With the SC. Good, solid reputation.'

'Precisely. We know where the rotten eggs are in the SAPS in the Cape, and Stellenbosch is not one of them. It's a good station. And if you're a good SC, and your people are investigating a disappearance that is going to bring the whole country's media down on you, then you speak strongly, and you tell them to make sure there are no *fokkops*.'

'Okay . . .' said Cupido. 'What's the punchline?'

'A very good investigation. And then they suddenly lose the laptop?'

Cupido digested this. 'Are you saying what I think you're saying?'

'When we're talking millions, and if we're talking drugs . . . Where do the big bosses of the Nigerian drug cartels live?'

'Parklands . . .'

'Near Blouberg.'

'Okay . . .'

'That storm Wednesday morning . . . They didn't think anyone would ever find Richter's body. But then it was found, and the Hawks got involved and the media went berserk. And they got worried. What would it take to bribe one of the detectives? Get that laptop for us, there is evidence that we don't want the Hawks to see. For fifty thousand, or a hundred thousand, that's small change to those guys.'

'*Jirre*, Benna, you're genuinely sober.'

'Only just,' said Griessel.

Cupido smiled and looked at Griessel for the first time, with a mixture of relief and surprise.

At the entrance to the Jonkershoek grounds Griessel said, 'There was nothing in the newspaper this morning . . . about the Fireman's . . .'

'We just stick to the story, Benna.'

'Thanks, Vaughn.'

Cupido nodded.

'For everything.'

The Stellenbosch SAPS Christmas *braai* was a jolly affair. Music thumping from a car boot, people laughing and talking, glasses in hand, paper plates with remains of barbecued lamb chops and potato salad on a table, beside two boxes of wine. Smoke lazily drifting from the cooling coals, and the faint smell of boerewors hanging in the air.

When they saw the two Hawks approaching, the noise level dropped.

Griessel and Cupido stopped a little way off and waited for the SC to come to them.

Griessel thought their approach worked well. Let everyone see them. Let the guilty ones start worrying. Force them out into the open.

The colonel put down a can of beer and walked over to them. They knew him, and he knew them, from crime prevention seminars and provincial meetings and training courses.

'Gentlemen . . .' said the colonel, with a concerned expression, because he knew this visit meant trouble.

'Colonel, sorry to bother you . . .'

'What's going on?'

'It's about the laptop, Colonel.'

'I thought so.'

'We believe it was stolen. And not to sell.'

He didn't react, but from his frown they could see that he must have considered this possibility already.

They waited for him to say something else.

'It's difficult,' he said. 'I have fifty-four people.'

'We think we should start with the two detectives.'

He immediately shook his head. 'It's not one of them.'

'Colonel, we know it's . . . awkward,' said Griessel, but the SC interrupted him, adamant.

'It's not them. I know those two men, and I can tell you now, nobody can bribe them. They are the best that I have. That's why I put them on the Richter case.'

'We're going to have to investigate them. We're going to put their cellphone numbers through the system . . .'

'You can, but it's a waste of time.'

'Who should we look at then?'

'I really don't know. You'll have to take all our numbers.'

Griessel merely nodded. 'If you could get them for us, please, Colonel.'

The SC's stiff neck showed that he didn't like this one bit. And they understood. If you were a good policeman, who ran a good station, you didn't want to hear stuff like this, because it reflected on you, it would be in your record forever. It broke down morale, in these difficult times when police got so little respect anyway.

Before the SC could respond, Cupido's cellphone rang. He took it out and looked at the screen. 'It's Bones,' he said.

*   *   *

'Bones just says Bingo, we must come and see,' said Vaughn as they got into the car.

Griessel's cellphone rang too and it was Captain Philip van Wyk of IMC: 'We found the number that called your regional bank manager on the eighth of May. So we put it through the system. And it gets interesting . . .'

'How interesting?' Griessel asked.

'The thing is RICA-ed with a false ID and a fake proof of address – a Telkom account. But it is Ernst Richter on the ID photo, doctored a little but it looks like a very good forgery. Which makes sense, if you look at the cellphone number's activation date. According to the IMEI details that are linked to the number, he bought the phone in November last year in Brackenfell, and activated it immediately. It's within the time frame when RICA was enforced more strictly. You couldn't buy a sim card then without an ID.'

Griessel thought about the forged aeroplane tickets and hotel bills Alibi made, and Ernst Richter's interest in that division of his company.

Everything fitted.

'And the call register?'

'From November last year until the last call in May this year there were only seventeen calls from this number, and eleven SMSes. One call and one SMS was to your regional bank manager. We are busy extracting the other numbers now. Oh, and Lithpel Davids brought us a duplicate of the Alibi database last night. We are running the numbers through that too.'

'No calls after May?'

'Nothing. It's as though he got rid of the phone then.'

When they stopped at the Alibi offices, Griessel said: 'I have to see the shrink, Vaughn. But I'll come back as soon as I've finished.'

'Take your time, Benna.' Cupido climbed out and held the door open as he spoke: 'Last night, I was sitting here in my office, and I was really pissed off at you, and I was asking myself, but why, really? If you really want to *suip*, why should I care? It's your life. And then I got it, Benna. It's comradeship and all that shit, but actually, the heart of the matter is, I can't be Vaughn the Terrible if you aren't Benna the Sober. It's like that line in the movies: You complete me.'

'And now you're going to kiss me?'

'That's the Benny Griessel I know and love. *Fokkof.* Go sort out your *kak.*'

'Take a look,' said Bones Boshigo, pointing a finger at his computer screen. 'The year 2012 was a really good one for the late Mr Richter.'

Cupido peered over Bones' shoulder. Then he leaned forward even further and whistled. 'Is that accurate?'

'Of course it's accurate. I have a degree and all. And Excel can't lie.'

'Four point three million?'

'That was what he had in October of 2012. But wait, there's more. He came back from South East Asia in 2011, *nè*?'

'Yes. November.'

'See, that was his bank balance in November 2011: six hundred and seventy thousand. Lots of money spent on travelling, that's what he had left. And, one year later, four point two million. Which he received in just three payments: August 2012, one million thirty-one thousand and change; September 2012, one million thirty-one thousand and change; October 2012, two point one six million and change.'

'Where did he get it from?'

'There's always a bit of bad news, *nè* . . .'

73

Ernst Richter asked Francois du Toit to fake ten thousand bottles of 2010 Château Lafite Rothschild.

That's impossible, Du Toit said. It's Château Lafite Rothschild. It's a unique blend, a unique vintage from a unique terroir, an ancient vineyard. Impossible.

Richter said: Look at the bottle. What do you see?

Du Toit looked, but didn't understand.

You see the red seal with the black-and-white logo, Richter said, and pointed out each item with his index finger. You see the shape of the bottle and the vintage and the five little arrows that are cast on the outside of the bottle, above the label. You see the colour of the wine behind the glass. And you see the label, the old etching of people working in the field in front of the chateau, and you see the words *Mis en Bouteille au Château*, then *Château Lafite Rothschild*, and then *Pauillac*. That is what you see. Have you got a corkscrew? And two glasses?

'We can't drink that . . . It must be laid down, for several more years still.'

'I have another eleven of them,' Richter said. 'Do you have a corkscrew?'

Richter opened the bottle and poured the divine liquid into two glasses. 'Look at the colour of the bottle now. We are going to have those bottles made exactly like this. And I am personally going to duplicate the labels and the seal. Precisely. No one will see the difference. All you have to do is to match the colour of the wine, so that it looks exactly like this in the bottle. And you must make the best wine that you can. Do you really think that in two or five or ten years a Chinese millionaire who bought twenty cases of *our* Château Lafite, is going to taste the difference? And let's say there are a few that think they may just have been taken for a ride. Do you think they are going to say anything? Those guys will never lose face. And besides, there will be no way they will be able to trace it to you.'

'That's . . . against the law.'

'To make wine?'

'To fake wine.'

'You're not faking anything. You are just copying. You are copying the best wine in the world. Isn't that what everyone is trying to do? To make wine like the French? Just as good, or better? That's why you all go there to work and learn. I'm asking you to deliver the best possible Bordeaux blend. I will do the forgery. And the shipping.'

Francois du Toit sat there, dumbstruck.

'You don't have to give me an answer now. Sleep on it.'

Du Toit tasted the wine.

'Two million,' Ernst Richter said. 'That's what you will make. Two million rand. And within a week you will receive half a million to renovate your cellar and buy your vats.'

'How did you know . . . ?'

'I'm an entrepreneur. I do my research.'

74

'The payments were made from a foreign bank. The statement only provides the SWIFT code, but if you go to the swiftcodes dot com website, you can trace it, which is what I've done,' said Major Bones Boshigo.

'Richter received those amounts from Guangdong China Banking Corporation in Guangzhou. That's a city in China. And that is really bad news because the chances are very slim that they will provide us with information about the origins of the money, or who that account belongs to, *nè*. I've also had a look at the amounts, per se, and I'm pretty sure it was paid in dollars. If you multiply a hundred and twenty-five thousand dollars with the exchange rate of August 2012, you get one point zero three million and just about that exact change. Same for September. And if you multiply two hundred and fifty thousand dollars in October, that gives you the two point one six million rand.'

'So he was paid in dollars,' said Cupido slowly.

'Yebo yes.'

'From a bank in China.'

'Yip.'

'Bad news.'

'That's what I said.'

Benny Griessel sat and stared at the teddy bear in the shrink's office while she read to him from a thick book: 'Without treatment, or overcoming it, a person suffering survivor guilt may begin a downward spiral that might include self-medication with drugs and/or alcohol; regression in recovery from post-traumatic stress disorder; major depression; increased anxiety, and suicide.'

She looked up at him, this attractive woman with the soothing voice. 'Does that sound familiar to you?'

Griessel nodded reluctantly.

'You are trying to drink it all away. Self-medicating. And you are right when you say your colleague Adjutant van Vollenhoven would not have committed that family murder if he had been a drinker. But alcohol abuse only delays the inevitable . . .'

'Vollie didn't have survivor guilt, he had . . .'

'Survivor guilt is one of the four conditions or subscales that we associate with the fear of harm to others. The other three are separation guilt, omnipotent responsibility guilt and self-hate. Policemen and soldiers are just about the only ones who are exposed to all four. I think . . .'

'I don't know what all those terms mean.'

'I think you do know, but you don't want to know, because it makes you afraid that you might be suffering from all four. Like Van Vollenhoven. Separation guilt in this instance is your pathological fear that something bad will happen to your loved ones if you're not with them. Most mothers have this in a mild form, when their children are far away . . .

'Omnipotent responsibility is separation guilt on steroids. Omnipotence is when you feel that you – and only you – have the power to do everything, to protect everyone. It is common with policemen, because they become accustomed to the power of protecting, enforcing justice, even the right to kill people who break the law. But when it comes to your loved ones, that omnipotence lets you down. You see all the gruesome things, but you feel powerless to protect your loved ones from them. And then the self-hatred . . . The combination of all those things is what drove Adjutant van Vollenhoven to destroy his family and himself.'

'*Jissis*,' he said, under his breath. She was right. That was precisely what was going on in his fucking head, what was driving him crazy.

'Let's not forget to add post-traumatic stress to this unholy brew,' she said. 'You didn't pick an easy profession.'

A thought suddenly occurred to him. 'But there's one of my colleagues . . . One specifically, who doesn't seem to be bothered by any of these things . . .'

She smiled sympathetically. 'What you are exhibiting is the "why me" syndrome. That's normal. I have a theory . . . I've been treating policemen for six years now. I think it has everything to do with the capacity for altruism. Not all of us have the same degree of altruism. The interesting phenomenon is that the detectives with greater altruism, work on the one hand considerably better in certain circumstances as a consequence, and on the other hand they suffer more from depression because of it. It's a double-edged sword . . .'

'I'm not a better detective than Vaughn . . .'

'I said in certain circumstances. It's a big subject this, but let's talk about it for a moment: You are good at putting yourself into the shoes of the criminal, aren't you?'

He just shrugged.

She smiled. 'There's the self-hate again. Embrace your talents.'

He said nothing.

'The ability you have to identify with the criminal is a form of altruism. In certain circumstances it gives you a great advantage in the approach to solving a case. But it's not the only weapon that a detective must have in his arsenal. Analytical reasoning, the ability to process large swathes of data, social skills, the ability to read people, to put them at ease . . .'

'That's Vaughn, all right . . .'

'Precisely. Why do you think it's a world-wide practice to make detectives work in teams? Because no two people have precisely the same talents.'

The heart of the matter is, I can't be Vaughn the Terrible, if you aren't Benna the Sober. Like that line in the movies: You complete me.

'Okay,' said Benny Griessel.

'Is that acceptance I hear?'

'I probably don't have a choice.'

'That's a big step forward.'

'How do I stop drinking?'

'Therapy is the only successful treatment for all four of these subscales that we associate with the fear of harm to others. We can look at anti-depressants as an interim measure, but you were opposed to them when I last saw you.'

'I don't want pills. That's just another sort of addiction.'

'Then you will have to come for therapy. Intense therapy.'

'For how long?'

'How long do you still want to be a detective?'

'*Jissis.*'

'The purpose of therapy is to analyse the traumatic events with you, until you understand that you are not responsible for the damage that's been done. The dilemma is that your job is one long string of traumatic experiences. You told me yourself how you experience the last moments of the victims' lives, every time you arrive on a murder scene. But it isn't all as terrible as it sounds. With hard work you can master the techniques to handle this on your own in due course. With the emphasis on hard work: in therapy, twice a week, for the next month or two. Then we can scale it back.'

Was he up for that?

'Oh, and another thing that helps a lot is to involve your family in it.'

'They have to come and sit here too?'

She smiled. 'No. Although a single session with your family would make sense. But you at least have to tell them about your condition. Their love and understanding can make a big difference.'

When he left the building, it was already dusk. The southeaster had begun to blow: a bleak, inconsolable wind. There was an SMS from Cupido. *Come to the office when you are done.*

It was a fifteen-minute drive from the psychologist's office in Stellenridge to the DPCI, but it took twenty. He felt drained, dog-tired, blunted.

He would have to tell Alexa and the children. If Alexa was willing to take him back.

Anna hadn't been. Even after he had dried out, back then, she'd left him for that little shit of a lawyer with his silver BMW and his shiny suits. Maybe Alexa also had a plan B somewhere. How would he know?

Fok, best not to go looking under rocks like a baboon. Don't need a nasty surprise . . .

He must tell Mbali too.

The shrink's opinion was that he couldn't tackle this long road without the support and understanding of his commanding officer. 'I will contact her as well, but with your permission.'

Complications. Something like this could kick up a real fuss, and he didn't like people getting in a flap. He preferred to just get on with his life, do his work, without people faffing over him. And Mbali would faff. She was also one of the altruistic types, though she hid it better than he did.

The trouble was, if he told Mbali, she would know that Vaughn had lied about the other night.

Or would she? If he could approach this thing properly and cleverly and carefully . . . They could say that he was just a bit tipsy on Wednesday, that's how he'd bashed his face.

He would have to discuss it with Vaughn first.

And he would have to tell Doc. That was the easy part, because Doc would say, 'How long have I been begging you to see a shrink regularly? But no, you're an Afrikaner man. Too clever and strong and macho.'

They both knew it wasn't true, Doc was just messing with him.

He just didn't like anyone probing into his mind. He had never been important enough for that.

Therapy twice a week. Just him and the teddy bear and the shrink.
Jissis.

75

Transcript of interview: Advocate Susan
Peires with Mr Francois du Toit

*Wednesday, 24 December; 1604 Huguenot Chambers,
40 Queen Victoria Street, Cape Town*

FdT: People rationalise. If two million rand is lying there in front of
you and that's the solution to all your problems, you see it as fate, as
if the universe is putting right all the evils of the last two generations, the stars realigning. You think about making the wine, the
incredibly thrilling challenge, you think about what the man said.
Who will know? Who is being hurt by it? A bunch of nouveau riche
Chinese who won't know the difference between Château Lafite
Rothschild and Château de Boxwine. You think of your wife-to-be,
who has found herself part of a family with so many troubles. You
think about the dreams she has, dreams that you would so love to
help her realise. You think, next year you want to get married, and
you want to be able to offer her something at last.

That's how you rationalise.

And you decide to do it. You lie to your future wife, and you lie
to your good, loyal neighbour, Dietrich Venske, and you feel bad,
but only for a day, about the disappointment in his eyes when you
tell him that you've decided not to sell your harvest to him after all.
Because the next day you remember that he's a wealthy man with a
brand that is drawing increasing attention in Britain and America;
he can do without this harvest, but you can't.

And then you make the wine.

And you know, it was fun. If I end up sitting in jail, I will try and
remember that. It was an unbelievable experience. A fantastic
apprenticeship. Ernst Richter was right. We all try to copy the best

French wines. The whole world – California, Chile, Australia, New Zealand . . . Because through this process of copying we learn to find our own wine voice.

Hopefully. Eventually.

And here I sit now, with my own wine voice, knowing what notes I can reach, but with a very good chance that I will never be able to sing like that again.

76

They all walked together to Mbali's office where she sat waiting for them. They sat down around the conference table. The entire team was there. Bones Boshigo as well.

Cupido said they had a lot of information, but still nothing to get excited about. He summed up the main points.

One. Ernst Richter's financial hourglass had practically run out. This December the bank would have called in Alibi's overdraft. And Richter's personal funds were exhausted. Alibi would have had to close and Richter would have been bankrupt. He would have lost everything – the business, his car, his big house. But more: he was a man who loved his status and reputation. He would have lost that as well. This of all things was perhaps more than his ego could stand.

Two. He had begun to behave criminally in order to save his butt. Since at least November of last year Richter had tried to blackmail his own clients. He had forged an ID document and proof of address to acquire a cellphone. Those were two crimes that they knew of. If you followed the old detective principle of 'former behaviour determines future behaviour', there was a strong possibility that he had committed other crimes as well. Including trying to blackmail other people but:

Three. Since November last year he had had no payments into any of his own accounts. Therefore they could assume that none of his blackmail attempts had met with success.

Four. From February to November 2011 Richter had been travelling through South East Asia. In June and July 2012 a Chinese bank paid him three amounts to the value of four point two million rand. In dollars. Of which his mother knew nothing. That was significant. Taking everything into account, it was highly probable that the money had been acquired criminally, most likely through some drug deal.

Five. All the above-mentioned suggested that a month ago, in November, Ernst Richter did something in order to get his hands on a large sum of money quickly, in an attempt to save Alibi. And that caused his death. But they still didn't know what that was.

Did they all agree, so far?

Yes, they all agreed.

'So far, so good,' said Cupido. 'So how do we find out what he did? Where he went? Who he met? Basically, what we have is the forensics from what we think is the actual crime scene, and that's not very specific. We have the laptop that was stolen from the Stellenbosch evidence locker that can link to the killer or killers. We have the other calls he made from the cellphone he faked an ID to buy, and we have the Chinese bank. Which isn't really useful, so we might as well forget about that . . .'

'Why?' asked Mbali.

'Major, the bank is all the way over there in China. They're this Communist state; it's not like we can call them up and say hey, *pêllies*, there's this guy who ran a website for wife cheaters who went and got himself killed, how about showing us all your secret bank files . . .'

'I think you are wrong,' said Mbali.

Cupido held himself back. He merely lifted sceptical eyebrows.

'The Chinese are our biggest trade partners,' she said. 'Our president was there just the other day. They want to build us nuclear power stations. I think if the brigadier talks to the national commissioner, and the commissioner talks to the minister, and the minister talks to the Chinese ambassador, you might be surprised at what could happen.'

Cupido's eyebrows knitted into a scowl. 'Major, with all due respect, that's a big if.'

'Stranger things have happened,' she said with quiet self-assurance.

'We . . . That would be great . . .' He pulled himself together again and addressed the team: 'In the meantime, we need to look into the calls on the fake-ID cell, and that laptop. Uncle Frankie, you're a family man, if you want to take the Sunday off, and Benna, you too . . .'

'No,' said Benny Griessel, much louder than he'd intended, because if he were to sit totally alone and idle at Alexa's house tomorrow, he would go off his head, and straight back to the bottle. He had to suppress the 'please'.

'Cool,' said Cupido. 'Then I'll see you guys tomorrow. Let's start at nine . . .'

*   *   *

When everyone had left, and the light was soft and pale gold outside her window overlooking Boston Street and the Bellville library, Major Mbali Kaleni locked her office door. She sat down again, and unlocked the third drawer of her desk. Under the bag containing her emergency cosmetics, lay the slab of chocolate. Lindt Excellence 70% Cocoa. Dark chocolate. According to many studies it was very good for one: for the heart, for the mood.

She respected Professor Tim Noakes. He was a clever man. But one should never forget that he was a man. And men don't really understand the heart of a woman.

Once a week she had to feed her heart as well, after the low-carb, high-fat Banting regime promoted by Prof Noakes, with all the full fat yoghurt, the meat and fish and chicken and cauliflower.

She put the slab down on her desk. She would get to that in due course. One last task first.

She picked up her phone and called Brigadier Musad Manie.

'Good evening, Mbali,' he said, his voice deep. In the background she could hear a TV being quickly turned down.

'Good evening, sir, I am happy to report that we have a new lead in the Richter case. It is one of those that might be big or it might be nothing, but we need your help in exploring it to the fullest.'

'Yes?'

She explained about the payments that had been made to Richter from a Chinese bank. And she asked him to call the National Commissioner of the SAPS, so that the request for cooperation would go through official channels to the Chinese ambassador.

'Let me see what I can do . . .'

Only then did the ritual unwrapping of the slab of chocolate begin.

Griessel didn't turn right at the intersection of Voortrekker Road and Mike Pienaar Drive to take the N1 to the city.

He drove straight on, to Parow.

It was a spur-of-the-moment decision. Something drew him, and he was too weary to resist. From Voortrekker he turned right into Tallent Street, then left into Second Avenue. He slowed, and stopped in front of the house where he had grown up. Switched off the engine, opened the window.

The wind blew in, along with the sounds of suburban Parow, here where the houses and gardens were small, where blue-collar workers like his father had been able to afford to buy.

Their house – long since someone else's – was surrounded by a cream-coloured concrete wall, but it was still the same house. Here in the street they had played cricket until late, under the street lights. There, in that room in the middle, he had sat learning to play his bass guitar for hours on end. The dreams and stirrings of teenage love, Lord, how many hours? So many dreams, of the fame and riches and happiness that lay in the future.

He sat there for nearly forty minutes, reminiscing. He smoked two cigarettes and longed for the simplicity of that existence, amazed by the journey he'd taken to this point. And the disappointment that was his life.

Then he drove home. Alexa's home really, though she talked about 'our house'.

The city centre was aglow with Christmas lights.

He thought about the last Christmas that his family had been whole, when he was still reasonably sober. Ten years ago? When he and Anna had brought the children here so they could enjoy the spectacle of the lights.

This year Christmas should just rather pass him by. It was going to be a lonely one. The children were with Anna, as they were every year, because with her and her little lawyer it was a 'warm family atmosphere, no one living together in sin'. As if she and the little legal eagle had never got up to mischief before they were married. As if he and Alexa could never be a family.

There was a chicken and broccoli dish on the kitchen table, with a note stuck to it: *35 minutes at 180 degrees. You must eat.* In Alexa's handwriting.

She had been here. But she was gone again.

Through the fatigue he felt a tiny bit of hope. Tomorrow Doc would phone Alexa . . .

He switched on the oven and waited for the food to cook. He ate it out of the packaging. Then he showered and got into bed.

He sent Alexa an SMS, even though Doc had said 'leave her alone'. *One day without a drink,* he wrote, and lay and waited. Perhaps she would answer.

The phone was silent. He slept restlessly, because the withdrawal and the day and everything would not go away, no matter how tired he was.

Mbali was already in bed with her iPad when Musad Manie phoned back.

'Major, we have a slight problem,' he said.

'What is that, sir?'

'The commissioner spoke to the minister, and the minister apparently spoke to a few of his colleagues. He wanted to proceed through the correct channels, and it took a while before the message came back to the commissioner. Mbali, do you know that we have one ANC Member of Parliament, two provincial MEC's, a deputy director general of foreign affairs and an ANC town mayor all implicated as clients of this Alibi thing?'

'Cloete has kept me posted, sir. Lots of other people too.'

'Well, apparently the top hierarchy does not care about the other people. But they *do* care about the whole mess. So the message I have to give you is that they will ask the Chinese for their help. But they expect us to catch the person or persons who published that database on the internet. And they demand that we prosecute him or them to the full extent of the law. And they will monitor our progress, they say. And they will evaluate our performance in this matter. Mine, and yours, and that of your team.'

'Yes, sir. We will see what we can do.'

After she had rung off, she uttered one loud '*Hayi*.' And then she decided she would pass this news on to Vaughn Cupido in the morning. Let him have a good night's sleep first.

**Transcript of interview: Advocate Susan
Peires with Mr Francois du Toit**

*Wednesday, 24 December; 1604 Huguenot Chambers,
40 Queen Victoria Street, Cape Town*

Sound file 16

SP: The Lafite bottles, are they unique?

FdT: Yes. The five arrows that lie across each other, with the vintage year cast over it. And the shape, the colour . . .

SP: How did you get the bottles? Is it possible . . . ?

FdT: It's possible and it's easy. You take an example of your bottle to one of the local manufacturers, and tell them that is exactly what you want. He had the bottles made here. It's the—

SP: But they, the bottle people would surely see—

FdT: Lafite's bottles aren't known here. I wonder if there are ten people in the country who would really recognise a Lafite bottle for what it is without its seal and label. The chances that the glass company would know are very slim. And if you order ten thousand bottles, fewer questions are asked. The greater problem is the corks, because every Lafite cork has a stamp with the name on it. Richter never said where he had the corks made, but he delivered ten thousand. I think they were manufactured in China. Or maybe in Portugal, because here . . . You would have had to bribe someone at the Stellenbosch cork producers to make them in the factory at night, and I don't think the . . . I think the risk would have been too great. But money is a funny thing . . . The seals and labels were definitely made in China. He said something, the night we bottled, about how cheap it had been . . .

SP: And you simply put your wine into the bottles?

FdT: It was done on Klein Zegen, by . . . There are a whole bunch of guys who have mobile bottling units nowadays. They come to the farms and bottle right there. Richter had a guy, the man knew my father, they worked together years ago. He must have paid him well, because he brought his unit at night . . . and because more and more of our wine exports are unbottled, wholesale exports, the bottling guys are under pressure, work is getting scarce. Then they don't ask questions . . .

SP: How . . . Richter must have worked with people in China, then? To get the wine there, and sell it . . . ?

FdT: Absolutely. Not just the distribution and sales, but . . . the money, he said a few times he was just waiting for the money. I think someone financed him. It was a large amount, to make everything work. And my money, the two million that I received – it came from a bank in China.

SP: What would ten thousand bottles have brought him in . . . ?

FdT: I can only guess. At that time Lafite was selling for between five and eight thousand rand a bottle. Let us say he and his financier got a thousand per bottle. That is ten million income, three or four million profit? But I think they got more. I think it was in the region of two thousand per bottle. Then it starts to be profitable, if you cover all your production and transport costs. But . . . I think Richter was just a sort of middle man. I don't think he was the top dog.

SP: Why?

FdT: When he took his wine away, when I had been paid, I didn't hear from him again, not for over a year. Then one Sunday I bought the *Rapport*, and there was a photo of him on the front page. I got quite a fright. But then I read he had started this website for cheaters. Then I thought, you don't start something like that if you have ten or twenty million in the bank. And I thought he might not have got much more than I did after all, if that was the best he could do.

SP: And then?

FdT: Then I went on with my life. Until Monday 24 November. Now, a month ago. Ernst Richter arrived on my farm. This time in an Audi TT, the Corolla probably sold long ago. I was afraid San would recognise him from all the newspaper stories, and I took him to my office and asked him what are you doing here?

And he said he wanted money. He wanted five hundred thousand rand. I said I don't have that sort of money lying around. And he said I had better get it. Or he would tell the whole world what I had done.

78

Sunday 21 December. Four days before Christmas.

Sunday. The day of rest. A day for church, for visiting family, long, heavy Sunday lunches, and long, deep afternoon naps.

But not for the Serious and Violent Crimes Group of the Directorate for Priority Crimes. For them it was a difficult day for the investigation, because nobody wanted to be disturbed: not witnesses or suspects or informants or off-duty policemen.

A day of loneliness, because there was something about a Sunday, as Kris Kristofferson used to sing, that made a body feel alone. And you felt it in your body and your bones if your name was Benny Griessel, and you got up alone and ate your Weet-Bix alone – because Alexa wasn't there to make her usual morning omelette for him. Alexa couldn't cook, the omelette was always too runny, or overcooked, or too salty, or too bland, but she made it with so much love and commitment that it didn't matter. Benny thought how he would eat it every time, and how two hours later at work he could still taste the odd flavour in his mouth, and how he would think of her then.

But not on this solitary Sunday.

If you're Benny Griessel on this sombre, sober Sunday, you drive alone through the quiet streets and you see the newspaper posters on the lamp posts: WIFE SHOOTS FARMER OVER ALIBI and MAYOR DENIES ALIBI CLAIM. But you don't fret over it. Your mind – without a headache this morning, but fuzzy from the medication and the withdrawal and the fear of the thirst – and your longing is focused on Alexa. All the things that sometimes irritate you beyond measure, don't matter at all this Sunday. Such as the way she introduces you to the music folk in her circle as her 'master detective'. The way all her creams and mascaras and lipsticks and mysterious bottles and tubes and pencils spread themselves around the bathroom like an amoeba, occupying an ever larger surface every day and pushing your meagre few toiletries into an ever-shrinking corner of the cupboard under the basin.

And this morning there was more space than usual for your stuff, and you thought, just come back, I don't mind. There's too much space here without you.

Sunday. The day of loneliness, if your name is Vaughn Cupido. Get to work early, to fight the loneliness, to keep your mind from straying to thoughts of the lovely Desiree Coetzee. Who might just have a thing for whiteys, but then again might not. And how are you going to wangle seeing her today, because yesterday you couldn't, and it was like there was a big black hole here inside you, and you can't understand it, because you last felt like this in *fokken* high school in Mitchells Plain, over Elizabeth 'Bekkie' November, and whatever happened to that chick anyway?

And then *Major* Mbali Kaleni walks in and gives you a premature Christmas gift: a reason to phone Desiree Coetzee.

'Captain, we'll have to investigate the guy who published the Alibi database. That's the price we will have to pay for reaching out to the Chinese.' All apologetic-like, *nogal*.

Then you say: 'I'm cool with that, Major,' with more enthusiasm than is appropriate, and your commanding officer looks at you a little funny, but you don't worry, 'cause why you don't feel so alone any more. This Sunday is suddenly looking up.

And you phone her number, and she answers, her voice a little bit sleepy and husky, sexy, and you apologise for disturbing her at such an early hour, and you say, really sorry, but I have to come and see you, about the case.

And she says then you must come to the house. I'm here with my child.

The first seventy-two hours of your normal murder investigation is all adrenaline: excitement and action and hurry and focus. Organised chaos, a driven team of detectives blowing in like a hurricane to propel the ship of justice across stormy waters.

But if there are no breakthroughs, if the winds die down after five days, then you're in the dreaded doldrums. The waters settle, go still.

The ship bobs directionless, becalmed. The drudgery, the footwork, the phone work and the endless admin begin. Hopes of an outcome, a solution and an arrest begin to fade. And that is the thing that detectives the world over hate most. The paperwork: sitting down and writing reports and filling out forms and dockets and documents.

Griessel and Liebenberg had to compile a document to send to Durban, Bloemfontein and Johannesburg. The document had to serve as a guideline during interrogation. Because the adjutant at IMC (Captain Philip van Wyk was spending Sunday at home with his family) explained to Benny and Mooiwillem that Ernst Richter made seventeen calls with his 'secret' cellphone.

One of them was to the regional bank manager.

IMC had compared the other sixteen unknown numbers with client details in the Alibi database.

Only fifteen yielded positive results.

The sixteenth was not an Alibi client. He was the second last number that Richter called on the secret cellphone. It only lasted ninety-four seconds, considerably shorter than any of the other calls that he made. The number belonged to one Mr Peter McLean of Kuilsriver. He had no criminal record.

In fact, none of the sixteen people that Richter had contacted had records.

Five were in the Cape, nine in Gauteng, one in Bloemfontein and one in Durban.

And so the drudgery began, the administration and frustration, because the detectives first had to compile the document laying out the nature of the interrogation. Then they had to track down their colleagues at the DPCI branches in other cities on the most difficult day of the week. And ask for the kind of help that no Hawk wanted to give just before Christmas, because they all had dockets and routine work and holiday plans of their own. Then Griessel and Liebenberg had to explain over the phone what they wanted, and send the document through.

Only in KwaZulu-Natal was there enthusiasm. 'Shane Pillay? I know this guy,' said the Durban Hawk. 'Very rich, owns four car dealerships. Real arsehole. So he was cheating on the missus? Sure, I'll go talk to him.'

It was just before lunch when Benny and Willem started calling the Cape numbers.

On the way to Stellenbosch Cupido phoned Lithpel Davids.

'Cappie, it's the sacred Sunday.'

'No rest for the wicked. Tell me, my genius, would you be able to find out who the people are that leaked the Alibi database?'

'As in track and identify?'

'Follow his digital footprints, I hear that's what you techies have to do.'

'Cappie, I am many things, but that is next-level shit, for a network and internet specialist. I'm a jack of all technological trades. I can try, but it will take a month or so.'

'We don't have that sort of time.'

'Then I'm not your man, I'm happy to say.'

'Have a *lekka* Sunday, Lithpel.'

Desiree Coetzee lived in Welgevonden Estate, on the northern side of Stellenbosch, on the R44 to Paarl. Among the whiteys.

Cupido got out in front of the townhouse and looked around. It was a well established property development, the houses closely-packed, the gardens tiny. His old house in Bellville-South at least had a yard where a *laaitie* could play.

It was the *laaitie* who opened the door. Tall and skinny, with knobbly knees. Inquisitively shy blue eyes with a café-au-lait skin, dark hair like his mother.

'I'm Vaughn Cupido,' he said and put out his hand.

'The policeman,' said the child, giving him a long look as they shook hands.

'You say your name, Donovan,' Desiree's voice preceded her hurried footsteps.

'I'm Donovan.'

'Pleased to meet you,' said Cupido and then there was Desiree, her hair still wet, the lipstick fresh.

She'd taken trouble, he thought, despite the short notice. White blouse, denim, barefoot. Breathtaking.

They said hello. He apologised. She said it was okay, it's a quiet Sunday. He said it was a tough week, you deserve a quiet Sunday.

Donovan stood staring at him, then asked: 'Uncle, have you got a gun?'

Cupido wanted to say, yes, I'll show it to you; he wanted to impress the kid. But chicks were funny. Just now she might not like the idea of him showing her boy a gun. He just said: 'I have.'

'Will you show it to me, uncle?'

'Donovan, have you made your bed?'

'No, Mommy.'

'Now then. The uncle isn't here to chat, he's working.'

Donovan was reluctant to leave. He peered at Cupido in the hope of getting a glimpse of the gun. Then he went up the stairs.

'You have a nice place.'

'Thanks. It's a rental, but we love it. If I can just get another job around here . . . Donovan is in a good school. Coffee? I only have instant, sorry.'

'That will be nice, thanks.'

'Did you find anything?' she asked over her shoulder as she filled the kettle with water.

'Maybe. Richter . . .' He had to change gears, adjust his tone of voice, for to him the murder victim was also a criminal now, but to her he was still a deceased employer. 'It seems to us that he made a lot of money in China, and . . .'

'In China?' Frowning, astonished, so that the water ran out of the kettle spout.

'He never said anything? About his travels?'

'He talked a lot about his travels. How crazy he was about the Far East. How hard-working the people were. But not a word about money.' She turned off the tap.

'Anyway that's not why I'm here. It's about Rick Grobler.'

Again she stopped what she was doing and looked at him. 'You're kidding.'

'No, he's not a prime suspect any more. His car and phone tested clean. It's about the database. Do you know if he's made any progress yet? In his quest to find the leak.'

'Why?' she asked sternly.

''Cause now it's pertinent to the case.'

'How is it pertinent to the case?'

'It's complicated . . .'

'Why don't you ask him yourself?'

'After Thursday . . . He's not going to fall into my arms, if you know what I'm saying.'

'You were like the Gestapo on Thursday. That white detective who had the cheek to tell me I wasn't shocked enough over Ernst's death . . .'

'He had a bad week . . .'

'So you keep telling me.'

'Will you be able to help? With Grobler?' He wanted to say, it looks as if you have a special bond, but she would know it was jealousy, and that would let the cat out of the bag.

She was busy measuring instant coffee into two mugs with a teaspoon. 'It's going to take some grovelling on your part. And you don't look like the sort of *klong* who is that good at grovelling.'

**Transcript of interview: Advocate Susan
Peires with Mr Francois du Toit**

*Wednesday, 24 December; 1604 Huguenot Chambers,
40 Queen Victoria Street, Cape Town*

FdT: Then I told him there was nothing I could do. I didn't have the money. All that I made on the deal was put into the farm and San's restaurant and into the next crop. I might be able to help him next year sometime, when my cash flow improved, with a hundred thousand or so. Then he said he needed the money now. I must go and borrow it. He basically lost his cool; I could see this guy was desperate now. So I asked him where all his money had gone? And he said things didn't work out so well with the business. Please, I had to help him.

Then I said no, I wasn't going to borrow the money to lend to him. And if he couldn't wait then he would just have to tell the world. But then everyone would know what he'd been up to too.

I just hoped he couldn't see how I was shaking inside. Because if it all came out now . . . This is a big year; I've just released my first wine. I went to New York and London to launch it. I'm still waiting to hear if I can get distribution, we worked very hard . . . If all this came out now . . . I'll never recover . . .

SP: And then?

FdT: Then he swore at me and said I would regret it. And he left. The next thing, I read in the newspapers that he's disappeared. I believed then he had run away, you know, from his creditors. And I thought that was also a way out, and I felt a bit bad that I hadn't been able to help him. And then, last week, they found his body, and it's a helluva thing, with all his clients' names on the internet, and the whole world wanting to know who murdered him . . .

SP: Mr du Toit, you never saw him again after he left the farm alive? On . . . Monday 24 November, is that correct?

FdT: That's right.

SP: That's . . . When did he disappear?

FdT: That Thursday the news broke, but he went missing on Wednesday already.

SP: And you had no, absolutely no, further contact with him?

FdT: That's right.

SP: Then why are you here?

FdT: My mother . . . The day he was there, when he came to ask me for money. I think my mother overheard us.

Griessel phoned the first number on the list, the only one who wasn't an Alibi client.

A man answered quickly. 'Hello?'

'Is that Mr Peter McLean?'

'Yes? Who's speaking?' A Cape Flats accent.

'My name is Benny Griessel, I am calling from the Police Directorate for Priority Crimes . . .'

'Is it about Sammy? I told you last time, Sammy doesn't work here any more. Let him sleep it off, I'm not coming to fetch him.'

'No, Mr McLean, we are investigating the murder of Ernst Richter . . .'

'Who?'

'Ernst Richter. We have on record that he phoned you, on Friday the twenty-third of May this year . . .'

'Twenty-third of May?' Annoyance in his voice now.

'That's right, we . . .'

'You want me to remember who phoned me . . . what is it . . . six, seven months ago?'

'We want to ask you if you would come and talk to us about the call, please. Our offices are in Bell . . .'

'Vernon, is that you? *Fok* knows, Vernon, you nearly had me. Nice one, you can go work for Candid Camera now. Schustered. Twenty-third of May, *nogal* . . .'

'Mr McLean, my name is Benny Griessel of the Hawks. If you want to call me back . . .'

'The Hawks? Now you're from the Hawks?'

'Yes, mister, the DPCI, the Hawks . . .'

'Vernon, it's not you . . .'

'Mr McLean, call me back. Here is the number.' He read it out slowly and emphatically.

A silence, then: 'I could swear it was Vernon trying to Schuster me. Listen, pally, it's Sunday, my mother-in-law is here for lunch and I have to go carve the leg of lamb. I don't know this Griessel *ou*, never heard of him.'

'*My* name is Benny Griessel. The victim was Ernst Richter, the man who ran Alibi dot co dot za. His death has been in the news over the past few days.'

'That thing the farmer's wife shot her husband over yesterday, that thing in the *Rapport?*' he asked in surprise.

Liebenberg had told Griessel that a woman in Bela-Bela had shot her cattle farmer husband yesterday, after his name appeared on the leaked Alibi client list. The farmer was in a critical condition, the wife under arrest.

'That's right. Ernst Richter. He phoned you on the twenty-third of May, according to his cellphone records.'

'Why?'

'What do you mean?'

'Why did he phone me? I don't know the man.'

'You can't remember such a phone call?'

'Pally, do you know how many people phone me every day? I am the only manager left at VBC; they phone me like it's going out of fashion . . .'

'You don't know Ernst Richter at all?'

'Now I know him, when you said it's that *Rapport ou* that was shot by his wife . . .'

'No, no, it's not . . . Mr McLean, thank you, thank you very much. Enjoy your lunch.'

Cupido listened to Desiree Coetzee phone Tricky Ricky Grobler. She was one tough cookie, that he already knew, but when she talked to Grobler there was a softer side, a patience and he heard a little playful-ness – a flirtatious touch even? – in her voice. Again he wondered – was Tricky the current or the next whitey in her life?

He heard her say: 'The detective would like to talk to you.' And then she said 'Yes', a few times and 'I don't know', and 'I understand, Rick, I understand that very well . . .'

She looked at Cupido and shook her head slightly, to say the conversation wasn't going well. She said: 'What if I'm there too? Will you talk to him if I am there?'

Eventually: 'Yes, I promise. Thanks, Rick.'

She rang off, looked dubiously at the phone in her hand. 'He's not keen, that's for sure.'

'But he will come?'

'Yes. He says he's going to shower first.' She put the cellphone down on the breakfast counter, shifted the two coffee mugs to the middle, the sugar bowl too. 'Come, sit,' she invited him and took a carton of milk out of the fridge.

He sat at the counter.

She took her place on the tall chair opposite him and pointed at the milk and sugar: 'Help yourself.' She drank her coffee black and bitter, it seemed, because she simply picked up her mug and blew on it.

'Let me tell you about Ricardo Grobler,' she said then. 'When I began at Alibi . . . That place is really all programmers, that's the heart and soul, the rest are just support staff, actually. And programmers are a breed of their own. Very exclusive, very male dominant, if you don't know about MySQL and PostgreSQL and DDL and DML, then you're the village idiot, and they show you no respect. And there I come, a coloured, *and* a girl. MBA or not, I tick all the wrong boxes, so they show me no respect. So I called this meeting with them all; I wanted to lay down the law, but I made absolutely no headway. Then Rick Grobler stands up. Now you have to understand, he's the senior programmer there; he's a bit of a legend because of his freelance work, he carries a lot of weight. And Ricardo says this attitude ends now. He told them he had worked at quite a few companies, and nobody treats their employees better. They were well paid, and Desiree there in front, she has to make this business work, and she's qualified to do it. Give her a chance. Show some respect. So that we can keep getting paid.'

She sipped her coffee carefully. 'That was a speech that Ernst should have made, but he was too much of a people pleaser, and he was too scared to upset the programmers, because they already looked down on him, because of his smart-aleck techie T-shirts and his wannabe attitude. But Ricardo Grobler stepped up to the plate.'

Another sip of coffee.

'He's an odd one,' she said. 'I'll give you that. And a bit of a sad one. He has this social interaction problem, like in zero social intelligence. He will sit there all morose in a meeting, but if anything is interesting to him, then he gushes on and on. You can't get him to stop. I think it's from too much sitting alone in front of a computer, for too many years. He sees a shrink, once a week; he's working on it . . .'

'And the schoolboy crush . . . ?' asked Cupido.

'Yes,' she sighed. 'Social outcasts like Ricardo . . . When you show a little empathy, they grab onto it big time. It can get complicated; you have to manage it nicely. And I think I've always done that.'

Music to his ears. 'So how do I approach him?'

She shrugged. 'He lost face badly. Everyone at Alibi knows that the *Cape Times* was writing about him. Those are his peers, and you humiliated him . . .'

'That's not true. We didn't cuff him, and we took him out the back . . .'

'Explain that to him,' she said and took a big gulp of coffee.

There was one advantage to carrying out an investigation on the holy Sabbath.

If you phoned a man – and they were men, without exception – who was an Alibi client, and you gave him the choice of coming to the DPCI offices, he grabbed it. They all did. And they came without legal representation, because it was Sunday, and lawyers are expensive on Sundays, or else they were simply unreachable.

There were four left to contact after Griessel had his surreal conversation with Peter McLean.

All four were wealthy – a fast food king with seven KFC concessions, an actuary at a big life insurance company in Pinelands, the owner of four massive scrapyards in Stikland, and a property developer in Somerset West.

Three of them admitted that they had received a call from an unknown person, on the date in question – someone who had tried to blackmail them. Three of them refused to pay, for more or less the same reason: once you paid a blackmailer, there was a very strong possibility that the demands would not end there. So you took a chance. As the KFC man put it: 'I called his bluff. And he threw in his hand.'

The fourth was the scrapyard owner. He was a not a sophisticated man. He was overweight, with small piggy eyes and massive hands. There was dirt under his nails. '*Ja*, I paid the *donner*. Fifty thousand rand. Cash. What could I do? My Vera would have shot me, like that cattle farmer at Bela-Bela yesterday – she's one helluva jealous woman. And if I made a bank transfer, Vera would have seen it. She does our books . . . But I put a note to him in the envelope with the money. I wrote to him, I'm going to find you, you *bliksem*, and I'm going to slowly *moer* you to death with a shifting spanner if you threaten me again.'

'How did you hand over the money?'

'I posted it, to PostNet in Stellenbosch. For attention: Martinus Grundlingh. Then I looked for a Martinus Grundlingh in the phone book and on Google, but I couldn't find anything.'

'Did you know it was Ernst Richter?'

'No, how would I know it was him behind this thing? The *drol* said he was Grundlingh.'

'Did he want a bank transfer?'

'*Jong, ja*, I don't remember all the details, I think I pretty quickly said I will send you cash.'

'And you didn't hear from him again?'

'No. He must have been scared off by the shifting spanner business.'

'Where were you on the evening of Wednesday the twenty-sixth of November?'

'I was at home. With my Vera. But if you want to check with her, you'd better tell her some lie. I don't want to be shot.'

What gave Cupido the final assurance that Tricky Ricky Grobler was not the whitey in Desiree Coetzee's life was the fact that young Donovan didn't know the man.

Grobler arrived in an old Citi Golf.

'And *this* car?' asked Desiree.

'It's my neighbour's. They' – and he pointed an accusing finger at Cupido – 'still have mine.'

'We'll go and fetch it now, Rick,' said Cupido conciliatory.

'Now, *ja*. Now that you want something. Now I'm Rick. But Thursday, then I was Tricks.'

'That is just how we work. I'm not going to apologise. You were a legitimate suspect, with that angry email. I can't take responsibility for that.'

Cupido caught Desiree's eye, saw that she was trying to show him this was not the right approach. And he thought, it's the truth, why should I lie now?

'You are going to apologise to me,' said Rick Grobler stubbornly. 'You are going to say you're sorry in front of everyone at Alibi. If you ever want to find out who leaked the database, that is.'

81

Transcript of interview: Advocate Susan
Peires with Mr Francois du Toit

Wednesday, 24 December; 1604 Huguenot Chambers,
40 Queen Victoria Street, Cape Town

FdT: My office on the farm . . . It's in the old cellar building. Pa sub-divided it – into an office, bathroom and storeroom. We keep a lot of supplies in the storeroom for the labourers: sugar and flour and tinned food, things like that. Ma was visiting us, because my son Guillaume was born six weeks ago and she comes over to help San . . . Ma must have come to fetch something, because I saw her walking away . . .

    I walked Richter to his car. Then I went back to the office, just to calm down before I went back into the house. I was standing look-ing out of the window, still upset about the whole thing. My window was half open, about forty-five degrees, so I could see the reflection if someone came out of the storeroom. And then Ma came out, holding some things in her hands. But the thing is, when she came out, she looked towards the office first. I don't know . . . It was like she was afraid I would see her . . .

SP: Would she have been able to hear what you were discussing?

FdT: That's what I was wondering. So I turned on the radio in the office, about as loud as someone would speak, and I went into the storeroom, and stood there listening. It's possible. Definitely possi-ble. I . . . It's hard to remember how loudly we were speaking. I was upset, I think I raised my voice . . .

SP: Mr du Toit, you are telling me you think your mother had some-thing to do with Ernst Richter's death.

FdT: I know, I know . . . Look . . . the police are waiting at my house. I committed a crime; I was involved in illicit international trade. It's going to come out. I need a lawyer. But if they . . . If my mother did anything . . .

SP: How did the police connect you to Ernst Richter?

FdT: I don't have the faintest idea. I went to Agrimark this morning. When I got there, San phoned me and said there was a whole task force of policemen at the house, they were looking for me. Hawks, she said, the man said he was from the Hawks and it was to do with Ernst Richter.

SP: How can they link you to Richter?

FdT: I don't know . . . There were other people involved with the whole wine business, I don't know if any of them . . . That's all that I can think of.

SP: Surely your mother is not capable of . . . Do you really think . . . ?

FdT: My mother . . . Remember the story of Oupa Pierre and the *dop* system. Remember how she handled Paul's psychopathy. My mother is a doer; my mother is . . . You don't mess with her. And how can you blame her when life has treated her and her family so harshly, and perhaps she says, up to here and no further. You will not send another son of mine to jail, you will not ruin my grand-son's life as well . . . That's why I told you everything from the beginning, from Oupa Jean onwards, so you can understand the whole history that lies behind this. So that you can . . . I don't know, I suppose I'm looking for extenuating circumstances for myself, and for my mother . . .

SP: How could she know about the French wine?

FdT: I don't know . . . She must have wondered how I got my start. She hinted once or twice that she would love to know, but I said it was all down to that vintage of 2012 . . . I thought then that she believed me.

82

That Sunday didn't end with a bang, but a whimper.

Vaughn Cupido had lost face in front of Desiree Coetzee. He'd had to swallow his pride – visibly and with great difficulty – and promise Tricky Ricky Grobler he would apologise to him in front of the whole Alibi team.

And Grobler said: 'Do it first, then we'll talk again.'

And then Cupido had to leave.

At least the boy asked, when he got to his car: 'Are you coming back again, uncle?'

'Maybe . . .'

On the road back to Bellville he thought he should have gone straight to Grobler. He shouldn't have involved Desiree in it. Look where that had got him. Bloody fool, couldn't wait to see the chick. You must think, Vaughn, you must think. But no, head over heels in love, then you think like an idiot.

Main problem was he said he would apologise, 'cause why he wanted to show Desiree he was a modern man, not just some macho guy.

And now he would have to eat humble pie in front of all those people. When he knew true as God he had nothing to apologise for.

He found Griessel still at work. Benna was doing paperwork, writing reports on all the interrogations. Benna looked the way Cupido felt. Down and out. Then he already knew . . .

He sat down with a sigh opposite his colleague. 'Hit me with the bad news.'

Griessel told him.

'This thing is going nowhere, Benna. First JOC chance I get and it's a *fokkop*.'

'The McLean number, the one who isn't an Alibi client. He says he doesn't know Richter . . . that's the one I'm still wondering about.'

'Do you believe him?'

'Yes ... The problem is, the call lasted ninety-four seconds. A minute and a half. It doesn't sound long, but I timed it just now on my watch ...' Griessel picked up his cellphone. 'I'm going to call you. Just play along, then we see how long it takes. You're Vaughn Cupido, but you don't know who's calling, you don't recognise my voice. Just talk the way you would handle a call like that ...'

'Okay.'

Griessel called. His colleague's phone rang. When Cupido answered with 'Hello, Vaughn speaking', he checked the second hand on his watch and said: 'Hello, can I talk to Pietie, please?'

'Pietie? Pietie who?'

'Pietie Pieterse.'

'Sorry *pêllie*, I think you have the wrong number.'

'There's no Pietie Pieterse?'

'No, this is the Hawks.'

'Oh. Okay. Sorry. Bye.'

He checked the watch again. 'Twenty-six seconds.'

'The dude could be busy on another phone, and keep the wrong number on hold.'

'What do you do when you ring a wrong number? What do you do straight after that?'

'I phone the right number.'

'Exactly,' said Griessel. 'But the next number that Richter phoned on that secret phone, was a whole two days later. A completely different number.'

'Weird,' said Cupido. 'What exactly did this McLean say?'

Griessel told him everything he could remember.

'And he sounded genuine? It wasn't an act?'

'If it was an act, he deserves an Oscar.'

'And you don't mean the Pistorius version.'

Griessel smiled, for the first time in days. 'No, I don't mean that one.'

'Maybe it was first someone else's number. Maybe it was a client who put a wrong number in the database. Maybe Richter forgot it was a secret phone, and he wanted to call garden services at ABC ...'

'VBC ...'

'Whatever. Shit happens. Let's move on.'

'Maybe we'll get something with the Stellenbosch station people. Vusi brought all the numbers here to IMC, they said maybe the day after tomorrow. It's a lot of work.'

But they both knew the chances were slim. There were a lot of drug lords and gang members with unlisted, unknown cellphone numbers.

Both of them were reluctant to go back to their own houses, to this Sunday's solitude. They sat and talked and brought the docket up to date, until well past four.

Griessel phoned Doc on the way home.

'Are you still dry?'

'Yes, Doc.'

'I'll phone her. But you'll have to be patient, there's a lot of damage.'

'All right, Doc.'

Then he drove to the city. There was a meeting of Alcoholics Anonymous, five o'clock on a Sunday at the Union Congregational Church on the corner of Kloof Nek and Eaton. The Green Door group, as they called themselves. A few blocks from the house. He and Alexa had been there a few times. Maybe she would come tonight.

She wasn't there.

He stood up first. He walked to the front. He said: 'My name is Benny Griessel, and I am an alcoholic.'

'Hello, Benny,' they said.

'I know I am powerless against alcohol. I know my life is out of control. I have gone one day without a drink.'

There was a Woolies ready meal on the kitchen table: Luxury Smoked Trout en Croute, with a note in her handwriting on how to cook it.

And three kisses.

How did she know he hadn't been at home? How did she know when to come here?

Three kisses. That was better than yesterday. It gave him hope.

He fetched his bass guitar. He put on Cream's *Fresh Cream* on Alexa's hi-fi system, so that he could play along with the incomparable Jack Bruce.

83

The Huguenot Chambers building was casting a long shadow over the Company Gardens as Advocate Susan Peires stood looking out of the window. 'Let me think first,' she had said to Francois du Toit.

He sat patiently waiting, staring at his hands clasped on the table in front of him.

It had been a long time since she'd been taken so unawares. Her suspicions had migrated from father to brother to Francois himself. She had not seen the revelation of the mother coming at all. Maybe she should have, when he'd told her of Helena's rebellion against her own father and the *dop* system. She should have known that wasn't for no reason.

Why wasn't she convinced?

She turned to him.

'I'm going to ask you one last time. Are you telling the truth?'

His utter stillness, the way he didn't look up – just nodded his head slightly – was what made her decide to believe him.

She sat down again.

'You have problems. If the police have sufficient evidence, there is a strong prima facie case against you. You participated in a fraudulent act and Richter tried to blackmail you just before he died. You have a strong motive, because you have a lot to lose if it all comes out. And the only other suspect that you know of is your mother. You don't want to talk about her.'

'No.'

'We don't know what they know, and the only way to find out is to go back to the farm. I suggest I go with you. But there are a lot of things we must agree on before we go. You have the right to remain silent and you will have to use it. It's bad news that there's a whole swarm of Hawks on the farm. They don't normally turn up in force unless they are ready to make an arrest. But an arrest gives us the opportunity to find out how strong the case against you is. My advice is, leave all the talking to me . . .'

'I am guilty of the wine fraud . . .'

'You are innocent until the opposite is proven in court, should it ever make it to court. The jurisdiction is complicated; the organiser of the scheme is dead. And in my experience no industry likes to admit that ten thousand items of expensive product that have already been sold are fakes. I would be surprised if you are prosecuted.'

84

Monday 22 December. Three days before Christmas.

The doldrums.

Even though Captain Vaughn Cupido woke with a mission.

The doldrums because the Richter case was at a standstill.

There were storm winds elsewhere: a new case, four bodies found in a house in Kraaifontein. Crime in the Cape of Good Hope had no consideration for the festive season, no sense of rhythmic ebb and flow. The new murder-flame drew the usual moths – the local SAPS, then the media and the Hawks and Forensics and ambulances and curious onlookers. New energy, a new sensation, new headlines that temporarily pushed Ernst Richter and the Alibi clients off the front pages.

A new investigative team: Liebenberg and Fillander and Ndabeni went to support other colleagues in Kraaifontein so as to make the first seventy-two hours count.

The Richter docket was in the doldrums and in the hands of the miserable Benny Griessel and man-with-a-mission Vaughn Cupido.

He woke with a realisation, a moment of clarity, with deep insight. He was Vaughn Cupido. In love or not, he was what he was. Direct and honest and very unconventional. Unpretentious.

Your greatest problem with relationships is always this initial period, when each party put their very best foot forward, when they tried to be what the other one wanted them to be.

Now, that was dishonest, it was pretentious, and he wasn't going to fall into that trap.

That's why he was now on a mission.

He reported back at the morning parade, comprehensively and professionally, doldrums be damned. From Brigadier Musad Manie and Major Mbali Kaleni he heard that there was nothing but deathly silence on the Chinese diplomatic front. He asked Benny

Griessel – whose eyes were a bit brighter this morning, his weathered face a little less red – to keep an eye on IMC, and on the lookout for the reports expected from the Hawks in Gauteng, the Free State and KwaZulu-Natal. Then he drove to Stellenbosch.

He walked into Alibi and bounded up the stairs two at a time to Desiree's office: he could see her at her desk, concentrating on the PC screen. He rapped his knuckles on the glass door, pushed it open and closed it behind him, all before she could even say hello.

'I like you,' he said.

'Excuse me?' she said.

He realised he was leaning right over her desk. It must seem pretty aggressive, he thought and sat down, now that he had her attention. 'I like you – a lot,' he added. 'But I scheme you've already worked that out for yourself.'

She started to speak, but he didn't want her to say anything just yet. 'I don't expect you to say anything; I just ask that you listen. Homicide investigation is a rough business. It's not for sissies. Man's got to do what a man's got to do. And there's one thing that this man's got to do and that is catch the killer. And if that means I have to get *rof* with an *ou*, then I get *rof* with an *ou*. But now I like you *kwaai*, and I start second-guessing myself. I'm not true to myself, *versta' jy?*'

She stared at him, eyes wide.

'So let me be true to myself. I will not apologise to Tricky Ricky Grobler, not in front of him, not in front of you, and not in front of all these people. 'Cause why, if I apologise, it will just be to impress you with a quality that I don't have. And that quality is pretension. That's not my scene. What you see is what you get. Rough around the edges, I come from Mitchells Plain, after all, but here inside I'm one of the good guys . . .'

Again she wanted to speak. He held up a palm to stop her. 'When this is all over I am going to phone you, and I'm going to ask you out on a proper date. Candlelit dinner for two, at a place a policeman can afford. And then you can politely decline, and I'll take the hint. Or you can gracefully accept, and then I am going to woo you, all romantic and proper. 'Cause I like you *kwaai*; you're beautiful and classy and you care about people, and you're smart enough to know when an *ou* is pretending, which I'm not going to do.'

'I see,' she said, her voice neutral.

'You ain't seen nothing yet, but let's leave it there. I'm going to talk to Tricks Grobler now. I will be Vaughn Cupido, Captain of the Hawks, investigating a murder. Nothing more, nothing less.'

Miserable Benny Griessel. The tedium scared him: the sitting and waiting, knowing how the Demon Drink always finds work for thirsty mouths.

He walked up and down to IMC, kept an eye on his email for the reports from other centres, went to ask Mbali Kaleni four times if there was any news from the Chinese. And he thought about the two miniature bottles of Jack that were still in his drawer, the remnants of Friday's scheme.

He reminded himself of the complexity that came with a life of lies; if you drank on the sly, you had to hide and deceive. It took so much concentration and energy, and he forced himself to be grateful that he was past that, that he was, albeit shaken and uncomfortable, back on the wagon.

He thought about the two little bottles in his drawer. How could he get rid of them?

He wondered how Alexa had known he was at the bar. And how she knew when he wasn't at home.

Why hadn't Doc phoned with news from Alexa?

Would he have to start looking for a new place to stay? Now, at Christmastime?

He walked back to IMC.

In the privacy of Richter's empty office Cupido asked Rick Grobler: 'You did get your car, *nè*?'

'I did.'

'Cool. Everything okay with your car?'

'Yes.'

'Cool. Then we're all square, me and you.' And as tactfully as he could, Vaughn Cupido told Tricky Ricky that there would be no apology. If Grobler hadn't written the threatening email, the Hawks wouldn't have had to treat him as a suspect. He got what he deserved. And that was how life worked, everything taken into account, at the end of the day. And here was how things were going to happen: The people who published the database were guilty of theft. A criminal offence. The law worked like this. If a member of the public withheld information about a criminal offence, that member of the public could be prosecuted. It wasn't a threat, it was just a statement of fact.

But here was the offer: If Grobler could identify the guilty parties, Cupido would make sure that Rick Grobler would get all the praise and credit in public, in the press and in the programmers' office at Alibi.

'That's the deal, take it or leave it.'

The DPCI Commissioner phoned Brigadier Musad Manie from Pretoria, to hear whether anything had been done about the illegal publication of the Alibi database, which had done so much damage to the country and its reputation.

Manie, in his deep voice and with great patience, explained that his team had done as much as they could, but it had not yet produced results. Was there any news from the Chinese?

No, there was no news.

The doldrums.

IMC had to process the Kraaifontein murders; the Richter case was put aside. Griessel went trawling through the docket again. And caught a small fish: in his interview yesterday the scrapyard owner had said he'd sent the package of money to PostNet Stellenbosch, to a Martinus Grundlingh.

He looked up the PostNet number and phoned. Yes, they said, if you collected a letter or a parcel you had to show an ID, unless you had a post office box there. No, there was no Martinus Grundlingh renting a post box from them.

When Cupido came back, he told him Ernst Richter most probably had a false ID: Martinus Grundlingh.

'Maybe another secret cellphone? It bugs me that the one he used to blackmail went off the air so suddenly. I scheme he was worried that someone might trace him. So he dumped it and got a new one.'

'That's possible. I'll ask IMC to do a RICA search.'

'And then we go home, because they won't be doing that today, or tomorrow.'

★   ★   ★

When he arrived home and opened the door, his cellphone beeped. An SMS from Alexa: *In J'burg. Order pizza.*

'*Fok*,' he said and walked out onto the veranda, looked up and then down the street, and at the houses opposite and next door. Could she see him? How had she known he had walked in *now*?

She wouldn't lie about Johannesburg; did she have someone watching him?

He walked into the street.

Saw nothing.

Walked back in to order pizza and play his bass guitar. And think about the two little bottles in his drawer at work.

85

Two days before Christmas – 23 December – and Cape Town was a seething, scurrying ants' nest, a massed press and rush as hordes of local and international holidaymakers descended on the city in their tens of thousands.

They had to buy their last gifts and cards and wrapping paper, and the turkeys and chickens and hams and legs of lamb for Christmas Eve or Christmas Day feasts. Or they streamed to the beach, or up Table Mountain, or to Cape Point or the wine estates, to enjoy the sunshine, to have fun, take selfies, because in the Cape you could never be sure when the wind or clouds would roll in to ruin your fun. It was a city of four seasons in one day, as fortune willed.

Griessel left early to avoid it all. Also because he had slept badly, unused these days to being alone, doing midnight battle with the demons and the bottle, and his anxiety over whether Alexa would return.

He had to do some shopping of his own. The Weet-Bix was finished, the milk too, the coffee tin was almost empty. Those were things that Alexa took care of and he didn't know if she was ever coming back. Nor could he blame her, because if you are an alcoholic, and you live with an alcoholic, it can be like crossing a deep chasm on the thinnest of cables, without a safety net.

Doc had said if you are forty-six years old and you go back to drinking uncontrollably again, it'll be the death of you. Your blood pressure will shoot up, and you will suffer uncontrollable diarrhoea. You will develop alcoholic cardiomyopathy of the heart, alcoholic hepatitis of the liver, inflammation of the pancreas, and you'll fuck up your stomach lining, your small intestine and your kidneys.

Alexa was a fraction older than he was. She was aware of all these things, and her head wasn't filled with altruistic depression, and survivor and other collective guilts. She wasn't on a mission to destroy herself.

He wouldn't blame her if she didn't come back.

Cupido got up in a bad mood. Not enough sleep; a restless night. He was cross with himself. Bull in a china shop, walking in like that and telling Desiree I like you *kwaai*, I'm going to woo you. *Jirre*, Vaughn, impulse control had never been his strong suit.

And he was JOC leader of a dead docket, and the day stretched out before him like a vacuum.

And he said to himself, it's par for the course. In the movies and on TV a cop's life was all action and satisfaction, but in real life, things worked a little differently: 10 per cent action, 90 per cent drudgery, grind, admin.

This is the 90 per cent, *pappie*. Suck it up.

And he did. He and Benny Griessel did the drudgery and grind, and the admin. And the last minute Christmas shopping. Until 16.56 on the 23 December.

Then they hit the 10 per cent.

They were sitting in Vaughn's office, a packet of Speckled Eggs on the desk, eating and chatting. Cupido was on the point of saying Let's go. Because he struggled with impulse control, he wanted to ask Benna, What do you do with a dolly who is out of your league, but you think about her night and day; he please just wanted to talk to someone, get it off his chest.

The *tsip-tsap* of Mbali Kaleni's almost silent, sensible shoes came down the passage. They stopped talking and shot each other a meaningful glance. Cupido thought this is either very good news or very bad news, if she's in this much of a hurry.

She came in, papers in hand. She looked at the Speckled Eggs and Cupido thought he saw lust in those eyes, just for a second. But she pulled herself together.

'All the way from China,' she said, holding the document out to him.

'*Jissis*,' he said before he could stop himself. 'Sorry, Major. Thanks, Major,' he said, up and out of the chair in an instant. He took it from her, looked at it.

'Look at the last page,' said Mbali, ignoring the swearword. Which meant that it was good news. 'The account belonged to a company called Qin Trading. It was registered as an import export company in Guangdong in China. It existed from December 2011 to March 2013. Both the company and the bank account. The other pages are all the payments received and paid out.'

Griessel stood up to look over Cupido's shoulder at the document. From the black stripe down the right-hand side and the quality of the type he could tell it was a fax. A header with the bank's name, and the company's name. and under that tables with dates and codes and amounts. Of which he understood very little. Here and there someone had circled a few figures in ink.

Cupido apparently also didn't understand, because he said: 'How do we know what these codes are?'

'I've left a message for Benedict, but he's on holiday,' said Kaleni, referring to Bones in her customary fashion, and came around the desk. She pressed a finger on the document. 'But look at the currency, in the right-hand column. I've circled all the payments that went through in South African rand. See, the ZAR . . .'

'Okay,' said Cupido and Griessel, a deep-voiced chorus.

'The column just to the left is the dollar amount. There were three amounts that corresponded to the amounts Bones identified in Richter's account. See? Here, here, and here. Hundred and twenty five thousand dollars, twice. And two fifty.'

'Right.'

'But there are four more payments converted to ZAR. I've underlined them. The total is about two million rand. And they are not to Ernst Richter's account.'

Cupido looked at the codes of those payments. They were indecipherable. He quickly glanced at his watch and had to bite back the '*fok*' on the tip of his tongue.

'The banks are closed for the day. Even if we can get hold of Bones, we'll have to wait until tomorrow.'

'Yes,' said Mbali.

Cupido picked up the packet of Speckled Eggs and held it out to her.

'No, thanks. Prof Tim says that's poison,' she said.

★   ★   ★

Bones called back, just before six. 'I'm on vacation here, *nè*. I promised Baba no work; she'll kill me . . . I'm not the only guy at Statutory Crimes.'

'Baba' was an abbreviation of his wife's name, Babalwa.

'But you are the best,' said Cupido, because he knew where Boshigo's weakness lay. 'So where did you take the missus?'

'Hermanus. She wants to do the sea and sand and moonlight thing.'

'Hermanus? You're a darkie, Bones. That's all white, all Boer territory.'

'Not any more. Listen, Baba's in the shower, so can we make this quick?'

Cupido told him about the Chinese bank statements and the indecipherable codes.

'Snap them with your phone and send them to me. I'll see what I can do. Maybe early tomorrow morning, Baba is going for an aromatherapy massage at the Birkenhead.'

'Thanks, Bones.'

On the kitchen table was a packet of cold meat, Woolies Wafer Thin Selection, beside a packet of Low GI Mediterranean Chickpea Salad, and Griessel could swear it was still cold, fresh out of the fridge.

There was a note.

I am glad you are dry again. xxx

86

They walked together out of the lift of Huguenot Chambers in Queen Victoria Street, and Advocate Susan Peires said to Francois du Toit, 'You said your mother is small of stature.'

He stopped and looked at her. 'That's right.'

'And she's sixty-one now?'

'Yes . . .'

'She wouldn't have been able to do it alone, would she?'

'I . . . I also . . . You think so many things when you're stressed, when you wonder . . . The labourers would do anything for her. She is like a mother to them. If she went and talked to one or two of them, told them that . . . I don't know, maybe if she said their future and their children's futures were on the line . . .'

Peires took that in, and nodded. 'Let's go. Where are you parked?'

He pointed. 'Just down here . . .'

'I'm in a red Jaguar. Wait until I come, then I'll drive behind you.'

'Okay.' He turned and walked away, took out his cellphone and turned it back on, for the first time since that morning.

Peires walked to the stairs to get to the basement where her car was. She was already thinking about the mother and the labourers, suddenly quite sceptical about it all, about his story.

She was already down the first flight of stairs when she heard him call. 'Advocate!' his urgent voice falling strangely on her ear. She stopped and called: 'Here!'

He appeared at the top of the steps, holding up his cellphone. 'I think you need to see this . . .'

87

On the 24th of December the ship of the Ernst Richter investigation sailed out of the doldrums.

The first brisk breeze in the sails was the deciphering of the Chinese bank statements – thanks to Babalwa Boshigo's aromatherapy massage, and her husband's knowledge.

But the sudden squall that made all the difference was the desire for drink that overwhelmed Benny Griessel.

Bones phoned Cupido just before eight, with the news that the four payments from the Qin Trading account were made to a person or a company at the Stellenbosch branch of First National Bank, with the indecipherable abbreviation DTFT. The bank would give him full details, if he could produce a warrant, of course.

So Cupido headed first to the Bellville magistrate's court to get the warrant, and then raced through to Stellenbosch to be at the door of the bank when it opened.

This morning Griessel was – thanks to the holiday city traffic – a few minutes too late to go with Cupido. Now he was sitting and waiting impatiently in his office. With the two miniature Jack Daniel's bottles haunting him. Idleness and the Demon Drink were now dancing together. He had to get rid of the bottles. He couldn't just toss them in his waste paper basket; he would have to make another plan.

At ten past nine he made up his mind. He would discard them in the garbage bins behind the DPCI office.

He closed his door, opened the drawer, scooped up the bottles, felt the cool glass in his palm. He shoved one each into his jacket pockets to stop them clinking, in case he ran into Major Kaleni in the passage.

He opened the door, went out. The passage was empty. He walked quickly towards the stairs.

His cellphone rang.

Fok.

He stopped, took out his phone, saw that it was Vaughn calling.

'Vaughn?' he answered.

'Benna, we've got him. The account belongs to the Du Toit Family Trust, and the Du Toit Family Trust belongs to, lo and behold, a wine farmer, Francois du Toit. Klein Zegen is the name of the estate, it's just here, other side the town.'

The name Klein Zegen rang a bell. Griessel searched for its echo in his memory banks. He knew he'd heard the name when he'd already knocked back a few, but he would find it. Cellphone at the ear, in the middle of the passage, he mouthed the words. 'Klein Zegen, Klein Zegen . . .' he repeated to jog his memory.

'*Jis*, I think what we must do . . .'

'There was a bottle . . . No, I think more than one bottle of Klein Zegen wine in Richter's drinks cabinet.'

'Benna, it all makes sense. The payments, the forensic detail about pesticides, and the baling twine and the plastic and the vine leaves – all that says wine estate to me. We must just find that jacaranda tree. I have a theory, but I'll tell you when you get here. Can you organise a search warrant for us? I went to magistrate Cynthia Davids this morning for the bank warrant; she already has the details, you can just fill in the new info. And then I scheme, Benna, we hit this guy with the full force of the Hawks, scare the bejaysus out of him. Hear from Mbali if Uncle Frankie and them are still on the Kraaifontein case, get everyone you can. Vusi is the great jacaranda expert, if he can come too. I'll phone Forensics so long, so they can send people. But call me, Benna, I want to orchestrate it so that we all arrive at the same time, if you get my drift.'

Cupido waited for the procession at the same Engen garage where they had bought food during the search of Richter's house.

He addressed them all first, in full JOC leader mode, a man with a new mission. Vusi, Mooiwillem, Griessel and Frank Fillander were there, along with four other Hawks, and Lithpel Davids, for the technology – the cellphones and computers. Thick and Thin from Forensics in their little white bus. Cupido said he had a theory. The wine farmer had imported something from China. Machinery, or harvesters or distillers or whatever shit wine farmers use. And inside those harvesters or barrels or whatever, were drugs. Richter was the middleman, he made contacts in South East Asia, *dagga* smoker that he is, and then he looked for a partner, someone who imports big machines or whatever from China. And then the wine farmer got his two million, and Richter got something like double that. But Richter's money ran out, and he tried a shakedown with Du Toit, just like he tried with all the others.

And that's what got him killed. Under the jacaranda tree.

'*Under the Jacaranda Tree*,' said Arnold, the short fat one from Forensics. 'That could be the name, if they make a film about Ernst Richter one day.'

Cupido looked sternly at Arnold. 'This is serious stuff. We are looking for evidence of the drugs. You swab and test all you have to swab and test. It's eighteen months since the big smuggling operation, but you never know.' Then to the detectives: 'We're looking for the papers from the imports, we're looking for the plastic and the baling twine and the jacaranda tree.'

'And the fungicide,' said Jimmy, the tall, skinny forensic investigator.

'Right,' said Cupido. Then to Lithpel: 'And all the cellphones and laptops and all that jazz.'

They drove in convoy, Cupido in front, because he had the directions, on the Blaauwklippen road. Just beyond the Dornier estate they turned left, and Cupido turned on his siren and flashing blue lights. The road narrowed, up the valley, the mountains brooding and beautiful to the left. The sky was a bright clear blue.

High up on the slopes of the mountain, through a gate, with a sign that said: *Klein Zegen. Wines. Restaurant La Bonne Chère. Traditional French Cuisine.*

The farmyard was beautiful, well-tended, with green lawns and flower beds and shrubs and the elegant Cape Dutch homestead at its centre, the restaurant and outbuildings alongside. Below, towards the river, was a newer structure, large, like a cellar, but carefully designed to blend in with the historic.

A few cars were parked in front of the restaurant. They stopped, Cupido turned the siren off and they all leapt out, except for Thick and Thin from Forensics, who waited to see if there would be shooting.

A woman walked out of the front door of the homestead. Small, frail, somewhere past fifty, maybe sixty, but still attractive, with a thick bush of grey hair. She held a wailing baby in her arms and gave them a look of stern reproach.

Cupido walked up to her, feisty, determined, the warrant in his hand, and opened his mouth to speak.

'*Ag* no, man, why did you have to make such a racket?' asked the woman. 'Now you've gone and woken little Guillaume.'

An anti-climax. Francois du Toit wasn't home, though his wife was. She was very pretty, dressed in her white chef's apron. Not yet thirty. She introduced herself as San, her eyes frightened.

'What's going on?' she asked.

Cupido said they were here about the murder of Ernst Richter. They wanted her husband for questioning, and they had a search warrant that covered the whole farm. Where was her husband?

She was confused. Ernst Richter? Francois? But why? Ernst Richter, the one who had been all over the news?

'Yes, ma'am.'

'But we don't even know him.'

'Ma'am, where is your husband?'

'He went to town. Ernst Richter? We have nothing to do with Ernst Richter.'

But they could see she was worried that perhaps there was something she didn't know.

The older woman with the baby came and took San du Toit by the arm. 'Come in, my child,' she said calmly. 'It's a mistake, they will realise later, it won't help to talk to *these* people now.'

'When will your husband be back?' asked Cupido.

'He'll be back soon,' she said, her voice shaking and let the older woman lead her away.

'Then we will begin our search so long. I ask you to choose one room in the house and stay there. Don't touch anything. And we want someone to show us all the jacaranda trees.'

The older woman stopped. 'Jacaranda trees?'

'That's right,' said Cupido.

She pointed to the side of the house. 'There,' she said. 'That's the only one.'

All the detectives' heads turned. The tree stood at the corner of the house. Beneath it was a lush green lawn.

Thick and Thin from Forensics walked quickly through the outbuildings, stores and the cellar and then phoned Plattekloof for reinforcements, because there was much more work than anyone had anticipated. They began with the cellar, and did their tests while they speculated which Hollywood actors would star in the film *Under the Jacaranda Tree* – and who would play which detective. Mooiwillem was easy: George Clooney. Fillander was definitely Morgan Freeman. Vusi was Denzel Washington. Cupido's casting led to heated debate, until they settled on Chris Rock. They themselves – non-negotiable – were represented by Brad Pitt (Jimmy) and Bradley Cooper (Arnold) respectively, however Jimmy said Zach Galifianakis was his stout colleague to a T. But they kept scratching their heads over Benny Griessel.

Chris Rock and Lithpel Davids set to work on Du Toit's office.

Morgan Freeman and George Clooney searched the house, because they could 'handle angry women the best'.

Griessel was grateful that he could be on the team that walked across the farm looking for the other jacarandas, because none of them believed the aunty with the hair, as Cupido had christened her.

He still had two 50 ml bottles of Jack Daniel's, one in each jacket pocket. In the heat of the moment, when Vaughn phoned him, Griessel had forgotten about his mission to dispose of them and only remembered the whisky when they were already on the road.

Now he could throw them away somewhere between the vines.

But on Klein Zegen the stars never lined up quite the way you planned.

88

He walked down a dirt road, a hand in each jacket pocket, clutching the bottles while his eyes searched for the purple-blue flowers that Vusi had described. 'But it's late in the season, so the flowers may be over, but the blossoms would still be lying under the trees. So look for this shape.' He showed them a photo of a tree on his phone.

Young grapes on the vines, rows and rows of them. The mountains looming behind. The silence: just the birdsong and the buzz of insects. Peaceful. He had been in places like this before – idyllic, breathtaking, you wouldn't believe a murder had been committed here. You couldn't believe that someone's final death scream had gone up from this place.

Don't mess with that stuff now. Follow the shrink's advice.

He turned his attention back to the possible jacaranda trees.

His phone rang sudden and shrill in his pocket, making him jump.

That was the thing with the drying-out process and the medication and poor sleep and the tension of the job and Alexa and all: it put him on edge.

He took out his phone. Recognised the number. Answered.

'Griessel.'

'Captain Benny Griessel? From the Hawks?' A man's voice that he didn't recognise.

'That's right.'

'I'm phoning from the *Son*, Captain. The newspaper.' He spoke the words in a rush, as if he were afraid Griessel would interrupt him. 'I just want to confirm with you where you were last Wednesday night, around six o'clock.'

Benny's heart missed a beat.

What did they know? Why now? *Jissis*, why now that he was dry?

He had to stay calm; he mustn't let the journalist hear what a fright he'd got.

'Where did you get this number?'

'From a contact, Captain. Can you confirm where you were last Wednesday evening?'

Stay calm, But his resistance was low. The implications of a news report about his drunkenness, about his fighting, hammered through him. Much worse, now that he had stopped drinking again and he could see the terrible outcome all the more clearly. Now, just when things with Vaughn were back to normal. When he still had a faint hope of Alexa returning.

He took a deep breath. He didn't want to wait too long before answering, that would suggest certain guilt. 'I am busy with an investigation, sir. Please call Captain John Cloete of the DPCI. He handles the media. Goodbye.'

He ended the call, but his heart kept racing.

What did they know?

He pushed the phone into his jacket pocket. It clinked against the Jack Daniel's.

His phone rang again.

The same number.

Again his fingers brushed against the Jack.

He would drink one, just to calm his nerves.

Not here. There were colleagues around. He clutched the bottle tightly as he walked blindly downhill, to the little stream below. *Can you confirm where you were, last Wednesday evening?* He had to think about the question when his nerves had settled, it was asked in a specific way. First he must just regain control.

He walked fast, stumbled over a stone. *Fok.* There was a place to hide, down by the stream. He was nearly there, he thought, narrowly avoiding walking into a wire fence. He turned right along the fence; there was dense plant growth here. He stopped, looked around. Nobody could see him. Water babbled against the bank beside him. He pulled the bottle out, unscrewed the cap with one swift movement, raised it to his mouth, lifted his head.

That's when he saw the jacaranda tree, across the river. Here and there a pale purple flower still clinging to the branches.

★   ★   ★

Griessel stood transfixed, bottle at his lips, his eyes on the tree barely ten metres from him. Something behind it. It looked like a shed: he saw a metal wall, corrugated iron.

Nothing grew under the tree. Just brown dirt and rotting plant material and those purple-blue flowers.

Secluded. Quiet. Far away from everything.

He looked around him. On the opposite bank of the river a dirt track ran past the tree, towards the shed.

He focused on the area under the tree. Drag a body there and you would get jacaranda flowers and sticks and vine leaves in the back pocket.

He looked at the bottle in his hand.

Can you confirm where you were, last Wednesday evening?

Not 'Were you at the Fireman's Arms?' or 'Were you in the cells at Cape Town Central?'

The journalist was fishing. Like he also did, when questioning a suspect. Clever. And he'd nearly fallen for it.

He let out a long, slow breath. He turned the bottle over and let the alcohol pour out onto the ground at his feet, then threw the empty bottle into the water. Took out the other one, did the same.

Then he walked upstream, looking for a bridge over the river.

He walked at least sixty metres before he found it. He followed the dirt track on the other side of the river and walked downstream back to the jacaranda.

The area under the tree was undisturbed. A month had passed; the possible drag marks would be long gone. But everything looked like it could fit.

He judged that the shed was about ten metres away. He walked up to it. It was a metal structure, big. He walked around the corner of the building, saw the big sliding door, wide enough for a tractor. It was closed, but not locked. He pushed it open. The door groaned.

There was a deep twilight inside. Only a few small windows on the northern side, beams of light falling onto the contents of the shed.

He stepped in. It was hot and the air was filled with strange odours. A tractor, unusually small and narrow – he had seen them in the vineyards. A trailer with a big yellow tank on it. Another implement that he suspected was to remove weeds.

He loosened his tie, uncomfortable in the heat, and waited for his eyes to adjust to the dim light. He saw the shelves against the walls, stacked full. Tins and drums and cans. Irrigation equipment.

He went closer. Portable sprayers, spades and forks. On one shelf pruning shears lay in a neat row, fifty or more of them.

Dark cylinders. He walked to them. Rolls of black plastic.

And below, five big rolls of baling twine. Blood red.

He touched the rolls to make sure, ran his hand across the plastic.

He took a quick look at the drums on the shelf. He couldn't read the labels. He took out his phone, used the torch function.

He saw the words: *Triazole.*

It was here that Richter had been bound and wrapped. The tree outside was the murder scene.

Had to be.

He needed to phone Vaughn, tell him they've just nailed Du Toit. He turned to the door, looking for Vaughn's number.

A figure appeared in the doorway startling Griessel. The man was startled too.

'*Wat maak jy hier?* What are you doing here?' The voice was sharp. A coloured man in overalls.

'Police,' said Griessel.

'Police? Does Meneer know you're here?'

'He's not back yet.'

Griessel saw the sign beside the labourer, just inside the door. It was an advertising board, half a metre wide, fixed to two metal poles, as if made to be pushed into the ground. Green background, white letters. There was a logo of a wine bottle, with four wheels. Something about it drew his attention, but the man was speaking, distracting him.

'What did you say?' asked Griessel.

'I better fetch Meneer,' he answered nervously.

'Is he back?'

'Meneer has been in his office all morning. It's Christmas bonus day today. I'll call him . . .' He turned and walked away.

'What meneer?' Griessel called after him, and wondered whether there was a foreman here.

'Meneer Venske.'

'What does he do here?'

'He's the owner of this farm.'

'Klein Zegen?' asked Griessel.

The labourer stopped for a moment. 'This is Blue Valley, here,' he said indignantly and then began to jog away, clearly upset.

Griessel didn't immediately register the implications; he was staring at the sign. Below the bottle with wheels stood three big letters: *VBC*. And below that: *Vintage Bottling Company*. In even smaller letters: *Estate Mobile Bottling & Labelling. Call Peter McClean*. And a cellphone number.

89

He stood in front of the shed, in the bright sunlight. He was still talking to Cupido on the phone when the labourer returned, along with a tall man in glasses.

'What are you doing on my property?'

Griessel held a hand up in the air to show he would answer soon and said to Cupido: 'The owner is here now. Will you find it? Blue Valley. It's just next door, across the river.'

'I said, what are you doing on my property?' the tall man asked again, his voice and body language aggressive, the indignant land baron. Now Griessel could see he was in his sixties, a powerful man with a hooked nose like a bird's beak under the glasses, and a thick moustache camouflaging a somewhat weak mouth. His skin was weathered by the sun.

'We're on our way,' said Cupido. 'Great work, Benna.'

Griessel rang off. The man was right up against him, intimidating, chest pressing forward.

'I'm from the police, sir.' Griessel put out a hand to greet him. 'Benny Griessel . . .'

The man ignored his hand. 'You have no business here.'

The labourer stood a few steps away and endorsed his employer's words with a nod.

'Are you the farm owner?'

'I am, yes, and I'm telling you now, to get off my farm.'

'I am busy with a murder investigation, and I have just identified the possible murder scene here on your property. What is your name?'

'Where is your permission to come sniffing around here?'

He had seen this kind of behaviour often. The only way to handle it was to remain calm, stay in control. And protect the investigation from attacks that might end up in court.

'My permission is in Articles Twenty-Five and Twenty-Six of the Criminal Procedure Act, sir. Article Twenty-Five point Three says I may access any area without a warrant during an investigation, if there are reasonable grounds to believe that in the circumstances I would obtain a warrant and a delay might hinder the investigation. I ask you again, what is your name?'

His words had the desired effect. The man's shoulders slumped slightly and he stepped back a fraction.

'My name is Dietrich Venske.'

'Mr Venske, I have reason to suspect that Ernst Richter was murdered here on your property. My colleagues are on their way. We are going to cordon off this area, and we are going to obtain a warrant for a full search. We hope we can rely on your cooperation.'

'Ernst Richter? Who is Ernst Richter?' he asked with absolute disgust, as if he was personally insulted by the name. Then he snorted through his nose like a bull and said: 'This is rubbish. I'm going to phone my lawyer.'

Only Cupido and Ndabeni and the men from Forensics came; the rest of the Hawks carried on with their search of Klein Zegen.

'Makes sense,' said Cupido, 'you ambush Richter on your neighbour's land, so that you don't leave evidence on your own farm.'

Griessel just nodded and led him and Vusi to the signboard, which was leaning against the wall just inside the shed door. 'This is the guy Richter phoned on his secret phone. The guy who had never heard of Richter.'

'Well, I'll be damned,' said Cupido.

'I'm going, Vaughn. I'm going to question him.'

'Okay. Take Uncle Frankie along.'

They were still making their way through Stellenbosch when Captain Philip van Wyk of IMC phoned. 'Sorry we took so long, the Kraaifontein thing kept us busy, but I have good news. We found your Martinus Grundlingh in the RICA database. It's another Richter forgery of an ID document and proof of address. He bought a phone with it, in June this year – just after the other clandestine phone went off-air.'

'Thanks, Philip,' said Benny, with feeling.

'We are just waiting for the subpoena to plot the new number.'

'Philip, what I also want to know, is whether the Grundlingh number phoned Peter McLean.'

'We will look. I'll call when we find something.'

They stopped in front of the house in Kuilsriver. Suburban, middle class, neat. On the green lawn three little boys and a girl, all between the ages of four and seven, ran after a ball, screaming and laughing. Through the open sitting-room curtains they saw the flickering lights of a Christmas tree. In the driveway, behind two other cars, was a Fiat bus, painted green, with the letters VBC and, after that, *Vintage Bottling Company. Estate Mobile Bottling & Labelling.*

Fillander and Griessel got out, walked up the driveway to the front door. The children stopped and stared at them. The oldest boy ran towards the front door. 'Oupa,' he shouted, shrill and excited, 'here's two uncles.'

But it was Ouma who came out with a tray of biscuits. She was an attractive coloured woman, maybe late fifties, who smiled in welcome.

'Good morning, are you looking for Peter?'

'Please, ma'am,' said Fillander.

'I'll call him now.' She looked at the cluster of children. 'Come you; Ouma has made *essies* and *rulle.*'

Her words caused great excitement, and they rushed at her. 'No, no, come and wash your hands first . . .' Then she called inside: 'Peter! Here are people for you.'

He appeared in the door, took them in at a glance, the coloured man and the white man, and something changed in his face: a realisation, and insight.

'Let's go and talk there by the car,' he said quietly.

All three of them walked out to the street where the Hawks car was parked. The woman called from the front door: 'Everything all right, my darling?'

'Hunky dory,' Peter McLean called back to her.

'You were really good over the phone, Mr McLean,' said Griessel. His problem was that he had nothing apart from a ninety-four second call, an advertising sign and a suspicion. He would have to fish. Cleverly, like the *fokken* reporter from the *Son*.

McLean stood by the car, arms crossed. He was somewhere around sixty, hair grey and short, his chest and arms strong from a lifetime of work. Fillander leaned on the Hawks car.

Benny took a chance. 'We found Richter's other cellphone as well,' he said.

No reaction.

'We will be able to see if he phoned you.'

Stoic silence.

'We're going to get a warrant to obtain your bank statements.'

McLean just looked at him. He would have to take a bigger gamble. Griessel hesitated, because if he was wrong the man would know he was feeling his way in the dark. 'We know about you and Francois du Toit.'

Now something moved again in McLean's face. Griessel knew he was heading in the right direction.

'Right now we're searching Klein Zegen. Everything, from one end to the other.'

McLean looked to the right, into the distance, then at Griessel, then at Fillander, and then he turned around, facing the house, and pressed his lips together.

When he spoke, it was to Fillander, as if he would get more sympathy from the coloured detective. 'Here's the deal,' he said. 'We talk here, by the car. You don't put me in handcuffs, and you don't take me away from her. You leave me to have Christmas with my children and grandchildren. Boxing Day I will come and hand myself over.'

'Did you kill Richter?' Fillander asked in astonishment.

'No. But I'm not an innocent man.'

Peter McLean asked them first to understand, over the last few years bottling companies had been under great pressure, because it had become much more profitable for wine farmers to export wine in bulk, to be bottled abroad, as the European demand for wine increased. He had to retrench people, from 2011 on. People who had worked with him for years. People with families, children at school, people with debt on houses and cars.

'And I'm four years from retirement. I haven't had a raise in thirty-six months, my nest egg is small.'

And then Ernst Richter turned up in January 2012 and made Peter McLean an offer. The bottling of ten thousand bottles of red wine; he would pay full price, plus a bonus of a hundred thousand rand. But then McLean mustn't ask questions about the origin or the destination or the nature of the wine.

'Then I said, fine, but I want it in cash, fifty thousand now, and fifty thousand when the job is finished. Cash, because I don't want it going through the books. I met him in Stellenbosch two days later, and he gave me the first fifty thousand. Then he asked me where he could find a farmer to make him a special red wine, no questions asked. I said I would think about it and phone him. Then he gave me a number, and I went away and thought about it. I have been working now forty-two years in the wine industry, and when you drive from farm to farm to bottle or to sell your services, then you hear all the stories. At the time it was only a month after Du Toit senior and his son died in the car crash, and I knew young Francois wanted to take over, and I knew about his harvest, because I had been there to tell him we are the best and the most cost-effective, if he was ready to bottle. So I phoned Richter and said, talk to young Du Toit.

'A week later he called me back, and he said thank you very much, Du Toit is in. We bottle in June or July. And that's what happened. That winter on Klein Zegen we filled, corked, sealed and labelled ten thousand bottles. Fake wine. Fake French wine. 2010 Château Lafite Rothschild. Ten thousand bottles. It must have earned Richter a fortune. A fortune.'

McLean stopped. He let his eyes drift back towards his house.

'And then?' Fillander asked.

'Then I got my other fifty thousand, and I thought that was that. But it wasn't. Nearly two years later, Richter phoned me again, out of the blue. He wanted money . . .'

'That was the call in May?' Griessel asked.

'Yes.'

'And then?'

'Then he wanted money, or he would tell my boss about the bottling in 2012. I asked how much, because if I lose my job now . . . then he said a hundred thousand rand, and then I said I don't have that sort of money, I can give him ten thousand. That's all that I have. Then he cut the call off.'

'Did you know about his Alibi business?'

'No, nothing. I'm not one for the newspapers.'

'So, when did you hear from him again?' Griessel was sure there must have been more.

'Monday twenty-fourth of November, I walked in to work, our head office is in Devon Valley, and my boss called me in and he asked me if I knew anything about French wine that was bottled in June 2012. I got such a fright then, and I said, no, nothing, but why the question? Then he said some guy had phoned and said he was from SARS and he was investigating a case, and my boss must talk to Peter McLean. And I said I don't know anything. But I was worried, the whole day. And that afternoon, Richter phoned me again, and he said, Are you ready now to pay me my money? And I said I genuinely didn't have any money. But I do have a story for him.'

'What story?'

'A story that would get him his money.'

90

Francois du Toit ran down the steps to where advocate Susan Peires stood waiting. She couldn't read the expression on his face; only his voice betrayed his emotion. He had his cellphone in his hand, and held it out in front of him like the Holy Grail.

'Look!' he showed her, but his hand was shaking so much that she had to take the phone from him to read the message.

There was an SMS on the screen from San. *The police have gone again. Said they were very sorry, big mistake. Where are you? Phone me, please. We are VERY worried.*

She looked at him, saw the emotion coursing across his face.

'Thank God,' he said. 'Thank God.'

'Don't trust too much in the stars,' she said.

He shook his head, self-conscious about the tears that welled up so close to the surface.

'I assume you no longer need me today.'

'I hope . . . I don't think so.'

'What are you going to tell your wife?'

'The truth. I'm going to tell her the truth.'

'That's good,' said Susan Peires. 'The truth is always the best.'

The Blue Valley homestead was modern, set high up against the mountainside, overlooking the Blaauwklippen Valley. The view from the sitting room, with the early evening sun setting over a distant Table Mountain, was indescribably beautiful.

But nobody was looking at the view.

The four detectives sat beside each other on the long couch: Ndabeni, Fillander, Liebenberg and Griessel. Their JOC leader Vaughn Cupido sat beside them on an easy chair, a happy man.

Opposite sat the indignant Dietrich Venske, and beside him, his legal representative Wynand van Straaten, a man with a sharp jackal-like face – an animal association that was heightened by two pointy ears, and eyes that darted from detective to detective.

'It's your show, Benna,' said Cupido.

Griessel paged through his notebook, found the correct page. He nodded and looked at Venske. 'Mr Venske, when did you buy this farm?'

Venske looked at Jackal van Straaten. The lawyer motioned with his head that yes, Venske could answer the question.

'In 1994.' Morose and sullen.

'And before you bought the farm, what did you do?'

The Jackal nodded, Venske spoke. 'I worked for KWV.'

'What did you do there?'

The Jackal nodded. 'I was the head of the accounts department, at Legal Administration, by the time I left,' said Venske.

'What was your salary then?'

'I don't see how that is in any way relevant,' said The Jackal.

'The question is how Mr Venske could purchase this farm on the salary from KWV,' said Griessel. 'Can you tell us how much you paid for the farm?'

'You don't have to answer that,' said Van Straaten.

Venske stroked his moustache, said nothing.

'I don't understand you lawyers,' said Vaughn Cupido. 'All you manage to do is to make us more suspicious. If your client is innocent, why the big silence?'

Van Straaten addressed himself to Venske. 'Anything that you say, they can use in court, Dietrich. And you know how things are going with our legal system.'

'There is nothing wrong with our legal system,' said Vusi Ndabeni.

The Jackal and Venske ignored him.

'Are you going to answer my question, Mr Venske?' Griessel asked.

'I think I have said all I want to say,' he said, stroking his thick moustache.

'What is your problem with my client?' asked Van Straaten. 'He's a respected farmer and businessman. He never made use of Ernst Richter's sinister services.'

'Sinister services,' echoed Cupido. 'There's one for the classics.'

'He didn't know Richter at all.'

'Let me tell you what our problem with your client is,' said Griessel and leaned forward, his notebook open in front of him.

Transcript: Interview and Sworn Statement

Name: *Mr Peter McLean*
Date: *26 December 2014*
Place: *Directorate of Priority Crimes Investigation, Market Street, Bellville*
Present: *Captain V. Cupido (DPCI), Captain B. Griessel (DPCI), Advocate A. Prinsloo (State Prosecutor)*

Peter McLean: Just so we're on the same page here: I'm turning state witness, and you don't arrest me for anything . . .

Advocate Prinsloo: The immunity is only relevant to crimes committed as part of what you refer to as Project Champ, between 1990 and 1994. I want to state that very clearly.

Peter McLean: That's all I ask. And Project Champ was all over by the end of '92. Just for the record.

Advocate Prinsloo: Then we're on the same page.

V. Cupido: Okay. Let's get this show on the road. What happened in '92?

Peter McLean: It began in 1990.

V. Cupido: Okay, cool. Start from there.

Peter McLean: I think it was around March of 1990, when Mr Venske came to talk to me . . .

B. Griessel: That would be Mr Dietrich Venske, who is today the owner of Blue Valley?

Peter McLean: That is correct. At that time I was foreman of Bottling at KWV, and he was the chief in charge of the Accounts Department . . .

B. Griessel: Also at KWV.

Peter McLean: That is correct . . .

V. Cupido: Mr McLean, this is not a court. You don't have to *gooi* that 'that is correct' every time.

Peter McLean: Okay. But I'm a bit nervous . . . Anyway, Mr Venske came to talk to me, January of 1990, at the KWV bottling plant. He talked about the sanctions first. Back then the anti-apartheid sanctions were biting *kwaai*, the KWV lost a lot of business because we couldn't export wine. Mr Venske said how hard times were, the sanctions were killing us. And the politicians overseas didn't understand; they were hurting the people they wanted to try and help. The coloured people, the black people. Because take me, for example. There I was, foreman at KWV, and when last did I get a raise? Because of sanctions, and business being so bad. I knew then, he wanted to soften me up, but I didn't see what was coming.

Then he asked me, if there was an opportunity for a fat pay cheque, and we could give sanctions the finger, would I be interested? So I asked, how fat, Mr Venske? And he said, a hundred and fifty thousand. Cash, in my pocket. I feel ashamed now when I think of it. That money made me feel weak, that day. A hundred and fifty thousand was more than two years' salary, to me. A hundred and fifty thousand was more than a house cost, back then. My children were small – four of them. That money was . . . it was a fortune, to a coloured man.

So I said, I'm in, Mr Venske. And he asked, can I trust you, Peter? Because we want to play this very close to the chest – because of the overseas newspapers, and sanctions and things. The money buys your silence. If you talk, if you say a word, even to your wife, you get nothing.

I said again, I'm in.

Then he said to me we are going to make nine hundred thousand bottles of champagne, and we are going to bottle them there with you, at night. They call it Project Champ, and it will take a year or so to make the champagne . . .

B. Griessel: Who is the 'we' that he was talking about?

Peter McLean: He and a couple of his mates, and guys like me, lower down on the KWV food chain . . .

B. Griessel: His mates were all from the KWV?

Peter McLean: No, it was just him.

B. Griessel: So, it wasn't an official KWV project?

Peter McLean: Never.

B. Griessel: Did he tell you who the champagne was going to be delivered to? And what sort of champagne?

Peter McLean: Not that day. Actually he never explained the whole deal to me. But if you work for two weeks with him and his mates through the night, then you pick up all these things. And I mean, I'm in the wine industry. I know about Moët & Chandon en Dom Pérignon, some of the most expensive champagne in the world . . . And so here, about the third last evening of the bottling, there was this guy from America. He'd come to look. He took one of the bottles of Moët off the line, and he inspected it from top to bottom, and then he opened it, poured it in glasses and they tasted. And the American man was very happy, and then I heard them talking. So I put the whole thing together, at the end of the day. Mr Venske and his mates bought surplus wine from the KWV; I don't know what that part of the deal was. And then they made champagne, there in the cellar, here in 1990–91. End of '91, over the December holiday when it was *lekker* quiet, we bottled it.

Those bottles Mr Venske brought in, they weren't local; we took them out of boxes that said 'Imported from France'. And the corks were from Portugal. But the labels and the foil were made here. We bottled nine hundred thousand bottles of Dom Pérignon en Moët & Chandon, and we crated them, and those bottles went to Las Vegas. Via Panama, that's what the waybill said . . .

V. Cupido: All nine hundred thousand bottles went to Las Vegas?

Peter McLean: As far as I know.

B. Griessel: And then?

Peter McLean: Then I got my money, and everything was hunky dory, back in January of '92. And then, early February, Mr Venske called us all together, the Project Champ team, and he said, there's an agent from America, from the AFT or something . . .

Advocate Prinsloo: ATF? The Bureau for Alcohol, Tobacco, Firearms and Explosives?

Peter McLean: Sounds about right. He said, the guy was there with SAP detectives at KWV, because they were looking at fake champagne that the Las Vegas Mafia had imported from us; they found a lot of cases in Panama. And Mr Venske said, if anyone talked to us, then we say we don't know a thing.

B. Griessel: And then?

Peter McLean: Then nothing. Because the world had changed. F.W. de Klerk made that big speech in parliament, February of 1990. By '92, nobody cared any more, because the New South Africa was happening. The whole thing just went away ...

B. Griessel: And that was the story you told to Ernst Richter? On 24 November this year?

Peter McLean: That's the one ...

91

In the sitting room of the Blue Valley homestead Benny Griessel told The Jackal: 'Your client was an employee of KWV in 1990, in the time that KWV was struggling under sanctions and had a huge surplus of wine in their cellar. Your client made a plan to get rid of the wine, and make a lot of money for his own pocket. Enough money to buy this farm – because a man on a salary could not have done that. According to my information Blue Valley cost at least six million rand, back in '94 . . .'

'I inherited money,' said Venske angrily. 'From my wife's side.'

'Dietrich, no,' said the lawyer.

'Duly noted,' said Vaughn Cupido. 'By five members of the Hawks.'

'The problem, Mr Venske, is that we are going to seize all documentation and I am reasonably sure we will find no record of such an inheritance, because you were one of the brains behind Project Champ. To tell the truth, a few hours ago I spoke to a man who said he is prepared to give evidence in court that you stood beside him while the champagne was bottled. Nine hundred thousand bottles of fake champagne . . .' Griessel looked at his notes: '. . . French champagne. Moët & Chandon. And Dom Pérignon. Nine hundred thousand bottles. That's a lot. And there was an American citizen from Las Vegas with you who wanted the champagne for their hotels.'

'Ridiculous,' said The Jackal.

Venske said nothing.

'Nine hundred thousand bottles,' Griessel repeated. 'That's big money, even if you sell it for 10 per cent of what that champagne would have gone for in those days. Enough money to pay for the champagne, the bottles, the labels, and smuggling it to Las Vegas. To pay the guy who bottled it one hundred and fifty thousand rand in cash. And to buy a farm like Blue Valley.'

Now both the farmer and the lawyer were silent.

'But that's not where it ends, Mr Venske, because twenty years later the thing comes back to bite you. Now you're a big wine farmer, and your biggest income is from America because . . .' and again Griessel consulted his notes '. . . your red wine was named by an American, Robert Parker, as the best out of Africa. Is that right?'

No reaction.

Griessel continued. 'So, if a guy comes to you and says he's going to tell some American newspaper about you and Project Champ if you don't give him money, then you lure him to your farm and you strangle him under your jacaranda tree . . .'

'That's enough,' said Van Straaten. 'You have no evidence.'

'We do,' said Griessel, observing Venske closely. 'We have a witness who says he told Ernst Richter the whole story of Project Champ, on Monday 24 November. Does that date sound familiar, Mr Venske? We have forensic evidence that he was strangled under that tree. We have evidence that he was buried with your plastic and your baling twine, and your Triazole was on it.'

'That says nothing,' said Venske. 'It could have been anyone.'

'Don't say a word,' warned The Jackal.

'We have further evidence that Ernst Richter had a secret cellphone that he used to phone you on your wine tasting centre's number, on Monday 24 November, just before five. He must have left an interesting message for you, because at a quarter past five you phoned that number with your cellphone, and the conversation lasted eleven minutes. That's a long time to talk to someone that you don't know at all.'

Something shifted, subtly, in Venske's body language.

'But that's not where it ends, Mr Venske. The day that Richter disappeared, the day that he was murdered, you spoke to him again three times on that same cellphone. At 16.42, at 17.18 and at 19.34. Our Information Centre tells us that that cellphone was static, here near Stellenbosch, till after eleven that night. And then it travelled all the way to Blouberg. And then it went off, just after midnight. Permanently off, never switched on again. Our Information Centre is now busy plotting your cellphone number. And I think we're going to find exactly the same pattern on it. Stellenbosch, to Blouberg, back to Stellenbosch. Will you be able to explain that?'

Deathly silence.

'You lured him here with the promise of money. But you did not intend to pay him. You crept up on him from behind while he waited for you under the tree. You strangled him with baling twine. If you strangle a man, he kicks wildly; we see that a lot. Richter's trainers came off in the kicking. You buried him without the shoes, as far from you as you could, in a place where the sand was loose and soft, because you wanted to do it as fast as possible. I think you burned the trainers and the other cellphone, the one that you communicated on, and buried them together in another place. You left his Audi TT here in Plankenbrug. I wonder if you were wearing gloves? There are two sets of fingerprints that we haven't identified yet. Maybe you were stupid, maybe not. But it doesn't matter. Plankenbrug is exactly ten point four kilometres from here; I measured it this afternoon. It's too far to walk, Mr Venske, so late at night, for a man who is in a hurry to dispose of a body. I think you phoned someone to come and pick you up there: a foreman or a labourer or maybe your wife. Your phone records will give us that number, and we will also talk to that person.'

Venske took off his glasses and wiped his fingertips over his eyes.

'And one last thing,' said Benny Griessel. 'The man who will testify for us about the bottling said that in 1992 and again in 1997 there were questions about the counterfeit champagne, from the American ATF, the Bureau for Alcohol, Tobacco, Firearms and Explosives. And it was reported in a South African newspaper. Our witness said he told Ernst Richter about it. I think there were emails as well, Mr Venske. I think Ernst Richter sent you an email, perhaps with a reference to one of the articles that appeared in the *Mail & Guardian* in 1997. I think you were so worried about that email, that you bribed a member of the SAPS at Stellenbosch station to steal Richter's laptop for you. We are busy going through your cellphone to see which SAPS member you communicated with. And that's how we are going to nail you. When he also testifies to us to save his own backside.'

Venske fought against his temper. It was an interesting show to watch. The Jackal held his hand in the air to stop him, but for one moment Venske let the mask slip. 'Fuck you,' he spat, with naked rage.

'Arrest him, Benna,' said Vaughn Cupido. 'Our work here is done.'

★   ★   ★

'Benny Griessel?' the journalist from the *Son* asked over the phone. 'You're not shitting me?'

'That's right, Maahir,' said Captain John Cloete. 'Cupido was JOC leader, but Griessel made the breakthrough. Your little bird is singing a very false tune. About the time of Richter's death, and about the alleged drunken assault. If you ask me, and off the record, it's jealousy. The SAPS also have their share . . .'

'Well, I . . . John, you know how it is, I'm just doing my job. If the birdies sing, then I just do my job.'

'I understand that, but you must think long and hard about this particular birdy.'

'Fair enough . . . My apologies. I had it wrong.'

'No harm, no foul, Maahir. Merry Christmas.'

There was a small Christmas tree on a coffee table in Alexa's sitting room and his heart leapt. He called her name, but she didn't answer. The house was empty.

92

Christmas.

San du Toit woke before sunrise on Klein Zegen and realised her husband was no longer in the bed.

She found him on the veranda with a mug of coffee in his hand.

She sat down beside him, put her arm around him. 'Happy Christmas,' she said.

He didn't answer. She looked closely at him and saw the tears running down his cheeks.

'Francois, I understand. About everything. It's okay.'

He shook his head. And when he had regained control, he said: 'It's because of the Christmas present. From the stars.'

Only later, when they saw the sun come up together, did he tell her what he meant.

The music woke Griessel.

He thought at first he was dreaming, but then it dragged him from his sleep: it was very clear and close.

In the street?

He got out of bed, walked to the window.

Alexa's car was parked in the street.

The music was coming from downstairs, from her hi-fi.

Then he recognised it. A golden oldie: Vince Vance & The Valiants and 'All I Want for Christmas Is You'. One of Alexa's favourites.

His bladder was full, but he grabbed a dressing gown, and jogged down the stairs to the sitting room.

She was standing there, with Carla and Fritz, his children. Each had a present for him.

⋆　⋆　⋆

At four o'clock, as Vaughn Cupido drove back home from his parents' house in Mitchells Plain, his belly full after the big festive meal, he received an SMS. From Desiree Coetzee.

Vaughn Stroebel leaked database. No doubt.

And he thought, that's it? That's all that Desiree had to say to him?
Okay. So be it.
Vaughn Stroebel *nogal*. The little scoundrel. Probably thought he had to do something to boost his ego after he lost face so badly with his big confession about the *dagga*. He should have seen it, because it was Tricky Ricky Grobler who said the wonderful data security, as Ernst Richter presented it to the media, was a myth. *Any of the programmers could scratch around in the database as they liked.*
Still, should have known. But he hadn't been focused on the database leak.
Never mind.
That was tomorrow or the day after's worries anyway.
Then his Christmas present arrived.
From Desiree again:

Merry Christmas. Waiting for your call.

EPILOGUE

It was a Woolies Christmas dinner in Alexa Barnard and Benny Griessel's house in Brownlow Street, Tamboerskloof, but nobody minded, because Alexa was generous with her gifts again, as she had been the previous year.

Carla received an envelope with a contract in it. For a small role in a new Afrikaans music film that Alexa had invested in.

Griessel received an iPhone 6. And his son Fritz a PlayStation 4, that he unpacked immediately, connected to the TV and turned on. So that he could play *Need for Speed: Rivals*.

Griessel sat and watched. And thought. He was remembering his unease in Ernst Richter's house, something that didn't fit. Only when they sat down at the table to eat, did he ask Fritz whether one could play Xbox games on the PlayStation as well.

Fritz was used to his father's technological ignorance. He laughed and said: 'Duh.'

'What does that mean?'

'No, Pa, you can't, because then Bill Gates wouldn't make so much money.'

'So, if you have an Xbox *and* a PlayStation, then you won't just have games for the PlayStation?'

'Only if you're a moron.'

'Why do you ask, Pa?' Carla piped up, feeling she ought to come to her father's rescue.

'I think I know where someone hid cellphones and false ID documents,' said Griessel. 'Inside an Xbox casing.'

'Cool,' said Fritz.

When they dropped the children off again at Anna and the lawyer's house, and he was driving back with Alexa, she said to him, 'You can

just put your old sim card in the new phone. I have already synchro-
nised everything for you.'

And Griessel remembered that she had done that with his iPhone 5
as well, a year ago. And he thought he knew now how she could
pinpoint where he was. Something to do with the phone . . .

'Thank you,' he said and smiled at her. 'Thank you so much.'

ACKNOWLEDGEMENTS

Icarus is pure fiction. Not a single character in this book is based on or inspired by real people.

The intrigue, however, is partly a highly fictionalised version of events that allegedly took place in the nineties in the then KWV – at that time still a semi-governmental institution. For the sake of credibility I was obliged to have my fictional characters 'work' in specific positions in that institution, but I wish to be very clear that there is no connection whatsoever between them and any real personnel from the KWV.

Nor did I talk to any former or present employee of KWV about any relevant intrigues that took place in the nineties. Newspaper archives were used almost exclusively as sources.

I also wish to explain that the KWV of the apartheid era and the new dynamic private company with the same name are two completely different entities. The present KWV is in fact controlled by a Broad-Based Black Economic Empowerment (BBBEE) shareholder.

Another aspect that has been partly fictionalised, is the way Apple's Touch ID technology works on iPhones. Of course, when an iPhone is completely switched off, a pin code *and* fingerprint is needed to unlock it. I have taken a little poetic licence with this order of events in an effort to make the book more interesting.

I acknowledge with much gratitude and appreciation the many people who shared their valuable time, help, advice, knowledge, insight, goodwill, support and encouragement during the research and writing of this book.

Many thanks to:

• Neil Pendock, for his time, his encyclopaedic knowledge and his insightful books: *Biography of a Vintage*, Cuspidor Press (Mayfair, 2010), and *Sour Grapes* (Tafelberg, Kaapstad, 2008).

- Hannes Myburgh of Meerlust, for his story of growing up – and farming – on one of the oldest and most respected wine estates in South Africa.
- Jacques du Preez, whose memories as quota inspector at the KWV were shared so entertainingly.
- Roy Peires, who contributed so generously to the Loxton I Am Living Trust, so that the name of his wife Susan Peires could be used in the book. And thank you to Jerry Graber who mediated it.
- Professor Dap Louw, Catherine du Toit, Dr J.D. Nel, Rudie van Rensburg, Danie Small, Francois Erasmus, Leslie Watson, Etienette Benadé, Eamon McCloughlin, Nadia Engelbrecht, Martin Smith and Sophia Hawkins.
- My translator Laura Seegers, editor Nick Sayers, and agent Isobel Dixon, for their brilliance, immeasurable loyalty, wisdom, patience and insight. Thank you too to Sharan Matharu for going the extra mile.
- Marianne Vorster, Diony Kempen, Lida Meyer and Johan Meyer, for their patience and support. A big thank you.
- The people whose names were lost among notes, digital notes and cut-off phone calls.
- The wine estates Dornier, Rustenberg, Vilafonté and Tokara, where I went to steal with my eyes – and could taste your excellent products. All in the name of research, of course.
- My translator Laura Seegers, editor Nick Sayers.

BIBLIOGRAPHY

This book began in two places. The first was the documentary film *Red Obsession* by David Roach and Warwick Ross (2013). The second was: http://fortune.com/2014/04/17/with-technology-an-easier-path-to-infidelity-in-france.

I also wish to acknowledge the following references:

- Tim James, *Wines of the New South Africa*, University of California Press (Berkeley, 2013)
- Jan-Bart Gewald, Andre Leliveld, Iva Pesa, *Transforming Innovations in Africa: Explorative Studies on Appropriation in African Societies (African Dynamics)*, Brill Academic Pub (November 2012)
- Lynn E. O'Connor, Jack W. Berry, Joseph Weiss, Paul Gilbert, 'Guilt, fear, submission, and empathy in depression', *Journal of Affective Disorders 71* (2002) 19–27
- Jessica H. Lee, 'The Treatment of Psychopathic and Antisocial Personality Disorders: A Review', Risk Assessment Management and Audit Systems (London, 1999)
- Franklin R.W. van de Goot, Mark P.V. Begieneman, Mike W.J. Groen, Reza R.R. Gerretsen, Maud A.J.J. van Erp & Hans W.M. Niessen, 'Moisture Inhibits the Decomposition Process of Tissue Buried in Sea Sand: A Forensic Case Related Study', *Journal of Forensic Research* (2012), 3:10
- *Classic Wine*, Classic FM (May/June 2014)
- *The Big Issue*, South Africa (25 June–24 July, 2014)
- http://blogs.psychcentral.com/childhood-neglect/2014/11/4-things-psychologists-know-that-you-should-know-too
- www.sahistory.org.za/1900s/1970s
- www.gov.za/documents/constitution/1996/a108-96.pdf
- www.citypress.co.za/news/csi-plattekloof-style

- www.cityam.com/1418155740/desert-island-wines-bordeaux-index-foundergary-boom
- www.dieburger.com
- www.farmersweekly.co.za
- www.osxdaily.com
- www.justice.gov.za/legislation/acts/1977-051.pdf
- http://mg.co.za
- http://forensicjournals.com/2010/02/02/late-postmortem-changesdecomposition
- http://en.wikipedia.org/wiki/Neuroscience_of_free_will
- www.forensicpathologyonline.com/e-book/post-mortem-changes/postmortem-hypostasis
- www.capl.sci.eg/ActiveIngredient/Penconazole.html
- http://wynboer.co.za/technical/a-south-african-perspective-of-powderymildew-in-grapevines
- https://bonesdontlie.wordpress.com/2013/04/11/preservation-when-bodies-dont-decompose
- http://en.wikipedia.org/wiki/Château_Lafite_Rothschild
- www.exploreforensics.co.uk/rigor-mortis-and-lividity.html
- www.capewineacademy.co.za/dissertations/Rise-of-the-Dragon-The-Chinese-Wine-Market-Raymond-Paul-Noppe.pdf
- www.fin24.com/Tech/News/SA-hackers-as-good-as-international-cybercriminals-20141020
- www.saps.gov.za/faqdetail.php?fid=273
- www.markwynn.com/wp-content/uploads/death-by-strangulation.pdf
- http://bandbacktogether.com/survivor-guilt-resources
- www.fin24.com/Tech/News/Technology-vital-in-fight-against-crime-20141020
- www.theguardian.com/commentisfree/2014/oct/14/age-of-loneliness-killing-us
- http://mg.co.za/article/2014-04-23-the-capes-top-20-wineries-of-2014
- http://time.com/2909847/facebook-twitter-job-hunting-social-sweepster
- www.winemag.co.za
- www.enca.com/opinion/blog/weather

- www.health24.com/Lifestyle/Healthy-you/What-happens-when-you-die-20130916
- www.thinkmoney.co.za/insurance/life-insurance/life-insurance-and-suicide

GLOSSARY

Ag – Ah!, oh!; alas, pooh!, mostly used with resignation. (Ag, man = Oh, man!)

Ai – Ah, oh; ow, ouch, mostly used a little despairingly. (Expression of frustration or resignation.)

Baie dankie – Thank you very much. (Baie = much; dankie = thank you).

Bakkie – Afrikaans popular term for a pick-up truck.

Ballies – Slang, meaning 'old farts', referring to older or old men.

Boekevat – Literally meaning 'to take the books', it is a term used in Afrikaans to indicate a small religious gathering.

Berg en Toerklub – 'Mountain and Touring Club', a student club at Stellenbosch University.

Bergie – Cape Flats Afrikaans for a homeless person, often a vagrant, living on the side of Table Mountain (berg = mountain).

Biltong – Very similar to beef jerky, but the recipe is different, using more spices. South Africa's signature (and most popular) snack.

Bliksem – Mild profanity, used as an exclamation or adjective ('Damn!' or 'damned'), a verb (I will 'bliksem' you = I will hit you hard).

Bo blink en onder stink – Shiny on top, but stinking underneath. An Afrikaans saying to imply that beneath someone's flashy lifestyle is but an illusion.

Bobotie – Very traditional South African mild curry and mince meat dish, of Malaysian origin.

Boerewors – 'Farmer's sausage', a very South African recipe of mainly beef, some pork, and lots of spices. Often prepared over the coals.

Boetie – Diminutive of 'broer', which means 'brother'.

Boy'tjie – Slang term, diminutive of 'boy', referring endearingly to a man, or young man.

Braai – South Africa's national pastime, to barbecue meat over the coals, mostly outdoors.

Cape Afrikaans – or Cape Flats Afrikaans refers to the Afrikaans spoken on the Cape Flats, a vast area east of Cape Town, where the majority of 'Cape Coloured' people reside. 'Coloured people' refer to the descendants of Malaysian slaves in South Africa (forced migration by the Dutch East India Company), who intermarried with white farmers and local Khoi people – as opposed to Blacks (descendants of the Bantu people) and Whites (descendants of European settlers).

Chaffing – To woo, to flirt with someone, to get their romantic attention.

Chlora – Cape Flats slang for a coloured woman.

Daai moet jy mooi verstaan – 'You have to really understand this'.

Daai's niks – 'That's nothing / That's trivial'.

Dagga – Afrikaans for marijuana

Dewani – Shrien Dewani, a British businessman accused – and acquitted on 8 December 2014 – of conspiring to murder his wife Anni in South Africa.

Die een se dood is die ander se brood – One man's death is another man's bread.

Donner – Mild Afrikaans expletive, literally meaning 'thunder'. Often used as 'damn!', or in the sense of 'I am going to donner you' – I am going to hurt / hit you.

Doos – Literally the Afrikaans translation for 'box'. Slang expletive, comparing someone to female genitalia. Closest English translation would be 'cunt'.

Dop – A drink, a shot of booze.

Dorp – A town, or referring to midtown.

Drol – A turd.

Dronkgat – A drunkard.

Een dag sal jy versta – Cape Flats Afrikaans vernacular: 'One day you will understand.'

Ek sê dit – 'I say it.'

Ek soen jou sommer! – I could kiss you!

Essies and rulle – Traditional Cape Malay sweet treats. Essies are baked biscuits with nutmeg and ginger. Rulle are deep-fried with cinnamon, cardamom, ginger and mandarin peel.

Finish and klaar – Tautology: 'Klaar' is a synonym of 'finished; denoting that something is truly finished.

FNB, ABSA – FNB = First National Bank. ABSA = Amalgamated Banks of South Africa. Both are major banks in South Africa.

Fok – Fuck.

Fokken – Fucking.

Fokkit – Fuck it.

Fokkol – Fuck all.

Fokkops – Fuck-ups.

Fyn brag – Bragging in such a way that it seems humble, but bragging nonetheless.

Fyndraai – Sexual climax.

Gat – Arse.

Gautrain – The Gautrain is a high speed train service (South Africa's first) between Johannesburg and Pretoria. The name is derived from the province Gauteng, and the word 'train', of course.

Makro – A chain of South African box retailers, partly owned by the American Walmart company.

Gooi – Literally, Afrikaans for 'throw', but used as a slang verb substitute for, inter alia, 'sing for us', or 'tell me'.

Haai – Hi (informal greeting). But also as an exclamation of surprise, similar to 'oh!'

Haai nee, boetie – 'Oh, no, little brother.'

Haas – Direct translation: rabbit. Police term for a member of the public.

Hardegat – Literal translation: Hard arse. Meaning, cocky, full of it.

Hase – Plural of Haas (see above).

Hoeka – 'All along', long since, long ago.

Hoog en lag – High and low.

Hotnots – Racist, derogatory term referring to coloured people.

Hyahi – IsiZulu for 'No!' (South Africa has 11 official languages: Afrikaans, English, IsiNdebele, IsiXhosa, IsiZulu, Sepedi, Sesotho, Setswana, SiSwati, Tshivenda, Xitsonga. Township slang transcends all 11).

Hy skrik sy gat af – Literal translation: 'He was so startled, his arse fell off'. To be very startled.

Ja, gooi – Yes, throw.

Jip – Yup.

Jirre – Cape Flats slang for God, approximates 'Gawd'. (Afrikaans.)

Jis/Jissis – Jeez (as in harsher version of the exclamation Jesus!) (Afrikaans.)

Jong, ja – Well, yes/ The 'jong' literally means 'young', but is often used as an address, such as 'Yea, man'.

Jonkershoek – A nature reserve outside the town of Stellenbosch.

Jonkmanskas – Single cupboard (usually antique), often with two drawers. Literal translation: A young man's cupboard.

Kak – Shit.

Kat se gat – Cat's arse.

Katvoet – Cautious.

Kêrel – Boy/friend.

Kêrels – Plural of kêrel, often used to informally address a group of men – 'guys'.

Kêreltjie – Youngster.

Klippie – Pebble.

Klong – Person.

Kwaai – Mostly used in slang form to indicate coolness, it is an Afrikaans word with a very wide application. Literally meaning someone who is hot-tempered, bad-tempered, ill-natured, harsh or severe, it is also often used as an exclamation: 'Kwaai!' = 'Cool!' (or 'Heavy!')

Laaitie – (Boy.) Slang for 'lighty', a young man, inexperienced.

Lekka, lekker – Afrikaans word widely used for anything that is 'good', 'delicious', 'tasty'. ('Lekka' is Cape Flats vernacular, 'lekker' is formal Afrikaans.)

Lig en lekker – Happy-go-lucky.

Lobola – (Or Labola, an isiZulu or isiXhosa word, sometimes translated as 'bride price'.) A traditional Southern African custom whereby the man pays the family of his fiancée for her hand in marriage. The custom is aimed at bringing the two families together, fostering mutual respect, and indicating that the man is capable of supporting his wife financially and emotionally. Traditionally paid in heads of cattle, but cash is now widely accepted. (Source: http:// en.wikipedia.org/wiki/Lobolo).

Los en lekker – Another variation of happy-go-lucky. Literal translation: Loose and good.

Magtig – Good grief.

Malherbe – Afrikaans surname.

Matric – Final year of high school.

Meneer – Mister.

Moer – 'Moer' is a wonderful, mildly vulgar Afrikaans expletive, and could be used in any conceivable way. Its origins lie in the Dutch word 'Moeder', meaning 'Mother'. 'Moer in' means 'to be very angry', but you can also 'moer someone' (to hit somebody), use it as an angry exclamation (Moer!, which approximates 'Damn!'), call something or someone 'moerse' (approximates 'great' or 'cool'), or use it as an adjective: I have a 'moerse' head-ache – I have a huge headache. 'Moer toe' means 'fucked up', or even 'dead'.

Moerse – See 'moer'.

Moleste – Commotion.

Mooi – Pretty, beautiful.

Mos – Surely/evidently.

Mosbolletjie buns – A South African sweet bun.

My China – Slang, similar to my brother, my bro', my friend.

Nè – Hey.

Net mooi fokkol – Just fuck-all.

Njaps, njapsed – Mild synonym for sexual intercourse.

Nogal – Sufficiently, enough, plenty, quite.

Nogal lekker – Quite good.

Nou ja – Well.

Oom – Oom: Respectful Afrikaans form of address to a male ten or more years older than yourself. Means 'uncle'.

Ou – Old.

Ouens – Guys.

Oupa – Grandfather.

Outjie – Guy, diminutive form.

Pappie – Pappy.

Pedi – One of the ethnic groups in South Africa, bantu people, also known as Northern Sotho.

Pêllie – Buddy.

Poepdronk – Shitfaced.

Poppie – A little doll, a pretty girl, or a bimbo.

Rand – South African currency. The Rand value – over the past two years, the value of the South African currency (Rand, or R) has fluctuated between 7 and 12 to the US $, 9 and 15 to the Euro, and 14 to 18 to the British pound.

RDP House – A house built as part of the Reconstruction and Development Programme, usually Spatan, one of two bedrooms.

Regmakertjie – The shot of alcohol you take the morning after, hair of the dog.

Rof – Rough.

Roker – Smoker.

SARS – The South African Revenue Services, the tax authority.

Schuster – Leon Schuster, South African comedian and performer, best known for his Candid Camera jokes.

Se gat – 'Bullshit'.

Sjoe – 'Wow'. (Afrikaans.) With wide, broad application.

Skedonk – A really beaten up old car.

skelmpie – Extra-marital lover, male or female, derived from 'skelm', which means illicit.

Snotkop – Literally, snot head. Refers to a young, inexperienced person. Derogatory.

Snot snoek – Snoek = Snook, a delicious fish found in South African waters. Snot snoek is a snook gone bad.

Sommer – Just.

Stank vir dank – Literal tanslation – stink for gratitude. (It stinks.)

Stoksielalleen – Utterly on your own.

Suip – Drink/drinking.

Takkies – Running shoes.

Tik – Crystal meth.

Tjaila – Go home.

Tjoekie – Jail.

Tommy Gentles – A real person, who played for the South African national rugby team.

Versta' jy? – Do you understand?

Vreeslik – Beastly.

Wat maak jy hier? – What are you doing here?

Windgat, maar bang-gat – Cocky scaredy-cat.

Windgatgeit – To be cocky.

Wraggies – Really!

Wyd en syd – Widely.
Zol – Joint.
Zuma – Pres. Jacob Zuma, South Africa's head of state.